UNIVERSAL ACC[...]
AN AMAZING NE[...]
NALO HOPK[...]

> Winner of the Aspect First Novel Contest
> Finalist for the Philip K. Dick Award

MIDNIGHT ROBBER
An Alternate Selection of Quality Paperback Book Club®

"It's been many a day since I've read anything so bursting with robust, inventive energy and singing language . . . a wonderful job."
   —Suzy McKee Charnas, author of *Walk to the End of the World*

"A lovely novel and a rousing adventure, with a unique setting and complex, intriguing characters."
   —Vonda McIntyre, author of *The Moon and the Sun*

"Transports you not only to a different world, but to a different way of looking at the world. This is what SF is supposed to be and so often isn't: provocative, intelligent, original."
   —Delia Sherman, author of *Through a Brazen Mirror*

"In rich and vibrant language, Hopkinson tells a universal tale of a young woman's struggle to reclaim her life from dark forces."
   —Candas Jane Dorsey, author of *Black Wine*

BROWN GIRL IN THE RING

"An impressive debut precisely because of Hopkinson's fresh viewpoint."
   —*Washington Post Book World*

"Simply triumphant."
   —Dorothy Allison, author of *Bastard Out of Carolina*

"Fusing Afro-Caribbean soul and speech in an intriguing landscape of spirits . . . a terrifying battle between good and evil."
   —*Black Issues Book Review*

"A wonderful sense of narrative and a finely tuned ear for dialogue . . . balances a well-crafted and imaginative story with incisive social critique and a vivid sense of place."
   —*Emerge*

more . . .

MIDNIGHT ROBBER

NALO HOPKINSON

ASPECT®

WARNER BOOKS

A Time Warner Company

Grateful acknowledgment is given to David Findlay for permission to reprint his poem "Stolen" © 1997 by David Findlay.

Aspect® name and logo are registered trademarks of Warner Books, Inc.

Warner Books, Inc.
1271 Avenue of the Americas
New York, NY 10020

Visit our Web site at
www.twbookmark.com

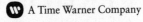 A Time Warner Company

Printed in United States of America
First Printing: March 2000

10 9 8 7 6 5 4 3 2 1

Library of Congress Cataloging-in-Publication Data

Hopkinson, Nalo.
    Midnight robber / Nalo Hopkinson.
    p. cm.
    ISBN 0-446-67560-1
    I. Title.
PR9199.3.H5927 M53 2000
813'.54—dc21   99-043008

Cover design by Don Puckey
Cover illustration by Leo and Diane Dillon

Stolen

I stole the torturer's tongue
it's the first side of me some see
the first line you hear
first line of defense when I say
"See this long tongue illicitly acquired—doesn't it suit me well?
hear these long words assiduously applied—
     don't I wield them well?
wouldn't you be foolish if you tried to tackle me in anything so
     complex as a kiss or a conversation?"
I stole the torturer's tongue!

hear this long tongue!
feel this long tongue!

this tongue sometimes my only tool not mine entirely but what is?
I was raised protectively of/as/by other peoples' property—
     I got over that
this tongue is yours too if you can take it

I stole the torturer's tongue!
man wouldn't recognize this dancing, twining, retrained flesh
if it slapped upside the empty space in him head—
it will, it has; he'll pay for the pleasure;
watch him try an' claim as his own this long, strong old tongue's
new-remembered rhythms. . . .

hear this long tongue!
fear this long tongue!

know this tall tale to be mine too, and I'll live or die by it.
I stole the torturer's tongue!

Oho. Like it starting, oui? Don't be frightened, sweetness; is for the best. I go be with you the whole time. Trust me and let me distract you little bit with one anasi story:

It had a woman, you see, a strong, hard-back woman with skin like cocoa-tea. She two foot-them tough from hiking through the diable bush, the devil bush on the prison planet of New Half-Way Tree. When she walk, she foot strike the hard earth *bup!* like breadfruit dropping to the ground. She two arms hard with muscle from all the years of hacking paths through the diable bush on New Half-Way Tree. Even she hair itself rough and wiry; long black knotty locks springing from she scalp and corkscrewing all the way down she back. She name Tan-Tan, and New Half-Way Tree was she planet.

Yes, this was a hard woman, oui. The only thing soft about Tan-Tan is she big, molasses-brown eyes that could look on you, and your heart would start to beat time *boobaloops* with every flutter of she long eyelashes. One look in she eyes, and you fall for she already. She had a way to screw them up small-small like if she angry, just so nobody wouldn't get lost in the melting brown of them, but it never work, you hear? Once this woman eyes hold you, it ain't have no other woman in the world for you. From Garvey-prime to Douglass sector, from Toussaint through the dimension veils to New Half-Way Tree, she leave a trail of sad, lonely men—and women too, oui?—who would weep for days if you only make the mistake and say the words "brown eyes."

But wait—you mean you never hear of New Half-Way Tree, the planet of the lost people? You never wonder where them all does go, the drifters, the ragamuffins-them, the ones who think the world must be have something better for them, if them could only find which part it is? You never wonder is where we send the thieves-them, and the murderers? Well master, the Nation Worlds does ship them all to New Half-Way Tree, the mirror planet of Toussaint. Yes, man; on the next side of a dimension veil. New Half-Way Tree, it look a little bit like this Toussaint planet where I living: same clouds in the high, high mountains; same sunny bays; same green, rich valleys. But where Toussaint civilized, New Half-Way Tree does be rough. You know how a thing and the shadow of that thing could be in almost the same place together? You know the way a shadow is a dark version of the real thing, the dub side? Well, New Half-Way Tree is a dub version of Toussaint, hanging like a ripe maami apple in one fold of a dimension veil. New Half-Way Tree is how Toussaint planet did look before the Marryshow Corporation sink them Earth Engine Number 127 down into it like God entering he woman; plunging into the womb of soil to impregnate the planet with the seed of Granny Nanny. New Half-Way Tree is the place for the restless people. On New Half-Way Tree, the mongoose still run wild, the diable bush still got poison thorns, and the mako jumbie bird does still stalk through the bush, head higher than any house. I could tell you, you know; I see both places for myself. How? Well, maybe I find a way to come through the one-way veil to bring you a story, nuh? Maybe I is a master weaver. I spin the threads. I twist warp 'cross weft. I move my shuttle in and out, and smooth smooth, I weaving you my story, oui? And when I done, I shake it out and turn it over *swips!* and maybe you see it have a next side to the tale. Maybe is same way so I weave my way through the dimensions to land up here. No, don't ask me how.

New Half-Way Tree is where Tan-Tan end up, and *crick-crack*, this is she story:

TOUSSAINT PLANET

Quashee and Ione? For true? His good good friend and his wife? Mayor Antonio of Cockpit County stepped up into the pedicab. "What you staring at?" he growled at the runner. "Is home I going."

"Yes, Compère," the runner said through a mouthful of betel nut. She set off, and every slap her two feet-them in their alpagat sandals slapped against the ground, it sounded to Antonio like "Quashee-Ione, Quashee-Ione." He could feel his mouth pursing up into a scowl. He sat up straight, tapping impatient fingers on one hard thigh. Not there yet? He slumped back against the seat. A trickle of sweat beaded down from the nape of his neck to pool at his dampening collar. *Ione, running a fingertip down he head-back and grinning to see how the touch make he shiver.* Antonio muttered, "What a thing to love a woman, oui?"

The runner heard him. She glanced back over her shoulder. Corded muscle twisted along her back, stretched on either side from her spine to the wings of her shoulder blades. Grinning, she panted out, "What a great thing for true, Compère. Three z'amie wives I have. Woman so sweet, I tell you."

Nothing to say to that. Antonio made a sucking sound of impatience between his teeth. He tapped his temple to alert his earbug; started to identify himself out loud to the pedicab's ancient four-eye, but remembered in time that pedicab runners only used headblind machines. This cab couldn't transmit to his earbug. He sighed, powered the transmission console on manually and selected a music station. Old-time mento rhythms gambolled noisily in the air round him. He settled back against the soft jumbie leather seat, trying to get into the music. It jangled in his ears like "Quashee-Ione, Quashee-Ione, eh-eh."

Ione, mother of his one daughter. Ione, that toolum-brown

beauty, the most radiant, the loveliest in Cockpit County. When Ione smile, is like the poui trees bloom, filling the skies with bright yellow flowers. A laugh from Ione could thief hearts the way mongoose thief chicken.

Ione and Antonio had grown up neighbours on two wisdom weed farms. Fell in love as children, almost. Time was, Ione used to laugh her poui flower laugh for Antonio alone. Time was, Antonio and Ione were the night cradling the moon.

Maybe all that done now? How it could done?

Antonio tapped the music off. Under his breath, he ordered his earbug to punch up his home. It bleeped a confirmation at him in nannysong, and his eshu appeared in his mind's eye.

"Hot day, Master," grumbled the house eshu.

Today the a.i. had chosen to show itself as a dancing skeleton. Its bones clicked together as it jigged, an image the eshu was writing onto Antonio's optic nerve. It sweated robustly, drops the size of fists rolling down its body to splash *praps!* on the "ground" then disappear. "What I could do for you?" The eshu made a ridiculously huge black lace fan appear in one hand and waved it at its own death's head face.

"Where Ione?"

"Mistress taking siesta. You want to leave a message?"

"Backside. No, never mind. Out." Antonio flicked the music station on again, then nearly went flying from his seat as the pedicab hit a rut in the road.

"Sorry, Compère," laughed the runner. "But I guess you is big mayor, you could get that hole fill up in no time, ain't?"

Runners didn't respect nobody, not even their own mother-rass mayor. "Turn left here so," Antonio said. "That road will take we to the side entrance." And it was usually deserted too. He didn't fell like playing the skin-teeth grinning game today with any of his constituents he might run into: Afternoon, Brer Pompous, how the ugly wife, how the runny-nose little pickney-them? What, Brer Pompous, Brer Boasty,

Brer Halitosis? Performance at the Arawak Theatre last night? A disgrace, you say? Community standards? Must surely be some explanation, Brer Prudish, Brer Prune-face. Promise I go look into it, call you back soon. No, Antonio had no patience for none of that today.

Slap-slap of the runner's feet. *Quashee-Ione.* Jangling quattro music in the air. *Quashee-Ione, eh-eh.*

Too many hard feelings between him and Ione, oui? Too much silence. When she had gotten pregnant, it had helped for a little while, stilled some of her restlessness. And his. He had been delighted to know he would have a child soon. Someone who would listen to him, look up to him. Like Ione when she'd been a green young woman. When little Tan-Tan had arrived, she'd been everything Antonio could have wished for.

In a hard-crack voice, the runner broke into a raucous song about a skittish woman and the lizard that had run up her leg. Antonio clenched his teeth into a smile. "Compère!" he shouted. She didn't reply. Blasted woman heard him easy enough when it suited her. "Compère!"

"Yes, Compère?" Sweety-sweety voice like molasses dripping.

"Please. Keep it quiet, nuh?"

The woman laughed sarcastically.

"Well, at least when we get closer to my home? Uh . . . my wife sleeping."

"Of course, Compère. Wouldn't want she for hear you creeping home so early in the day."

Bitch. Antonio stared hard at her wide, rippling back, but only said, "Thank you."

Antonio knew full well that his work as mayor was making him unpopular to certain people in this little town behind God back. Like this pedicab operator right here.

And like she'd read his mind, the blasted woman nuh start

for chat? "Compère, me must tell you, it warm my heart to know important man like you does take pedicab."

"Thank you, Compère," Antonio said smoothly. He knew where this was going. Let her work up to it, though.

"Pedicab is a conscious way to travel, you see? A good-minded way. All like how the cab open to the air, you could see your neighbours and them could see you. You could greet people, seen?"

"Seen," Antonio agreed. The runner flashed a puzzled look at him over her shoulder. She made a misstep, but caught herself in the pedicab's traces. "Careful, Compère," Antonio said solicitously. "You all right?"

"Yes, man." She continued running. Antonio leaned forward so she could hear him better.

"A-true what you say. Is exactly that I forever telling Palaver House," he said in his warmest voice. "In a pedicab, you does be part of your community, not sealed away in a closed car. I tired telling Palaver House allyou is one of the most important services to the town."

The runner turned right around in her traces and started jogging backwards. She frowned at him. "So if we so important, why the rass you taxing away we livelihood? We have to have license and thing now." Her betel-red teeth were fascinating. "I working ten more hours a week to pay your new tariff. Sometimes I don't see my pickney-them for days; sleeping when I leave home, sleeping when I come back. My baby father and my woman-them complaining how I don't spend time with them no more. Why you do this thing, Antonio?"

Work, he was forever working. And the blasted woman making herself such a freeness with his name, not even a proper "Compère." Antonio ignored her rudeness, put on his concerned face. "I feel for you and your family, sister, but what you want me do? Higglers paying their share, masque camps paying theirs, pleasure workers and rum shops paying theirs. Why pedicab runners should be any different?"

She had her head turned slightly backwards; one eye on him, one on the road. He saw the impatient eye-roll on the half of her face that she presented. "Them does only pay a pittance compared to we. Let we stop with the party line, all right?"

"But . . ."

"Hold on." She wasn't listening, was jogging smartly backwards to the road's median to avoid a boulderstone. Her feet slapped: *Quashee-Ione. Quashee-Ione?* She pulled the pedicab back into the lane, turned her back to him, picked up speed. Over her shoulder: "Truth to tell, we come to understand allyou. The taxes is because of the pedicabs, ain't?"

Antonio noted how businesslike her voice had become, how "me" had multiplied into "we." Guardedly he asked her, "How you mean, sister?"

"Is because we don't use a.i.'s in the pedicabs."

An autocar passed in the opposite direction. The woman reclining inside it looked up from her book long enough to acknowledge Antonio with a dip of her head. He gave a gracious wave back. Took a breath. Said to the runner, "Is a labour tax. For the way allyou insist on using people when a a.i. could run a cab like this. You know how it does bother citizens to see allyou doing manual labor so. Back-break ain't for people." Blasted luddites.

"Honest work is for people. Work you could see, could measure. Pedicab runners, we know how much weight we could pull, how many kilometres we done travel."

"Then . . ." Antonio shrugged his shoulders. What for do? A-so them want it, a-so it going to stay.

The woman ran a few more steps, feet slip-slapping *Ione? Ione?* An autocar zoomed past them. The four people inside it had their seats turned to face one another over a table set for afternoon tea. Antonio briefly smelt cocoa, and roast breadfruit.

He barely had time to notice the runner give a little hop in the traces. Then with a jolt and a shudder the pedicab clattered through another pothole. Antonio grabbed for the armrests. "What the rass . . . ?"

"Sorry, Compère, so sorry."

"You deliberately . . ."

"You all right, Compère? Let me just climb up and see."

"No . . ." But the woman was already in the cab beside him. She smelt strongly of sweat. She hummed something that sounded like nannysong, but fast, so fast, a snatch of notes that hemidemisemiquavered into tones he couldn't distinguish. Then Antonio heard static in his ear. It faded to an almost inaudible crackle. He tapped his earbug. Dead. He chirped a query to his eshu. No answer. He'd been taken offline? How the rass had she done that? So many times he'd wished he could.

The woman was *big,* her arms muscled as thighs, her thighs bellied with muscle. Antonio stood to give himself some height over her. "What you do that for?" he demanded.

"No harm, Antonio; me just want to tell you something, seen? While nanny ear everywhere can't hear we."

"Tell me what?"

She indicated that he should sit again. She planted her behind in the seat next to him. Antonio edged away from her rankness. "The co-operative had a meeting," she said.

"Co-operative?"

"Membership meeting of the Sou-Sou Co-operative: all the pedicab runners in Cockpit County; Board of Directors, everybody."

Why hadn't he known they were organized? Damned people even lived in headblind houses, no way for the 'Nansi Web to gather complete data on them. "So you have a communication from your co-operative for me?" he asked irritably.

"A proposal, yes. A discreet, unlinked courier service. Special government rate for you and the whole Palaver House. We offering to bring and carry your private messages."

Private messages! Privacy! The most precious commodity of any Marryshevite. The tools, the machines, the buildings; even the earth itself on Toussaint and all the Nation Worlds had been seeded with nanomites—Granny Nanny's hands and her body. Nanomites had run the nation ships. The Nation Worlds were one enormous data-gathering system that exchanged information constantly through the Grande Nanotech Sentient Interface: Granny Nansi's Web. They kept the Nation Worlds protected, guided and guarded its people. But a Marryshevite couldn't even self take a piss without the toilet analyzing the chemical composition of the urine and logging the data in the health records. Except in pedicab runner communities. They were a new sect, about fifty years old. They lived in group households and claimed that it was their religious right to use only headblind tools. People laughed at them, called them a ridiculous pappyshow. Why do hard labour when Marryshow had made that forever unnecessary? But the Grande 'Nansi Web had said let them be. It had been designed to be flexible, to tolerate a variety of human expression, even dissension, so long as it didn't upset the balance of the whole.

But what the runners were offering now was precious beyond description: an information exchange system of which the 'Nansi Web would be ignorant. The possibilities multiplied in Antonio's mind. "The whole Palaver House?" he asked.

"Seen, brother. Some of we did want to extend the offer to you one, oui? But then we start to think; if we putting we trust in only you, what kind of guarantee that go give we? Not to say that you is anything but a honest man, Compère, but this way we have some, how you call it, checks and balances in the deal, right?"

"And what guarantees you offering we?" asked Antonio petulantly.

"Contract between we and you. On handmade paper, not datastock."

"Headblind paper too? How?"

"We make it from wood pulp."

Like very thin composition board, Antonio imagined. Koo ya, how these people were crafty. "And what your terms would be?"

"Some little payment for we services, and reduction of we taxes to the same level as the pleasure workers and them."

Crafty, oui. Turn right away round from paying the government to having the government pay you. Palaver House would have to mask the activity as something else, probably a government-dedicated taxi service. Only the Inner Palaver House could be privy to it, but it ain't have nothing unusual in something like that. Antonio found himself whispering, "We could do it . . ."

"Me know so. You going to come to terms with we?"

"Maybe. You have ahm, a private place where me and some next people could meet with your board?"

"Yes, man." They set a meeting time. She told him the place. "One of we go come and get you. Look smart, partner. You coming online again." She warbled again in impossibly intricate nannysong. Antonio's ear popped. In a voice schooled to convey worry the runner said: "Sorry man, too sorry. It working again?"

"Yes." He was still marvelling at the few minutes he'd been dead to the web. Never before since birth. He chirruped in nannysong for his house eshu.

"Master," said the eshu, "you want me?" No visuals this time. It was capricious sometimes.

"Yes. Something . . . malfunction in the blasted headblind four-eye in this pedicab, and I was only getting static for a second. I just making sure you still getting through."

On the screen, the eshu appeared, spat. "Cho. Dead metal." It winked out.

"I name Beata," the woman said. She stuck out a paw. He shook it. Her palm was rough. From work, Antonio realised. How strange.

"Seen." They had an agreement. Silently, she leapt onto the roadway, stepped into the traces and set off again.

They were at the entrance to Antonio's house in minutes. "Here you go, Compère. Safe and sound and ready to ferret out your woman business."

Quashee and Ione? Antonio felt jealousy turning like a worm in his belly. He didn't like the weight of the cuckold's horns settling on his brow. His mind was so worked up, he barely remembered to pay Beata. He got down from the cab and would have walked away, but she hauled it into his road and stood there sweaty and grimy, blocking his path. She poked a bit of betel out from between two teeth with a black-rimed nail. Flicked it away. Smiled redly at him. He threw some cash at her. She caught it, inspected the coin insolently and tucked it into her bubby-band. "Walk good, Compère. Remember what I say."

He was sure he could still smell the sweat of her even though she had jogged off. He opened the white picket gates and walked up the long path towards the mayor house.

This day, Antonio couldn't take no pleasure in his big, stoosh home, oui? He didn't even self notice the tasteful mandala of rock that his Garden had built around the flag pole near the entrance when he first took office. The pale pink rockstone quarried from Shak-Shak Bay didn't give him no joy. The sound of the Cockpit County flag cracking in the light breeze didn't satisfy him. His eye passed right over the spouting fountain with the lilies floating in it and the statue of Mami Wata in the middle, arching her proud back to hold her split fishtail in her own two hands. The trinkling sound of the fountain didn't soothe his soul. Is the first time he didn't notice the perfection of his grounds: every tree healthy, every blade of grass green and fat and juicy. He didn't remark on the snowcone colours of the high bougainvillaea hedge. He didn't feel his chest swell with pride to see the marble walls of the mayor house gleaming white in the sun.

Quashee and Ione? For true?

On the way, Antonio found Tan-Tan playing all by herself up in the julie-mango tree in the front yard. Her minder was only scurrying round the tree, chicle body vibrating for anxious; its topmost green crystal eyes tracking, tracking, as it tried to make sure Tan-Tan was all right. "Mistress," it was whining, "you don't want to come down? You know Nursie say you mustn't climb trees. You might fall, you know. Fall, yes, and Nursie go be vex with me. Come down, nuh? Come down, and I go tell you the story of Granny Nanny, Queen of the Maroons."

Tan-Tan shouted back, "Later, all right? I busy now."

Antonio felt liquid with love all over again for his doux-doux darling girl, his one pureness. Just so Ione had been as a young thing, climbing trees her parents had banned her from. Antonio loved his Tan-Tan more than songs could sing. When she was first born, he was forever going to watch at her sleeping in her bassinet. With the back of his hand he used to stroke the little face with the cocoa-butter skin soft like fowl breast feathers, and plant gentle butterfly kisses on the two closed-up eyes. Even in her sleep, little Tan-Tan would smile to feel her daddy near. And Antonio's heart would swell with joy for the beautiful thing he had made, this one daughter, this chocolate girl. "My Tan-Tan. Sweet Tan-Tan. Pretty just like your mother." When she woke she would yawn big, opening her tiny fists to flash little palms at him, pink like the shrimp in Shak-Shak Bay. Then she would see him, and smile at him with her mother's smile. He could never hold her long enough, never touch her too much.

Antonio called out to his child in the tree: "Don't tease the minder, doux-doux. What you doing up there?"

Tan-Tan screwed up her eyes and shaded them with one hand. Then: "It ain't have no doux-doux here," the pickney-girl answered back, flashing a big smile at her daddy. Sweet, facety child. "Me is Robber Queen, yes? This foliage is my subject, and nobody could object to my rule." Tan-Tan had become fascinated with the Midnight Robber. Her favourite game was to play Carnival Robber King. She had a talent for the patter. "Why you home so early, Daddy?"

In spite of his worries, Antonio smiled to see his daughter looking so pretty. His sweetness, his doux-doux darling could give him any kinda back-talk, oui? "I just come to see your mother. You know is where she is?"

"She and uncle taking tea in the parlour, Daddy. Them tell me I musn't come inside till they call me. I could go in now?"

"Not right now, darling. You stay up there; I go come and get you soon."

Antonio dragged his feet towards the parlour, the way a condemned man might walk to a hanging tree. As he reached inside the detection field, the house eshu clicked on quiet-quiet inside his ear. "You reach, Master," it said. "Straighten your shirt. Your collar get rumple. You want me announce you?"

"No. Is a surprise. Silence."

"Yes, Master Antonio." The eshu's voice sounded like it had a mocking smile in it. Like even self Antonio's house was laughing at him? Where Ione?

When Antonio stood outside the door, he could hear his wife inside laughing, laughing bright like the yellow poui flower, and the sound of a deep, low voice intertwined with the laugh. Antonio opened the parlour door.

Years after, Antonio still wouldn't tell nobody what he saw in the parlour that day. "Rasscloth!" he would swear. "Some things, a man can't stand to describe!"

Mayor Antonio, the most powerful man in the whole county, opened up his own parlour door that afternoon to behold his wife lounging off on the settee with her petticoat hitched up round her hips, and both feet wrapped round Quashee's waist.

Antonio stood there for a while, his eyes burning. He knew then that whenever he shut them from now on, he would see that pretty white lace petticoat spread out all over the settee; Quashee's porkpie hat on Ione's head; the teasing, happy smile on her face; and Quashee's bare behind pushing and pushing between Ione's sprawled-opened knees.

Antonio never noticed that Tan-Tan had followed him to the parlour door. She stood there beside him, eyes staring, mouth hanging open. She must have cried out or something, because all of a sudden, Ione looked over Quashee's shoulder to see the two of them in the doorway. She screamed: "Oh, God, Antonio; is you?"

Soft-soft, Antonio closed the parlour door back. He turned and walked out his yard. Tan-Tan ran after him, screaming, "Daddy! Daddy! Come back!" but he never even self said goodbye to his one daughter.

Little after Antonio had left, Ione came running alone out the house, her hair flying loose and her dress buttoned up wrong. She found Tan-Tan by the gate, crying for her daddy. Ione gave Tan-Tan a slap for making so much noise and attracting the attention of bad-minded neighbours. She bustled Tan-Tan inside the house, and the two of them settled down to wait for Antonio to come back.

But is like Antonio had taken up permanent residence in his office. Ione took Tan-Tan out of the pickney crèche where she went in the mornings to be schooled: said she wanted some company in the house, the eshu would give Tan-Tan her lessons. So Antonio couldn't come and visit Tan-Tan during siesta like he used to. He had to call home on the four-eye to talk to her. He would ask her how her lessons with the eshu were going. He would tell her to mind not to give Nursie or the minder any trouble, but he never asked after Ione. And when Tan-Tan asked when he was coming back, he'd get quiet for a second then say, "Me nah know, darling."

Well, darling, you know Cockpit County tongues start to wag. Kaiso, Mama; tell the tale! This one whisper to that one how he hear from a woman down Lagahoo way who is the offside sister of Nursie living in the mayor house how Ione send Quashee away, how she spend every day and night weeping for Antonio, and she won't even self get out of bed and change out of she nightgown come morning. Another one tell a next one how he pass by Old Man Warren house one afternoon, and see he and Antonio sitting out on the porch in the hot hot sun, old-talking and making plans over a big pitcher of rum and coconut water. In the middle of the day, oui, when sensible people taking siesta!

All the way in Liguanea Town, people hear the story. They have it to say how even the calypsonian Mama Choonks hear what happen, and she writing a rapso about it, and boasting that she going to come in Road March Queen again this year, when she bust some style 'pon the crowd with she new tune "Workee in the Parlour." And Sylvia the engineer tell she daughter husband that somebody else whisper to she how he see Quashee in the fight yard every day, practising cut and jab with he machète. But eh-eh! If Antonio going to call Quashee out to duel come Jour Ouvert morning, ain't Antonio shoulda been practising too?

What you say, doux-doux? You thought this was Tan-Tan story?

You right. My mind get so work up with all that Antonio had to suffer, that I forget about poor Tan-Tan.

In fact it seemed like nobody wanted to pay any mind to Tan-Tan no more. People in her house would stop talking when Tan-Tan went into a room, even old Nursie. Ione was spending all her days locked up in her room in conference with Obi Mami-Bé, the witch woman. It looked like Antonio wasn't coming back at all at all.

But truth to tell, Tan-Tan wasn't so lonely, oui. She was used to staying out of Ione's way, and playing Robber Queen and jacks with just the fretful minder for company. She liked leaning against the minder's yielding chicle, humming along with the nursery rhymes it would sing to her. She had nearly outgrown the minder now, yes, but it did its level best to keep up with her. Tan-Tan used to play so hard, it come in like work:

"Minder, you see where my jacks gone? I could find the ball, but not the jacks. You think I left them under the settee yesterday?"

"Maybe, Mistress. Make I look." And the old construct would flatten its body as best it could and squeeze itself into tight places to retrieve the jacks Tan-Tan was always losing.

Or, "Minder, let we play some old-time story, nuh? I go be Granny Nanny, Queen of the Maroons, and you have to be the planter boss."

So the minder would access the Nanny history from the web and try to adapt it to Tan-Tan's notions of how the story went.

Tan-Tan had a way to make up tales to pass the time, and like how time was hanging heavy on her hands nowadays, she started to imagine to herself how sweet it would be when her daddy would come to take her away from this boring old place where everybody was sad all the time, their faces hanging down like jackass when he sick. She was going to go and live with Daddy in the mayor office, and them would play Robber King and Queen in the evenings when Daddy finish work, and Daddy would tickle her and rub her tummy and tell how she come in pretty, just like her mother. And come Carnival time, them would ride down to town together in the big black limousine to see the Big Parade with masqueraders-them in their duppy and mako jumbie costumes, dancing in the streets.

Finally, it was Jonkanoo Season; the year-end time when all of Toussaint would celebrate the landing of the Marryshow Corporation nation ships that had brought their ancestors to this planet two centuries before. Time to give thanks to Granny Nanny for the Leaving Times, for her care, for life in this land, free from downpression and botheration. Time to remember the way their forefathers had toiled and sweated together: Taino Carib and Arawak; African; Asian; Indian; even the Euro, though some wasn't too happy to acknowledge that-there bloodline. All the bloods flowing into one river, making a new home on a new planet. Come Jonkanoo Week, tout monde would find themselves home with family to drink red sorrel and eat black cake and read from *Marryshow's Mythic Revelations of a New Garveyite: Sing Freedom Come.*

But Antonio still wouldn't come home.

This Jonkanoo Season was the first time that Tan-Tan would get to sing parang with the Cockpit County Jubilante Mummers. She and eshu had practised the soprano line for "Sereno, Sereno" so till she had been singing it in her sleep and all. And she had done so well in rehearsals that the Mummers had decided to let her sing the solo in "Sweet Chariot." Tan-Tan was so excited, she didn't know what to do with herself. Daddy was going to be so proud!

Jonkanoo Night, Nursie dressed her up in her lacy frock to go from house to house with the Mummers. Nursie finished locksing Tan-Tan's hair, and took a step back to admire her. "Nanny bless, doux-doux, you looking nice, you know? You make me think of my Aislin when she was a just a little pickney-girl. Just so she did love fancy frock, and she hair did thick and curly, just like yours."

"Aislin?" Tan-Tan dragged her eyes from her own face in the mirror eshu had made of the wall. She had been trying to read her daddy's features there. "You have a daughter, Nursie?"

Nursie frowned sadly. She looked down at her feet and shook her head. "Never mind, doux-doux; is more than twelve years now she climb the half-way tree and gone for good. Let we not speak of the departed." She sucked her teeth, her face collapsing into an expression of old sorrow and frustration. "Aislin shoulda had more sense than to get mix up in Antonio business. I just grateful your daddy see fit to make this lonely old woman part of he household afterwards."

And all Tan-Tan could do, Nursie wouldn't talk about it any more after that. Tan-Tan just shrugged her shoulders. Is so it go; Toussaint people didn't talk too much about the criminals they had exiled to New Half-Way Tree. Too bedsides, Tan-Tan was too nervous to listen to Old Nursie's horse-dead-and-cow-fat story tonight. First parang! Nursie had had all the ruffles on Tan-Tan's frock starched and her aoutchicongs, her tennis shoes-them, whitened till they gleamed.

Tan-Tan's bedroom door chimed, the one that led outside to the garden. She had a visitor, just like big people! "You answer it, doux-doux," said Nursie.

"Eshu, is who there?" asked Tan-Tan, as she'd heard her parents do.

"Is Ben, young Mistress," the eshu said through the wall. "He bring a present for you."

A present! She looked at Nursie, who smiled and nodded. "Let he in," said Tan-Tan.

The door opened to admit the artisan who gave her father the benefit of his skill by programming and supervising Garden. As ever, he was barefoot, console touchpen tucked behind one ear and wearing a mud-stained pair of khaki shorts and a grubby shirt-jac whose pockets held shadowy bulges like babies' diapers.

Weeds hung out of the bulgy pockets. He had an enormous bou-
quet of fresh-cut ginger lilies in one hand. The red blooms
stretched on long thumb-thick green stalks. Tan-Tan gasped at
the present that Ben was balancing carefully in his other hand.

Nursie chided, "Ben, is why you always wearing such dis-
graceful clothes, eh? And you can't even put on a pair of shoes
to come into the house?"

But Ben just winked at her and presented her with the lilies.
She relented, giggled girlishly and buried her nose in the blossoms. Finally he seemed to notice Tan-Tan gazing at the present. He smiled and held it out to her: a Jonkanoo hat. It was
made from rattan, woven in the torus shape of a nation ship. "I
design it myself," Ben told her. "I get Garden to make it for
you. Grow it into this shape right on the vine."

"Oh, what a way it pretty, Ben!" The hat even had little
portholes all round it and the words "Marryshow Corporation: Black Star Line II" etched into a flat blade of dried vine in
its side.

"Look through the portholes."

Tan-Tan had to close one eye to see through one of the
holes. "I see little people! Sleeping in their bunk beds, and a little crèche with a teacher and some pickney, and I see the bridge
with the captain and all the crew!"

"Is so we people reach here on Toussaint, child. And
look . . ." Ben pulled six candles out of a pocket and wedged
them into holders woven all along the ring of the ship. "Try it
on let me see."

Careful-careful, Tan-Tan slid the hat onto her head. It fit
exactly.

"When you ready to go," Ben said, "ask Mistress Ione to
light the candle-them for you. Then you going to be playing
Jonkanoo for real!"

Nursie fretted, "I don't like this little girl walking round
with them open flame 'pon she head like that, you know? You

couldn't use peeny-wallie bulb like everybody else, eh? Suppose the whole thing catch fire?"

"Ain't Ione go be right there with Tan-Tan?" Ben reassured her. "She could look after she own pickney. This is the right way to play Jonkanoo, the old-time way. Long time, that hat woulda be make in the shape of a sea ship, not a rocket ship, and them black people inside woulda been lying pack-up head to toe in they own shit, with chains round them ankles. Let the child remember how black people make this crossing as free people this time."

Tan-Tan squinched up her face at the nasty story. Crèche teacher had sung them that same tale. Vashti and Crab-back Joey had gotten scared. Tan-Tan too. For nights after she'd dreamt of being shut up in a tiny space, unable to move. Eshu had had to calm her when she woke bawling.

Nursie shut Ben up quick: "Shush now, don't frighten the child with your old-time story."

"All right. Time for me to get dressed, anyway. Fête tonight! Me and Rozena going to dance till 'fore-day morning, oui." Ben knelt down and smiled into Tan-Tan's eyes. "When you wear that hat, you carry yourself straight and tall, you hear? You go be Parang Queen–self tonight!"

"Yes, Ben. Thank you!"

When everything was ready, Nursie fetched Tan-Tan to Ione. Nursie carried the Jonkanoo hat in front of her like a wedding cake, candles and all.

Ione was too, too beautiful that night in her madras head wrap and long, pale yellow gown, tight so till Tan-Tan was afraid that Ione wouldn't be able to catch breath enough to sing the high notes in "Rio Manzanares." She looked so pretty, though, that Tan-Tan ran to hug her.

"No, Tan-Tan; don't rampfle up me gown. Behave yourself, nuh? Come let we go. I could hear the parang singers practising in the dining room. Is for you that hat is?"

"From Ben, Mummy."

Ione nodded approvingly. "A proper Jonkanoo gift. I go give you one from me tomorrow." She put the nation ship hat on Tan-Tan's head, and then lit all six candles.

"Candles for remembrance, Tan-Tan. Hold your head high now, you hear? You have to keep the candles-them straight and tall and burning bright."

"Yes, Mummy." Tan-Tan remembered Nursie's posture lessons. Proper-proper, she took Ione's hand, smoothed her frock down, and walked down the stairs with her mother to join the Cockpit County Jubilante Mummers. The John Canoe dancer in his suit of motley rags was leaping about the living room while the singers clapped out a rhythm.

Tan-Tan was Cockpit County queen that night for true! The Mummers went house to house, singing the old-time parang songs, and in every place, people were only feeding Tan-Tan tamarind balls and black cake and thing—" Candles for remembrance, doux-doux!"—till the ribbon sash round her waist was binding her stuffed belly. Everywhere she went, she could hear people whispering behind their hands: "Mayor little girl . . . sweet in that pretty frock . . . really have Ione eyes, don't? Mayor heart must be hard . . . girl child alone so with no father!" But she didn't pay them any mind. Tan-Tan was enjoying herself. All the same, she couldn't wait to get to the town square to sing the final song of the night. Antonio would be there to greet the Mummers and make his annual Jonkanoo Night speech. For days he had been busy with the celebrations and he hadn't called to speak to Tan-Tan.

At last the Mummers reached the town square. By now, Tan-Tan's feet were throbbing. Her white aoutchicongs had turned brown with dust from walking all that distance, and her belly was beginning to pain her from too much food. Ione had blown out the candles on the nation ship hat long time, for with all the running round Tan-Tan was doing, the hat kept falling from her head. She had nearly set fire to Tantie Gilda's velvet curtains.

Tan-Tan was ready to drop down with tiredness, oui, but as they entered the town square, she straightened up her little body and took her mummy's hand.

"Light the candles again for me, Mummy." Hand in hand with Ione, Tan-Tan marched right to her place in the front of the choir. She made believe she was the Tan-Tan from the Carnival, or maybe the Robber Queen, entering the town square in high state for all the people to bring her accolades and praise and their widows' mites of gold and silver for saving them from the evil plantation boss (she wasn't too sure what an "accolade" was, oui, but she had heard Ben say it when he played the Robber King masque at Carnival time the year before). Choirmaster Gomez smiled when he saw her in her pretty Jonkanoo hat. He pressed the microphone bead onto her collar. Tan-Tan lost all her tiredness one time.

The square was full up of people that night. One set of people standing round, waiting for the midnight anthem. It must be had two hundred souls there! Tan-Tan started to feel a little jittery. Suppose she got the starting note wrong? She took a trembling breath. She felt she was going to dead from nerves. Behind her, she heard Ione hissing, "Do good now, Tan-Tan. Don't embarrass me tonight!"

Choirmaster Gomez gave the signal. The quattro players started to strum the tune, and the Cockpit County Jubilante Mummers launched into the final song of the night. Tan-Tan was so nervous, she nearly missed her solo. Ione tapped her on her shoulder, and she caught herself just in time. She took a quick breath and started to sing.

The first few notes were a little off, oui, but when she got to the second verse, she opened her eyes. Everybody in the square was swaying from side to side. She started to get some confidence. By the third verse, her voice was climbing high and strong to the sky, joyful in the 'fore-day morning.

Sweet chariot,
Swing down,
Time to ride,
Swing down.

As she sang, Tan-Tan glanced round. She saw old people rocking back and forth to the song, their lips forming the ancient words. She saw artisans standing round the Mercy Table, claiming the food and gifts that Cockpit Town people had made for them with their own hands in gratitude for their creations. Every man-jack had their eyes on her. People nodded their heads in time. She swung through the words, voice piping high. The Mummers clapped in time behind her. Then she spied a man standing near the edge of the crowd, cradling a sleeping little girl in his arms. He was the baby's daddy. Tan-Tan's soul came crashing back to earth. Tears began creeping down her face. She fought her way to the end of the song. When she put up her hand to wipe the tears away, an old lady near the front said, "Look how the sweet song make the child cry. What a thing!" Tan-Tan pulled the mike bead off and ran to Ione. The nation ship hat fell to the ground. Tan-Tan heard someone exclaim behind her, and the scuffing sound as he stamped out the flame of the candles. She didn't pay it no mind. She buried her head in her mother's skirt and cried for Antonio. Ione sighed and patted her head.

Soon after, her daddy did come, striding into the town square to give his speech. But he didn't even self glance at Tan-Tan or Ione. Ione clutched Tan-Tan's shoulder and hissed at her to stand still. Tan-Tan looked at her mother's face; she was staring longingly and angrily at Antonio with bright, brimming eyes. Ione started to hustle Tan-Tan away. Tan-Tan pulled on her hand to slow her down. "No, Mummy, no; ain't Daddy going to come with we?"

Ione stooped down in front of her daughter. "I know how you feel, doux-doux. Is Jonkanoo and we shoulda be together, all three of we; but Antonio ain't have no mercy in he heart for we."

"Why?"

"Tan-Tan, you daddy vex with me; he vex bad. He forget all the nights I spend alone, all the other women I catch he with."

Tan-Tan ain't business with that. "I want my daddy." She started to cry.

Ione sighed. "You have to be strong for me, Tan-Tan. You is the only family I have now. I not going to act shame in front of Cockpit County people and they badtalk. Swallow those tears now and hold your head up high."

Tan-Tan felt like her heart could crack apart with sorrow. Ione had to carry the burst nation ship. Scuffling her foot-them in the dirt, Tan-Tan dragged herself to the limousine that had been sent to the square to wait for them. They reached home at dayclean, just as the sun was rising. Tan-Tan was a sight when Nursie met her at the door: dirty tennis shoes, plaits coming loose, snail tracks of tears winding down her face.

"Take she, Nursie," Ione said irritably. "I can't talk no sense into she at all at all."

"Oh, darling, is what do you so?" Nursie bent down to pick up the sad little girl.

Tan-Tan leaked tired tears, more salt than water. "Daddy ain't come to talk to me. He ain't tell me if he like how I sing. Is Jonkanoo, and he ain't self even give me a Jonkanoo present!"

"I ain't know what to do for she when she get like this," Ione told Nursie. "Tan-Tan, stop your crying! Bawling ain't go make it better."

Nursie and Ione took Tan-Tan inside to bed, but is Nursie who washed Tan-Tan's face and plaited up her hair nice again so it wouldn't knot up while she slept. Is Nursie who dressed Tan-Tan in her favourite yellow nightie with the lace at the neck. Nursie held to her lips the cup of hot cocoa-tea that Cookie sent from the kitchen, and coaxed her to drink it. Cookie was an artisan too, had pledged his creations to whoever was living in the mayor house. Usually Tan-Tan loved his cocoa, hand-grated from lumps of raw chocolate still greasy with cocoa fat, then steeped in hot water with vanilla beans and Demerara sugar added to it. But this time it was more bitter than she liked, and she got so sleepy after drinking it! One more sip, and she felt she had was to close her eyes, just for a little bit. Nursie put Tan-Tan to bed with the covers pulled right up to her neck, and stroked her head while sleep came. Ione only paced back and forth the whole time, watching at the two of them.

But just as sleep was locking Tan-Tan's eyes shut, is Ione's sweet voice she heard, singing a lullaby to her from across the room.

> *Moonlight tonight, come make we dance and sing,*
> *Moonlight tonight, come make we dance and sing,*
> *Me there rock so, you there rock so, under banyan tree,*
> *Me there rock so, you there rock so, under banyan tree.*

And her earbug echoed it in her head as eshu sang along.

Tan-Tan slept right through the day until the next morning. When she woke up Ione told her irritably, "Your daddy come by to see you while you was sleeping."

Tan-Tan leapt up in the bed. "Daddy here!"

"No, child. He gone about he business."

The disappointment and hurt were almost too much for breathing. Unbelieving, Tan-Tan just stared at Mummy. Daddy didn't wait for her to wake up?

"Cho. Me ain't able with you and your father. He leave this

for you." Ione laid out a costume on the bed, a little Robber
Queen costume, just the right size for Tan-Tan. It had a white
silk shirt with a high, pointy collar, a little black jumbie leather
vest with a fringe all round the bottom, and a pair of wide red
leather pants with more fringe down the sides. It even had a
double holster to go round her waist, with two shiny cap guns
sticking out. But the hat was the best part. A wide black sombrero, nearly as big as Tan-Tan herself, with pom-poms in different colours all round the brim, to hide her face in the best
Robber Queen style. Inside the brim, it had little monkeys
marching all round the crown of the hat, chasing tiny birds.
The monkeys leapt, snatching at the swooping birds, but they
always returned to the brim of the hat.

"Look, Tan-Tan!" Ione said, in that poui-bright voice she
got when she wanted to please. "It have Brer Monkey in there,
chasing Brer Woodpecker for making so much noise. Is a nice
costume, ain't?"

Tan-Tan looked at her present good, but her heart felt like
a stone inside her chest. She pressed her lips together hard. She
wasn't even going to crack a smile.

"Yes, Mummy."

"Your daddy say is for he little Jonkanoo Queen with the
voice like honey. You must call he and tell he thanks."

"Yes, Mummy."

"You ain't want to know what I get for you?"

"Yes, Mummy."

Smiling, Ione reached under Tan-Tan's bed and pulled out
the strangest pair of shoes Tan-Tan had ever seen. They were
black jumbie leather carved in the shape of alligators like in the
zoo. The toes of the shoes were the alligators' snouts. They had
gleaming red eyes. The shoes were lined inside with jumbie
feather fluff. "Try them on, nuh?" Ione urged.

Tan-Tan slid her feet into the shoes. They moulded themselves comfortably round her feet. She stood up. She took a

step. As she set her foot down the alligator shoe opened its snout wide and barked. Red sparks flew from its bright white fangs. Tan-Tan gasped and froze where she was. Ione laughed until she looked at Tan-Tan's face. "Oh doux-doux, is only a joke, a mamaguy. Don't dig nothing. They only go make noise the first two steps you take."

To test it, Tan-Tan stamped her next foot. The shoe barked obligingly. She jumped and landed hard on the floor. The shoes remained silent. "Thank you, Mummy."

"You not even going bust one so-so smile for me, right?"

Tan-Tan looked solemnly at her mother. Ione rolled her eyes impatiently and flounced out of the room.

Tan-Tan waited till she could no longer hear Ione's footsteps. She went to the door and looked up and down the corridor. No-one. Only then did she try on the Midnight Robber costume. It fit her perfect. She went and stood in front of a bare wall. "Eshu," she whispered.

The a.i. clicked on in her ear. In her mind's eye it showed itself as a little skeleton girl, dressed just like her. "Yes, young Mistress?"

"Make a mirror for me."

Eshu disappeared. The wall silvered to show her reflection. Aces, she looked aces. Her lips wavered into a smile. She pulled one of the cap guns from its holster: "Plai! Plai! Thus the Robber Queen does be avengèd! Allyou make you eye pass me? Take that! Plai!" She swirled round to shoot at the pretend badjack sneaking up behind her. The cape flared out round her shoulders and the new leather of her shoes creaked. It was too sweet.

"Belle Starr . . ." said the eshu, soft in her ear.

"Who?" It wasn't lesson time, but the eshu had made her curious.

"Time was, is only men used to play the Robber King masque," eshu's voice told her.

"Why?" Tan-Tan asked. What a stupid thing!

"Earth was like that for a long time. Men could only do some things, and women could only do others. In the beginning of Carnival, the early centuries, Midnight Robbers was always men. Except for the woman who take the name Belle Starr, the same name as a cowgirl performer from America. The Trini Belle Starr made she own costume and she uses to play Midnight Robber."

"What she look like, eshu?"

"No pictures of she in the data banks, young Mistress. Is too long ago. But I have other pictures of Carnival on Earth. You want to see?"

"Yes."

The mirrored wall opaqued into a viewing screen. The room went dark. Tan-Tan sat on the floor to watch. A huge stage appeared on the screen, with hundreds of people in the audience. Some old-time soca was playing. A masque King costume came out on stage; one mako big construction, supported by one man dancing in its traces. It looked like a spider, or a machine with claws for grasping. It had a sheet of white cotton suspended above its eight wicked-looking pincers. It towered a good three metres above the man who was wearing it, but he danced and pranced as though it weighed next to nothing.

"The Minshall Mancrab," eshu told Tan-Tan. "Minshall made it to be king of his band 'The River' on Earth, Terran calendar 1983."

"Peter Minshall?" Tan-Tan asked. She had heard a crèche teacher say the name once when reading from *Marryshow's Revelations*.

"He same one."

The sinister Mancrab advanced to the centre of the stage, its sheet billowing. Suddenly the edges of the sheet started to bleed. Tan-Tan heard the audience exclaim. The blood quickly soaked the sheet as the Mancrab opened its menacing pincers wide. People in the audience went wild, clapping and shouting and screaming their approval.

Tan-Tan was mesmerised. "Is scary," she said.

"Is so headblind machines used to stay," eshu told her. "Before people make Granny Nanny to rule the machines and give guidance. Look some different images here."

The eshu showed her more pictures of old-time Earth Carnival: the Jour Ouvert mud masque, the Children's Masquerades. When Nursie came to fetch her for breakfast, Tan-Tan was tailor-sat on the floor in the dark, still in her Robber Queen costume, staring at the eshu screen and asking it questions from time to time. The eshu answered in a gentle voice. Nursie smiled and had the minder bring Tan-Tan's breakfast to her on a tray.

For two days straight Tan-Tan insisted on wearing her Robber Queen costume. She slept in it and all. Neither Ione nor Nursie could persuade her to change out of it. But she never called Antonio to thank him. Let him feel bad about boofing her on Jonkanoo Night.

She missed the crèche, missed Crab-back Joey and Vashti, and the brightly coloured minders that would sing and play games of "Brown Girl in the Ring" and "Jane and Louisa" with them. No-one else would play with her, so she talked to the eshu. Not just for her lessons in maths and history and art, but for all the questions the grownups wouldn't answer for her.

"Why Daddy gone away, eshu?"

"He mad at your mother and Quashee, young Mistress. Them shouldn't have been hugging up behind Antonio back."

"He mad at me too?"

The eshu said, "It look so, don't it? Me can't calculate no other reason for him to stay away from you. But Nanny say is classic jealousy behaviour, it don't have to do with you. I tell you true, I don't always understand people so good. Allyou does do things for different reasons than we. You certain you never do nothing to vex your father, young Mistress?"

Tan-Tan thought back to the day her daddy had left; the time when she'd been playing Robber Queen in the julie-mango tree and talking back so breezily to Daddy. Like slugs squirming in salt, she felt her lips twisting into a sad bow. "Maybe because I ain't stay up in the tree when he tell me?"

"I not sure. Maybe is that, oui. 'Nuff respect, Mistress, but sometimes you hard ears, you know. You don't always obey when adults talk to you."

"No," Tan-Tan agreed in a small voice.

"You want me to ask Antonio if is that why he vex?"

"No! Don't tell he nothing!" When she felt like this, Nursie told her she was acting too proud. But she couldn't bear to let Daddy know how bad she was pining for him.

"Seen," agreed the eshu. It played a cartoon for her instead. Tan-Tan laughed at Brer Anansi, the cunning little man who could become a spider. Her heart eased for a time.

Jonkanoo Season ended as Old Year's Night came round. Tan-Tan heard Nursie and Cookie talking about how Ione had scandalized the crowd at the Cannes Brûlées Ball by showing up dressed off in black like a widow ("Except that widows ain't supposed to show off they chest in all kinda see-through lace," said Cookie), and hanging on to the arm of a young swaggerboy, even more dressed up than she. But eh-eh! And she married to the mayor!

Tan-Tan had finally come to understand why her daddy wasn't coming back: Ione had been bad, and Tan-Tan had been bad, and he didn't want to be with them no more. He was disgusted at them. Sometimes Ione would get sad and drink too much red rum. Then she would bawl, and tell Tan-Tan how Antonio was a thoughtless, ungrateful man; look how he bring down all this scandal on he wife head! Sometimes Ione would

say through tears, "But I miss he, child. Even with all he slack-
ness and he plenty plenty women, I miss he too bad."

Tan-Tan heard Ben telling Cookie that "A man have him
pride, you know! How you could expect him to live with a
woman who horning he steady? And he the mayor too besides!
You don't see the man have to have some respect in he own
house?"

Tan-Tan didn't understand all of that, it was big people
story; all she knew was she wasn't going to cry or complain, she
was going to try to be real, real good so Daddy would come
home again.

Come Carnival time, Antonio called to tell her he would
take her to the Children's Masquerade, as he had every year
now since she was four. She opened her mouth to say, yes
Daddy, thank you, Daddy. So why was her mouth saying politely, "No thank you, Daddy. Mummy go take me"? Pride.
Nursie was always telling she she too prideful. Daddy's face
fell.

"All right, doux-doux," he said sadly. "If is so you want
it."

The words chilled Tan-Tan's heart to a ball of ice in her
chest. But she set her lips together and nodded solemnly at her
daddy. When he had signed off, Tan-Tan whispered to the air,
"Eshu? Come and play with me." That day, whispering directions through her earbug, eshu directed Tan-Tan out to the
fountain to examine the pale pink rockstones from Shak-Shak
Bay. It showed her how to see the fossils trapped in some of the
stones. It told her about the animals that used to live on Toussaint before human people came and made it their own.

"You mean chicken and cow and so?"

"No, Mistress. Them is from Earth. I mean the indigenous
fauna: the mako jumbie-them, the douen. The jumbie bird allyou does farm for meat and leather is a genesculpt. Allyou
grow it from the original stock. It didn't used to be small so."

"Small! Eshu, jumbie bird does be big like cow, ain't?"

"The mako jumbie could eat a cow for breakfast and be hungry again come noon." The eshu must have heard the small noise Tan-Tan made in her throat, for it said; "Don't frighten, young Mistress. It ain't have no more mako jumbie on Toussaint no more. You safe."

"And the douen? You said it had douen."

"Searching..." the eshu whispered quietly. Usually it could get information instantly from the web data banks. "I don't know plenty about them, young Mistress," it said finally. "Indigenous fauna, now extinct."

"Extinct?"

"No longer in this existence."

"Why, eshu?"

"To make Toussaint safe for people from the nation ships."

"Oh."

Tan-Tan saw Antonio on the broadcasts, opening Carnival season for another year. Watching him on the screen she felt a little sad and vex. At him, at herself. But eshu always knew how to help her feel better. And Ione was trying to be nice to Tan-Tan, in a kind of a way. She was forever buying her new toys, even though she wouldn't play Robber Queen or any old-time story, for she didn't like to "bother up sheself with stupidness."

Nursie was throwing word steady behind Ione's back, whispering to Cookie and Ben that the mayor wife had bring all of this on she own head. Nursie took care that Ione never heard her, though. The eshu could hear, but it would only reveal private conversation if it judged the speakers meant harm to anyone. Simple badmouth didn't warrant its attention.

One day before the big Carnival parade, the eshu told Nursie that Ione wanted to see Tan-Tan. When they reached Ione's dressing room, they found Ione with a seamstress lacing her tight into her riding leathers. Tan-Tan could never understand why her mother had riding leathers, when she didn't even self have a horse. But she looked pretty in them.

"Nursie," Ione said, "ain't the eshu tell you to get Tan-Tan ready?"

"No, Compère. You know it does make mischief sometimes."

"Cho. Well, take she back and dress she up nice. I taking she to the fight yard to watch the practice."

Tan-Tan could scarcely believe it. "For true, Mummy?" She had never seen the practice, just heard about it from Ben.

Mummy looked down at her, smiling. "You would like that, eh doux-doux?"

"Yes!"

Ione held out her arms, gleaming strong and firm through the translucent white linen of her best pirate blouse. The seamstress looked appraisingly at the blouse. "I think is soon time you stop wearing that style, Compère," she said. " 'Nuff people see you inna this shirt plenty times already."

"Well, is you have the eye for these things, Annie," replied Ione. "Tell me what you think."

"A new blouse. I go make you something pretty in lace." She fastened the cuffs of the blouse.

"I would be honoured to wear your creation, Compère." Ione looked down at Tan-Tan.

"I know you been asking your daddy to take you to the fight yard from since, and he never pay you no mind. Well he not here now. I going take you. Go and get dressed, doux-doux."

The fight yard! The place where challengers trained to fight in the Jour Ouvert morning duels on the first day of the Carnival parade. On Jour Ouvert morning, besides the street dancing, anybody who had a quarrel with someone could call their enemy out to fight. "Young Mistress," said the eshu in her ear, "you understand the word 'archaic'?"

"No, what it mean?"

"Old. Very old. When people does fight in a Jour Ouvert duel, them does fight in the old ways, with machète and bull pissle and stick and thing. All to remind them of their history, of times back on Earth. Them does even fight with hand and foot."

Nursie bustled Tan-Tan back to her room, chatting the whole time about the training at the fight yard:

"Tan-Tan, if you see it! When me was young me did train to be a fighter, you know? Well, a dancer. Stick fight dance. The yard big so like a sugar cane field, but pack down flat all over; just dirt, no pavement. The chicle fetches does sweep the yard flat every morning. And the practice! Lord, it sweet for so! It have three kinds: stick fight, bare hand and machète. Your own labour, you understand? Body and mind working together to defeat an enemy, like old-time days. Woi, Nanny. A laying on of hands. Don't mind people who tell you labour nasty. Some kinds is a blessing for true, a sacrament." Nursie's eyes got big-big, and she was waving her hands round in the air, trying to describe how the fighters-them looked.

"Stick fight pretty to watch, you see? When the fighters and them does practice, and the stick fight marshall call out the steps, it come in just like a dance. Man and woman, everybody know they place, and even though you might think say them will lash each other by mistake, them does scarcely do it, you know?"

"Bare hand is the type I really like; is that I used to play when I was young. Capoeira."

Click in Tan-Tan's ear. "When you come back, young Mistress, I go tell you about capoeira."

Nursie said, "You know is fight you fighting when you could feel your opponent muscles sweaty beneath you hand. Mama, that is fight! It take skill! The bare hand marshall we got now does only train with two-three people at once, and she don't make fun to make example of them. One time, I see she haul one big, hard-back man over she shoulder, and drop him *boops!* on the ground like a sack of cornmeal, just because she catch he giving a kidney blow. She don't make joke, oui?"

"Machète fight different, though; it ain't a clean type of fighting. When them practice, the marshall make everybody wear the leather armour and use the wood blades. Even so, I see people get bruise-up bad in machète practice. I don't like to watch the machète duels so much. One crazy motherass so-and-so only have to fetch you one chop for you to end up dead. Oh—excuse my language, doux-doux."

Tan-Tan couldn't wait to see the fight yard with her own two eyes. She made haste to get dressed; she even laced up her aoutchicongs by herself, instead of begging Nursie to do it for her. By the time she reached the front yard, Ione was already waiting for her in a pedicab.

"Hurry up, nuh, Tan-Tan?" Ione pulled her into the cab. She made sure Tan-Tan was settled, then tapped her foot on the floor of the cab for the runner to move off.

Ione's eyes were bright. She sat straight and tall in the cab, waved at passers-by on the long avenue, cut her eyes at the ones who scowled at the mayor's cheating wife. Ione just smiled: Granny Nanny's ears and eyes everywhere kept people's actions to one another respectful. Ione was running her mouth off steady like water from a tap: "I so love to watch the practice. The fellers does look too nice, oui, with the sweat shining on their muscles, and them tiny dhoti them does wear like loin-cloth."

"Compère Ione," came the runner's deep voice. He glanced back at them over his shoulder. "Me bring one message for you. You will hear it?"

"You? A message for me? From who?"

"The Obi-Bé." The witch woman. "She say must tell you

to go where it have plenty people today, not to stay in your house and grieve for your man."

Ione smiled, a pleased look on her face. "And ain't is that I doing?"

"She say the shells tell she a former love making plans to change your life."

"Koo ya! Look at that now. I know say Quashee been practising in the fight yard since before Jonkanoo Time. I bet you he getting ready to call that blasted Antonio out to duel. It woulda serve Antonio right if Quahsee kill he dead! I spend too many nights crying over that man and he worthless ways!" Ione's eyes were bright and shiny. Excitement or fear, Tan-Tan couldn't tell.

They were passing through the heart of Cockpit Town now. Tan-Tan took in the Carnival sights. The runner took them up Main Street, past the town square, where the big calypso tent was erecting itself with the aid of tiny, agile chicle fetches. Calypsonians had been touring all the cities and towns on Toussaint. They went from one calypso tent to the next, singing their best new kaisos, competing for the title of Road March Monarch. There was a billboard in front of the tent. Its message: "Woi, Mama; Is a Calypso Fight; Piquant for So Tomorrow Nite!" Behind the words flashed vids of the reigning Road March Monarchs, Mama Choonks and Ras' Cudjoe-I. Piquant was a competition of skill and wit. The singers had to make up insults for one another in song, right there on the stage.

"Mummy, Mama Choonks going to sing 'Workee in the Parlour' tomorrow night?"

"Stop it, Tan-Tan; where you hear such rudeness? You musn't mind wicked people with nothing better to do than fast themself in other people business."

Tan-Tan didn't understand. More big people story. But

she'd heard people in the house softly singing the chorus to "Workee":

This woman greedy for so, you see?
One lover ain't enough for she!
She little bit, but she tallawah, oui!

Tan-Tan didn't understand all the words, but she liked the tune. Nursie had told her that "tallawah" meant somebody tough, somebody who could take hard knocks. Then she'd laughed a nasty laugh.

Little bit down the road they passed the masquerade camp. From inside came one set of hammering and drilling and cuss-word flying like breeze.

"You hear that?" Ione said. "Them building everything by hand, oui? The old-time way." She shook her head in admiration.

"Who, Mummy?"

"Fimbar and Philomise. They making the costumes for Carnival Day. Send-off parade here in Cockpit County Jour Ouvert afternoon, then them have a mag-lev train to carry everybody to Liguanea Town for the big jump-up; all the bands from every parish in the county competing.

"One big mako secret what theme them two men come up with for the float this year, oui? Even though everybody who jumping-up in the parade done pay for their costumes already." Ione smiled. "Is so them does always do it. People fenneh for know what they going to be wearing; no way to tell."

"Their eshus wouldn't tell them?"

"Nah. Fimbar and Philomise have special dispensation to lock out data from the spider web till they done."

The runner shouted: "You see them five hard-face men and women guarding all the entrances? Just for show, oui; the camp eshu give better security."

The only clue to the parade theme was a big banner across the front of the building with the words "Wail for Marley."

"Man," the runner chuckled, "Fimbar and Philomise been life partners and business partners since God was a boy, oui? Two people, one mind."

Tan-Tan stared at the camp until they had passed it. The banner flapped in the breeze, slapping the side of the building.

Finally the pedicab was at the fight yard all the way at the opposite edge of the town. While Ione was paying the cabbie, Tan-Tan jumped down and ran to the big wrought iron gates.

It had an old man guarding the entrance, standing in between the two stone pillars on either side of the gates. His face was nothing but wrinkles. He had a red kerchief tied and knotted on his old bald head. He was wearing a dirty white singlet. A dhoti flapped loose round his skinny matches stick legs-them. He was holding a long wood staff, but his wrinkly brown arms were meager so till you couldn't be sure what was staff and what was arms. He looked to Tan-Tan like a stick insect. She didn't get to see too many people too old for telo rejuve.

"Good afternoon, young lady," he said to Tan-Tan in his shaky old-man voice. "Don't you is the mayor little girl?"

"Yes, mister."

"And is what I could do for you this fine day?" The old man smiled down at her. His teeth looked white and perfect and new.

"Me and Mummy come to watch the practice, mister."

"Good afternoon, Bogle," Ione said. "You keeping well?"

"Yes, ma'am; thank you, ma'am. The hot sun does make the old bones feel young, oui? Like I could dance the stick fight again." Bogle opened the gates so mother and daughter could pass inside. "Mind allyou stay on the yellow walkways, all right?"

Baps! A man landed on his back on the ground just in front of Tan-Tan and Ione. Berimbau music jangled to a halt. Before they could move out of the way, a woman strode up. She looked at Ione, who stepped back, pulling Tan-Tan along with her.

"Get up!" the woman said to the man on the ground. "Get up, you lazy so-and-so!" Her voice was two rockstones cracking together. "Tomorrow when you fighting for real, you can't lay down so every time you get throw. Get up, I say!"

"Must be the bare hand marshall, she," Ione said to Tan-Tan in a low voice.

The marshall's chest was a bull chest. Her bare arms and legs-them were thick like poui tree trunk. She hauled the man to his feet. "Every Carnival them send me one set of allyou soft-hand people, say you learning how for fight. Well, go back and fight then, nuh!" With a hard slap to the man's shoulder she sent him stumbling back into the ring. The man who'd thrown him all that way looked determined and cocky. The berimbau player began his tune again. The two men faced off, grappled, began to tumble around the ring of the roda.

"Lord have mercy," Ione said. "What make anybody want to labour so?"

Tan-Tan could barely hear her for all the yelling and shouting, the scraping of the berimbau, the sounds of sticks crashing together. Over to the right they could see the stick fight ring. It had about twelve men and women standing in two short lines, facing one another. They each had one short stick and one long one. The stick fight marshall was shouting out the measures: "Lemme see you do the Scarlet Ibis!" The stick fighters turned and jumped, swinging their sticks high in air and hitting them against their opponents' sticks. It was more performance than fight, and Tan-Tan could see the pattern of the dance. It looked like birds flying for true.

"All right! Now the Dip and Fall Back!" One line crouched down low and ran behind the other. The people in the standing line leapt up high, crashing one another's sticks together at the apex of the jump. The marshall sang out, "Canboulay-Oh!" and the dance turned into a free-for-all. Fighters jabbed at one another with their long sticks and used the short ones to fend off blows. One set of comess and confusion!

"Mummy, they going to get hurt!"

"No, child; you ain't have no sense? Long time ago, the stick fight was real, but is just a pappyshow now."

It ain't look like no pappyshow to Tan-Tan; it looked like serious business.

Ione pointed to the middle of the fight yard. "Look the machète practice there so. That is what we come to see." She hustled Tan-Tan over to the barrier. "Peel your eye, girl. Me will look too. Tell me if you see your Uncle Quashee."

True to old-time tradition, the machète fighters-them were wearing full antique leather armour and face plate and thing, so it wasn't easy to see who was who. They were sparring in twos, slicing at each other with wood machètes. The marshall went from one pair to the next, moving an arm or a leg, stopping people sometimes to demonstrate a move.

Suddenly, one fighter tripped a next one to the ground and kicked the machète out of the fallen one's hand.

"Bloodcloth!" the downed one cursed, cradling the kicked hand. His voice was muffled by the face plate.

"Hold on; hold on!" the marshall yelled. The sparring stopped.

"Quashee, man, I tired tell you about cheating! Kicking not allowed; tripping not allowed! If you can't fight fair, get your ass out of my blasted yard, you hear?"

The cheater swiped off his helmet and face plate and dashed them to the ground. It was Quashee for true. It had dust in his hair. His face was covered in sweat and mud. Ione was only waving her handkerchief, trying to catch his eye, but he wasn't paying her no mind. He was too busy arguing with the marshall.

"Don't vex, Boss," Quashee say. "Is forget I did forget. I know you tell me before, but this thing ain't no joke, you hear? We only playing fight today, but if Antonio decide to challenge me, tomorrow I go be catching my nen-nen."

"Man, what you frighten for?" The man on the ground had picked himself up and entered into the argument. "You ain't even self know if Antonio going to challenge you. Today is he last chance to lay challenge. Is five months gone, and you ain't hear from he. I bet you he don't show up."

A real machète flew through the air and jooked into the leather helmet lying at the mens' feet, nearly slicing the helmet in half. Quashee cried out and jumped back.

"Well, Master Don, you lose your bet. I here." One of the other fighters in the ring was unbuckling his face plate. Tan-Tan knew that voice. It was her daddy. He had been practising beside Quashee all along, disguised by his helmet.

A woman in the crowd of spectators sang out joyfully, "Oh, God! Look story now!"

The marshall scolded: "Antonio, what the ass you doing making masque in my machète ring? Is Potoo supposed to be he in here, not you! And what you mean by throwing bare steel at one of my students like that?"

Antonio frowned, but the marshall continued his harangue: "You is mayor of Cockpit County, yes, but in this machète yard, even the mayor don't break my rules."

When Antonio replied, he did so in a respectful voice: "Sorry, Marshall; my head get too hot when I see that cheating son of a bitch who disgrace my wife and insult my hospitality!" (Quashee moved behind the marshall's back.) "I can't let it pass; I come to announce my intentions to challenge Quashee to a fair fight on Jour Ouvert morning!"

Outside the barrier, the spectators began to whisper to one another. Tan-Tan heard: "Lord, how Antonio think he could win a machète fight when Quashee been practising for five months now?"

Obviously the same thing was on the marshall's mind; he kissed his teeth, shook his head and said, "Allyou know I could cancel a challenge if I think one fighter have a unfair advantage, right? Antonio, you don't have no practice fighting with machète."

Antonio laughed. "No? What make you think so? You remember Warren, Marshall? The man you replace as machète master when he retire from the yard last year? Well, Warren is my good, good friend and he been giving me private lessons since before Jonkanoo Time."

Oh, yes: scandal break again in Cockpit County! The crowd was *ssu-ssu*ing so till the marshall had to shout for silence. It ain't have nothing for him to do but shrug and ask Quashee and Antonio if they understood the rules of the challenge: "The two of you going to fight with machète, leather armour your only protection; a fair fight, until one of you surrender or can't fight no more. And Quashee, listen good; the rules say you can't refuse a Jour Ouvert challenge if you healthy. So: you accept the challenge, or you refuse?"

Sweat was beading Quashee's forehead like when you put salt on a slice of z'avocat pear.

"I accept, Marshall."

Antonio just nodded.

Tan-Tan couldn't stand to keep silent any more. "Daddy! Daddy! I over here!"

Antonio turned at the sound of her voice. He strode over to Tan-Tan and Ione. Tan-Tan felt suddenly shy. Was he still vex with her?

But Antonio bust one big grin and patted Tan-Tan on her head. "Well, doux-doux, long time I ain't see you. You miss me?"

"Yes, Daddy," Tan-Tan whispered. Yes, she had been missing him too bad.

"Don't mind, Tan-Tan; as soon as I teach that young boy name Quashee a lesson, I go come back home to live with you. You would like that?" He was speaking to Tan-Tan, but is Ione the tamarind-brown beauty he was looking at.

Mummy frowned. She didn't say anything. She would make Daddy vex again! Desperately, Tan-Tan asked, "We go be together again, Daddy?"

"Yes, doux-doux. Soon." To Ione he said, "You looking after my child good, woman? I too angry with you already; you wouldn't want me to vex even more." His smile had an edge to it now.

Ione's look changed from I-don't-business-with-you to I-best-take-care. She pressed her lips together and made a little step back. "Yes, Antonio, I taking care of she. You don't see how good she looking?" Then a pleading look: "You going to come back to we, doux-doux?" she wheedled. "I sorry too bad for what I do."

Daddy's face softened. Mummy smiled like she'd just won a game of jacks. She reached out a hand to Daddy. He took it and squeezed it gently. Then harder, until his heavy leather gloves creaked. Don't that must hurt? Tan-Tan looked to her mother, but Ione just stood there with her mouth set in a smile. She hissed a little through her teeth. A tear was worming its way down her cheek. See, she really was sorry for hugging up with Quashee!

Still tightly holding her hand, Antonio smiled tenderly at his wife. "Yes, darling, I go come back, after I deal with that young boy there. He pee ain't even start to make froth yet, but still he casting he eye 'pon my woman like he is big man."

He raised Ione's hand to his lips and kissed it. He released her. He left them and went to where Quashee and the marshall were standing. Ione rubbed her hand. She looked as though she were going to cry for real, but instead she shook her head and gave a little laugh.

"What a thing eh, Tan-Tan?" she said in a high, shaky voice. "To have two men fighting over me! Ain't? I think your daddy really love me, sweetheart. I must try to be a good wife to he after this. Is me make him vex, and is me must fix it. Come let we go home, child; I have to dress to puss-foot tomorrow morning, oui!"

On the way home in the pedicab, all Ione's talk was about how Quashee is a nice man, young and tireless; but on the other hand, how Antonio is a mature man who know he own mind, and too besides, you see how fit and strong Antonio looking nowadays? She ain't really know which one to wish would win, after them both have them good points.

Tan-Tan was frighten too bad, oui.

"Mummy," she asked. "Daddy go dead?"

Ione sighed. "Tan-Tan, you does worry too much about stupidness. The machète marshall ain't go let Quashee kill we mayor, doux-doux. The rules say you ain't supposed to kill in a Jour Ouvert challenge. For you to win, your opponent have to be hurt too bad to keep fighting, or he have to beg you to stop. Okay? So what you think I should wear tomorrow? I have to look nice for the fight!"

Ione and Antonio had always had a stormy relationship. *"Love so sweet it hot,"* people said. They quarrelled often. It added spice to the subsequent making up. It was their favourite game. But over the years the sweetness had soured. To keep it juicy they'd had to raise the stakes on the fights. Now they each had too much to lose. Neither would give ground. People used to think that Ione was the one suffering, oui? Cockpit County knew about Antonio and the way he lied about his womanizing. The old people who had seen everything in their lives happen two and three and four times would just shake their heads and mutter, "He going to run aground, just like a Garvey ship."

People thought say was only wicked Antonio horning Ione, for Ione had been too sly to make anybody know her business.

But the game had gotten stale on her. Once Antonio had become mayor he was soon too busy with the work to pay their games much mind. Some days Ione felt say she could have paraded naked through Antonio's office with three of her lovers and he wouldn't notice. Singing with the Jubilante Mummers distracted her busy intellect a little. Being on the committee that organized the annual Mercy Table helped too, but she missed Antonio. She found herself longing for the young people days when the two of them would meet after a day of farming and hold hands and walk and talk in the setting sun and make plans for their life together till the frogs in the wisdom weed bushes were wooing *krek-ek!* in the dark.

Ione decided to try a new way to catch Antonio's attention again. She got pregnant. So that is the piece of comess that Tan-Tan had been born into. Two people who loved each other fiercely but had forgotten how to do it without some quarrel between them. Ione and Antonio thought say is baby they were making oui, but they were really only creating one more thing to quarrel over.

It had sweet Antonio can't done to know he was going to be a father. And it was a good thing he liked the idea, for from the first birth pangs hit Ione, it was as though she realised she didn't have the taste for hard labour, oui. As soon as she pushed the baby out of her, Ione took one look at it and shouted at Antonio to activate the wet-nurse, purchased to help Ione with the breastfeeding. The midwife Babsie took the baby, held it out for Ione to give it one dry kiss on the tiny cheek, and that was that for mother-love.

Antonio followed Babsie as she went into the next room and parked the baby in the carry pouch of the wet-nurse. The nurse's calming blue chicle gel body hummed reassuringly. "Is all right," he said to Babsie. "I go stay with she little bit."

With trembling hands, he made sure his new daughter was snug and comfortable in the carry pouch. She stopped crying. He guided her mouth to the teat of the wet-nurse. The tiny lips locked on and began to suck.

Antonio sat for two hours straight by the baby's side. He marvelled to watch the new little thing eat, sleep. Watched her wake crying at the feel of the soiled bedding wadded round her. The wet-nurse had come with instructions. He played the ones for changing the swaddling and followed them meticulously, afraid at every turn that he would hurt the child. He fed her again. Then he sat and stared at her for another long hour.

"I still getting pain," a voice from the next room said.

"But no more contractions?"

Antonio climbed slowly out of his reverie into awareness. Ione was next door in the lying-in room, talking to the doctor. Is how long he had left her alone?

He jumped to his feet. He picked up the baby and hurried into the next room. His wife's skin was grey with fatigue, her eyelids-them drooping. Is two hands she was using to hold the glass of water to swallow the pills the doctor was giving her.

Doctor Kong turned and smile at him. "Congratulations, Daddy."

Antonio looked to Ione, but the cut-eye of contempt he got in return was enough to slice skin, oui. She reached out her two arms to claim her property. Antonio put the baby into them. But Ione grasped her too roughly. The pickney woke up and started to cry.

"No," Antonio said. "Hold she so."

"Back off from me. You make any pickney?"

And it was Ione who held her child as Doctor Kong syringed the nanomite solution that would form her earbug into the baby's ear. From then on, what used to be sweet hotness between Ione and Antonio turned to nuclear war, yes.

Ione would look in on Tan-Tan once a day and pat the tiny shoulder, just a little bit too hard. She would always startle Tan-Tan awake, and the baby would start to cry. Quick-quick, Ione would set the wet nurse on "rock." "Ssh, baby, ssh. You musn't cry. Don't make so much noise, or the Midnight Robber will come and take you away."

In years to come, the little girl Tan-Tan would ask the eshu to show her images of the Midnight Robber. Fascinated and frightened at the same time, she would view image after image of the Midnight Robber with his black cape, death-cross X of bandoliers slashed across his chest, his hat with its hatband of skulls. The Midnight Robber, the downpressor, the stealer-away of small children who make too much mischief. The man with the golden wooing tongue. She would show him. She would be scarier than him. She would be Robber Queen.

All Ione knew was that she was no good at being a baby-mother. She told her husband, "Hear nuh? You have one pickney now, so don't expect me to be stretching out my figure trying to make no more for you."

Antonio pushed out his lip when she said that, and his brow got dark as thunder clouds, but he didn't say nothing, nothing at all. After that, no sweet words for Ione any more.

Is all right though. Ione had better fish to fry, oui? Mayor Antonio was always bringing sweetie and dolly for his little girl Tan-Tan, but he never had anything sweet no more for his hot-blooded, lonely wife. Ione pitched her cap for a youth named Evan, a tall, sweet-talking swaggerboy. Who coulda blame her? Such a nice boy, so polite, so attentive. Such long, strong legs. She hoped for Antonio to see the glances between them and counter with a passion of his own. The game was on again.

Well, doux-doux, Ione was a woman who got bored easily. Couple months down the road, Evan made his eyes rest too long on a pretty young man he met while playing dominoes. And is not like he and Ione coulda had any fidelity pact, but Ione didn't want to be one of two people vying for Evan's loyalty. Next day, Ione abandoned Evan for Franklyn and his green, bitter-melon eyes.

About a half-year later, Ione's favourite parasol flew away from her in the garden, and Franklyn laughed to see her running after it. Just for that little piece of mako, Franklyn gave way to Jairam. Jairam was a dougla boy, Indian and Euro blood from Shipmate Shiva that had settled two continents away. Jairam's mammy was descended from the longtime ago East Indians, the ones who had crossed the Kalpani, the Black Water on Earth to go and work their fingers to the bone as indentured labour in the Caribbean. Jairam was a pretty, pretty man with curly black hair and sweet, pouty lips. All the same though, he could never get a joke. Ione soon tired of his long, serious face, so Jairam lost his place to Quashee. By coincidence, it was about the same time that Antonio threw over a certain Shanti for a pretty piece of sweetness name Aïsha.

Now, Quashee was to hang around a little longer. He was the first one of this string of lovers to really sweet Ione: his skin was smooth, black and hot; just so cocoa-tea will warm your body on a cool morning. He managed to keep Ione entertained for a few years well. By then, Tan-Tan was seven, and she was so used to seeing Quashee round the place, she was calling him "uncle." Nice arrangement for Ione, oui. Hard-working husband and a harder lover.

Things couldn't go on so for good. Cockpit County is a small place, and you know how them back-a-wall, smalltown people stay. Eventually, Antonio came to find out about his wife and Quashee. Jealous Jairam whispered some badmouth something in his ear one day.

At first, Antonio didn't believe, but all day long he kept seeing Quashee in his mind's eye. That good-for-nothing grin.

The long, lanky way he would lope after the ball on the soccer field that would have people sighing and fanning themselves for how pretty he was. If Ione was horning him in their own house Granny Nanny would have the images in her data banks, but no-one could override Nanny's privacy protection. Nanny only chose to reveal information that she judged would infringe on public safety.

Like plenty people in Cockpit County, Quashee had a way to pass by the house in the evenings to pay his respects to Mayor Antonio and wife, Ione. Antonio had always felt say Quashee was really paying respects to their good red rum, but now he was wondering. Quashee and Ione? For true?

And that is how the story start.

"Is a argot of she operating language, seen?" Maka's voice was muffled through the filter he wore over nose and mouth. He inspected the beaker on the stove, frowned at it.

"Nannysong? How you mean, 'argot'? All this time me think say it *is* her operating language." Antonio longed to take his own filter off, but Maka said the fumes could be harmful. He stayed close to the door, ready to run outside if it looked like the experiment was getting away from Maka. He touched the nearby wall of Maka's house, still bemused at there being no eshu, at the way that runners chose to live inside dead material.

Maka smiled. Laugh lines ran deep grooves beside his mouth, making his leonine features even more arresting. With one foot he hooked a stool closer to his worktable. Looked at it approvingly. "Is my cousin make this, you know? Work the wood with she own two hands. First one she make that ain't give nobody splinters."

Labour. Back-break. Antonio grimaced at the memory of

the calluses on Beata's palms. "Me nah understand oonuh, but your way is your choice. Tell me about this creole then, nuh?"

Maka sat on his cousin's stool. In their terrarium on the worktable, mice scurried around. "When Nanny get create, she come in like a newborn adult; all the intelligence there, but no knowledge. You follow me?"

"Hmm."

"She had was to learn, she had was to come to consciousness. Them days there, the programmers and them had write she protocols in Eleggua, seen—the code them invent to write programmes to create artificial intelligence?"

"Yes, me know." Old-time story. Antonio sipped at the rum he'd brought to share with the Obi-Bé's son. He savoured its sweet burning at the back of his throat. Maka raised his own glass to him, threw back a swallow.

The liquid on the burner was bubbling. Maka consulted the notes on the table beside him, written on stained, wrinkled sheets of the headblind paper that Antonio found so wondrous. Code that Nanny couldn't automatically read!

Maka turned down the heat, added another substance to the mix. "Well," he continued, "something start to go wrong. It get to where the programmers would ask Nanny a question, and she would spew back mako blocks of pure gibberish. Them think say the quantum brain get corrupt. Them prepare to wipe it and start over."

"Them kill Granny Nanny?" The thought was obscene.

"Nearly. But she save she own self. Is Marryshow she break through to first. You know he was a calypsonian, yes? Just trying a thing, he run the Nanny messages through a sound filter; tonal instead of text-based, understand? The day them was set to wipe she memory, Nanny start to sing to Marryshow. She brain didn't spoil, it just get too complex for Eleggua to translate the concepts she was understanding no more; after Nanny was seeing things in all dimensions—how a simple four-dimensional programming code would continue to do she? So she had develop she own language."

"Nannysong."

"Nah. If you was to transpose nannycode to the tonal, humans couldn't perceive more than one-tenth of the notes, seen? Them does happen at frequencies we can't even map. Nanny create a version we could access with we own senses. Nannysong is only a hundred and twenty-seven tones, and she does only sing basic phrases to we; numbers and simple stock sentences and so."

"Like the proverbs she used to sing to we in crêche."

"Seen. Same way so." Maka read in his notes again, took the beaker off the burner.

"So is what I hear allyou runners doing? When you turn off Nanny?"

"Not turn we turning she off. Not possible. We just know more nannysong than the rest of oonuh, we more fluent, seen? If you sing the right songs, so long as Nanny don't see no harm to life nor limb, she will lock out all but she overruling protocols for a little space."

"Rasscloth," Antonio breathed in amazement.

Maka laughed. "Nice thing to know, eh? And we learning little more nannysong every day. We could ask she to do things nobody else could even think of."

"And how come allyou runners know all this?"

"Is who you think we descend from? We was programmer clan." Maka pulled the filter off his face, used a dropper to suck up some of the paste from the beaker.

"What, it ready?" asked Antonio. His heart started a pan jam beat. He stepped closer to the worktable. Took his own filter off.

"Me think so. If me understand the old knowledge right. If me follow the instructions right. Making casareep juice for pepperpot stew is one thing, but me ain't know about this woorari.

Me tell you straight, Compère, this herb science I teaching myself is a ancient skill for true." He stuck a hand into the terrarium, pulled out a kicking mouse. He dropped it into the deep pan of a nearby scale, weighed it. Consulted his notes. Picked the mouse up again. Forced its muzzle open. Squeezed a measured drop of the woorari onto its tongue. The mouse struggled and worked its mouth, foam forming on its snout. Maka put it down on the table. It ran a short distance, then flopped to the ground and lay still. Maka inspected it. "Good. Still breathing." He looked at Antonio and smiled.

Come Jour Ouvert morning, Tan-Tan was afraid to even self get out of bed. She had asked her mother the rules of the fight over and over till Ione got fed up and refused to repeat them any more. Tan-Tan knew the rules in her own head by now. As she opened her eyes she started to recite them like a mantra. Daddy would be all right.

"Young Mistress," said eshu softly. "Ione say is time to get up now. She say to clean your teeth and take a shower, then put on your best frock, the white one with the sailor collar."

Tan-Tan got out of bed. She went outside through the bedroom doors that led to the back verandah. The morning was looking dreary, oui. Papa Sun was hiding his face behind one big mako cloud. Rainflies flitted everywhere, dancing on their wings in anticipation of a wetting. Tan-Tan went to her bathroom, washed herself and brushed her teeth. She reached into her closet for the white dress with the blue-piped collar, but her hand touched her Robber Queen outfit instead. She put it on. It covered up some of her scared feelings.

Nursie bustled into the room, carrying combs, ribbons and fragrant coconut oil for Tan-Tan's hair. "No, child. Put on the white dress, you ain't hear what your mother say?"

"I wearing this."

"Tan-Tan . . ."

"Mistress say is okay," chimed the eshu out loud. It confused Tan-Tan. She hadn't had any message from her mother.

Nursie sighed with exasperation. "Let me just get some red ribbons then. These blue ones not going to match."

Nursie oiled and parted Tan-Tan's hair, wove it into plaits, then rubbed some of the coconut oil into her elbows and knees so they wouldn't be ashy. "My pretty little girl." She kissed the top of Tan-Tan's head and took her to have breakfast with Ione.

Tan-Tan's mother was sitting at the table, staring off into the distance. "Oh, you prefer to wear that instead, doux-doux?" she said absent-mindedly. "All right."

Nursie narrowed her eyes. "Compère, eshu tell me that you give permission for Tan-Tan to wear this."

It was a second before Ione replied. "Eh? No, but is all right." With a sigh she got to her feet and pulled out a chair for Tan-Tan. "Just ask Ben if he will please do a synapse wash on the eshu, nuh? It must be past time." She stood and patted Tan-Tan's shoulder, a little too hard. She smiled nervously, muttered at the air, "Eshu, we ready to eat."

Mummy was wearing a beautiful white dress that left her shoulders bare. It had puffy sleeves and a deep flounce from knee to ankle. Tan-Tan thought Ione was the most beautiful woman in the whole world.

A chicle fetch slid into the room, loaded with covered trays. Ione took them and put them on the table. Bammy bread and saltfish with cabbage and thyme. "Oh, what a creation! Eshu, thank Cookie for we, please."

But Ione only nibbled at breakfast. She kept asking Tan-Tan if she looked okay, kept checking her hand mirror all the time.

Outside, the threatened passing shower broke. Drops

pounded like fists at the windows and thunder shouted at lightning.

As soon as the meal was over, Ione had the eshu make a full-sized mirror on the nearest wall. She put a colourdot from her purse onto one lip, then pressed both lips together. Her lips flushed with her favourite oxblood burgundy.

The eshu said out loud, "The limousine waiting, Mistress."

"Oh God," Ione whispered. "Time to go." She hugged Tan-Tan to her, a little too hard. "Don't fret eh, doux-doux? One way or another, it go work out all right." Silently Tan-Tan repeated the rules of the duel to herself. They bustled out into the front yard.

The shower was over. Tiny so like babies' fingernails, transparent rainfly wings were everywhere, held pasted in place by drops of water. Outside twinkled. Flightless as ants now, the rainflies were crawling off to wherever they went after a downpour. The sun had come out, was burning down full. Registering the way Tan-Tan's pupils contracted against the glare, the nanomites swimming in the vitreous humour of her eyes polarised, dimming the light for her.

Plang-palang! Plang-palang! Cockpit County was in the full throes of Jour Ouvert morning revelry. People beat out their own dancing rhythms with bottle and spoon, tin-pan and stick. What a racket! Bodies danced everywhere: bodies smeared with mud; men's bodies in women's underwear; women wearing men's shirt-jacs and boxers; naked bodies. They pressed against the car, pressed against one another, ground and wound their hips in the ecstatic license of Carnival. Someone grinned into the limo at Tan-Tan and Mummy. The woman had temporarily cell-sculpted her skin to be Afro on one side, Euro on the other. The Euro side was already sunburnt. She licked the length of the window with her tongue, which had been pierced with a star-shaped platinum nugget. The metal scraped against the window glass.

The limo crept along, slow as a chinny worm. A mako jumbie strode through the crowd, picking his way on his tall stilts. His tattered motley had been made into pants that clothed the stilts all the way to the ground. His chest was bare and he'd tied a long, pointy beak onto his face.

A Robber King stepped into the road in front of them, brandishing pistols almost as long as he was tall. He blew a shrieking whistle that brought to a halt the comess and carrying-on all around him. A circle of space cleared for him. People called out to him cheerfully and drew closer to see what he would do. The limousine braked, tried to go round the man. He stepped into their path again. Ione sighed. "Let he give he speech," she told the car.

Tan-Tan could have lain comfortably under the expanse of the Robber's hat. It had small white skulls bobbing all round its brim. The skulls' lower jaws yammered, but it was too loud in the street to hear if they were saying anything. The Robber's black and red outfit was the essence of Robber King style: bandoliers, holsters, chaps, alligator skin boots with enormous spurs. For a second, Tan-Tan felt the old fear: had he come to take her away for being bad?

The Robber gestured with his guns, spat his whistle from his mouth and broke into the nonsensible rant he had written especially for this day. "Arrest thou compunctively, embroilèd despoilers. Dip and fall back, and hear my sultry cry." He turned his head towards the car as he spoke, and it was as though he were sitting right beside them. He must have been wearing a pointmike. Tan-Tan leaned forward to get every word of his speech. Maybe she could pick up some new ones for hers.

"My seraphic dam was a very queen of Egypt; mine pater its monarchical magnate, and I, a son of the sun, a coddled cocotte in my child's robes of ermine and cloth-of-gold. Who would curdle my kingly boy's joy, who mash me down and steal me away like jacks from a ball?"

And so it went: the classic tale, much embroidered over the centuries, mirrored the autobiography of Olaudah Equiano, an African noble's son stolen into slavery on seventeenth-century Earth. The Robber Kings' stream-of-consciousness speeches always told of escaping the horrors of slavery and making their way into brigandry as a way of surviving in the new and terrible white devils' land in which they'd found themselves.

". . . and then," the Robber went on, "I wrestle the warptenned flying ship from the ensorcelled dungmaster, the master plan blaster in his silver-fendered stratocaster with wings of phoenix flame, and I . . ."

Ione opened the window, stuck her hand out. "Here," she called to the Robber. "Take this, and make we move on." She held out money in her hand.

He was supposed to stop when offered payment, but he wouldn't reach for it. "Avaunt!" he shouted. "Get thee behind me, horny horning whore of Babylon!" Someone in the crowd giggled. "Thine gelt shall not tempt me, too wise am I to be clasped by your thighs."

"Take it," Ione growled. "Is fight yard we going, you hear me?"

Fight yard. Fight yard . . . was whispered through the crowd. "Robber man," someone yelled, "take she blasted money and let she get through. She going to see she husband duel."

Ione threw the coin. The Robber leapt, swept off his hat, bent on one knee to catch the coin between his teeth and came up smiling. Tan-Tan clapped her hands and whistled to salute him. "Shut up, pickney," Ione snapped. Tan-Tan pouted and slouched back against the seat.

The Robber stepped back to let them through, bowed and flourished his hat as they passed. The ring-bang ruction and the dancing started up round them again.

They reached the fight yard to find Quashee standing in the

machète circle already, looking stiff and serious in his leather armour gleaming with jumbie oil, and holding his helmet under his arm. Ione made to wave to him, but pulled her hand back before the gesture was finished. She sucked in her bottom lip and hurried with Tan-Tan to a seat. Some people glared at her, some smiled. An old, white-haired woman with a cane made the kiss-teeth sound of disgust and leaned over to whisper with her companions, another old woman and an old man.

The fight yard had been rearranged to accommodate the only activity it would feature today: the duelling circle. The circle dominated the whole yard. It had rows of benches erected all round. Spectators sat on one side, everybody dressed to puss-foot, everybody excited. The duelling parties sat in two separate boxes on the other. A team of medics sat beside the fighters in one box, a stretcher propped up nearby. Higglers moved through the crowd of watchers, shouting, "Roast peanut? Topi-tambo? Chataigne? Who going buy my fresh roast peanut?"

Tan-Tan craned her neck, trying to see the fighters better. "Mummy, is where Daddy there?" Tan-Tan asked.

"I don't know, darling. I don't see he. Mama Nanny, tell me that after all this fret I fret, the blasted man not going to just forfeit."

The fighters were all dressed differently, according to their fighting style: some armoured like Quashee; some in leotards; some in dhotis with bare chests or bubby-bands. They all looked jittery.

Daddy finally came striding out from the change rooms. Ben the gardener was running in front as squire, carrying Antonio's helmet and machète.

Quashee ain't have a squire.

The crowd went silent. Daddy walked into that ring tall and proud. You could tell he wasn't 'fraid nobody. Tan-Tan's heart was thumping like drums.

She had never seen Daddy look so fine as this day. His leather armour was all in black with silver joints for the elbow and knee. His matching black leather helmet had a silver mouth guard. His machète was sharp so till it caught the little bit of sunshine that had graced the day and flung the light into Tan-Tan's eyes, sharp like a razor cut.

Tan-Tan could see the fear-sweat already on Quashee's brow.

Quashee and Antonio stood opposite each other. The machète marshall examined both their armour, ran a black box over their bodies. "Mummy, what he doing?"

A woman beside them answered. "He checking to make sure them ain't using electronic fields to protect themself."

"Granny Nanny," the marshall chanted in nannysong to the air, "let the record show: the combattants dress fair to fight fair." His enhanced voice echoed. He put a hand on either man's forearm and switched to patwa. "Gentlemen, I want you to inform the crowd who issue this machète challenge this Jour Ouvert morning."

"Is me, Marshall. Antonio, mayor of Cockpit County, against Quashee, the man who take away me wife honour from me."

Somebody muttered, "Eh-eh. Like her honour is yours to have or lose."

Mummy shot a quick glare at the man, her lips set hard together. He returned her gaze sheepishly, shrugged. Mummy looked back at the ring.

The marshall boomed, "Quashee, you accept the challenge?"

"Yes, Marshall." His voice trembled a little.

The marshall nodded and looked up at the stands. "People, listen good, for though Granny Nanny hearing we, you is the human eyes of the law this morning. This fight must go according to these rules:"

Tan-Tan whispered the rules along with the marshall.

"Them could only use bare machète, no other weapon or device.

"Them could wear leather armour for protection.

"If the fight going fair, nobody must interfere.

"The thing must continue until one of them beg mercy or can't fight no more.

"The winner shouldn't kill, but should show mercy.

"Them is the rules. Allyou go be witness?"

"Yes, Marshall," the crowd yelled back. As the marshall turned and walked to safety at the edge of the ring, Tan-Tan could hear the excited voices of people all around her:

"Quashee, man, is Quashee go win! Put a ten rupees on Quashee there for me."

"You know so! He been practising! He sure to beat out Antonio. Look my five rupees."

"Nah, man. Is fool allyou fool. Antonio have more life experience. I bet you the dog have some tricks in he. I putting down twenty on Antonio, oui?"

From the edge of the ring the marshall called to the two fighters: "All right; allyou ready?"

They nodded. Quashee put on his helmet. Even from where she was sitting Tan-Tan could see how his trembling hands fumbled with the chin buckle. Ben made to put on Antonio's helmet, but Antonio stopped him cool-cool. He swaggered over to Mummy and Tan-Tan. Ione giggled like a sob. She put her hand to her mouth.

"Doux-doux," Antonio called out to his wife, "give me your favour, nuh? Your lace handkerchief to tie back me hair from out me eyes?"

Ione put her hand on her bosom. Her lips wavered into a smile. She reached into her bodice with two fingers, slow, the way molasses does run down the side of the bowl. She drew out a pretty lace kerchief from her blouse, dabbed it against the moisture gathered between her breasts, and then flung it to Antonio. He caught the little piece of lace and held it up to his face, inhaling the perfume of Ione's skin. "Oh God," a man whispered from the crowd. "Look how he love she, even though she did horn he."

"Never mind that at all," somebody replied. "Ain't you would give anything to be that kerchief, and rest where it does rest?"

Antonio smiled at Ione and tied back his long black hair with the kerchief. Only then would he let Ben put on the helmet. Tan-Tan clutched at the Robber Queen cape Daddy had given her. She closed her eyes and said silently, *The winner can't kill. He must show mercy. The winner can't kill . . .*

Daddy and Quashee shook hands. Ben jogged to safety beside the marshall. Daddy and Quashee drew their machètes. They started to circle each other.

And the fight start! Quashee made the first feint. Antonio danced out of the way easy-easy. He swung his machète through the air. Quashee stumbled out of the way just in time. Somebody in the stands muttered, "Quashee too craven, oui."

Antonio came back for another jab, but Quashee lunged beneath it. Antonio cried out as Quashee's machète grazed across his thigh.

"Daddy!" screamed Tan-Tan, jumping to her feet.

Ione pulled her firmly into her lap and held her still. "Quiet, pickney. Don't distract your daddy." Tan-Tan bit her lips against the sobs that threatened to break through.

A sharp line of red blood was oozing through the slice in Antonio's black armour. He ran a hand through it, then shook his head like a bull snorting in anger. He leapt vigorously at Quashee, slicing and slicing through the air. Quashee didn't let a single thrust through. He jumped, he dodged; he used his machète to block all the chops Antonio was throwing for him. He was good, and young, and fast. Tan-Tan held Mummy's hand tight-tight. Ione curled her arms round Tan-Tan, never taking her eyes off the ring. She mumbled, "Chop he, doux-doux; mash he down!"

Antonio got inside Quashee's block. He chopped off a piece of Quashee's forearm guard clean. But the cut barely grazed the skin. Antonio dropped to the ground and swept the blade of his machète at Quashee's ankles-them. Quashee jumped up over the blade but got tangled in midair in his own two feet. He crashed down. Antonio was on top of him one time; he pinned Quashee and put his machète right up under Quashee's chin guard, where his neck was exposed. Quashee wailed, "Ai! Mercy!" He dropped his machète and froze, his palms spread rigid in front of him. A trickle of blood was running down his neck. Antonio had nicked him.

"You want me to stop?" Antonio roared into his face.

"Yes, yes! I done, I done!"

"All right, little boy, Mama man; I go stop." The scorn in Antonio's voice was how you would speak to some stray dog you kick in the street. He slapped Quashee on his ear with the flat of the machète. Quashee howled again.

"Ey!" shouted the marshall in his enhanced voice. "Enough of that!"

Antonio stood up. Ben rushed over and unbuckled Antonio's helmet to reveal his triumphant, sweaty grin. "Oh," said Ione softly. She loosened her hold on Tan-Tan a little.

The marshall hurried over to the two fighters, face black as a passing shower.

"Antonio, you know the rules. Once Quashee ask you to stop, you had no right to box he like that!"

"Man, don't give me no umbrage today. I win the fight fair, and I taking my wife and my child and going home."

Somebody in the stands shouted out, "Bloodfire! What wrong with Quashee?"

Quashee hadn't gotten up, was lying limp as do-do in the dirt.

Ione sniggered. "All that just for a little pin prick? Quashee!" She yelled, "You could stop making mako now! Fight done!"

Quashee started to make a horrible choking noise. Alarm jumped plain onto the marshall's face. He lifted Quashee's helmet, then shouted for the doctors. The team jogged to Quashee's side, carrying a stretcher between them. They assessed the information they were getting from his earbug and began to minister to him. The marshall got the listening look of someone getting a message from an eshu. He scowled at Antonio, who looked confused and angry.

"You coward dog you!" The marshall motioned to the sheriffs. "Arrest he."

All the way home in the sheriffs' car, sitting with Antonio between the two guards, Ione was only beating her breast and carrying on, holding on to Antonio like she would never let go. Antonio reached out from time to time to pat Tan-Tan's head where she sat crying in the front seat. "Maka get it wrong," he fumed. "The poison was only supposed to slow he down, not make he sick so."

The streets were a little clearer. Everybody would be following Fimbar and Philomise's band "Wail for Marley" as it made its first lap through the Cockpit County parade route. Then it would be time to see the band off to Liguanea Town for the competition. Nanny's guidance was for the sheriffs to take Ione and Tan-Tan home, then drive Antonio to the shift tower in Liguanea and confine him there. Whether Quashee lived or died, things weren't going to go good with Antonio.

"That blasted Quashee. He constitution too damn weak, yes?"

Tan-Tan was so frightened she couldn't think. They were going to lock Daddy away! She kept reaching out her hand to touch Antonio's sleeve, but he wasn't paying her plenty mind, only stroking Ione's hair and saying, "Don't cry, doux-doux, don't cry."

They reached the mayor house. "Compère," said one of the sheriffs, "you have one hour to pack up your necessaries for the jail."

"Pack? Why?"

"You just pack up what you need, oui? Provincial Mocambo not going to waste resources on you, you must bring your own. And make haste, yes? Sooner we get you there, sooner we get to jump-up this Carnival."

"Nanny save we! Antonio!" Ione moaned in grief, taking Antonio's face between her hands and kissing it all over.

"Doux-doux . . ." Antonio picked her up and took her inside, Ione holding on to him and sobbing for dear life. Tan-Tan tried to follow them inside the bedroom, but they closed the door in her face.

"Daddy! Mummy!" She threw herself to the floor and cried like her heart would break. She was still weeping when she felt the touch on her shoulder. She looked up through bleary eyes. Nursie and the sheriffs. Nursie shook her head sadly. "I hope your parents find enough drama to suit them this time." She pounded at the door; no answer. She sucked her teeth in disgust. "Them two have one solution for every problem, oui?" One of the sheriffs sniggered. Nursie silenced him with one look. She picked Tan-Tan up and rocked her. Tan-Tan threw her arms round Nursie's neck and blubbered.

"Oh, doux-doux darling, don't fret so, nuh? Nursie go take care of you. Come lie down."

"No! I want Mummy! I want Daddy!"

"They go come and see you soon, darling. Come now."

She put Tan-Tan to bed, but when the fetch brought in the

cocoa-tea, Tan-Tan remembered how it had made her sleep the last time. She only took couple-three little sips. She pretended to be drowsy. Slowly she closed her eyes and made like she was asleep.

Nursie stayed. Tan-Tan was frantic. Nursie had to go away! Finally Nursie sighed and left the room. When Tan-Tan couldn't hear her steps retreating any more, she swung herself carefully out of bed and began to put her shoes on; a quiet pair, not the barking alligator shoes. Then quickly, just in case eshu decided to check with Nursie or Granny Nanny, Tan-Tan ran out through the porch door and round to where the sheriff's car was parked. Her earbug clicked as she moved out of the house's detection field. The trunk was open. Tan-Tan stood on tiptoes to look inside.

"You is Tan-Tan."

Tan-Tan jumped. The voice was deep and sad as a potoo-owl's cry. She peeked out from behind the car. The man who stood there had the massive chest and tree branch arms of a runner. His forehead sloped back to his peaked hairline, giving him the appearance of royalty. His brow was creased like ugli fruit skin, his mouth turned down in a forlorn bow. He looked like everybody in the world had decided to stop talking to him. "You is Tan-Tan, ain't?" he repeated.

"Yes."

"I name Mako." He whistled a tune. Her earbug crackled into static, then faded away. "Your daddy in trouble," he said.

"Yes."

"I sorry too bad for it."

Why was he sorry? He wasn't Quashee.

"I could help he. You want that?"

"Oh, yes please, Compère."

"Then you have to help me." He held out a small playback machine wrapped in what looked like datastock.

Tan-Tan reached for it. As she took it from him, she felt the callus on his fingers. "What I must do?"

"Find a way to give he that when nobody ain't looking. And mind you don't talk about it out loud, not you and not your daddy. You must keep quiet, quiet about it like a mus-mus, like a mouse. Seen?"

"Seen."

"Put it in your pocket."

She did, and when she looked up, the man's eyes were brimming over. "I pray it going to work. Is two nannytunes we just now invent, nobody ain't have opportunity to test them out yet. But this might be he only chance to live out he life on he own terms, so try not to make a mistake, pickney. Me and your daddy was friend. Tell he I going to be following he presently." He turned and jogged away, leg muscles flexing with each step.

Tan-Tan peeked inside her pocket. The package was safe.

There was a big cloth bag full of Daddy's clothes and some folded-up blankets beside it. People were coming, she could hear Nursie talking to somebody. She clambered into the trunk and tucked herself into a dark corner of it, pulling the folded blankets over herself as neatly as she could.

Somebody plopped some heavy things down round her, probably more bags for Daddy. One landed on her foot. Quietly she squirmed the foot out from under it.

"So is what he use to poison the man?" asked one of the sheriffs.

"Me nah know. Nanny say woorari, curare; something so. I wonder is where he get it?"

"Cho, me ain't business. He coming or what?" said one of the sheriffs.

"Yes, look he here."

In a few seconds Tan-Tan heard more sets of footsteps, her

mother's sobs, then Daddy's gruff voice saying, "Where Tan-Tan?"

"I put she to sleep in she room, Compère," said Nursie. "She was too distressed. She could come and see you later."

"Seen. Then I ready. Make we go." The trunk was slammed shut, leaving Tan-Tan in total darkness. The autocar dipped with the weight of people getting into it. Mummy's sobs got louder. Daddy's voice said, "Is all right, sweetness. I go come back to you soon. Look after Tan-Tan."

The car moved off. Tan-Tan felt it turn out of the driveway then pick up speed. She rolled around helplessly whenever the car turned a corner. She hung on to the luggage, but it only slid round with her. She was starting to feel dizzy. She bumped her head. She was locked in—how would they ever find her? Suppose they didn't take Daddy's bags out right away? "Daddy!" she shouted, but no-one heard her over the noise of the autocar. "Eshu," she whispered. No answer. The car lurched around another corner. She tumbled. The car picked up speed. "Eshu!" There was static like before, then a pop. Eshu clicked on reassuringly in her ear.

"What happen, young Mistress?"

"I frighten."

"Checking . . . Nanny say you in the trunk of the car, child. That not good. Hold on, young Mistress, help coming soon."

The autocar stopped moving. She heard the sound of running footsteps then saw light as the trunk was thrown open. Tan-Tan fought her way free of the blanket she was tangled in. A voice said, "Granny farts! The pickney mad or what?"

One of the sheriffs was there, and her father. They reached in and lifted her out of the trunk. Cars were zipping by. They were on the highway, parked over to the side. Daddy pulled her into his arms, hugged her hard. He was shaking. Tan-Tan hugged back. "Oh, my child, my child," Antonio said. "Own-way just like your mother. How you convince eshu to let you do this thing, eh?"

"He never know about it, Daddy."

"Back inside the car," said the sheriff. He sounded angry.

They started on their way again. Should she show him the package the man had given her? She reached into her pocket and touched it, then remembered: she couldn't do it while people were looking on.

The sheriffs sent word to Ione to come and collect Tan-Tan from the shift tower. "We ain't go be able to bring she back for you. Our day contract done long time, and we hear the jump-up sweet down in the city." Then they accessed the road marches that were playing in Liguanea. Songs blared out from the car's console. The two men sang and beat air steel pan along with the tunes, ignoring Tan-Tan and her daddy.

Antonio paid them no mind, just hugged Tan-Tan and rocked her. He didn't look good. His skin was grey with fright, and his body only trembling, trembling. "What if Quashee up and dead on me?" he whispered into Tan-Tan's hair. "When I get my hands on that Maka . . . !"

They entered the city limits, seat of the Provincial Mocambo. The outskirts were deserted, every man-jack in Liguanea centre was jumping-up with the bands. The long, wide avenues lined with gris-gris palms were quiet. Dog- and mongoose-sized fetches were going peacefully about their business, searching out and devouring trash. No need to dodge people and traffic today. The larger fetches made Tan-Tan think of her minder. The big peeny-wallie street bulbs bobbed and hovered above the city, their egg shapes clustering and glowing where there was most shade, flickering off whenever the sun caught them.

The car took them past low, graceful buildings, past a wooded park with a statue of Nanny of the Maroons and one of Zumbi. They pulled up in front of the tallest building in sight. It was ugly, thick and arrogantly high. "Your *hotel*, Compère," one of the sheriffs joked.

Daddy's skin was clammy. He looked ill. "What allyou go do with me?"

"So many people you must be send here already and you don't know what happen inside?"

"I never been inside, just by four-eye."

"Come. Get your things."

They all got out of the car. One sheriff hailed a chicle fetch, told it to be a porter. The fetch flipped parallel to the ground, indented its surface to hold Antonio's luggage. They loaded it up then approached the building, which greeted them when they reached inside its detection field. "Your i.d. and business verified," the building told them. "This Antonio Habib that you bring me must be confined here until official notice. All the holding cells free. Them start third door on the right. Please to tell me, Masters, the pickney coming in too?"

The two looked at each other uncomfortably for a second. "Yes, until she mother reach. Expect Ione Brasil, Cockpit County, mother to Tan-Tan, who is this pickney here so. Tan-Tan will have to stay in the holding cell with she father."

"Seen, Masters. Nanny judge she go be safe there till she mother reach. Ione Brasil could enter once today and leave once." The doors swung open for them.

Cement and bars; the whole inside of the place was only cement and bars, oui? Tan-Tan took Daddy's hand. He held on tight. There was a long, empty corridor with big metal doors flanking each side. Some of the doors had signs on them. Tan-Tan didn't understand all the words: TO DEPORTEES' HOLDING CELLS; LIMITED ACCESS AREA; COURTROOM A; COURTROOM B; LOWER COURT (FOR THOSE WITHOUT COUNSEL).

The third door on the right was open. The sheriffs took them inside. The cell was bare, felt almost dead. The sheriffs took Daddy on a quick tour of its empty rooms: bedsitting room with its food dispenser; bathroom. "We going now," they said.

The building assented. It let them out of the cell and then locked the door. The men left, fetch following them.

Daddy sat on the bed, shoved his face into his hands. "What to do, girl; what to do?" He looked so frightened, it made Tan-Tan frightened too. She went and stood by him, patted his knee. He looked up at her and gave her a shaky smile. "Come. Come and sit by me."

She clambered onto the bed. He put an arm round her shoulders, hugged her tightly. "What a thing, eh? What a thing. I was only fighting for my dignity and now the blasted man might up and dead on me. And then what, eh?"

He rocked them both, looked off bleakly into the distance. The building's eshu spoke from the air. "Antonio Habib," it said, "Quashee Cumberbatch just pass away."

"Nanny have mercy."

"Uncle Quashee, Daddy?"

Antonio whimpered. "What going to happen to me now?"

"Nanny don't find no extenuating circumstances, Master. Is up to the Provincial Mocambo. Life imprisonment or exile."

"Daddy? What going to happen?"

"Me nah know! Me nah know! Mama Nanny, you going to lock me away for true?"

"You a danger, Master," said the building eshu. "Is so the law go."

Antonio's face crumpled, horrifyingly, into tears. Her daddy wasn't supposed to cry. He wasn't supposed to be frightened. What could scare him? Terrified, Tan-Tan clung to him and started to wail too. Antonio rocked and rocked, clinging to her so hard she could feel his fingertips bruising her arm. She didn't care.

Something was hurting her chest where it was pressed against Daddy's body. The package the man had given her. She pulled it out of her pocket. Never in her born days had she seen datastock like that. It was dirty, and stayed crumpled. She pulled off the box, uncrumpled it, tried to flatten it against her thigh.

"A-what that, pickney?"

They weren't supposed to talk about it in words. She put a finger to her lips so Daddy would know to stay quiet. Then she handed the box and the datastock to him. His eyes opened big when he saw the writing on the paper. He read it. His tears dried. He sniffed snot back into his nose, swallowed. "Bumbo cloth! You mean that will work for real? I did swear say was only drunkenness talking when Maka tell me that thing."

"What, Daddy?"

He didn't reply, just looked right through her as though his mind were somewhere else. "Freedom . . ." he whispered. Then he grabbed her, hugged her tight. "I have to do it, girl."

"Do what, Daddy?"

"You ever hear people say the only way out is through?"

"No." She didn't understand.

Antonio stood, a dithery energy animating his body. "Freedom is the thing, eh? Is freedom me don't want to lose." Something lit his face, like relief, like hope. He stood up, squared his shoulders. He activated the box. Tan-Tan heard a burst of too-fast nannysong; a soft, high-pitched whine in her ears, then a fading static. The cell door swung open. "Koo ya! It work! Fooling a house eshu is one thing, but the shift tower? Bless you, Maka." He reached for Tan-Tan's hand. "Come. Time for we to do we business."

They headed briskly down the corridor. "Daddy, where we going?"

"To freedom, child. We going where nobody could tell we what to do. Maka say he will come after, and what the two of we could do in that world, with all we know! You want to come with me, right?"

"Yes, Daddy." She didn't understand, but she wasn't going to make him leave her again. "Mummy could come with we too?"

"Probably later, doux-doux. Hurry now."

Antonio took them into Courtroom A. Inside it was row after row of uncomfortable-looking seats. They all faced a big chair with a desk. There were two other chairs on either side of the desk.

"That is where the judge does sit," Antonio said, hustling them past a big chair. "When he pass sentence, the people to deport does go through here."

Behind the judge's seat was a door marked TO SHIFT TOWER. DEPORTEES AND DETENTION OFFICERS ONLY BEYOND THIS DOOR. They went through.

"Daddy, let we go home, nuh?"

"Can't do, sweetness. Quashee dead. Me try to go home and them will pop me. Maka saving my ass, darling. Can't get out, but I can get through."

They were in a long, dark cement corridor. Their footsteps rang on the concrete floor like the dead-gong in Cockpit County.

"Daddy, what 'deportee' mean?"

"When people do bad things, we does send them away so they can't hurt nobody else. Killers, rapists . . . people we don't know what to do with, and like so."

"And is which part New Half-Way Tree is?"

Antonio gave a small, tight laugh. "Where? You know what, doux-doux? It right here." He explained about the dimensional shift, how there were more Toussaints than they could count, existing simultaneously, but each one a little bit different. "We going to a next Toussaint, one we can't come back from again, nobody know how. It going to be hard to live, no comforts. But I think we can survive. Is a big chance I taking for you, doux-doux."

All Tan-Tan heard was *can't come back*. She imagined deportees walking down this same corridor, hearing their footsteps echoing in this world for the last time, and knowing they would never see home again.

They reached a room marked SHIFT TOWER. They went inside. The room was tall and narrow and the ceiling was so high that it disappeared in the shadows above. In the middle of the room was a tall-tall column with four doors all around it.

"That is how we going," Antonio said. "That is the halfway tree. You see the four pods?" He pointed to the doors. "We go get inside that one there—just like peas in a pod, right?" He tickled her to make her laugh, but it didn't work this time. "It will take we in, and point we at New Half-Way Tree, and fling we there like boulderstones from a slingshot."

Tears started to run down Tan-Tan's face; she had promised Daddy to be good, but she was scared.

"Don't frighten, sweetheart; it going to be a nice ride." His voice shook. He picked her up, took her over to one of the pods, stepped inside. "This is it, Tan-Tan. Pray that it going to work." Daddy activated the box again. Came another burst of song.

The door to the pod slid soundlessly closed. It was bare inside; just one dim light in the ceiling. Antonio had barely set Tan-Tan down when a wave of nausea swept through her. "Daddy!"

Antonio sat down hard beside her. Tan-Tan felt like a big hand was pressing her down onto the floor of the pod, its fingers stirring up her insides. "My ears block up," she complained.

"Hold your nose and blow hard," Antonio said. His voice was trembly. Tan-Tan looked at him. His face was grey with fear. He looked like he wanted to vomit. Her daddy wasn't supposed to 'fraid nothing.

The first shift wave hit them. For Tan-Tan it was as though her belly was turning inside out, like wearing all her insides on the outside. The air smelt wrong. She clutched Antonio's hand. A curtain of fog was passing through the pod, rearranging sight, sound. Daddy's hand felt wrong. Too many fingers, too many joints. Antonio coughed nervously. The wave passed through them and went. Daddy's hand felt all right again. "We climbing into the Tree for true," he said.

A next veil swept through them, slow like molasses. Tan-Tan felt as though her tailbone could elongate into a tail, long and bald like a manicou rat's. Her cries of distress came out like hyena giggles. The tail-tip twitched. She could feel how unfamiliar muscles would move the unfamiliar limb. The thing standing beside her looked more like a man-sized mongoose than her father. He smelt like food, but food she wasn't supposed to eat. Family. Tan-Tan sobbed and tried to wrap her tail tightly around herself.

But the veil was gone. She had only thought she was a big manicou. Antonio was a man again. He made a little noise in his throat, like a whimper. He skinned up his teeth at her in one big false grin. "That wasn't so bad, eh, doux-doux?" His voice was high. "We going to a good place." But under his breath he started to sing,

> Captain, Captain, put me ashore,
> I don't want to go any more.
> Itanami gwine drownded me,
> Itanami gwine bust me belly,
> Itanami is too much for me.

"That one is a old sailor song," he mumbled, almost as though he wasn't talking to Tan-Tan, but just to hear his own voice. "Itanami was a river rapids. People in ships would go through it like we going through dimension veils. Itanami break up plenty vessels, but them long ago people never see power like this half-way tree."

They were trapped in a confining space, being taken away from home like the long time ago Africans. Tan-Tan's nightmare had come to life. "Daddy," she started to bawl, "I don't like this. I want to stop. Let we get off, nuh?"

"I can't do that, sweetheart. Now I activate it, I can't control it from the inside, you understand? This is the half-way tree, this is exile! When you go through the shift, we is new people, not Marryshevites no more. We never going to belong in Toussaint again."

Click came the eshu into Tan-Tan's ear. Antonio got the listening look that let her know eshu was talking to him too. "Young Mistress, is what a-go on?" It was her eshu, the one from their house.

"Is all right, eshu," Daddy lied before Tan-Tan could say anything. "She eat some pepper mango is all. It making she sick little bit." He chuckled weakly. "She could never stand pepper, oui?"

Eshu was responding, but his voice was crackly. She couldn't understand him. Antonio was shaking his head like a dog with fleas in its ear. "We losing the connection to the web," he muttered. "Oh, God, like this is it, oui."

Another veil. The light inside the pod turned pink. The air got hot. Very faintly both her eshu and the building eshu said together, "Hold on, young Mistress, shift aborting."

"No!" shouted Antonio.

Tan-Tan felt a little *pop!* inside her ears. She felt dizzy. "Abort fail . . ." whispered eshu.

There was an itch at the back of her throat. Her ears popped painfully; once, twice. There was a ringing in them. Antonio moaned in fear. He took Tan-Tan in his arms and held her close. "Whatever happen, you is my little girl, you hear? My doux-doux darling, come in just like Ione when she was a sweet little thing. Don't care where we go, you is always my little Ione." Antonio buried his head against Tan-Tan's shoulder, a heavy weight.

Another veil washed over them. It was hot, fire hot. The ringing in Tan-Tan's ears was so loud, it was pain. She cried.

The tears running down her face felt too cold, like ice water. They were leaving Marryshow's paradise, shifting to a new world, her and her daddy.

Little by little, the ringing and itching went away. The pod door clicked open. Antonio picked Tan-Tan up and reached for the hatch, but his hand went right through it. The image of the pod faded away, leaving the two of them standing in the bush.

Tan-Tan looked at Antonio to see if he'd changed plenty now that he was no longer a Marryshevite. He was crouching down beside her. His face was the same, and his body, but in his eyes was a look like the fear in Quashee's eyes when he had felt Antonio's machète at he neck. Is so a man face does stay after he look at he own death, and he could never be the same again. Tan-Tan felt say she must have changed too.

Antonio stroked Tan-Tan's cheek and looked deep into her eyes. "You is all that leave to me now. You dear to me like daughter, like sister, like wife self."

Tan-Tan didn't like the way Antonio was talking. She tried to act normal, to make everything be normal again: "Eh-eh! Where the pod gone, Daddy?"

But the crazy look wouldn't leave her daddy's eyes. "It was never here, Tan-Tan. It just push we here from Toussaint."

Antonio ran his hands over his body. "Safe . . ." He looked around. "Ahm, let we take a look at we new home, all right?"

"This? This bush?" All around them it had some big knotted-up trees-them, with twisted-up roots digging into the ground like old men's fingers. The air was too cold, and it had a funny smell, like old bones. The light coming through the trees was red, not yellow. Even the trees-them looked wrong; the bark was more purple than brown. Some beast was making noise in one of the trees over her head; a grunting noise like Quashee made when Antonio hit him yesterday. This wasn't her home. This ugly place couldn't be anybody's home.

"Where we going to live, Daddy? What we going to eat? Where the people?"

"I ain't know, doux-doux. We just going to have to fend for weself." Antonio shrugged his shoulders.

No more Nursie with her 'nansi stories; no more Ione and her pretty dresses-them. No more eshu. Daddy gone stupidee, like he ain't know the answer to nothing any more. She and Antonio didn't look no different, but Tan-Tan could feel the change the shift tower had made inside her, feel her heart begin to harden against her daddy who couldn't tell her where they were, who couldn't make everything all right again. She felt she didn't know him any more. He was right. Once you climb the half-way tree, everything change-up.

How Tan-Tan Learn to Thief

Try and stretch out your spine straight. It go ease some of the pressure. Cho. I forget, you don't really understand what I talking about. Oh, but you doing it anyway. Yes, like so.

Well. The first time Tan-Tan hear anybody tell a 'nansi story about she, she was a big woman living in exile on New Half-Way Tree.

'Nansi story? Another time I go tell you about Brer Anansi, the spider man, the trickster. So much you have to learn! But me go teach you.

So anyway, Tan-Tan had was to stop off for a while in one of the prison colonies to trade smoked tree frog for a good knife. Come evening time, she was sitting on a box carton in a beat-up marketplace, eating two boiled gully hen eggs with some salt, when she hear the local griot spinning a tale for the pickney-them. And this is what she say:

Gather round, gather round, pickney! Come around, come around, pickney! Night come and work done; time for story now!

Come Patrick, my doux-doux, Mamee nice child. You is the littlest one; sit down right here beside Granny. Jocelyn and Sita, come! Oonuh not too old for listen to story, you know! Yes, all of you, sit.

Well, pickney, what story I must tell allyou today? Tan-Tan, you say? You want a story about Tan-Tan, the Robber Queen; the Midnight Thief with the heart of gold; the woman who had was to save two life for every one she take; the exile on New Half-Way Tree, this prison planet? All right; I go tell oonuh a Tan-Tan story: this one name "How Tan-Tan Learn to Thief."

Long time before, Tan-Tan was queen of the Taino people, and she live on the moon with she father, the king Antonio.

Each day Queen Tan-Tan and King Antonio stand outside the palace doors and call upon all the Tainos to sing praises of Kabo Tano, the Ancient One who give to them light and dark and all good things.

For the moon where they living was a wondrous place, a magical place. It shine like silver and gold all over, and the Taino people-them was rich and prosperous, oui? Kabo Tano give them food to eat, and make them strong: star apple, and guavas yellow and round like the moon it own self, and mamee apples, big and sweet and sun-orange inside. Now, Kabo Tano had make his people this way; as long as them eat what he gift them with, him could hear them when them call out to he. In them there days, Taino people ain't learn yet to kill animals for food. Is only plants and roots and fruits and vegetables them eat.

Tan-Tan and Antonio had everything them want. Them live in a castle with plenty servants and thing. The walls of the castle could talk.

The two of them would travel through streets paved with marble, in a cloud carriage that didn't even self touch the ground, oui? It float through the air. You don't believe me? But is the simple truth I telling you, oui?

Tan-Tan had a maid to bring she nice things, name of Ione, though sometimes people would call she Janisette. Tan-Tan had beautiful silk clothes for she body, and somebody to comb she hair. She spend she days playing jacks in the palace. Toss up the ball: *Whee!* Thief the jacks out from under it: *Swips!* The ball bounce: *Bap!* She catch it in she hand: *Wap!* Then she do it all over again. Tan-Tan could thief eight jacks out from under the ball before it bounce, and never miss a catch. And if the ball ever make fast and roll away, Tan-Tan and she maid would run to chase it, laughing as them search under the mahogany settee and the four-poster bed and thing in Tan-Tan bedroom.

King Antonio was a sorcerer too, seen. He give Tan-Tan a magic glass so that if she want he, she only had was to look in the glass and say, "Antonio, oh! Antonio!" and him face would appear.

"You calling my name, doux-doux? What my sweetness want?"

Tan-Tan would talk back to the glass. "Daddy, please Daddy, if is not too much trouble, I could have a new dolly?" (Tan-Tan was a nice child who did mind she manners, like allyou must do.) Next thing she know, a servant would come through the doors, carrying a new dolly on a silk pillow. And Tan-Tan would say thanks to the servant, for she daddy teach she always to be polite and never to put sheself above other people. She had a favourite dolly; the one wearing a red silk cape, black toreador pants, a white bandit shirt, and carrying two little tiny guns in holsters strap round it tiny waist.

King Antonio love he daughter can't done. He swear say the brightness of the moon shine from Tan-Tan eyes. If anything make Tan-Tan cry, for him is like bitter rain falling over the whole moon and him couldn't take no pleasure in him life until he make she happy again.

Now, when the Taino people look up into the sky, them could see other worlds floating all round them in space, pretty-pretty. Some yellow, some red, and some blue. Some gold and some silver, and all of them shining and clean, just like the moon where they living.

One night Tan-Tan was standing with she daddy outside the palace, gazing into the sky and admiring the beautiful worlds that great Kabo Tano make all round them. And Tan-Tan notice something she never see there before, for it was so dark and dingy it get hide in the brightness coming from the other worlds. The something was a ball like the shiny pretty worlds, but dusty and dull.

"Daddy, is what that one there?"

"It name Earth, sweetheart."

Next night, Earth look even worse. By the third night, Tan-Tan couldn't bear to look at it no more. It was spoiling the view. "Daddy, how come the Earth so dirty?"

"It make of dirt, my darling. It ain't have nobody there to clean it."

So Tan-Tan know what she have for do. "Daddy, please Daddy, is not right we let it get like that. If is not too much trouble, I want to go to the Earth and scrub it clean."

Well, King Antonio heart too soft to say no to he one daughter, but he 'fraid too bad to let she go to Earth alone.

"All right," he say, "but a queen can't go anywhere without she king, so I go come with you to keep you safe."

Then Tan-Tan laugh and clap she two hands, and give she daddy a big kiss on he cheek.

Tan-Tan and she maid Ione prepare everything for scrubbing the Earth clean. Them fill up a big basket with broom, and duster, and mop and bucket, and plenty, plenty soap.

"What about food, Mistress?" Ione ask.

"We ain't going for long," Tan-Tan tell she. "We go come back before we even self get hungry."

"Mistress, take this cutlass at least. You never know when you might need to defend yourself." And the maid gave Tan-Tan a cutlass with a blade that would never get dull.

Come early the next morning, Tan-Tan and Ione load the big basket into King Antonio best cloud chariot, the one that could fly through the air so smooth, you ain't even know when you leave and when you reach. The seats did soft as cotton, and when the night air get too cold on you, you could pull a piece of cloud over you to warm you like a blanket.

All the Taino people come to wish the king and queen a safe trip. Everybody waving. King Antonio sing the special song to make the chariot fly. It lift itself gentle into the air and take off. Some little children chase after it as it float up into the sky, higher and higher until Tan-Tan couldn't see them down on the ground no more.

Them fly past all Kabo Tano bright, shiny worlds twirling around in the air to delight the Taino people with their beauty. Them pass the world of the bristle star people, waving at them with all their plenty fingers. Them pass the world of the manicou people, hanging in the trees by their long tails. Then Antonio direct the cloud chariot towards the Earth with the power of he mind. When the two of them reach, them park the chariot in the sky and jump down to the ground.

Earth was in a bad way, oui? All she waters brown and foul. It ain't have no people living there, only dead fish floating on the surface of the oceans and rivers, stinking up the place. The land barren too; dry and parched. Tan-Tan and Antonio watch the sun hot up a patch of Earth so much that it burst into flames. The air above Earth full with grey, oily smoke. The only thing growing was a thin, sharp grass that would cut up them feet if them not careful. The beasts on Earth gaunt and hungry, for the grass wasn't giving them nourishment enough.

"This going to be a hard day's work for true," Tan-Tan say. She give Antonio the mop and bucket, and she take one of the brooms.

"Daddy, you must mop all the rivers and the oceans clean and throw out the dead fish. I go sweep the smoke from out the air."

King Antonio grumble little bit, for king not make to do hard labour. "Why I don't just magic it?" he say to she.

But when him try, nothing happen. Him wasn't on the moon no more, and him obeah magic wouldn't work. Antonio sigh and set about to clean, using him own two hands. What a bring-down for a king!

The two of them mop and sweep and scrub so till the Earth get clean and shiny again, the way Kabo Tano make it in the first place. Them throw the dirty mopping water on the parched ground, to moisten it up so it wouldn't catch fire no more.

Tan-Tan straighten up she back and look at what them do. "Righteousness. The grass growing back thick and strong again, and the waters clean now so the fish wouldn't poison. I hungry from all this work. Time to go home for supper. Call the chariot down, Daddy."

But them forget that on Earth, King Antonio wasn't no obeah man. All he call, he couldn't make the cloud chariot come. It only floating up in the sky with the other clouds. A breeze spring up and blow the chariot away.

"What we going to do?" Tan-Tan ask. She getting frightened now.

"We have to plea to Kabo Tano, doux-doux. He go help we."

And so them call on the Ancient One, begging he to save them. But remember, pickney, Kabo Tano could only hear he people so long as them have his food running through their veins. All like how Tan-Tan and Antonio ain't eat for a long time, them words come out weak and soft. Kabo Tano ain't hear them. Them call until them hoarse. No reply.

"When we don't come home for supper, somebody from the moon go come and get we," said Tan-Tan.

"No, darling. I is the only one could make the cloud chariots move."

Finally night come on, and all them could do was take two-three sips of water from the river and try to sleep. King Antonio curl up tight round he daughter to keep the night chill from she body.

So every day, them wander the Earth, looking for the kind of food Kabo Tano does provide and calling his name. But it ain't have no help for them. It had beasts on the Earth, but them couldn't eat beasts in them there days. Tan-Tan and Antonio get meager so till them arms and legs-them look like twig, and them bellies just a-stick out with starvation.

"Kabo Tano! Hear we! Kabo Tano! Save we!"

No reply.

In desperation, them dig up some dry red soil from the ground, and use some river water to make clay. Them shape it into the shape of fruits and vegetables, hoping Kabo Tano go make them real. Nothing happen. "Maybe we must eat them first," Tan-Tan say. So them bite into the clay food, but it was just clay. It leave a dusty taste in them mouth.

One day they climb up a mountain, thinking maybe if them get closer to the sky, Kabo Tano could hear them. Them had was to crawl, them was so weak with hunger. Them finally reach the top, and them join them voices in a last plea to Kabo Tano.

Well, pickney, Kabo Tano couldn't hear them, but him was casting his eyes about that day, and he spy them standing on the mountaintop, leaning on each other. He mark how them belly-them swell up with hunger, and how them arms and legs thin so like twig. Kabo Tano take pity on he children, but without his food in their bellies, him couldn't instruct them. So him cause some of the grass that did there 'bout to grow into a magic tree to sustain them. The tree had plenty-plenty branch, and each branch big so like one whole tree. Every branch had a different fruit or vegetable growing on it, a different gift from Kabo Tano: sweet brown naseberry and fat red otaheite apple; breadfruit and custard apple and peewa. In the shade under the great tree, Kabo Tano make all kind of good things grow: cassava root and yellow yam; dasheen leaf and pigeon peas; sorrel bush and grenadilla vine.

Him woulda make the tree grow on the mountaintop where Tan-

Tan and Antonio was, but it was too high for good plants to grow. So he plant the tree half way between the mountain them did climb and the river where them did drink. Them would have to find it. That is why it name the half-way tree.

One more day pass and Tan-Tan and Antonio never find the half-way tree, so Kabo Tano send a wild pig as a messenger. "Go to them quick," he say. "Tell them where the tree is."

But the pig greedy for so, you see? Him look way up into the branches of the half-way tree and him see hog plum and jackfruit growing, and he mouth start to water. But him couldn't climb tree with him trotter-them. So he push he nose into the ground, and root out sweet potato and yellow yam. He crunch them up with he sharp teeth. The food taste so good that he decide to keep the tree a secret. He eat so till he belly get round and hard like a drum, all the while Tan-Tan and Antonio groaning for hunger.

"Wild pig," Kabo Tano say, "why you ain't go to save my children yet?"

"Mm-scrumph," the pig say through a mouthful of food. "Is a long journey, O Great One. I just eating a little bit to get some strength to climb that mountain, oui?"

The pig figure he better make the thing look good, so he climb up the mountain to where Antonio and Tan-Tan did lying. He even pass by them, but all he say to them was "Mm-scrumph," and they ain't pay he no mind. When Kabo Tano ask he what Tan-Tan and Antonio say, he pull a next trick.

"What? Is you that, Kabo Tano? I can't hear you too good, oui? My belly must be getting empty again. I tell your children where it have food, but them want to lie down and rest little bit before them make the trek back down the mountain."

And the pig went and fill he belly up again at the half-way tree.

Tan-Tan watch at the wild pig. She tummy feel like it turning inside out from hunger. "Daddy, that pig fat. Maybe he know where to find food."

"I think you right, daughter, but I too weak to follow and see where he go."

Tan-Tan ain't want to leave she daddy side to go follow the pig, so she say to a woodpecker, "Bird-oi, please bird-oi, do; follow that wild pig for we, and see where he getting food, and come back and tell we."

The woodpecker find that Queen Tan-Tan so polite and nice, it would please him to do what she ask. So see him there, a-follow the wild pig waddling through the tall grass.

But the woodpecker is a stupid bird, you see? All heart and no brains. As him follow the pig, him start to forget the route, so him only stopping and drilling hole *tat-tat-tat* into the trees to mark where them pass. Him was making one set of racket. Mister Wild Pig realise that somebody following he. He hide so he wouldn't lead them to the food. The woodpecker had was to go back and tell Tan-Tan and Antonio how him lose the trail.

Tan-Tan was in despair, till she see a manicou rat slinking past. She notice how quiet the rat could go through the grass. "Mister Rat, you could help we, please?" But the manicou ain't business with she. He just flick he tail at she and keep going. He self too want to see where that wild pig getting food, but he ain't have no mind to bring anyone else in on the secret.

Tan-Tan still ain't give up. She watch at how silent the manicou slip *swips* through the tall grass without bending a single blade, and how he climb up a rockstone quiet-quiet, wrapping he tail around it so him wouldn't fall. Tan-Tan feel say she could be nimble and agile she self too. She choke down two-three extra handfuls of grass to give she little more strength. She pick some long blades and weave them into a pouch to hold any food she might find. Then she catch some water in she hands from the mountain spring. Some for sheself, and some for Antonio to drink.

"Daddy, lie still and guard your strength. I coming back when I find out where that wild pig getting food."

"Kabo Tano guide you, daughter."

And Tan-Tan set off through the bush quiet like breath, till she find the trails of the wild pig and the manicou.

As he watch the strange procession to the half-way tree, Kabo Tano realise that the wild pig had deceive he. He get vex, you see? But him couldn't speak to Tan-Tan to advise she until she find the tree and eat from it. She had was to help sheself.

The wild pig only stopping and listening all the time to hear if anybody following he, but neither Tan-Tan nor Brother Rat ain't make no sound at all at all. Tan-Tan follow, she follow. Them go down the mountain; Tan-Tan follow. Them cross a dead tree that had fall across a little brook; and Tan-Tan right behind them. Them go little more, and for the first time she lay eyes on the half-way tree, so big that she couldn't see around it, and so tall that the branches-them disappear up into the sky. And the food! Tan-Tan mouth start to water when she see ripe guava and june plum hanging in the branches. She crouch down in the tall grass where the beast-them couldn't see she.

Brother Rat twirl he whiskers in glee when he see all that food. He slip through the grass so quiet that the wild pig ain't suspect nothing. He climb up the tree and start picking z'avocat pear from one branch and stuffing it in he mouth. The wild pig waddle to the root of the tree. He only nosing out cassava root and yellow yam and swallowing them down. As she watch at the two of them eating, Tan-Tan belly growl.

"Is who that?" the wild pig call out.

Same time the manicou say, "Is what that I hear?"

Tan-Tan ain't reply. She pick some leaves off a piece of bush and chew on them to soothe she stomach. The wild pig look up and spy the manicou up in the tree.

"Brother Rat, like you been following me?"

"Seen, Brother Pig, but don't fret, all right? It have plenty for both of we. Look, I go only eat what in the tree; you could have everything on the ground."

The wild pig think about this. Him can't climb tree. The food up there would only rotten and fall on the ground. "All right then, my brother, but we can't make Tan-Tan and Antonio know."

Them continue eating. Tan-Tan swear she could see them getting fatter as she watch. Brother Rat have sharp, sharp teeth. Brother Wild Pig have pointy tusks curling round he snout. How to get to the food?

Tan-Tan think back to she jacks games, how she had was to snatch up the jacks-them fast before the ball bounce. To get the food she and she daddy need, she go have to move sly like that.

She get down on she belly and crawl through the tall grass to the foot of the tree, where the pigeon peas bushes growing thick-thick. She was mad to just pull off two-three handful of pigeon peas pods and jam into she mouth, but first she had was to deal with the wild pig.

Tan-Tan reach up and pull one of the bushes down closer to the ground, where the wild pig could almost reach it, if he only jump a little. She rustle the bush. The pig hear the sound. He come closer to see better, for pig eyesight ain't so sharp, oui? But Tan-Tan still couldn't quite reach he. She bend the bush down a little closer to the ground. When Brer Pig look good, he see a branch full of fat, sweet pigeon peas, just above he snout. Him couldn't resist. He take a little run, as fast as he short legs would go, and he leap into the air to reach the peas. And so he leap, is so Tan-Tan catch he.

"Eee-eee-eee!" The wild pig start one set of racket. Tan-Tan pull out the cutlass that Ione give she and slice off the wild pig head with one blow. Then she put the pig body in she pouch and crouch back down in the pigeon peas bushes.

"Brother Pig? Is you that?" The manicou start back down the tree to see what happen. Tan-Tan answer in the wild pig voice. "Don't fret yourself, my brother. I just catch my snout in some cassava root." Same way she steal the pig life, she steal him voice too.

The answer satisfy the manicou; him climb back up the tree. This time, him go to a custard apple branch. Him was so busy eating, him never see Tan-Tan shinnying up the tree, quiet like death. She inch out across the branch, wrapping she legs round it like rat tail, so she wouldn't fall. So noiseless she move, so soft, the branch ain't even self tremble.

When she reach the manicou, Tan-Tan reach out swift like grabbing jacks from out underneath a jacks ball. She catch the manicou long, hairless tail and swing he head *bup!* against the half-way tree trunk. That was the end of Brother Rat. Tan-Tan put the body in she pouch. She eat up two-three custard apple right there, sucking down the sweet white meat and spitting out the shiny black seed-them. She fill up she bag for Antonio.

Now that she have he food running in she veins again, Kabo Tano could make she hear he. From out of the sky he say, "You do good, my daughter. This half-way tree is for you and Antonio."

"Thank you, Kabo Tano!"

"Chop it down."

"What?"

"Chop down the tree."

Tan-Tan couldn't believe she ears. How she could do that? How them would eat after? She decide to try a thing.

"Ancient One, I too weak to chop down this thick tree. The trunk bigger than me and King Antonio put together."

Kabo Tano say, "Climb down and make a fire." So Tan-Tan do that.

"Fire burning good, Ancient One."

"Take the pig and the manicou out of your pouch. You must gut them and skin them and string them on a pole above the fire. And keep turning the pole so that the bodies burn even all the way through."

Tan-Tan think say this must be powerful obeah. She follow Kabo Tano instructions, and as she turn the meat on the fire, it start to cook. It smell so nice, Tan-Tan belly start to rumble again, even though she done full it up with food from the tree.

"What I must do now, Kabo Tano?"

"Do what your mouth and your belly telling you. Eat."

That is how Tan-Tan learn another way to feed sheself. She gorge on manicou and pork. She put aside a portion for Antonio, then she suck the fat from the meat and tear the meat from the bones. She even crack open the bones-them and suck out the marrow. When she done, she lie back on the ground and sigh, patting she belly.

"You full, my daughter? You strong?" Kabo Tano voice sounding soft, but Tan-Tan ain't pay that no mind.

"Yes, Kabo Tano."

"Cut down the tree."

She ain't have no more excuse. She had to do it. She go and stand beside the half-way tree. She hold she cutlass that would never dull in one hand and she place the next hand flat against the broad trunk. It had all different kinds of bark on the trunk, one for each kind of fruit and vegetable.

She decide to have faith in Kabo Tano. Everything he do, he do for a reason. Tan-Tan fetch one blow to the trunk of the half-way tree. And again! And again! She chop and she chop until the tree start to sway. She look up to see which way it go fall, and she stand aside. The great tree crash down to the ground, and is like the whole Earth tremble for the magnificent thing that Tan-Tan just destroy. Tan-Tan hear Kabo Tano voice, even softer this time.

"Is the flesh of the beast give you the strength to do this thing, my daughter."

"Yes, Kabo Tano. Thank you."

"But is lie you lie to me. I know you wasn't feeling weak once you done eat my food. You just ain't want to cut down the tree. Because you tell untruth, you have to stay down there on Earth. I going away and leaving you and Antonio."

Tan-Tan start to cry. "But Great One, how we go live here without you to help?"

"Even though you lie, you is still my daughter. The half-way tree is for you and your daddy. Pull one of every kind of twig from the tree, and one of every kind of plant that growing underneath it. Wherever you plant them, they go grow, and you and Antonio will always have food. Let the beasts have what leave from the tree to nourish themselves with."

That was the last time Tan-Tan ever hear Kabo Tano voice. She mourn, but she do as he tell she. She pick all kind of food for Antonio, then she break off a twig for each type of plant, and she bundle them up together with grass. She take everything back to she daddy, lying there faint beside the mountain stream.

"Daddy! Here, eat." Tan-Tan put little pieces of food and meat into Antonio mouth. He chew one-one piece at a time until he start to feel like a man again.

"What is this I eating, daughter?"

Tan-Tan tell he the whole story; how she follow the pig and the manicou to the half-way tree, how she ambush them and steal they life, and how Kabo Tano help she to feed sheself, even though she lie to he, and how she get them exile on Earth for good. Antonio couldn't be vex at she, though. She save he life, and he couldn't think of nothing better but to live out he days by he daughter side.

The two of them clear a space near the stream, and them plant all the twigs and plants-them. Them use mud and grass to build a wattle-and-daub hut.

And so Kabo Tano tell them, is so it go. Everything grow, and Tan-Tan and Antonio had food for their bellies and wood to build with. Tan-Tan learn to hunt and trap, so them always had meat for their table. The pieces of the half-way tree that get leave behind grow and spread all over the Earth. Earth get green and living again. The beasts in the bush had enough to eat.

King Antonio and Queen Tan-Tan live long on the new, clean Earth, and is Tan-Tan who give birth to the race of people on Earth, for it never had none there before.

But forever after, the beasts in the bush would run and hide whenever them see Tan-Tan coming, for them know she to be the greatest thief of all, the one who could steal them life away before them time come. She turn Robber Queen for true.

Is Tan-Tan make it so.

You like that story, sweetness? Tan-Tan ain't too like it, you know. It always make she mind run on how she daddy steal she away from her home.

The light was too red and the air smelt wrong. The shift pod had disappeared and left Tan-Tan and the daddy she couldn't recognise no more in this strange place. They were in a bush with no food and no shelter. Everything was changed.

"Allyou climb the Tree to visit we?" The high, clear voice was coming from behind Tan-Tan. She whipped round. Someone strange was standing there. Tan-Tan screamed and jumped behind Antonio.

Antonio grabbed Tan-Tan's arm and took a step back.

"What you want?" he asked.

It made a hissing noise *shu-shu* and said, "That all depend on what you have to trade."

"Not we. We come with we two long arms just so."

Tan-Tan peeked out. The creature was only about as tall as she. It smelt like leaves. Its head was shaped funny; long and narrow like a bird's. It was ugly for so! Its eyes were on either side of its head, not in front of its face like people eyes. It had two arms like them, with hands. Each hand had four fingers with swollen fingertips. Slung across its leathery chest was a gourd on a strap. It carried a slingshot in one hand and had a pouch round its waist. It wore no clothing, but Tan-Tan couldn't see genitalia, just something looking like a pocket of flesh at its crotch. A long knife in a holder was strapped onto one muscular thigh. But it was the creature's legs that amazed Tan-Tan the most. They looked like goat feet; thin and bent backwards in the middle. Its feet had four long toes with thick, hard nails. "Eshu," she muttered, "a-what that?"

Static, then a headache burst upon her brain. Eshu didn't answer.

The jokey-looking beast bobbed its head at them, like any lizard. "I think you two must be want plenty, yes? Water, and food, and your own people? What you go give me if I take you where it have people like you?"

At the word "water," Tan-Tan realised that she'd had nothing to drink since the cocoa-tea Nursie had given her that afternoon, and she'd only sipped that; a whole lifetime away, it seemed now.

"Daddy, I thirsty."

"Hush your mouth, Tan-Tan. We don't know nothing about this beast."

The creature said, "Beast that could talk and know it own mind. Oonuh tallpeople quick to name what is people and what is beast. Last time I asking you: safe passage through this bush?"

"Why I making deal with some leggobeast that look like bat masque it own self? How I know you go do what you say?"

"Because is so we do business here. Give me something

that I want, I go keep my pact with you. Douen people does keep their word."

Douen! Nursie had told Tan-Tan douen stories. Douens were children who'd died before they had their naming ceremonies. They came back from the dead as jumbies with their heads on backwards. They lived in the bush. Tan-Tan looked at the douen's head, then its feet. They seemed to attach the right way, even though its knees were backwards.

The creature made the *shu-shu* noise again. "Too besides, allyou taste nasty too bad, bitter aloe taste. Better to take you to live with your people."

Antonio made a worried frown. Then: "All right," he said. "Let me see what I have to trade with you." He searched his jacket pockets and pulled out a pen. "What about this?"

One of the douen's eyes rolled to inspect the pen. A bright green frill sprang up round its neck. It stepped up too close to Antonio. Antonio moved back. The douen followed, said, "Country booky come to town you think I is? Used to sweet we long time ago, when oonuh tallpeople give we pen and bead necklace. Something more useful, mister. Allyou does come with plenty thing when you get exile here."

"Nobody know we was leaving Toussaint. I ain't think to bring nothing with we."

"Me ain't business with that."

Worriedly, Antonio started searching his pockets again. Tan-Tan saw him ease a flask of rum part way out of his back pants pocket then put it back in. He patted his chest pocket, looked down at himself. "Here. What about my shoes-them?" He bent over and ran his finger down the seam that would release his shoe from his foot.

"Foolish. Is a two-day hike." Its frill deflated against its neck, leaving what looked like a necklace of green beads. "Leave on your shoes and come."

"What?"

"You will owe me. Come. Allyou want water?"

That was what Tan-Tan had been waiting to hear. "Yes, please, mister," she piped up. *Mister?* she wondered.

The douen laughed *shu-shu*. "This one barely rip open he egg yet, and he talking bold-face! Your son this, tallpeople?"

"My daughter. Leave she alone."

"He, she; oonuh all the same."

Antonio shot the douen a puzzled look.

"She want water," the creature said.

"Let me taste it first."

Antonio took a few swallows from the gourd the douen handed him. He nodded, then held it for Tan-Tan to drink. The water was warm and a little slimy. She didn't care, she drank until her throat wasn't dry any more.

The douen said, "Never see a tallpeople pickney climb the half-way tree before. What crime you do, pickney, to get cast away?"

"Never you mind," growled Antonio.

The creature didn't reply. It took the gourd back. It sniffed at Daddy, then at Tan-Tan. She moved away from its pointy snout, hands jumping protectively to cross in front of her body. But it just grunted at them and started off through the bush, hacking a path with its knife. Tan-Tan remembered Nursie's stories about how douens led people into the bush to get lost and die. She started to feel scared all over again. She called silently for eshu. Her headache flared, then quieted. She reached for Antonio's hand. "Daddy," she whispered. "Where eshu?"

"Back on Toussaint, child. We leave all that behind now."

She didn't understand. Eshu was always there. She bit her bottom lip, peered into the bush where the douen had disappeared. "We have to go with that funny man?"

"Yes, doux-doux. It say it taking we to we own people."

"For true? It not going to lost we?"

"I don't know, doux-doux. Just come."

They followed the path the creature had left. Red heat beat down. Branches jooked. The space the creature was clearing through the bush was short so till Antonio had to rip off the foliage above his own head to make room to pass through. By the time they caught up to the douen, Antonio was panting with the exertion and scratched from jutting twigs. "Is what you did call this place?" he asked.

"New Half-Way Tree oonuh call it."

"But," said Tan-Tan, "we not half way. We come all the way and reach now." The douen blinked at her. Its eyes were very large. She didn't like it looking at her. She shouldn't have said anything. Nervously she giggled at her own joke.

Antonio stopped her with a look. He said, "How you know where to find we? The shift pod does land at the same place every time?"

"No. Douen does know when and where a next one going to land. Taste it in the air. Whichever douen reach there first, him get first right of trade with the new tallpeople. Bring we good business, oonuh. A tallpeople gave me a shirt one time. Front does close up when you run your finger along it. I give it to the weavers in my village. Them will study how to make more."

"How come you could speak the same way like we?"

"Yes. Anglopatwa, Francopatwa, Hispanopatwa, and Papiamento. Right? We learn all oonuh speech, for oonuh don't learn we own."

"And why you call yourself 'douen'?"

"Allyou call we so. Is we legs."

The ringing in Tan-Tan's ears, which had never quite stopped since the shift pod had deposited them here, was getting louder. She shook her head to try to clear it. She had begun to feel chilly. She wrapped her arms round herself.

The douen noticed, sniffed in her direction. It raised one

twisted leg and scratched behind its shoulder blade. "Mister, watch at your pickney-girl. Is so allyou does do for cold."

Antonio stared down at her with a look like he didn't know what to do.

"Allyou people blood too hot for this place," said the douen. Now it was holding the foot up in front of its face, inspecting between its long toes to see if its scratching had unearthed anything. Its toes flicked, shaking dust off themselves as agilely as fingers. It put its foot back on the ground, looked at Antonio. "Give she something warm to wear."

"Me done tell you, me don't have nothing!"

The creature reached into the pouch at its waist and pulled out a cloth like the one it was wearing. It was saffron yellow, Tan-Tan's favourite colour.

"Here, small tallperson."

Tan-Tan pressed up against Daddy's legs. She looked doubtfully at the cloth. Antonio took it, peered at it, smelt it. He shook it out and put it round her shoulders. "Thanks," he said grudgingly.

"My wife make those cloths," the douen said to Tan-Tan.

A dead douen baby could have wife?

"With every thread she weave," the douen continued, "she weave a magic to give warmth to who wear the cloth. Is true; I does see she do it."

Tan-Tan took a hard look at the little person. She wished she could talk to eshu. The douen's eyes-at-the-sides couldn't look at her straight on; it cocked its head like a bird's to return the stare, like a parrot. She smiled a little. No, it didn't look like a dead child. Too besides, it didn't have no Panama hat like a real douen. She began to feel warmer, wrapped in its wife's magic cloth. "What you name?" she asked the douen.

"Eh-eh! The pickney offering trail debt." He bent, sniffed her hair. "You have manners. Me name Chichibud. And what you name?"

"Tan-Tan," she said, feeling shy.

"Sweet name. The noise Cousin Lizard does make when he wooing he mate."

"It have lizards here?"

Chichibud looked round the gloomy bush, picked up a twig and flung it at a crenellated tree trunk. A liver-red something slithered out of the way. It was many-legged like a centipede, long as Daddy's forearm, thick around as his wrist.

"Fuck," Antonio muttered.

"No, I make mistake," said Chichibud. "Foot snake that, not a lizard. *Shu-shu*."

He peered round again, then pointed to a tree in front of them. "Look." The tree had brownish purple bark and long twist-up leaves fluttering in the air like ropes of blood floating in water.

"I ain't see nothing."

"Look at the tree trunk. Just above that knothole there."

Tan-Tan squinted and stared at the tree, but still couldn't make anything out.

Chichibud picked up a rockstone from the ground and flung it at the tree. "Show yourself, cousin!"

A little lizard reared up on its hind legs to scuttle out of the way, then just as quickly settled still again on the tree.

Tan-Tan laughed. "I see he! He like the ones from back home, just a different colour." The lizard was purple like the bark, but with streaks of pink the same strange colour as the sunlight. When he was quiet he looked just like a piece of tree bark with the sun dappling it.

"Tallpeople say your world not so different from the real world," the douen told her.

Yes it was. Plenty different. "Why you call the lizard 'cousin'?"

"Old people tell we douen and lizards related. So we treat them good. We never kill a lizard."

Antonio said impatiently, "The place you taking we; is what it name?"

"We go keep hiking," Chichibud told them. They moved off through the bush again. He answered Antonio's question: "It name Junjuh."

The parasitic fungus that grew wherever it was moist.

"Nasty name," Antonio mumbled.

"One of oonuh tell me about junjuh mould. It does grow where nothing else can't catch. When no soil not there, it put roots down in the rock, and all rainwater and river water pound down on it, it does thrive. No matter what you do, it does grow back."

As they walked, Chichibud showed them how to see the bush around them. He took them over to a low plant with pointy leaves. In the dusky sunlight they could just make out dark blue flowers with red tongues. "Devil bush this."

"I know it!" Tan-Tan said. "We have it back home, but the flowers does be red."

"The one back home like this?" Carefully, Chichibud picked a leaf off the plant. He held it up to the light so they could see the tiny, near-transparent needles that bristled on its underside. "Poison thorn. If you skin touch it, bad blister. Skin drop off. Our bush doctors smoke it. Give them visions. It does talk to them and tell them which plants does heal. Some of oonuh smoke it too, but never hear the voice of the herb, just the voices of your own dreams."

From then on, Tan-Tan kept casting her eyes to the ground to make sure she wouldn't brush up a devil bush.

Chichibud said to Antonio, "You bring any lighter with you? Any glass bottle?"

"Nothing, me tell you!"

"Too bad for you. Woulda trade you plenty for those; bowls to eat out of, hammock to sleep in."

A few minutes later Chichibud pulled down a vine from a

tree as they were walking under it. The vine had juicy red leaves and bright green flowers. "Water vine. You could squeeze the leaves and drink from them. If you dry the vine, you could twist it together to make rope." Chichibud picked two-three of the leaves and squeezed them in his hand. "You want to try, pickney?" But before he could drip the water into her mouth, Antonio dashed the leaves out of his hand.

"Don't give she nothing to eat without I tell you to!" Antonio shouted angrily.

Chichibud fell into a crouch. He said nothing, but bobbed his head like a parrot. His eyes went opaque and then clear again, like someone opening and closing a jalousie window shutter. The frill at his neck rose. Somehow he seemed to have grown bigger, fiercer. Tan-Tan edged behind her daddy again. Them was going to fight! Maybe Daddy still had some of the poison he'd used on Uncle Quashee. That would serve the nasty leggobeast right.

"Man," Chichibud replied, his voice growly, "you under trail debt, your pickney declare it. Is liard you calling me liard?"

"I don't want her to eat nothing that might make she sick."

"Oh-hoh." Chichibud straightened up. He was back to his normal size. How he do that? "You watching out for your pickney. Is a good thing to do. But we under trail debt, I tell you. You go get safe to Junjuh. I won't make your child come to harm."

Antonio just grunted. Tan-Tan knew that particular set of his jaw. He was still vex. Chichibud tugged down a length of vine, showed it to Antonio first, then said to Tan-Tan, "Water vine only grow on this tree here, the lionheart tree with the wood too tough to cut. But if you see a vine looking just like this, only the flowers tiny-tiny, don't touch it! Allyou call it jumbie dumb cane. Juice from it make your tongue swell up in your head. Can't talk. Sometimes suffocate and dead."

They hiked on through the bush. It was sweaty work, but Tan-Tan still felt chilly. Her ears tingled. She was only watching the ground below her feet for the devil bush and the bush above her head for jumbie dumb cane. Chichibud stopped them yet again. "What you see?" he said, pointing to the ground ahead. Like all the ground they'd tromped so far, what wasn't covered with a thick carpet of ruddy dead leaves was blanketed with a fine, reddish green growth like moss. Gnarled trees with narrow trunks twisted their way out of it, reaching towards the too-red sun. It looked just like the rest of the bush.

Antonio sucked his teeth. "Look, I ain't business with your bush nonsense, yes. Take we to this Junjuh."

But as Tan-Tan had looked where Chichibud was pointing, she had slowly discerned something different through the mess of leaf and mould and stem. She tapped Chichibud on the shoulder. "Mister, I see some little lines, like the tracks badjack ants does leave in the sand."

Gently, Chichibud touched her forehead with the back of his hand, once, twice. "Good, little tallpeople. Sense behind you eyes. That is sugar-maggot trails. If you follow them, you could find their nest. Boil them to sweeten your tea." Chichibud looked at Antonio. "You must learn how to live in this place, tallpeople, or not survive."

They hiked and they hiked. They had to stop one time for Tan-Tan to make water. They kept walking. Tan-Tan pulled Chichibud's wife's cloth tighter round her, wishing she could feel warm. She peered through the dimness of the bush ahead. "Look, Daddy! Bamboo like back home."

Antonio turned wary eyes on the tall, jointed reeds growing thick as arms up towards the light. There was a whole stand of them. The shifting shadows caused by the narrow leaves blowing in the breeze hurt Tan-Tan's eyes. The hollow stems clacked against each other and made her head pound. Antonio frowned. "How bamboo reach here? Is from Toussaint." He looked to Chichibud for explanation.

"Tallpeople bring it. Plenty other bush too."

They hiked on and on until Tan-Tan couldn't make her legs move any more; Antonio had to carry her. As Daddy gathered her into his arms, Tan-Tan could feel how he was shivering too. He turned to the douen: "So where this village you only telling me about all the time? Like you is douen in truth, trying to lead we deeper into the bush and get we lost?"

"Your people tell me story. Where you come from, you could hire people to carry you where you going. You could go fast in magic carriage with nobody to pull it. Here, tallpeople have only your own two feet to carry you. By myself I get to Junjuh in one day. With new exiles, longer. Allyou making I move slow. Not reaching tonight. Tomorrow morning. After we sleep."

"And so is what? Where we going to stay?"

"Right here. I go show you how to make the bush your home for the night."

"And suppose it rain?" Antonio challenged him.

"It ain't go rain. I woulda smell it coming. We looking for a clearing with a tree spreading wide over it."

A few more minutes' walk. The douen passed one tree by; it had too many beasts living in its trunk. Then another; it would drop strange, wriggling fruit on their heads while they tried to sleep. Finally they came upon two trees growing close together. Chichibud pointed to lumpy brown growths in the branches of one tree. "Halwa fruit. Dinner." The other tree was broad-trunked with fire-red leaves. It had thick spreading branches, the shade of which made a clear space in the bush beneath them. "This one good. Let we make camp," Chichibud told them. He led them under its branches.

The sun was setting. The dying light reflected off the tree's leaves and made Tan-Tan's eyes ache, so she looked down.

Blood-red shadows were darkening and lengthening along the ground. She could hear things rustling in the gloom where they couldn't see. She was frightened. She shook her head to clear its ringing.

Antonio let Tan-Tan down. The douen told her, "Pickney, pick up as much dry stick as you could find for the fire. Don't go far. Stay around these two trees."

Chichibud went to the halwa tree and shinnied up its trunk. Tan-Tan could hear him moving through the branches.

"Down below! Catch!"

Daddy went and stood below the tree, hands stretched out. Chichibud threw down two heavy round fruits, big as Daddy's head. Daddy caught them, making a small explosion of air from his lips as he did. No sound came from the douen for a few minutes. Then from another part of the foliage came a *wap!* like something hitting against the tree trunk. He let something else drop into Daddy's hands, something big so like the halwa fruit, but floppy and flabby. Daddy looked good at the hairy body he was holding, cried out, "Oh, God!" and dropped it on the ground. In the incarnadine evening light the blood covering his hands looked black. Tan-Tan shuddered. Antonio was only whimpering, "Oh, God! Oh, God, what a place!" and wiping the blood off on his pants.

Chichibud sprang down from the tree, licking his hands. He peered at Tan-Tan and then at Antonio. "New tallpeople always 'fraid the dead." He laughed *shu-shu-shu*. "Is meat for dinner."

Antonio flew at the little douen man, yanked him into the air by the throat, and gave him one good shake. "Jokey story done right now," Antonio said. "What you do that for?" Chichibud snapped at Antonio's face and reached for his knife. Antonio let him go.

The douen's throat was smeared with blood from Antonio's hands. He wiped it off and sucked it from his palm. His tongue was skinny like a whip. "In the bush, you catch food when you see it. Manicou, allyou call that beast. Allyou bring it here."

The large rodent lying on the ground had a naked tail. Tan-Tan remembered the tail she'd hallucinated growing and losing again in the shift pod. The thing on the ground looked fat and healthy. Its head was all mashed up. "What happen to it?"

"I kill he," Chichibud replied. "Grab he quick by the tail and swing he head against the tree trunk. You hear when it hit?"

"Yes." She imagined the head splitting apart like a dropped watermelon. She felt ill.

"Every noise you hear in the bush mean something. Bush Poopa don't like ignorance."

"Bush Poopa?"

"Father Bush, master of the forest."

Antonio had had enough of the lesson. "We setting up this camp, or what?" He helped Tan-Tan find twigs for the fire. They made a big pile on the ground in the clearing, beside the halwa fruit and the rat-thing. Antonio crouched down right there, just watching Chichibud. Tan-Tan knotted Chichibud's wife's cloth around her shoulders. She picked up one of the heavy halwa fruit and pressed her nose against it. The smell made her mouth water.

Chichibud had come back into the clearing with three sturdy staves, fresh cut. He put them beside the trunk of the red-leaved tree and spread a cloth from his pouch on the ground. He jammed the staves into the ground round the groundsheet. They met and crossed in the air like steepled fingers. Chichibud pulled out one more cloth and shook it out. It was much larger than the others. How had it fit inside that little pouch? Like it was magic too, yes? Tan-Tan wondered what else he could have in there. He threw the cloth over the staves. It stretched down to the ground. He shook some pegs out of the endless pouch, looked round himself, saw Antonio watching at him. "Find a rock to pound these pegs in with."

Sullenly Antonio stood up and cast round until he'd found a good rockstone. "Here."

Chichibud pounded the pegs through the stretched cloth, solidly into the ground. They had a tent. Chichibud straightened up and stretched his back, just like any man.

"If you ever sleep out in the bush like this by yourself, check the tree first. Any hole in the trunk, look for a next tree. Might have poison snake or ground puppy living in there."

Chichibud showed them how to start a fire with three sticks for kindling and a piece of vine for friction. By the time the fire had caught it was full dark. The dancing flames were pinkish and the burning wood had a slight smell of old socks, but Tan-Tan felt cheered by the circle of flickering light the fire threw. She moved nearer, rinsed her chilled hands in the heat flowing from the fire. The itching in her ears eased if she turned them to the warmth, one side of her head, then the other. One ear was more itchy.

Chichibud built a wooden spit over the fire. He skinned and gutted the rat-thing. Tan-Tan's stomach writhed at the sight of the raw, split-open rat, but she couldn't look away. This was a thing she'd not seen before, how the meat that fed her was a living being one minute and then violently dead. The smell of it was personal, inescapable, like the scent that rose in the steam from her own self when she stepped into a hot bath. They had broken open the animal's secret body just to eat it.

Chichibud chopped off their supper's head. He smeared the empty body cavity with herbs from his pouch, then with a quick motion jooked the spit through it. Tan-Tan started at the wet ripping sound. Chichibud put the meat above the fire to cook.

"Here, Tan-Tan. Turn the handle slow, cook it even all around."

He wrapped up the guts and the head in the creature's skin. "I soon come back," he told them. "Taking this far away so other beasts don't smell it and come after we."

He disappeared into the bush, rustling branches as he went.

"Nasty little leggobeast goat man," Antonio muttered. "You all right, doux-doux?"

"I don't like the dark. My ears itching me. Let we go back home nuh, Daddy?"

"No way back home, sweetness. The shift pod gone. Here go have to be home now."

Tan-Tan sniffled and jerked the meat round and round on its spit.

"I here," Antonio said. "I go look after you. And I won't make the goat man hurt you, neither."

Tan-Tan was more 'fraid ground puppy than Chichibud, but she didn't say so. Antonio sighed and pulled out his flask of rum. He took a swig.

Chichibud returned just as the browning, smoking meat had begun to smell like food. He praised Tan-Tan for turning the spit so diligently, then took the halwa fruit-them and broke them open. Tan-Tan's belly grumbled at the smell. It favoured coconut, vanilla and nutmeg. Same way so the kitchen back home smelled when Cookie was making gizada pastry with shaved coconut and brown sugar.

"It best raw, this meat," Chichibud told her, "but oonuh prefer it burned by fire."

He hauled out three flat stones from his pouch and put them on top of some of the live coals close to the outside of the fire. "Far away from the meat, yes? So the meat juice wouldn't splatter?" He balanced the fruit on the stones. In the firelight, Tan-Tan could make out the brown fleshy inside of the fruit halves. Little-little, the sweet gizada fragrance got stronger. It floated in and round the rich scent of the cooking meat till Tan-Tan could feel the hunger-water springing in her mouth. She feel to just rip off a piece of manicou flesh and stuff it down, half-cooked just so. She reached towards the spit, but Chichibud gently took her fingers. Antonio stood up and came over to them. "It hot," said Chichibud. "You a-go burn your fingers and make me break trail debt." From his pouch he took a parcel wrapped in parchment paper and unwrapped it. It had a square of something dry and brown inside. With his knife, Chichibud cut off strips for the three of them. He distributed them then bit into his own. When Antonio saw Chichibud eating, he started to chew on his own piece one time. Chichibud said, "Is dry tree frog meat." Antonio cursed and spat the jerky out of his mouth. He tossed the rest into the bush. Chichibud just watched him.

Tan-Tan bit into the dried meat. It was salty and chewy. She tore off a piece with her teeth. It tasted good.

A little time more, and Chichibud told them that the meat was cooked. He set out three broad halwa leaves around the fire as plates. He pulled out a little brown cloth from his endless pouch and used it to juggle the hot fruit halves onto the leaves. Then with his knife he sliced off three slabs of rat-thing and put them beside the fruit.

"Pickney, everything hot. Go slow until it cool. Use your fingers to scrape out the fruit. Don't swallow the seeds, you might choke." He put two long fingers into his halwa fruit and pulled out a shiny purple seed, round like a pebble.

"I go be careful, Chichibud." Tan-Tan scooped out a piece of fruit, pulled out the seed and put it on her leaf plate. She put the fruit in her mouth. It come in sweet and sticky and hot. The lovely gizada taste slid warmly down her throat. The meat was good too, moist and tender, and the spice Chichibud had rubbed on it tasted like big-leaf thyme. Tan-Tan began to feel better.

Antonio picked up his halwa fruit half with both hands and dropped it again, blowing on his burnt hands. "Motherass!"

Chichibud laughed his *shu-shu* laughter. Antonio glared at him and started to dig out pieces of fruit, blowing on his fingers and spitting the seeds out everywhere.

"Don't spit them into the fire," Chichibud warned. But Antonio just cut his eye in contempt and shot one seed from his mouth *prraps!* into the middle of the flames-them.

"Back! Behind the tree!" Chichibud grabbed Tan-Tan's arm and they both scrambled quick to get behind the trunk of the tree, Chichibud hopping on his backwards legs like a kangaroo. But Antonio took his cool time, doing a swaggerboy walk towards them. "What stupidness this is now?" he grumbled.

With a gunshot noise, a little ball of fire exploded from the flames. Only because the sound made Antonio duck that the seed didn't lash him in the head. It landed on top of the tent. By its glow Tan-Tan could see the tent fabric smouldering. With shrill, birdlike sounds, Chichibud rushed over and quickly flicked the burning ember onto the ground. His ruff was puffed out full. Tan-Tan stared at it, fascinated. Chichibud growled at Antonio, who shrank back, muttering sullenly, "All right, all right! Don't give me no blasted fatigue. How I was to know the damned thing would explode?"

"I tell you not to spit it in the fire. I know this bush, not you. You ignorant, you is bush-baby self. If you not going to listen when I talk, I leave you right here."

Antonio made a loud, impatient *steuups* behind his teeth. He went back to the fire and continued eating his share of the meal. Chichibud inspected the tent. "Just a little hole," he said to Tan-Tan. "I can mend it." His ruff had deflated again. Tan-

Tan ran her fingers over the cloth and was surprised at how thin and light it felt.

They went back to their dinner. Antonio looked up as they approached. "All right," he said to Chichibud. "It have anything else we have to know to pass the night in this motherass bush behind God back?"

"Don't let the fire go out," Chichibud replied. "Light will frighten away the mako jumbie and the ground puppy, and grit fly like the flame. Fly into it instead of into we eyes. You and me going to sleep in shift."

"All right," Antonio said. He looked unhappy.

"You catch the first sleep," Chichibud told him. "Little bit, I wake you up."

Tan-Tan and Antonio curled up under their shelter, sharing the cloth Chichibud had lent to Tan-Tan. The firelight danced against the sides of the tent.

"Daddy? How Mummy go find we here? How she go know which Toussaint we come to?"

But Antonio was already snoring. Truth to tell, Tan-Tan was missing Nursie and eshu just as much as Ione. All now so, if she was going to bed back home, she and eshu would have just finished singing a song; "Jane and Louisa" maybe, or "Little Sally Water." Nursie would have had Tan-Tan pick a nightie from her dresser drawer to put on. Tan-Tan could almost smell the bunch of sweet dried khus-khus grass that Nursie kept inside the drawer to freshen her clothing.

She would pick the yellow nightie. Then Nursie would have hot eggnog sent from the kitchen for both of them, with nutmeg in it to cool their blood. The smell would spice the air, not like in this strange red land where the air smelled like sulphur matches all the time.

Tan-Tan swallowed, pretending she could taste the hot drink. Swallowing cleared her ears a little. *Now Nursie was combing out Tan-Tan's thick black hair. She was plaiting it into two so it wouldn't knot up at night. Nursie and eshu was singing "Las Solas Market" for her. When the song finished, Nursie kissed her goodnight. Tan-Tan was snuggling down inside the blankets. Eshu wished her good dreams and outed the light.*

The wetness on Tan-Tan's face felt hot, then cool against her skin. She snuffled, trying not to wake Antonio. She clutched her side of the yellow blanket round herself and finally managed to fall asleep.

It felt like she had barely locked her eyelids shut when Chichibud was standing outside the tent, shouting, "Tallpeople man! Your turn to watch the fire."

"Why the rass you can't use my name, eh?"

"You tell it to me yet?"

"Oh. Antonio."

"Time to watch the fire, Antonio."

"I coming, I coming."

In her half sleep, Tan-Tan felt Daddy move away from her and crawl out from under the tent. Chichibud crawled in. She heard him move to the opposite side of the tent. He had a strange, spicy-sharp smell; not human, but not unpleasant.

"Chichibud, you want some blanket?"

"You use it, child. The night warm for my blood."

His voice faded away. She was singing with Nursie: "Come we go down Las Solas, for go buy banana," but when it came to the chorus, Nursie's voice turned into a low, raspy buzz. Then Nursie bit her beside her eye with one tooth, sharp like needle. Tan-Tan woke up swiping at a stinging spot in the outside corner of her eye. A small, soft body popped under her fingers, leaving a granular smear. Grit fly? Tan-Tan scrubbed at her eyes, wondering if grit flies looked as nasty as they felt. It was pitch black in the tent. "Chichibud?"

From out of the dark Chichibud said, "The fire." She heard

a *whap!* like a hand against flesh, the sound of Chichibud getting to his feet. He twittered something, then:

"Your foolish daddy let the fire go out, child. Stay here so. Don't come out."

She heard him crawling out, then silence. What was happening? She stuck her head under the tent flap to look out. The only light was the blue-red glow of the coals from the dying fire. If she squinted she could just see Daddy asleep beside them. Chichibud must have been looking in the blackness for sticks and dry leaves to stoke up the fire. He was moving quietly, except for the occasional thump or crackle.

The fire ebbed a little more. Suddenly Tan-Tan had to be near her father's warmth. She crawled on hands and knees to Antonio, stopping on her way to swat at three more grit flies. She was at his side now. The breaths he blew out smelled sweet and thick. There were dark spots moving round his eyes. Grit flies.

"Daddy. Wake up."

Antonio knuckled at one eye; mumbled, ". . . ain't enough, Ben. Look, just put some more of the paste on the blade, oui?" He flung his arm out and caught Tan-Tan across her chest.

"Oof." The blow threw her backwards. She reached behind her to break her fall. She landed with a thump that set her ears to ringing again. Her hand touched the empty rum flask. Then Chichibud was there beside them. He threw some kindling on the coals and fanned them till the fire started to come back.

"Pickney," he whispered, "get back in the tent. Dangerous out here in the dark. I go look after this tallpeople man."

Tan-Tan was almost at the tent when Chichibud said with a low, urgent calm, "Child. Don't move." Tan-Tan looked back. Chichibud was holding himself in an alert quiet, staring up into the sky. Something rustled in the trees far, far above them. It sounded big.

"Me say don't move, Tan-Tan. Not a muscle. Don't even turn your head again. Stay just how you is. A mako jumbie just come out of the bush."

"What that?" Tan-Tan's voice was quavering out of control.

"Sshh. Talk soft. A bird, tall like this tree here. Stay still like the dead, pickney. It don't hear so good, but it eyes sharp."

Tan-Tan froze as she was, with one foot pointed in front of her and her head twisted back to look at Chichibud. Antonio was still unconscious on the ground beside him. From her blind side Tan-Tan heard the crash of twigs breaking. She shook with the effort not to turn her head to the sound. Snot filled up her nose. She panted shallowly through her mouth, tasting the salt tears that ran into it.

An enormous clawed foot landed *bap!* in her line of sight. Tan-Tan made a small noise in her throat. It looked like a chicken foot, but it was the same length as Tan-Tan's whole body. She turned her eyes up to follow the leg of the mako jumbie, long as a bamboo stem, but in the darkness she couldn't see the body way up in the trees. It was high like a house. The next foot slammed down beside the first. Tremble, she just a-tremble.

"Pickney, all you do, don't move. Them birds stupid, oui? Hold still, it will think you is bush or stick."

"Chichibud, I frighten."

"I know, pickney," he said in that eerily calm voice. "All we could do is wait until the fire catch. That go scare it away."

Tan-Tan nearly expired on the spot when the mako jumbie peered down low to look round the clearing. Its head was as big as their tent. A hungry, dead-cold eye rolled above its thick, sharp beak. Its snaky giraffe neck was covered in black feathers the length of Tan-Tan's arm.

It swung its monster head right by her, so close she could feel the breeze as it passed. The sulphur-stench of carnivore breath almost choked her. The mako jumbie looked round the campsite, cocking its head to one side to see better, just as Chichibud had done. Tan-Tan didn't laugh this time. It would take a step, it would crush them, she should run, hide. She heard her own prayerful whimpering, felt her body readying to flee. "Still, Tan-Tan, root yourself still like the halwa tree, like the lizard you see today. Yes, good pickney."

She and Chichibud remained frozen for a lifetime, watching the fire slowly get brighter. Her neck ached in its twisted position, her poised foot was cramping.

The fire leapt into flame. Spitting, the mako jumbie pulled its head back up into the treetops and took a step out of the clearing.

"Just two-three second more, little one. You being brave."

The smell of its hot, sticky spittle in her hair was worse than its breath. It stepped over them and shoved between two trees. It was leaving.

Antonio flung himself upright in his sleep and shouted, "Get away! You can't jail me!"

Quick as death, the mako jumbie turned and struck at Antonio. His scream turned Tan-Tan's blood to ice water in her veins. It had him by one arm, was yanking him into the air when Chichibud leapt onto it, wrapping his legs round its neck. The mako jumbie dropped Antonio like Chichibud had dropped the killed rat-thing. There was a snapping sound. He screamed again. The bird threw its head from side to side, trying to shake Chichibud off. Tan-Tan ran to her daddy. He was moaning and rocking on the ground, his arm bent back on itself. A white tooth of bone was sticking through the skin, with a red spongy tip. In desperation, Tan-Tan grabbed his shirt collar and tried to pull him away from the battle. The bird screeched, thickening the air with its dead-meat breath. Still howling in pain, Antonio helped Tan-Tan by pushing and pushing his heels against the ground to move himself until the two of them reached a low tree to cower against. Tan-Tan looked up in time to see the mako jumbie scrape its neck against the trunk of the halwa tree, but still Chichibud didn't drop off. He hauled out his knife from its holster and jooked it right into the mako jumbie's throat. With a gurgle the bird went silent, but its thrashing became even more destructive. It stepped on the tent, piercing its own foot on the staves. It screeched its agony without vocal chords, a stinking harmattan wind. Chichibud dragged his knife right through the bird's throat. In the firelight, its blood jetted out blackish in the air, thick and rank so till Tan-Tan nearly vomited when a gout of it, enough to fill a bucket, splashed to the ground nearby, splattering foul drops on her.

The mako jumbie's legs collapsed under it. Chichibud jumped down quickly just before it hit the ground. Its head landed with a thump. Its rolling eyes were still. The slash in its neck, still pumping blood, gaped a wet black. Then the flow stilled. Chichibud had chopped the bird right to its neck bone.

He put his knife away and started to limp across the clearing, favouring one leg. "Tan-Tan! Antonio! Where allyou?"

"Chichibud, please—Daddy arm break!"

Antonio was moaning and crying with pain. The sound scraped at her ears. The smell of stale rum from him reminded her of nights when he and Ione would fête till dayclean, shouting and singing all through the mayor house.

"He been drinking that bitter liquid allyou does make," Chichibud said.

His arm was scraped raw. He put a clawed palm on Antonio's chest. Antonio quieted a little, looking pleadingly up at him. "Tallpeople," Chichibud said, "I go help you, understand?"

Antonio nodded.

Chichibud went to the ruin of the destroyed tent and brought back a small packet and the water gourd from the wreckage. "Good the calabash ain't break, we go need the water." He unwrapped and picked out two-three pieces of dry bark. He put them in Antonio's mouth. "Chew this. Is for sleeping. It bitter bad." Antonio chewed, screwing up his face at the taste. He gagged. "No," Chichibud said. "Don't spit it out." The douen stared at Antonio. "You is pure botheration. Without trail debt, I might left you here just so."

Little-little, Antonio's two eyes-them closed down. His head rolled onto his chest and the piece of chewed-up bark fell from his mouth. He relaxed into Chichibud's arms. Chichibud lowered him to the ground.

"Little one, you must help." He sliced Daddy's shirt sleeve with his teeth, tore it away from Daddy's broken arm. Tan-Tan felt woozy, looking at it. "Cradle his head. Hold he jaw back so he could breathe easy."

Chichibud washed his hands then Antonio's arm, using his claws to pick out grit and leaf mould from the break. When he was done he shook the calabash. "Nearly empty. Tomorrow we find some water vine. That bark your daddy chew does make you thirsty."

He found a straight stick for a splint, and ripped the torn shirt sleeve into a bandage. Then he leaned over Antonio's two broken ends of bone and spat into them.

"You nasty!" Tan-Tan said.

"It will heal faster so. Is so we mouth water stay." He stretched Antonio's arm out straight and gently moved the two ends of bone back together. Tan-Tan screwed up her face at the grinding noise. She looked down at her daddy's face to see if he felt it, but he was sleeping peacefully.

Chichibud said, "Must reach to Junjuh before it start to rotten."

He bound Antonio's arm tightly.

"He go get better, Chichibud?"

"He go sleep quiet. The doctor in Junjuh go make he better." He held Antonio's head. "Take his feet."

They were heavy, but she could do it. They carried Antonio back to the wreckage of the tent. They passed the stiffening corpse of the mako jumbie on the way. The scent of its blood was sweet and sickly, like rotten frangipani flowers. They laid Antonio down. Chichibud burrowed into the mess that had been the tent and surfaced with the yellow cloth.

"Lie beside he and keep he warm." He covered them both. "Sleep now."

She sat up, throwing the cloth off in the same moment. "You going and leave we?"

"No. I watching the fire. And it have fresh meat lying out there. I guarding it." Chichibud laughed *shu-shu*. "Too besides, you musn't waste the gifts Bush Poopa does send you. I go smoke the mako jumbie meat over the fire tonight; as much as you and me could carry. And I taking the feathers, for my wife to make a hat to keep the sun off she face. Everybody go know what a brave husband she have." He made sure that Tan-Tan was comfortable beside her daddy, then covered them both with the fabric that had been their tent. Tan-Tan could hear him twittering and chirping as he tended to the bird.

They were safe. She closed her eyes.

"Tan-Tan! Tan-Tan! Wake up, nuh?" Antonio was cotched up on his good arm.

Tan-Tan sat up and blinked her eyes in the pink morning light. Daddy's face was grey and haggard-looking. His eyes were red and bleary. But he was smiling.

"You doing good, doux-doux?" he asked. She nodded.

"Tell me that I only had a bad dream last night, nuh? Tell me that I ain't see a bird big so like a mountain, and it ain't try to pull off my arm."

Tan-Tan giggled. Antonio made to sit up all the way, but he cried out and sank back down to the ground.

"It paining you, Daddy?"

"Yes, girl. It paining too bad."

"I go get Chichibud."

She scrambled out from under the canvas. The warm pink morning light made the whole forest glow. It had some things like big butterflies dancing in the air, gold and green wings flashing. They were tearing leaves from the bushes with their hands and eating them. A small something was working up inside the ground just in front of her. A head and body popped out of the little mound of soil. It was dark red and furry, with an intelligent face like a mongoose's. It saw her, *wheep*ed in alarm and jumped back into its hole. What came after five? Yes, six. She always forgot. The mongoose thing had had more legs than six, but it had gone before she could count them all.

Small busy beast noises came from the halwa tree; chucking and chuckling sounds. The air smelt better to her than it had the day before. The glowing light on everything made it hard to focus. Her head hurt a little from it. She squinted and looked round. There was Chichibud sitting by the fire, slicing at something with his knife and eating the strips he cut off.

The mako jumbie legs-them were jooking out of the bush, where Chichibud must have dragged its carcass. The branches over the spot were shaking and sometimes there was a growling and a scrabbling. Tan-Tan imagined animals tearing at the body. She would make sure to stay far away from the trembling branches. She wondered what Mummy was doing this morning, if she was getting ready yet to come and join them. This place ain't go suit Mummy so good, oui; with no Nursie and no seamstress and no eshu, and all kind of wild animal only looking to make a meal on your bones.

"Father Tree shade you, little one." Chichibud skinned his snout back in a smile. "You sleep good?"

"Yes." Yesterday his snarly, snouty grin would have frightened her, but she was coming to like how his face looked.

Chichibud had used branches to rig a net of vine over the fire. He was smoking strips of mako jumbie meat in it. It smelt nice. But he had the mako jumbie head in the net smoking too, with its beak cut off, ugly as the devil he own self. The beak halves stood nearby, like a canoe that had been sliced in half.

"Why you cooking the head?"

Shu-shu-shu. "Not cooking; drying. I go jam it on a stake and stand the stake up right here-so in this bush, so anybody who pass by going to know that a fine hunter win a battle here. Beak coming home with me to decorate my entranceway." His long tongue flicked out, licked his snout, the corner of one eye; slid back into his mouth. He held out a piece of gristle for her. "Here; piece of the mako jumbie tongue. The sweetest part to eat."

It had bumps on it like on her own tongue, but big. And it was dark blue. Her gorge rose. "No." Then she remembered her manners. "No, thank you, Chichibud." Oh, but she'd come to talk to him for a reason: "Daddy arm paining he. Come and fix it, nuh?"

"Yes. I have some hard words for he too. We nearly all dead because of he."

Chichibud stood. From beside him he picked up Daddy's empty rum flask. He'd found the lid, transferred the water from his calabash into the bottle. He saw Tan-Tan looking at him. "Precious thing this your daddy cast away. I take it as payment for my trouble."

The arm he had scraped the night before was all over scabs now. Tan-Tan wondered if he had spit on it the way he had spit on Daddy's broken bone. He began to limp towards where Daddy was lying.

"Chichibud, your leg hurt?"

He didn't answer. When he reached Antonio he stood by

his head, making Antonio scrunch his eyes to look up at him in the sunlight.

"Tallpeople, you know what we does do to people who break trail debt?" Antonio said nothing.

"We does break they two . . . arms and leave them out in the bush."

Tan-Tan's skin prickled. Chichibud would do that? Hurt Daddy and leave him like that? It was her fault. She shouldn't have made a noise when the grit fly bit; she should have just gone outside and lit the fire back her own self. Then Daddy wouldn't be in trouble.

Chichibud ask Antonio, "What I must do with you? Eh?"

"You ain't go do nothing with me. You go keep me alive so I could look after my little girl."

Chichibud skinned up one side of his snout. That looked to Tan-Tan like a growl, not a laugh. Is so mad dog does do before they jump you. Tan-Tan went and stood close to Daddy.

"Mister," Chichibud said, "best I leave you for Bush Poopa to take in truth. She go survive better without you."

"No!" Tan-Tan leapt into Daddy's arms. He cried out in pain. Horrified at what she'd done, Tan-Tan jumped up again. Antonio glared at the douen.

Chichibud jerked his snout up into the air two-three times, like a he-lizard throwing a challenge. His ruff started to swell out. Then he stopped.

"No. I liard. I not going to hurt you. Is just vex I vex."

Antonio's face was serious. "Look, you right. I do a stupid thing last night. I sorry. I make a long, long journey to this strange place, and it sitting heavy on my heart that I never going to see home again."

His tone of voice was familiar. It was the same one he used to use on the narrowcasts back home come election time. Mummy called it "speechifying." Antonio hung his head, looking shame. Tan-Tan felt bad. She was so much trouble.

"We could reach Junjuh today," Chichibud said, "if you mind everything I tell you."

"Yes. I go do that."

Antonio made as if to get up, but he sucked air and sat back down. "Tan-Tan say maybe you have something for pain. Is true?"

"Same bitter bark from last night. I could only give you little piece. You chew too much, you go fall asleep. You go be thirsty too, after chewing it last night. First thing, we go find some water vine."

By the time the shadows were getting long again, Tan-Tan was weary so till she thought she would drop. They had had to move slowly because walking jogged Antonio's arm badly. He came close to fainting away a few times. Chichibud was limping heavily on his injured leg, but even so, he had a net vine sling at his back with the smoked mako jumbie meat, and was carrying the dead bird's beak halves stacked inside each other and overturned on his head. He'd made a second sling in which Tan-Tan was carrying more smoked bird.

"For the way you was brave," he'd said. "Food to share with your daddy until he could hunt for the both of you." It was heavy. He'd had to remind her a few times not to drag it on the ground.

Junjuh village snuck up on Tan-Tan like a mongoose; one minute, the three of them were beating their way through bush, then the bush got less dense, fewer trees, more shrubs. Next minute they turned a corner to see cleared earth.

Two men were standing round a low round wall made of stone. It had a roller handle above it. A rope wound round the handle and extended down inside the wall. The wall had a thatch roof. One of the men, the big, brawny one, was winding the handle. So he turned so the handle creaked. Both men were chanting:

> *Oh, the donkey want water,*
> *Hold him, Joe!*

As Tan-Tan and Daddy and Chichibud approached, the men wrestled a dripping bucket up at the end of the rope. The bucket was strange, made of pieces of wood with iron bands round them. "Daddy, what they doing?" Tan-Tan whispered. By now she knew it was no point asking eshu. He'd gone and left her.

"I think is a well that, doux-doux," Antonio replied tiredly. "For getting water out of the ground."

Out of the ground? Why not from the tap in their house?

One man picked up a large calabash, one of two round-bottomed gourd containers that had been sitting in twisted rings of cloth on the ground. He put the cloth on his head then sat the calabash in the ring. The other man carefully poured water from the bucket into the calabash. He gave his friend the bucket to hold. His friend wove his head a little from side to side to counter the sloshing of the water. The second man arranged his own calabash on his head then went down on one knee so his friend could fill it. He began to stand with the full calabash of water. He would spill it!

But no, he made it safely to both feet. The men rested the bucket on the lip of the well then, steadying their calabashes with one hand, they turned and started walking down the path. Their hips and heads swayed like those of Bharata Natyam dancers as they balanced the shifting water. Tan-Tan laughed with glee to see it.

They stopped at the sound and turned, slowly, their heads sliding from side to side. One of them grinned. "Eh Chichibud, ain't see you for a while. I bet you been up to mischief, ain't, boy? And is who that with you? Like you mash them up bad, oui!" Tan-Tan frowned, confused. The man spoke to Chichibud the way adults spoke to her.

Chichibud said, "Evening, Master One-Eye, Master Claude. These two drop out the half-way tree."

Master? Only machines were supposed to give anybody rank like that. The two men beckoned them over. Daddy drew himself up tall as he limped up to them. "Good evening, Compères," he said in his official voice. "I name Antonio, and this is my daughter, Tan-Tan."

One of the men had an eye cloudy in its socket like guinèpe seed. He nodded at Antonio. "One-Eye, me. This is my partner, Claude." Claude said nothing, just spread his two feet-them wide for balance and stood there looking at them. He had a truncheon tucked into his waistband. One-Eye clapped Chichibud hard on his back. The douen man stumbled, favouring his injured leg. "Chichibud, you thieving little bastard, you!" One-Eye said. "I bet you you make these two give you something before you bring them here."

Chichibud cast his eyes down at his feet and mumbled, "Is so trade does go. If people ain't share their talents and gifts with each other, the world go fall apart."

One-Eye laughed and turned to Antonio. "Superstitious. Is so douen people stay."

"Boss," the douen say to One-Eye, "this man need the doctor bad."

Tan-Tan scolded, "He not your boss, Chichibud." She repeated her lesson exactly as Nanny had sung it to them in crèche: "Shipmates all have the same status. Nobody higher than a next somebody. You must call he 'Compère,' " she explained to the douen.

The men burst out laughing, even Daddy. "Pickney-child," said Claude, "is a human that?" His voice was dry and rough like after you eat stinkin' toe pods.

"No," Tan-Tan replied doubtfully.

"So how he could call we Compère?"

"I don't know." She felt stupid.

Chichibud headed off down the dirt path. "I taking them to Doctor Lin, seen?"

They needed a doctor. Daddy was swaying on his feet. He had rested his good arm on Tan-Tan's shoulder, and dark blood was seeping through the bandage on his broken arm. Tan-Tan patted his hand and looked up at him.

"Yes, doux-doux," he said. "Come make we go." One-Eye and Claude walked along with them, balancing their calabashes.

Farther down the road was one set of wattle-and-daub cottages squeezing up against the bumpy gravel path. Some of the houses had provisions growing in their front yards. Tan-Tan saw pigeon peas and sorrel bushes and a plant she didn't recognise, with big pink leaves and fat, tight buds like cabbages, only aqua blue. She could hear hammering and sawing off in the distance. As they passed one cottage, two men and a woman with thick heavy sticks were pounding some kind of paste in a hollowed-out tree stump, THUMP-thump-thump, THUMP-thump-thump. "Mortar and pestle," Antonio said quietly. "I only ever see that in pictures."

An old man was hanging out washing to dry on a clothes line strung up between one house and the next. He sang to himself in a cracky voice.

They drew level with another cottage, much like the rest. "Let we just put down this water," One-Eye said. "Then we go escort you the rest of the way." They rested their burden in a shady part of the porch. One-Eye ran round to the back and returned with a banana leaf that he'd just cut. It was the same height as him. He used it to cover the two calabashes. They set off down the road again. One-Eye spoke to Tan-Tan: "Your daddy say you name . . . what?"

"Tan-Tan."

"Tan-Tan. A pretty little girl with big brown eyes like toolum sweetie. What a sadness for a pickney to come here."

Antonio said to him, "So what you get exile for?"

The man replied gruffly, "We don't ask people questions like that."

"Oh, yes?" Tan-Tan knew that tone. You didn't cross Daddy when his voice got that edge. "So is who going to stop me from speaking what on my mind?"

"Me. And this." Claude had stepped between the two of them, was patting the truncheon he carried. He smiled a crocodile grin.

With one bright eye and his one dead one, One-Eye stared Antonio down. "Mister," he said soft and low, "it have rules here in Junjuh. No Anansi Web to look after we." Antonio looked startled, then thoughtful. "I is the one who does enforce the rules," One-Eye continued. "Claude is my deputy."

"And so? What I care for your rules?"

"After a day in the tin box, most people does care."

"A-what that?"

"You go see it soon."

Chichibud laughed *shu-shu-shu*. Claude challenged him: "You have something to say?"

"No, Boss. Is tallpeople business, oui?"

"You know so. Take that child sling from she. She looking tired."

Balancing the mako jumbie beak on his head with one hand, Chichibud made a whistling noise as he lifted her sling off her shoulder. He was limping more now. Now that she didn't have the weight dragging her shoulder, Tan-Tan felt a little less tired. She looked round more, paid more attention. She liked the way that the pinkish rockstones that made up the gravel path had glints in them. The lowering sun made them sparkle. A few people were sitting on their front verandahs watching them as they passed. A woman hoed in her garden. Her belly was big with baby, and her short-zogged hair was twisted up in little picky-plaits like she never had nobody to do it up nice for her. Everybody looked old and callous. Tan-Tan had never seen so much hard labour and so many tired faces.

"Nanny save we," muttered Antonio. "Is what kind of place I bring we to any at all?"

Some of the vegetable patches had bright flowers twining amongst the food plants. A morning glory vine clambered up the side of one cottage, flowers just opening up in the evening cool. Things mostly looked neat and clean, but Junjuh had a weariness to it.

Two-three of the houses had douen men working in the gardens, digging and hoeing. They all called out to Chichibud as he passed, in a language sweet like when your mother sing to you in your dreams. Glancing back at the houses to see if the humans would notice and stop them, some of the douens came hopping out to greet Chichibud. They crowded round him, nuzzling his shoulders and face and grooming his eye-ridges. Two of them took the mako jumbie beak halves and leaned them up against their bodies. A whole ring of them clasped arms with him and just stood there in a circle, twitching their heads from time to time in that jerky birdlike motion that Chichibud did. They opened and closed their mouths but no sound came out.

"What them doing, Daddy?" Tan-Tan asked.

"Me ain't know." Antonio looked at them with a sneer. "Them look bassourdie for true, like them crazy from the sun or something."

"Is so douen-them does greet one another," One-Eye said. "You could run a donkey cart through the whole pack of them right now, and them would barely notice."

And just so, quick as the circle had formed, it broke up. Two of the douens picked up the mako jumbie beak halves. They all started walking with Chichibud, talking steady-steady to him the whole time, looking in his pack and touching the beak. All Chichibud was limping, he was only making style in the street, dancing and waving the mako jumbie feathers in the air. Tan-Tan was mad with curiosity. She called out, "What them saying to you, Chichibud?"

"Glad I reach safe. And how me wife going to love me even more when she see the gift I bringing she."

For the first time, One-Eye seemed to really look at the douen man limping along beside them.

"But eh-eh, Chichibud, what stupidness you go and do to yourself? Is mako jumbie allyou meet up with in the bush?"

"Death bird herself, yes! And it done dead! Is me it buck up in the dark; me, Chichibud!" He did a little dance on the gravel path, hopping from side to side, bad leg or no. The other douens joined in. Tan-Tan giggled. Claude rolled his eyes. They kept walking, leaving Chichibud to catch up. Twittering the whole time, he and his friends came along behind.

With the truncheon, Claude pointed out a galvanized metal box on one side of the path, suspended between four wooden posts. It looked scarcely big enough to hold a grown man. It had a ladder leaning up against it, leading to a door in its side. Above the door, it had one little air hole drilled in the galvanized metal, about big enough for Tan-Tan to stick her fist in. The door had four big bolts all round to hold it shut.

"The tin box," One-Eye told them. "One morning in dry season I put a gully hen egg inside that box. When I open it up come evening, the egg did boil to a jelly, right inside it own shell. Man or woman, anybody break the rules, is at least a day in the box for them. I warn you so you know."

Something complicated happened to Daddy's face. Tan-Tan imagined being shut inside the dark box, no choice to leave, no room to move, drowning in your own sweat. Skin burning with from your own stinking piss, from the flux of shit running down your leg. Like crêche teacher had told them. Like her nightmares.

Antonio didn't say anything for a while, just leaned on

Tan-Tan as he walked, blowing a little from the exertion. Then he looked sideways at One-Eye and asked, "So how the rules go that allyou have in this place?"

One-Eye laughed. "I see you is a man does figure the odds fast. That go do you good. You have to understand, Antonio, that this is a prison colony. The Nation Worlds send all of we here because them ain't want nothing to do with we. Either we do something them ain't like, or we ain't do something them would have like we to do."

Antonio didn't say anything.

"Now you," One-Eye continued, "I mad to know is what make them send you here with a pickney. But by we code, you can't ask people why them get exile, but people could choose to tell you. You could share confidences, seen? Me, I lose my temper one day and beat up the lying, cheating, motherass mongrel who call himself my business partner. Bust him up bad before the sheriffs reach."

"You tell me wasn't the first time you hit he, neither," Claude interrupted. "Nanny and your Mocambo decide you too violent."

"But I woulda do it again too. That ain't any way to do business."

"I stab a man who thief my woman," Antonio said boastfully. Tan-Tan looked up at him. His eyes were bright. She remembered the sight of Uncle Quashee after Daddy had stabbed him; lying flaccid in the dust of the fight yard with his breath sticking in his throat. "Me and Daddy fool them," she said. "We run—"

"Hush up your mouth, Tan-Tan. This is big people story."

Stung, Tan-Tan pressed her lips together. They pushed out into a pout. Pride. She could just hear Nursie saying it. One-Eye frowned at her, flashed a strange look at her daddy, then said:

"Is just so. Most of we get send here because anger get the better of we too often. Almost any other crime the Grande

'Nansi Web could see coming and prevent, but Granny Nanny can't foresee the unpremeditated, seen?"

"Seen," Antonio muttered thoughtfully.

"A whole planet full of violent people," Claude told them.

"Everywhere? The shift towers send people to the poles too?"

"We nah know. Nobody have time for go exploring. Hard enough staying alive right here so. Granny Nanny sentence we to live out we days in hard labour."

"When I reach New Half-Way Tree," One-Eye said, "life in Junjuh Town was madness, you see? One set of comess. Everything you had, somebody else ready to take it from you. And take your life too, if them had them way. You couldn't close eyes and sleep in peace come nighttime. So when me and Claude find each other"—he flashed a warm smile at Claude—"we lay down some ground rules and we find two next people to help we enforce them: no fighting; if somemaddy mark goods as them own, nobody else could claim them; if somemaddy beat their spouse, the spouse could leave and go to a next somemaddy, and them could take them own goods with them. Anybody who break a rule, is the box the first time for them, and a hanging the next time. Oh, and it have one more: is only we could enforce the rules."

"How allyou get away with that?"

"Wasn't easy. We had was to stand up for weself more than once, and we always have to mind each other back. Is so I lose this eye, oui? But is only my one eye gone; the man that start that argument never draw breath again to start a next one. After a while, people come to see that we judgement fair, that we don't cheat them. I the one who usually make the judgements. And I listen to both sides before I make a decision. So Junjuh people acknowledge me as sheriff, and the next three people as deputies."

"And no Nanny to watch everything you do. No web nowhere." Daddy sounded like a man in prayer.

One-Eye grinned. "No nanoweb to mind you, but no-one to scrutinize you either."

Tan-Tan was bored. Chichibud and his friends had finally caught up with them. She patted his shoulder to get his attention.

"Chichibud, your wife coming to meet you?"

The douen men laughed and clicked their claws together *tick-tick-tick*. Claude guffawed too. Tan-Tan didn't understand what she had said to sweet them so.

"Pickney-child," One-Eye said, "the day I see a douen woman must be the day I go drop dead. Chichibud does talk about he wife like she is the living goddess; Pastora Divina she-self come down to Earth. Don't it, Chichibud? But none of we ever see she, nor any other douen woman. Douen don't live among we, and douen women don't come among we."

"Them 'fraid oonuh too bad," one of the douens said, arching a reptilian head towards One-Eye. "Them tell we all-you ugly like duppy!" And he laughed *shu-shu*, covering one eye with his hand to imitate the man he was speaking to.

One-Eye scowled. "All right, enough fête." He waved his hands at the douen-them to make them go away. "Go back to work."

One-one, they all left, except Chichibud and the two helping him. "We have to do for him, Master," one said to One-Eye. "He too lame to carry all this by heself."

"Hmm. All right." He spat onto the dirt path.

"You have to watch them all the time," One-Eye told Antonio. "Them like children."

Chichibud said nothing. He pulled his sharp bush knife from his waist and started cleaning in between his fangs-them with it.

In a few more steps they reached a bungalow that had a white flag waving on a pole out in the front. The two douens laid the mako jumbie beak halves down in the dust beside the house. They skreeked at Chichibud and left.

"This is where Doctor Lin does stay," Claude told them. He led them up the front steps. No house eshu clicked on to greet them. It felt strange, wrong.

It had a girl, older than Tan-Tan, sitting in a rocking chair on the verandah, rocking and singing to herself in a little girl voice. She held on tight to a tattered rag doll, so old that most of the embroidered stitches that had sketched its face were gone. Tan-Tan remembered the many dollies that Daddy had bought for her. She'd left them all behind; dollies that walked and talked and thing, and Babygreen, the special one, the one whose clothes would change colour when Tan-Tan ran a special wand over them. She missed them. Her heart hurt when she remembered all the things she missed.

The big girl in the rocking chair had her hair in two fat plaits on each side of her head. As she rocked she held on to one plait and twisted it round and round in her fingers. When she saw the procession, she grinned sloppily and called out, "Good evening, allyou. Allyou come to see Doctor Mummy?"

"Yes, Quamina," Claude said gently. Then quietly: "She ain't have all she wits. Lin tell we she have the mind of a four-year-old."

Antonio stared at Quamina, his lip curling up in disgust. Tan-Tan didn't understand. If the big girl was sick, why didn't they fix her?

One-Eye said, "She did even worse than that when she was little. Born bassourdie, and she couldn't learn to walk good, or talk; only wetting up sheself all the time."

"And what happen to she now?" Antonio whispered. He looked like he'd stepped in dog do-do.

Claude answered, "Asje, my douen, bring some bush tea for she. He tell Lin she must make Quamina drink a little every morning. Next thing you know, Quamina start to talk!"

"She might never come into she full age, though," One-Eye say. "I ain't know what Aislin make she live for. She only a burden."

Claude scowled at him. "Quamina quiet, and she sweet, and she does help Aislin round the place."

One-Eye hugged Claude to him, patted him on the back. "All right, sweetness! I ain't go badtalk your woman daughter." He kissed Claude on the mouth. Claude returned the kiss, his scowl clearing slowly. He took One-Eye's hand and went up to the door, stopping to tousle Quamina's hair. She smiled. He rapped on the door and called out, "Inside!"

"Claude? I here," a woman's voice called happily from inside. Claude's face lit up. "What crosses you come to bother my soul with today?" the playful voice said.

"We bring you a new boyfriend, Lin." He showed Antonio and Tan-Tan inside. "Only one thing, though; he reach in two pieces, and you have to put he back as one again." He stood with his arms round One-Eye, waiting for her reply.

Chichibud limped over to an examination table. He put his slings down beside it and climbed up onto it. The woman washing her hands in a bucket looked up and smiled at Chichibud. She didn't look pretty to Tan-Tan. She had little baby plaits sticking out of the kerchief she'd tied round her head. Her eyes were creased up at the corners as though she was used to frowning all the time. Although she straightened up from the bucket to greet her visitors, her shoulders had remained stooped. When she saw Antonio, a look of horror came over her face. Antonio sighed, then said, "Well, Aislin; is you? Like me and you meet up again."

Aislin! Nursie's daughter that had climbed the half-way tree! Tan-Tan tried to see Nursie's face in Aislin's.

Aislin looked good at Antonio. "Mayor Antonio? Is Antonio allyou bring to my clean hospital for me to treat?" Her voice rose. "This . . . this piece of *trash?*" She strode up to him, waved her fist in his face. "Yes, you hear me right! I glad Toussaint throw you away to this hell! You ain't mayor of nothing any more. Here I could name you for what you is—dung that dog does mash in the street! You do me wrong . . ."

"You mean to tell me your conscience really clear, Aislin?" Antonio asked softly. "You totally innocent?"

Aislin's face purpled with rage. "Don't give me none of that, I won't listen to it! You do me wrong, I say! Then you send me away from my old mother so you wouldn't have to look on your own deeds, send me away to rot here behind God back, and now look; you end up here your own self. I know it would happen; I know your liard ways would catch up with you one day." Aislin started to laugh, but it had tears running down her face. "Take he away, Claude. I ain't looking after he."

One-Eye frowned. "What he is to you, Lin?"

"My baby father." Aislin hugged Quamina, who had come in to see what all the comess was about. "You see, Antonio? You see what does happen to the child when you send a pregnant woman up the half-way tree? You greet your daughter yet?"

Antonio said nothing, just stared in repulsion at Quamina. Tan-Tan pulled on his pants leg. "Daddy? Why that lady so vex?"

"Hush, doux-doux. I go explain you later."

"Why you don't explain to she now, Antonio? Tell she she have a sister, nuh?"

A sister? Tan-Tan looked at Quamina. She didn't understand. Aislin wasn't her mummy. Quamina smiled her wet smile at Tan-Tan and held out her doll. Tan-Tan released Antonio's hand and went to stand in front of Quamina. She reached out and touched the dolly with the tips of her fingers. It was still warm from Quamina's clutch. Quamina released the dolly into Tan-Tan's grasp and Tan-Tan grabbed it like a lifeline. She held it and stroked its head. She said to Quamina, "You want to play with me?"

"Tan-Tan!" Antonio shouted, "get away from that mad girl!" He made to pull her away, but he forgot and used his broken arm. He bawled for pain and would have fainted dead away if One-Eye hadn't supported him and helped him onto the other examining table. Chichibud chewed on a piece of jerky from his pouch, simply watching.

"Aislin," One-Eye said, "I know how this must be paining you, but you is we doctor; you have to help this man."

Aislin just shook her head. Claude went and held her hand.

"Choonks, I know now who this man is. I know what he do to you, for ain't is me who shoulder you bawl on when Quamina did born bassourdie? But you have a job to do, darling."

Aislin just stood frozen, her face set hard. Tan-Tan had seen that expression plenty of times before. "Is just so Nursie does do she lip," she said.

Aislin's face softened. "Mamee still alive?" she asked Tan-Tan.

"Yes," Antonio muttered. "I taking care of your mother good-good in my house. And she visit she sister all the time. I ain't leave she lonely with no people to share she life with. She all right."

Aislin made a soft noise, like when you standing outside the sweetie shop window but your mummy won't let you go in.

"Maybe Tan-Tan should go outside and play with Quamina after all," Daddy said to her.

Aislin sighed. "Yes, Quamina; show your sister the swings, all right, sweetness? I have to do some doctor business now."

"All right."

"You better stay here, Claude; you and One-Eye. I need someone here with me to mind I don't poison this son of a dog instead of giving he medicine. Stay and watch me, or it might be me allyou putting in that galvanized box tomorrow morning."

Chichibud walked with them down the steps to the gravel path. "Trail debt between we done, pickney. You reach safe."

"Thank you, Chichibud."

Carrying his bounty, he limped back towards the bush.

Quamina took Tan-Tan to an almond tree in the middle of the village. A rope swing with a plank for a seat hung from one of its low branches. "I go push," Quamina said shyly. Tan-Tan climbed on, still clutching Quamina's doll in one hand. She squeezed its arm and the swing's rope together in one fist. She let the older girl push. "Where you come from?" Quamina asked.

"From the half-way tree. Yesterday morning."

"Mummy say you is my sister."

"I ain't know. Push a little harder, nuh?" Tan-Tan pumped and pumped her legs until she was swinging high over the village. But all she looked out over the bush, she couldn't see the shift tower. It was daylean; the sun was lowering to dark. The ringing in her ears was back. She shook her head, trying to clear it.

She pushed Quamina in the swing for a while, then she taught her how to play Midnight Robber. Quamina had to be the Faithful Tonto and just follow what Tan-Tan did. Her mind was too young for anything else. They made up brave deeds for the Midnight Robber: "And then, and then she say, 'Oh, bad mako jumbie, I going chop your neck for you and send you far away up in the half-way tree!' "

As it got darker a woman with a ladder came out and climbed the lampposts in the village square. She lit the lamps. The flickering light put Tan-Tan in mind of the nation ship hat she'd worn at Jonkanoo time. Were the tongues of flame singing, or was the sound just in her ears?

A little after nightfall, Aislin came to look for them, her

face set and unsmiling. She hugged Quamina tight, straightened her dress. Quamina chortled and kissed her mother. "Come, Tan-Tan," Aislin said. "You could have dinner with me and Quamina, and then I go take you to Antonio."

"Daddy staying by you in the doctor house?"

"No, child. I can't have that man near me. One-Eye and my Claude carry he over to the mash-up hut where old Zora used to live till she pass on last year. The two of you could stay there."

"Daddy go get better?"

"Yes, darling. Your father tough like old boot. In two-twos he go be back on he feet, up to he old tricks. And Granny Nanny help we then."

As they got close to the silent doctor house Tan-Tan could smell food cooking. Her tummy started to rumble. They went inside. There wasn't a lot of light there. Rusty iron chandeliers hung from the ceiling: smelly, smoky candles burned in them. Tan-Tan stroked a wall for light, but nothing happened. The voices in the candle flame were stronger now. She could almost hear what they were singing. Her ears itched, particularly the left one. She tunnelled her little finger into it to scratch it, but it didn't help.

"I been busy all day," Aislin told them. She went to something that looked like a stove, only flames were burning in the top of it. There was a big frying pan on the flames. Aislin reached for a cloth hanging beside the stove and used it to lift the lid off the frying pan. A fry-popping sound came from it, and a delicious smell. Aislin stuck a spoon inside. She tapped something from the spoon onto her hand and tasted it. "I ain't have time to do nothing fancy. Quamina, put down that dolly, nuh? Show Tan-Tan how to wash she hands, then allyou sit to table."

"Yes, Mummy." There was a big wooden barrel of water beside the wooden sink. A calabash dipper hung from a string on the wall. Quamina dipped water over Tan-Tan's hands while she washed them. The soap smelt nasty and made her skin dry. The cool water made her shiver. "Dip some for me now," Quamina told her. She did, awkwardly. "Now come to table."

Three rough, uneven chairs stood round a hand-hewed table. Tan-Tan's chair wobbled. The plates were a blue glaze with red birds painted on them. In the candlelight they seemed to flap their wings. Were they singing? *Ah, chi-chi bird, oi. Some of them a-holler, some a-bawl.* No, that's not what they were singing. Tan-Tan couldn't understand the words.

Aislin brought the frying pan over to the table and emptied its contents onto the three plates. "You like metamjee, child? Oil-down, some people call it? Chichibud give me some of he mako jumbie meat, and I fry it up with some ground provisions and coconut oil."

"What happen to your Cookie?" Tan-Tan asked her.

Aislin frowned. "Doux-doux darling, nobody here have any artisans to gift them with their skills. You and Antonio going to have to cook your own food that you grow in your own yard, or that you hunt and kill yourself. You going to have to fetch your own water, and take your own clothes down to the river bank to wash. Anything we have here, we make with we own two hand. You understand, Tan-Tan?"

"Back-break not for people," Tan-Tan quoted at her scornfully.

"We not people no more. We is exiles. Is work hard or dead."

"I does work hard," Quamina said proudly. "Is me get the stuffing for my dolly from the feather pod trees it have growing in the bush."

Aislin smiled at Quamina.

Tan-Tan said, "My daddy go take care of me. My daddy could do anything."

"Your daddy think he could get *away* with anything. Is a

different thing. And it look like them finally catch him out, oui? Junjuh Town go do for he." She seemed to shake the thought away. "Well, never mind, sweetness. Let we eat."

Tan-Tan thought she'd never tasted any food so good as the plate of oil-down she was eating with a beat-up old spoon at a rickety kitchen table. But after couple-three mouthfuls she lost her appetite for more. She still felt shivery from the cold water. Her head hurt like it had hammers inside. The voices in the candle flames were singing:

> *Dodo, petit popo,* (Sleep, little one,)
> *Petit popo pas v'lez dodo,* (But baby ain't want to sleep,)
> *Si vous pas dodo, petit popo,* (If you don't sleep, little
>   baby,)
> *Mako chat allez mangez 'o.* (Big tiger go come and eat you
>   up.)

"No!" she yelled at them. "Daddy won't let you!"

"Tan-Tan?" Aislin said.

Eat you up, beat you up, the candles told her. Her head pounded. *Brigand a miduit allez mangez 'o.* Everything looked blurry. "No," she whimpered at the candles.

"Tan-Tan, is what do you?" It was Nursie's voice, but young. Nursie's hand touched her forehead. "Me granny! You burning up with fever!"

"Nursie, I want to go to bed. I don't feel good."

Nursie picked her up. She closed her aching eyes and laid her head against Nursie's neck. The room was swinging, swinging in circles. Her supper flew up out of her belly and gushed acidic lumps past her lips, splattering Nursie's shoulder. Then blackness come down.

●　●　●

They never heard word of Maka, the runner who had made the poison that had killed Quashee. He'd promised he would join Daddy by climbing the half-way tree. Tan-Tan sometimes wondered what had happened to him. She had liked his face.

The year she turned nine, Antonio and his new partner Janisette threw a fête for Tan-Tan:

My little Tan-Tan get so big! You look just like my lost Ione.

The fête started when the three of them got home from working the cornfields that flanked Junjuh. They toted extra water, enough to wash their hair and all. When it was her turn to use the big wooden washbasin out back of the cottage, Tan-Tan sat still in the water and inspected her face reflected in it. Yes, Mummy's eyes had been brown so, had come to tiny turned-up points at the outsides like that. Mummy's hair had been mixup-mixup like that, some straight, some coiled tight like springs, some wavy. All the bloods flowing into one river. She looked like Mummy for true. Mummy was never coming to see her. Nor eshu, nor Nursie. They had just left her here in this place.

Janisette shouted through the window, "Pickney-child, make haste and done with that bath!" Tan-Tan looked up to see Daddy gazing at her through the mesh of the wet-sugar tree bark that formed his and Janisette's bedroom window. He drew his head back fast. Tan-Tan stood and dried herself.

Quamina came to her birthday, with Claude and Aislin. Aislin scowled the whole time and kept calling Quamina to her. Tan-Tan had asked for Chichibud to come too. "Nanny guard we," Janisette had said. "What you want that nasty douen in the house for?"

Tan-Tan had pouted and looked at her feet. "He tell nice stories."

"Is true, doux-doux," Antonio had said to Janisette. "We

could have him out in the yard. He could tell 'nansi story and keep the pickney-them entertained."

One-Eye dropped in after he had made his rounds of the town for the evening. When Chichibud arrived the whole fête moved to the yard out back. They drank sweet sorrel (Janisette gave Chichibud his in a calabash dipper, not a mug). They ate hot halwa fruit, and Chichibud told them duppy stories by the fire, about all kinda dead spirits and thing. Claude lay across One-Eye's and Aislin's laps, reaching up from time to time to kiss one or the other of them. Tan-Tan and Quamina screamed and laughed and held each other as Chichibud told them about the Blackheart man who steals away tallpeople girl-pickneys and chops out their hearts.

Ah, my little Tan-Tan, so sweet. Don't 'fraid. I not going to hurt you.

Quamina gave Tan-Tan a new dolly. "I make she like a Carnival Robber Queen for you, sister." Quamina had gained even more sense in these years. Aislin had told Tan-Tan that the douen medicine was still working on her, growing her up very slowly. The dolly had on a black jacket and pants like a masquerade Robber, and a big wide-brim hat with tassels hiding its face. Quamina had put a little wooden gun in the doll's waistband and had tied a tiny wooden knife in a holster round one thigh. "You know is a lady dolly because I give she two bubbies," Quamina said. And for true, the doll had two bumps of breasts like Quamina's. Tan-Tan wondered what it would feel like when she got her own.

Aislin kissed her and gave her some lavender perfume that she had brewed in the doctor house. "Doux-doux, remember the scare you give we the first day you come here? I so glad you here for we to enjoy your birthday." Aislin glared at Daddy. When adult exiles got punted to New Half-Way Tree, the trip through the warps of the dimension veils caused their earbugs to cease functioning. But Tan-Tan's earbug had still been growing with her growing body; its nanomites hadn't yet calcified permanently into a transmitter-receiver. The nanomites had become infected and had nearly killed her.

Chichibud gave Tan-Tan a plant from the bush. It had heart-shaped leaves and a deep red flower. A simple gift, but Tan-Tan had come to understand over the years that douens were simple people; Aislin had told her so. They did everything with their hands and never thought to advance themselves any further.

Chichibud held up the flower to show her, and Tan-Tan realised that she had grown taller than the little douen man. She inhaled the perfume of the flower, like roses and grapefruits.

"We does call it sky-fall-down-to-earth, for is the same colour as the evening sky," he say. Tan-Tan watched as he transplanted it into the garden.

"Thank you, Mister Chichibud."

"He is only douen. Don't be calling he mister." Janisette kissed her teeth. She had given Tan-Tan a pretty new dress in douen yellow, made by Chichibud's invisible wife. "I hope the bodice fit. You does outgrow everything so fast nowadays."

Antonio had given her his gold wedding band strung onto a leather thong to wear round her neck.

"This is yours, Daddy."

"Never mind. Is yours now. I give up everything to come here so we could be together, Tan-Tan; my wife, my home, everything. And look at how big you get. The ring is yours."

As Tan-Tan tied the thong round her neck she glimpsed Janisette's thundercloud-dark face. "You leave one wife and gone, but you have a next one now. And I suppose you ain't think to gift this one with gold ring." Janisette spent the rest of the fête knocking back one set of sorrel spiked with strong rum. Antonio had to half-carry her to bed when the fête was done and everybody gone home. Then he walked Tan-Tan to her bedroom.

Tan-Tan was feeling so happy. She gave Antonio one big hug, pressed against him and held on tight. "Thank you for my party, Daddy."

"Nanny bless, doux-doux. You know how much I love you." He stroked her shoulder, her hair.

My sweet little girl. You get so big now. Let me comb your hair for you. Let me put on your nightie. I go tuck you into bed, all right?

He took her face in his two hands and kissed her on the mouth. *Let me show you something special.*

Antonio laid her down on the bed. The "special" thing was something more horrible than she'd ever dreamt possible. Why was Daddy doing this to her? Tan-Tan couldn't get away, couldn't understand. She must be very bad for Daddy to do her so. Shame filled her, clogged her mouth when she opened to call out to Janisette for help. Daddy's hands were hurting, even though his mouth smiled at her like the old Daddy, the one from before the shift tower took them. Daddy was two daddies. She felt her own self split in two to try to understand, to accommodate them both. Antonio, good Antonio smiled at her with his face. Good Tan-Tan smiled back. She closed her mind to what bad Antonio was doing to her bad body. She watched at her new dolly on the pillow beside her. Its dress was up around its waist and she could see its thigh holster with the knife in it. She wasn't Tan-Tan, the bad Tan-Tan. She was Tan-Tan the Robber Queen, the terror of all Junjuh, the one who born on a far-away planet, who travel to this place to rob the rich in their idleness and help the poor in their humility. She name Tan-Tan the Robber Queen, and strong men does tremble in their boots when she pass by. Nothing bad does ever happen to Tan-Tan the Robber Queen. Nothing can't hurt she. Not Blackheart Man, not nothing.

Oh God, Tan-Tan, oh God, don't cry. I sorry. I won't do it again. We won't even tell Janisette, all right, or she go be mad at we. You wouldn't want she to send for One-Eye to put me in the tin box, right? That would kill your poor Daddy, Tan-Tan. Is just because I missing your mother, and you look so much like she. You see how I love you, girl? See what you make me do? Just like Ione. Just like your mother.

Tan-Tan looked at the dolly's knife holster. It would be nice if the little wooden knife inside it were really sharp steel. Baby-green, she would name the dolly Babygreen to replace the one she'd left behind.

The bad thing happened plenty of times after that. Antonio promised every time would be the last. But he couldn't help himself, is because she was the spitting image of Ione. Daddy said so. One evening she passed by Antonio and Janisette's room. Janisette was sobbing, "You love she better than me, ain't?"

"No, doux-doux," came Antonio's appeasing voice.

"She is your daughter, but I is your wife!"

"No, doux-doux, no."

"Auntie Aislin, you coming tomorrow?"

Tan-Tan rested her carry sack on the side table in Aislin's office and ran to give the woman a hug. She had to lean forward over Aislin's baby-big belly to put her arms around the doctor.

"Of course, sweetness! You think me and Quamina could miss your sweet sixteen?" Aislin chuckled and rocked her, singing about the sweet sixteen who'd never been kissed.

You wish, whispered a silent, mean voice in Tan-Tan's head. She ignored it. "Eh-eh, Aislin; them is your new shelf and thing?"

Tan-Tan went to inspect the wood shelves and cupboards Aislin had asked Cudjoe to build for her. The shelves were crookedy. Most of the cupboard doors didn't quite meet. Tan-Tan looked back at Aislin.

"Me know, me know," Aislin said. "One-Eye tell me how I fool-fool to make that man put hammer to nail for me, but I feel sorry for Cudjoe, man! He having a hard time learning how to be headblind."

Cudjoe had climbed the half-way tree just two months earlier. He had wanted to be a carpenter on Toussaint. He had learned the trade in a hurry, trying to cash in on the new fad amongst the Shipmate Houracan people from the south. Everyone wanted headblind cottages of real wood with nails, like the runners had. Gazebos and small huts were springing up everywhere beside people's main, aware homes. One of Cudjoe's shoddily constructed cottages had collapsed, killing a woman, a man and three small pickney. While the local Mocambo was still trying to decide what to do with Cudjoe, a treehouse he'd built had fallen in on itself. The boy and girl who'd been playing in it had been injured, but would live. Nanny's guidance to the Mocambo was that Cudjoe should be made to learn his trade properly, but the Mocambo disagreed. They judged that Cudjoe had already endangered too many people. They didn't even opt for exporting him, just shipped him up the half-way tree.

"One-Eye tell he if these shelves fall down, is the box for he! Cudjoe taking he real serious." Aislin laughed, holding the weight of her belly with two hands. "I swear, I never see nail long so in my life! It have more nails than wood in them cupboards there."

"But suppose them break in truth?" Tan-Tan asked. "You should have ask one of the douen-them to build them for you, Auntie Aislin. You know how them good with them hands."

"Is all right. I does only keep towel and gauze bandage in there, and some little small things. The medicines-them in the back room, where I could keep my eye on them."

Tan-Tan knew Aislin's back room well, with its neat rows of bottles and jars with labels, all lined-up on the shelves along the walls. The back room was where Aislin performed what operations she could manage with the tools she had. It was where Aislin had taken seven-year-old Tan-Tan that first night on New Half-Way Tree when her earbug nanomites had become infected. Aislin had had to fight to keep the fever down. Tan-Tan had lain in recovery there for days, reading the labels on the shelves: "Disinfectants"; "Anti-inflammatories."

"Melonhead give you he present yet?" Aislin asked teasingly.

"No." Aislin seemed to have forgiven Melonhead finally. Tan-Tan had lain in her back room again two years ago, staring at one label in particular: "Abortifacients." The memory of the rending pain was still strong in Tan-Tan's mind. Is only because the cramps and bleeding had her so sick after the abortion that Janisette hadn't striped her backside with blows over that one.

"Is Melonhead, ain't it? Say is he!" Tan-Tan hadn't answered.

"You little slut! You been hot for that that mamapoule boy from since, you know is true! You think because you get bubby now and your blood start to flow, you is big woman!"

Melonhead. Tan-Tan could have almost laughed out loud at the idea of making boobaloops with her friend Melonhead. He was her only agemate; tailor Ramkissoon's son who had chosen to come into exile with him when his daddy had been sent up the half-way tree. Melonhead was Tan-Tan's dearest friend next to Quamina, but he was about as sexy as a clod of dirt. He wasn't like some of the older men who were already casting their eyes at her then fourteen-year-old body; not like One-Eye's deputy Kenneth, or like Rick. Tan-Tan had smiled, thinking of how she could make them stare. And Janisette had shaken her finger in Tan-Tan's face, spraying her with rum-scented spittle as she hissed: "I thought so! Barely old enough to smell yourself, and you carrying on with Melonhead. You leggobeast you!"

"Is not Melonhead," Tan-Tan had mumbled. But Janisette hadn't believed. She'd gone to Ramkissoon. He'd kept his son away from Tan-Tan while she was healing, but when she met Melonhead a few weeks later under the acerola cherry tree in the middle bush around Junjuh, Melonhead had told her that Ramkissoon was only doing what Janisette had asked because she was his neighbour.

"He ain't believe Janisette," he said, the bobbin of raw fibre he always had with him dropping from his fingers to spin, spin thread just centimetres from the ground. "Daddy believe me. But he say Janisette crazy like dog in the sun hot, he ain't want to cross she. He say you and me must be careful and stay out from under she eye."

Melonhead had never asked her who she'd been making baby for. That's why she liked him. When she didn't want to talk, he didn't press her. People gave Melonhead static for making Tan-Tan pregnant, but he never defended himself, just let them think it had been him. He was a good friend.

Tan-Tan dragged her mind back to the present. "Aislin, Daddy send me. Is that same arm what he did break so long ago. He say it paining him again."

Aislin waddled over to one of Cudjoe's cupboards. She took a small woven basket out of it and shut the cupboard door, which promptly swung wide again, nearly catching her in the face. "Cho." The door closed the second time. Aislin pulled the cover off the basket. She took out two papyrus-wrapped packets and held them out to Tan-Tan. Antonio had had this medicine before; an infusion of particular twigs and leaves. The tea reduced inflammation. Aislin said, "Mix two pinch of this in with some z'avocat leaf tea for Antonio, three times a day. It go ease up some of the pain, and the tea good for he pressure. And tell he, he must work he joints so them wouldn't stiffen up. Now he stop working in the fields, he should be digging in the garden with Chichibud, or making something with he hands. It go do he good."

"Thanks, Doctor Lin. I go tell he, but you know how he does stay."

"Yes, sweetness, I know. Antonio have a little bit of arthritis but he only carrying on so Janisette wouldn't make he wash no more dishes."

Tan-Tan laughed. "For true! You should hear how he does go on: 'What kind of thing that is for a man to be doing; washing dish and feeding chicken? You and Tan-Tan more accustomed to manual labour than me. Oonuh could do that.' "

Aislin chuckled. "It have anything in that house that Antonio does do?"

Things for send he to the tin box, cackled the silent bad voice, like an insane eshu. Tan-Tan set her mouth hard. "I just pass Quamina swinging on the almond tree swing," she said. "She do some nice cutwork embroidery on she new dress."

"Yes. She show it to you? She getting real good with a needle, ain't? Ramkissoon training she to be his assistant. Glorianna and Janisette does trade she for basket and leather shoes and thing."

"I know. I think every chair in we house have a piece of Quamina cutwork decorating the back. She keeping Chichibud wife busy busy weaving more cloth."

"Quamina doing good for true. When she did born bassourdie so, I never think say one day she would be able to help sheself. I thank Nanny every day for that bush medicine that Asje give me. It working slow, but it growing she up little-little. She does act more like ten years now than only six."

Tan-Tan had outgrown her half sister. More often now, she was the one babysitting Quamina.

She chatted a little more with Aislin, left her the bread Janisette had baked in return for Antonio's medicine, then said goodbye.

It was drizzling outside, a light rain from a passing cloud. Tan-Tan stopped on Aislin's verandah for a minute to wait for the rain to pass. It gave her an excuse to enjoy a little bit of freedom before she had to go back home again. There was someone in the tin box today, Tan-Tan had heard him groaning as she passed. The rain would cool the box, ease the torture a little.

Asje and two-three other douens were working Aislin's garden in the rain. They didn't mind getting wet. They were chattering and twittering happily to each other. From the way their eyes were cloudy, Tan-Tan knew they had their second eyelids drawn down to keep the rain out. They greeted her and went back to their hoeing and weeding. One of them caught a worm as long as Tan-Tan's forearm and sucked it up like a noodle.

Tan-Tan went and sat in the old creaky rocking chair. She liked the ice-cream sweet scent of the frangipani trees Aislin had growing all around her home now. They used to be just some little fine-fine twigs jooking up into the air.

New Half-Way Tree had changed Aislin and all. The angry, bitter woman Tan-Tan had met nine years ago seemed content now, for all that hard labour had toughened her hands and wrinkled up her face. Whenever Claude came into the room Aislin lit up like is somebody turn on the sun. He was always bringing she and Quamina some nice thing: a jar of wet sugar he'd boiled down himself from tree sap; a new doll he'd carved for Quamina. Sometimes it was hard to believe this was the same Claude who would happily crack heads in the wine shop when things got too raucous.

It had stopped raining, the sun was out. A splinter in the weave of the rocking chair seat was jooking her. Time to go home, after she'd picked up her birthday present from Gladys and Michael's forgery.

Tan-Tan stepped off Aislin's verandah into the pink of

noonday. The red light of New Half-Way Tree used to seem strange to her. But she and all had changed-up too. Just like Antonio.

Eh-eh. She'd been feeling happy before. Not any more, for some reason.

Antonio hadn't said anything at first when Aislin and Quamina had brought Tan-Tan home after the abortion. Janisette had still been scolding her when Antonio showed up in the doorway. Fear had jumped in Tan-Tan's belly at the sight of him. Her womb had shuddered through another cramp, thanks Nanny a small one this time. Antonio had been carrying a steaming pail in one hand and folded-up rags in the other. Compresses. He'd boiled water. He, who left all the work round the house to her and Janisette. "She tired," he'd said to Janisette. "Let she sleep little bit."

Janisette had made a suck-teeth sound of irritation and left.

Tan-Tan wouldn't let Antonio hold the hot compresses to her aching back. "Leave them on the table," she'd told him, then turned her face to the wall.

She'd thought he'd left, but then she'd heard him whisper, "Doux-doux, I sorry this happen."

"I tired."

"I sorry too bad. I sorry you sick."

He didn't dare say it plain, what he'd done. She didn't answer, didn't trust herself to.

"I sad and I lonely and sometimes you is my only comfort, the only thing that come with me from back home. You know I love you, sweetness. I never want you to hurt."

Was this good Daddy or bad Daddy talking? Confused and angry, good Tan-Tan and bad Tan-Tan just lay silent. Finally they'd heard the sound of Antonio walking away. The rags stayed in the cooling water in the pail. Eventually the cramping had gotten less and Tan-Tan had fallen asleep.

She healed. Antonio still stroked the bad Tan-Tan from

time to time with too-familiar touches, but no more of the thing in the night that had sent her to Aislin. He never spoke about it again. Bad Tan-Tan knew that he'd stopped loving her because she'd gotten pregnant. Good Tan-Tan got increasingly jumpy with fright that the thing in the night would start again. Neither of them slept well, ever.

Never mind. Tomorrow she would be old enough to set out on her own. She was going to live in Sweet Pone Town, her and Melonhead. No hanging tree there, no tin box. Sweet Pone had running water. And no sullen, skulking Antonio. Melonhead could have left two years before, but they were friends. He had waited for her. The two of them had been pestering the douens, pumping them for news from Sweet Pone and for advice on how to get there.

Old Pappy was coming back from the riverside with his three goats-them. "Evening, Pappy. Walk good."

"Seen, sweetheart. Getting so pretty! You almost old enough to give this old man a kiss now, ain't?" He cackled and reached out to tap her under her chin.

Tan-Tan scowled and stepped back from his long, bony fingers. "Old enough to push you my own self through the door of the box," she threatened. Pappy glared at her. He spat to one side. The spittle landed in the mane of one of his goats. The animal shook its rank, smelly head. Pappy took his stick to them angrily, walked on without saying a word more to Tan-Tan.

Is messing with young girls why Pappy had climbed the half-way tree in the first place. Aislin had long ago warned Tan-Tan and Quamina to stay away from Pappy's wandering hands. Pappy had nearly died the time that One-Eye put him in the box for sticking his hand up Quamina's skirt. Three hours of that heat and they'd had to pump his chest to get his heart started again.

Round the corner, Tan-Tan bucked up Rick doing his

deputy rounds. His eyes slid slowly over her body, down to her crotch, back up to her chest. "Evening, Tan-Tan."

Tan-Tan smiled slyly at him and walked away, twitching her hips. She could almost feel his eyes on her retreating behind. Rick, Pappy, Antonio; you could rule man easy, with just one thing. Sometimes she wished for something more, wished that they wouldn't make it so easy. She'd get vex at all the stupidee men in stupidee Junjuh. Then she'd go and talk to Melonhead whose eyes met hers and who talked to her face, not her bubbies.

She took the riverside path to Gladys and Michael's iron shop to avoid passing the hanging tree. The woman's body was beginning to smell in the hot sun. One-Eye would have to cut Patty down soon before the maggots came. He kept bodies up on the hanging tree two-three days so everybody could see and learn. Patty had beaten her baby boy to death after she'd been up three days and nights from his crying. The child had been colicky from birth. One-Eye said he was sorry but in Junjuh, murder must always get repaid with murder. "Them is the rules," he'd said, then brought out his rope.

Tan-Tan had only gone once to see a hanging. She'd vomited out her lunch by the side of the road.

She had a brief vision of Antonio hanging from a rope, his swollen tongue protruding from his mouth.

What would she wear for her fête tomorrow? Oh yes; the new sarong and blouse that Chichibud's wife had sent for her. They were yellow, her favourite colour. Little black figures were woven all along the hem of the skirt. Some were dancing, some were climbing trees. One had a knife in its hand. Chichibud had said that as his wife wove the cloth for the sarong and blouse specially for Tan-Tan, she'd breathed on it and with her breath, Bois Papa had sent her the story she'd woven into it. "Is the story of your life, doux-doux. You go have plenty adventures."

It was loud at the iron shop today. Tan-Tan had always liked the clang of the hammer on the anvil, the red clouds of steam that would billow from the shop when Gladys or Michael quenched the metal. Husband and wife been running the smithy five years now, trading with the other human settlements for scrap iron and melting it down to make new things. They were in fierce competition with the douens, oui; many of the things they could make from iron, the douen people made better from wood. Douens were masters at that craft. Plenty prison settlement people preferred to trade with them for bowls and pot spoons and baby bassinets and so, rather than chance human iron, which had a way to rust. The few runner people on New Half-Way Tree were reviving hard labour crafts as fast as they could, but they hadn't yet perfected making steel with the primitive resources on New Half-Way Tree. Too besides, douen work pretty, seen. The douens etched indelible designs on the inside of their bowls: vine patterns; ratbats flying; douens leaping. They made baby bassinets from a lattice-work of smooth peeled twigs that they had trained to grow into a bowl shape. Every one had a different lattice design. The pliant wood that made them grew deep in the bush where only douens could go. On the days that Chichibud appeared in Junjuh Town with his cow-sized packbird Benta, people would mob him to see what douen woodwork he was carrying. When Tan-Tan was little Chichibud had told her that tallpeople couldn't help but like douen makings; it was because the douens had worked obeah magic upon the wood.

"Douen man grow them, douen woman paint them," he would say with pride. "The woman-them does work obeah into them as they painting them. Is for so the patterns come in like they alive. You don't think so?" He would hold up a beautiful bowl for her to admire, perhaps one that had a favourite douen symbol on its inside, a spreading banyan tree design.

"Men make things and women magic them. Is so the world does go, ain't, doux-doux?" Then he'd laugh *shu-shu*.

Old trickster! For years, Tan-Tan had believed him about douen magic, but now she knew he'd only been making mako 'pon her. It wasn't magic, it was craft and cunning. And it was vexing Gladys too bad. When she and Michael had come to New Half-Way Tree, the douens-them were still using bone-chip knives. Now every douen had at least one iron blade to call his own. There was good trade with the douens for sculpting tools; the tools the douens used to compete with Gladys and Michael. Gladys was always complaining about how ungrateful douens were. Chichibud laughed in private with Tan-Tan about it. "Yes, oonuh tallpeople show we plenty of new ways, and we does learn fast. Why you think we always right there to meet new exiles when them climb the half-way tree?"

Wouldn't have been Tan-Tan crossing Gladys. Gladys was big and beefy. Her tree-branch thick arms came from slamming that hammer down onto the anvil plenty times each day. Her temper was sour and too besides she ain't too like Tan-Tan already.

The tall, thick metal door to the iron shop was closed. Strange. It got too hot in there to do that. Tan-Tan turned the handle and pulled. It was bolted from the inside. Gladys and Michael must be burning up with heat. Were they all right in there? She leaned closer to the door. She could hear the roar of the flames, the ringing of metal on metal, then a mechanical noise, a kind of cough: "Kuh-hunh! Kuh-hunh!" Is what that? The sound reminded Tan-Tan of something, something from long time ago, back on Toussaint . . .

No matter. She slapped the door with the flat of her hand and shouted, "Inside! Allyou in there? Gladys? Michael?"

The coughing noise stopped one time. After a few seconds, the handle of the door turned in Tan-Tan's hands. Michael opened the door one little crack to peer out at her. A cloud of black, greasy smoke with the stench of burning oil floated out the iron shop and escaped on the breeze. Tan-Tan coughed and waved her hands to dispel the smoke, but she had to smile at the sight of Michael's soot-covered face, his reddened eyes glistening like guinèpe fruit. "Mister Michael," she said teasingly, "like one of your creations blow up in your face, or what?"

Michael tried to wipe away some of the soot, but all like how his hands were black with it too, he only smeared his face worse. "What you want, Tan-Tan? We busy."

Tan-Tan frowned at his tone. "Ain't you remember, Michael? You tell me was to come and get my birthday present today," she said in her sweetest voice. "It not ready yet?" She gave him a disappointed look, biting her bottom lip to make it fuller and riper. What were they doing in there that they wouldn't make her see?

"Nah, nah, is all right, Tan-Tan, I have your present right here."

Tan-Tan smiled and stepped forward, thinking Michael would open the door for her; instead he said, "Soon come," and shut it in her face. She heard the bolts slide over. What the rass . . . ?! Tan-Tan kissed her teeth. Nothing she could do about it, she just had to stand there and wait for Michael to come back out. She put her ear to the door. She thought she could hear Gladys's voice, then Michael's, but she couldn't make out the words. It fell quiet inside the iron shop.

In a little minute a clean-face Michael cracked the door again. He stepped outside fast-fast and shut it behind him. A quick blast of heat had followed him out. It dissipated on the breeze. Tan-Tan had only managed a glimpse inside before the bolts locked. There was something big like a donkey cart in there, covered right down to the ground in an oilcloth that had mako rockstones weighting it down. Tan-Tan was mad for curious. "Is a big something that," she said enquiringly.

Michael only smiled, caramel skin crinkling to cocoa along

his forge-weathered face. "Craven puppy does choke, Tan-Tan. When time come for you to know, you will know."

Oh, yes? She knew how to get what she wanted from him. She grimaced a little, made a small noise of pain, lifted one foot delicately off the ground and perched it on top of the other.

"What happen to you?" he asked.

"Is a long walk over here, you know. I think I must be blister my foot." She bent over, slowly slipped her alpagat sandal off her slim, brown foot. She spread her toes and inspected them. Michael gave a small intake of breath. She had him now. "You see any blister there, Michael? Between the big toe and the long toe? It paining me right there so."

Michael pursed his lips. He looked almost frightened. He wiped his hand on the leather apron tied round his waist. His smith's biceps jumped with the movement. He came closer and bent to look at her foot. The tips of his ears went ruddy with embarrassment. "You don't think maybe I should go inside and sit down?" Tan-Tan asked him. She nearly felt wicked, teasing him like this. For a big, hard-back man, Michael was shy and gentle so till he wouldn't even mash ants beneath his foot. For all her mischievousness, Tan-Tan liked him. He was a man who saved his strength for his work, not for brutalising people who didn't do as he wanted.

"I ain't see no cut," he said softly.

Enough. She wasn't going to torment the poor man any more. "Well, maybe is just a little soreness. You bring the knife?" She slipped her alpagats back on.

He straightened up, held his apron away from his thighs, kept wiping his hands in it as though they were wet. He took a long, chamois-wrapped package out of his apron pocket and held it towards her.

It had been Janisette's idea; a cooking knife.

"The way people always sweet after you," she'd told Tan-Tan, "you go have your own partner soon, and you go have to

do your share of the cooking. A good cook need a sharp knife."
She'd sent Tan-Tan to the iron shop to order it, so Gladys could
measure her grip. But as Tan-Tan had opened up her mouth to
tell Gladys to make a cooking knife, the image of the Robber
Queen dolly had popped into her head, and for some reason
she'd said "hunting knife" instead. She hadn't made Janisette
know. Too besides, it was time she owned her own hunting
knife. She and Melonhead were going to have to go through
bush to get to Sweet Pone.

Tan-Tan unwrapped the chamois. An oiled leather sheath
lay inside it. A shaped wooden handle protruded from it, rivets
still new and shiny. Tan-Tan slid the knife out of its sheath.
Light winked along the blade edge.

"When you not using it," Michael said, "you must clean it
with the chamois then oil it. And you must always store it in the
sheath, you understand me?"

Tan-Tan just watched at the knife. It was gun-metal grey. A
dark blue sheen chased itself round the blade. The tip of the
blade came to a sharp point. She touched her finger to it, hissed
as the point entered her skin.

"Careful!" Michael took the knife from her. "The point is
so you could use it for throwing. Gladys make the handle from
some Jamaica mahogany Chichibud bring we from Sweet
Pone."

The hardest wood, the most precious. It only had a few Jamaica mahogany trees growing on New Half-Way Tree, from a
cutting an exile had brought years back. The way the handle of
the knife curved, the way it was just the length of her palm and
looked smooth like a baby's cheek, Tan-Tan's hand was itching
to hold it again. She reached to take it from Michael.

"Mind now, girl. You must treat a knife with respect. You
is left handed, yes? Here. Take it."

The knife fit her hand like she'd been born carrying it. She
laughed and swung it through the air. It sang.

"Wait, wait! Not like that. You go hurt somebody, or drop it and cut off your own pretty foot. Let me show you how."

Michael stood behind her and reached over her shoulder to take her hand. He formed her fingers around the hilt of the knife. Shyly he said, "Like so. Feel the indentations for your fingers, and the one on top for your thumb? When your thumb slide into that space, you know you have the right angle for throwing."

Tan-Tan turned and made to throw the knife at the trunk of the big halwa tree in the yard.

"No, not like that! You have to cock your arm back like this." He bent her arm into the right position.

"Thanks, Michael." She gave him a seductive smile. He looked down at the ground. What a way this man was sweet! Tan-Tan too liked gentle Michael. He was no true exile, had followed Gladys for love. People like him and Melonhead would never try to catch her in a quiet corner and feel her up. Not like . . .

Suddenly angry, she grunted and threw the knife. It went wide of its mark and sliced through a branchlet of the tree before it tumbled to the ground.

Michael laughed. "You get power in that throwing arm, Tan-Tan!" He retrieved the knife and gave it back to her. "The way you stand is the most important thing. You must plant your right foot in front." He pointed at her foot, looked quickly away.

"Like you giving the girl-pickney a lesson, Michael?"

Michael started at the sound of Gladys's voice. He took a step away from Tan-Tan.

"Ah-hah. Showing she how to use she new present."

Gladys was leaning up against the front entrance, toffee-brown face flushed maroon from the heat and the exertion of forging iron.

Tan-Tan had always wondered what Michael saw in

Gladys's fat, round body, sturdy as a mother hen. How did Gladys even see over her own chest and belly to work on the anvil?

Gladys pulled off the scarf from her hair and used it to wipe her face. "I sure plenty of man already been teaching she how knife could jook." She smirked at Tan-Tan. "How do, sweetheart?"

Bad Tan-Tan was snarling silently. None of Gladys's blasted business. Tan-Tan skinned her teeth in a fine-fine smile. "Doing good, thank you, Gladys."

"And your father? How things with the ex-mayor?" Gladys was from Cockpit County. She had been right there in the fight yard when Antonio had poisoned Quashee. She never had a good word for Antonio. Is jealousy fuelled by hard liquor that had brought Gladys to New Half-Way Tree. She'd broken a next woman's back in a fight over Michael. She and Antonio were alike in that, oui. Maybe that's why she hated him so. Gladys still had a taste for the bottle. Sometimes when she went on a drunk, Michael had to lock her in the shed and make her sleep off her rage.

"Daddy all right. Arthritis bothering he a little."

"Too bad," Gladys replied, looking as regretful as the mongoose that eat the last guinea fowl in the pen. "Anyhow, don't make we keep you, Tan-Tan. I sure you have plenty to do to get ready for your birthday. Michael, time for we to take a break. My foot-them dusty. I want you to wash them for me. You know only you could do it nice the way I does like it." She turned and walked into the bungalow that she and Michael had beside the iron shop.

"Yes, doux-doux." Quick like fowl when it see corn a-throw, Michael followed Gladys into the house. As the door closed behind them, Tan-Tan heard Gladys's rich, throaty laugh, heavy with hard living and hard loving. Tan-Tan cut her eyes at the closed door. Then she crept to the door of the iron shop and quietly tried it. Still locked.

The sheath could be tied round her waist. She knotted it securely, tucked the chamois into her bodice and headed for home. At the turnoff that led to their house she spied their neighbour Cudjoe, the bad carpenter, hoeing up dasheen in his front yard. He was clumsy with the hoe, still accustoming his body to the linear tasks that ate up every waking hour on New Half-Way Tree. He was cursing and working with equal determination. He'd taken off his shirt, leaving only a pair of work pants covering him. Sweat had put a sheen on his black skin. Muscles in his back flexed with each turn of the hoe. *Like even bad carpenter can get good body, oui?*

Cudjoe saw her. He waved. Tan-Tan waved back; looked down at her feet as though from shyness; looked back at him again, smiling sweetly. Worked smooth like cool breeze. Cudjoe let the hoe fall and came over. He'd failed the first test.

Tan-Tan made shift to toy with a curl of her hair. She was proud of her waist-long plaits. Every morning she undid them and washed her hair good with a soapy piece of cactus plant. Then she oiled it with some shine oil from Chichibud's cart and plaited it up again.

"Good afternoon, Cudjoe. Like you working hard?"

"Yes, Tan-Tan, but then I see your beautiful self out catching the sun, and I come was to tell you that when I could see such a sight, all hard work get easy."

An edgy excitement warmed her, shot through with pique. Easy fish. Rise to the hook. "Not all hard work, I hope, Cudjoe."

Cudjoe quirked his lips into a small smile, stared provocatively into her eyes. "So," he said, "I hear allyou having big fête and thing tomorrow."

"Yes, my sixteenth birthday party. You coming?"

"I bet your boyfriend go bring you something real pretty."

Tan-Tan giggled and gave Cudjoe a delicate tap on his shoulder; a slap light like a kiss. "Get away! You too fast! Where you hear I have any boyfriend?"

"What, nobody to dance with you on your sixteenth birthday? Now, that is a crying shame."

He kept looking deep into her eyes. She met his glance full on and said, "You go come and dance with me then, Cudjoe?"

"What you going give me for a dance?" he asked playfully.

"Let we go for a short walk round the back and I give you little taste." She took his hand, led him to the back of his hut where passers-by couldn't see them. He hesitated, waiting to see what she would do. She put the front of her body up against his, put an arm round his waist. She could smell the man-sweat off him, the complicated scent that she loved and hated at the same time. "Kiss me then, nuh?" He put his mouth to hers. She sucked on his tongue. The silent, wicked Tan-Tan urged her on.

She heard Janisette shouting before she even self reached the house.

"You blasted motherass piece of shit! Get out here right now and face me, Antonio! Is where the dry fruits I been soaking in liquor for Tan-Tan cake? Eh? You mookoomslav! Don't tell me booze have you so bassourdie, you drink it out from the soaking fruits and all? Get out here, I say!"

Antonio raged back, "Woman, don't bother my ass with your stupidness. I been here sick in my bed all day. I ain't see no fruits in liquor."

"You liard son of a bitch!"

Tan-Tan ran inside the house, slamming the door as she entered. Sometimes if she did that, Janisette and Antonio would stop fighting and yell at her instead. It didn't work this time, though. Tan-Tan heard the sharp *wap!* of a wooden pot spoon connecting with somebody's flesh. She knew that sound too well. Is who throw the first blow this time? She flew inside the kitchen and grabbed the pot spoon out of Janisette's hand, just as her stepmother was about to slap it against Antonio's shoulder again.

"Janisette, stop! Daddy say he sick!"

Janisette turned and shoved Tan-Tan in her chest. Tan-Tan stumbled back against the kitchen wall. "Is only alcohol sick he! Why the rass you fasting yourself in my business? Is *your* birthday cake I trying to make, you know!"

Antonio flew at Janisette and threw his open hand across her face, *crack!*

"What you think this is, Janisette, laying a hand on my daughter? Eh?" He cuffed her in the belly. Janisette dropped to the ground, retching. Then she leapt to her feet again and flew at Antonio, screaming and kicking. He tried to trap her hands in his fists, shouted bitch and leggobeast at her.

"Daddy! Janisette!" They ignored her. "Oonuh have to stop, or somebody go send for the sheriff!"

Now Antonio had Janisette's hair. Her head was twisted at an uncomfortable angle. She was clawing at his crotch. Tan-Tan forced herself in between them. She could smell the heavy sweet staleness on Antonio's breath. "The sheriff coming!" she hissed desperately.

Antonio let Janisette go and stumbled back towards the bedroom. Janisette crumpled to the ground and lay there, gasping and holding her belly. Tan-Tan crouched down beside her.

"You all right, Janisette?"

She never saw the lash that creased her face.

"Facety girl-child!" Janisette hissed. "How you mean, 'You all right?'" After you just done take your daddy side against me, like always? You two-face, force-ripe bitch, you no better than he, with your sluttish self! I bet you if I make One-Eye know how you does carry on with half the men in Junjuh, him would have plenty to say about that!"

Tan-Tan's cheeks burned, from the slap, from shame. *You no better than your daddy.* She stood and looked down at Janisette. She fingered her mother's wedding ring hanging from the chain round her neck, the one Antonio had given her for her ninth birthday. She had earned that ring. The words burned her lips. She spat them at her stepmother: "Talk all you like, Janisette. Both of we know is which one Antonio really love."

Janisette's face crumpled into tears. Tan-Tan stalked out to the verandah, went round to the back verandah. Power thrummed through her so strong she could scarcely breathe. She had never stood up to Janisette like that before! Is the last time she would let Janisette shame her like that. *Oh yes*, Tan-Tan thought. *I big woman now, sixteen tomorrow. She go have to leave me alone.*

She heard the front door slam, and the tinkle of Janisette's gold ankle bracelets going away up the walk. *She must be going to weep on Glorianna neck. Good for she.*

She sat there on the back porch, legs swinging through the railings, taking in the afternoon sun and thinking about how she go talk plain around Janisette from now on. *Pride? I have every right to be proud. I speak my mind.*

Shame? You have every right to be shame. No better than your mother.

She ignored the silent voice.

Someone was coming round to the back house, whistling. It was Melonhead's favourite tune. Tan-Tan smiled, craned her neck. There he was, wearing as ever a much-mended pair of khaki shorts and a holey singlet. Dust powdered his bare feet to the ankle.

"Girl, is what you do Janisette, eh? I just pass she fleeing up the walk sobbing with she whole head bury in a kerchief." The dreads on his big round melon head bobbed with his stride. Tendons flexed in his bandy thighs as he walked. His broad smile was full of fun.

Tan-Tan chuckled. "But eh-eh. Ain't she is big woman and me only pickney? What I could do she?"

He leaned against the banister beside her, picked a wind-blown leaf out of her hair. "Not no pickney no more. Full adult come tomorrow. You bags pack?"

Tan-Tan got serious. "No. Later."

Melonhead frowned. "You tell them yet that you leaving?"

"No. Don't talk so loud, Daddy somewhere round the place." Tan-Tan rubbed her arms. Sun had gone behind a cloud. "I done tell you already, I just want to leave quiet-quiet tomorrow night. Daddy and Janisette go be bassourdie with liquor and the two of them going to be asleep. Let them wake up next morning and find we gone, nuh?"

Melonhead sighed, cocked a foot up onto the verandah floor. His legs were really too short to do that gracefully. Tan-Tan absent-mindedly brushed some dust off the knobby knee he presented. Melonhead said, "Girl, talk sense. How we going leave at night, eh? Is bush we go be walking through. You want ground puppy chew up we tail? You want grit fly to suck we eyeball-them dry?"

"It have trails to Sweet Pone."

"And bush all round. You have a water jug to carry?"

"I can't share yours?"

"What food you taking? You have dry bouilli beef and buju and congo peas and thing?"

"Some," she said quietly. "I thief little piece from Janisette."

"You have pot to cook in, and firestick?"

"I have a knife," she said, indicating the sheath at her waist.

"And what? You going to catch wild boar with that and

your bare hand? How you going eat? How you going sleep? Come to that, you have tent and bedroll?"

"I thought I could share your—"

"Nanny give me strength! Tan-Tan, you is big woman or you is pickney still? These is the same questions I been asking you for two months now, and still you ain't prepare. Like you ain't really want to go, or what?"

"Sshh!" Tan-Tan hissed. "Daddy go hear you!" Melonhead scowled at her, ran a hand through his hair. He always did that when he was upset. She tried to explain: "I just want to do this quiet, get away quick before they know."

"When you going to stop hiding from them?" he asked. Hesitated. Then softly: "I know them does beat you."

The flurry-fear of panic rose in her throat like wings beating. Hush it, mock it, make it small. She cackled, "Melonhead, is what that big head of yours working overtime on in truth? I get two-three little slap when I was pickney, same like you. Not for years now, man." She made a dismissive gesture with her hand, looked away from the hurt in Melonhead's eyes.

"Tan-Tan, don't make mako 'pon me, I not going let it confuse me. You frighten of Antonio and Janisette and you frighten to leave. I could see it, I know you too good."

Tan-Tan could only stare at him.

"You want me to tell them for you?"

"No! Don't say nothing!"

"I serious, girl. Then me and Daddy could help you get ready, if your family not going to do it." His look softened in a way she'd never seen before on Melonhead's jovial, easy-going face. He said awkwardly, "I, ahm . . . Nanny hear me, Tan-Tan; I would do anything for you."

"What?" The first "huh" of a laugh fell from her lips. Then she looked into his eyes, felt wonder rearrange her features. "What?" she breathed, scared to death of the answer.

He looked embarrassed, backed away a little. "Look, never

mind. I go come back later, all right?" With hurried, awkward steps he started away.

"Stay, Melonhead." He stopped, kept his back to her, looked down at the ground.

"Is what you saying?" Tan-Tan asked.

He returned slowly, still not looking at her. "You go laugh."

"I ever laugh after you yet? Tell me."

"I . . . so long I want to tell you, to ask you . . ." He took her hand, Melonhead took her *hand,* played nervously with one of the beads of her bracelet. He wouldn't meet her eyes. "You think you might ever want to partner with me?"

"Me?" The sound could have been a sob. She pulled her hand away from him. "Why you want me?"

"You and me does walk good together, talk good together. Me nah want that for stop, ever. You don't like me, Tan-Tan?"

This was not her friend Melonhead, this was a new creature standing in front of her. "I never think—"

He rushed to cut her words off: "I know we never talk about it before, I know you got plenty next boyfriend, I know my face favour jackass a-peep through tear knickers . . ."

A giggle bubbled to Tan-Tan's lips. "Don't say so! You not ugly!"

Melonhead's eyes searched her face. He smiled uncertainly. And waited. He always knew when to wait, just let her talk, or think. This wasn't a new Melonhead, she was just seeing him differently. He had always looked out for her. He cared for her. *Who could care for mud in the street,* whispered bad silent Tan-Tan, but for the first time in years the voice didn't wound, didn't matter. "When we would do it?" she dared to ask quietly.

Hope made Melonhead incandescent. "The ritual? Before we leave, so everybody could come."

"No. Not here. In a new place, with new people. Please, Melonhead, not here. When we settle in Sweet Pone we could send for your father to come and have it with him there. In we own house." *We own house;* was it her saying those words?

He smiled. "All right, if is so you want it."

"And what about . . ."

He was suddenly cheerful. "All the thousand and one boyfriend-them, you mean? We could be freehand partners, sweetness." He looked away shyly, her too, startled by the endearment.

Such a simple solution. He didn't scorn her, didn't call her names, wouldn't punish her. Bad silent Tan-Tan made unhappy sounds. She would consider that later. Gravely she said to Melonhead, "Let we do it." She could scarcely breathe for joy. Melonhead stepped closer to her, his hands warm on her knees. His breath smelled of cloves and sweetleaf. She leaned forward to touch her lips to his.

Crash! Shards of glass showered down over her and Melonhead. Jumping up, she saw Antonio holding a broken-off rum bottle neck in his hand. Antonio jabbed at Melonhead who leapt back.

"Mothercunt thiefing son of a bitch!" Antonio bellowed. "What you chatting she up for? Eh?" He staggered forward, tried to leap the banister. He slipped and caught himself, his bare feet sliding in the broken glass. So drunk he didn't even self notice his sliced, bleeding feet. "You want I tear up that pretty face for you? You ain't business with my daughter!"

Melonhead pulled himself up tall, his face cold. "Your daughter old enough to do what she please, man."

Antonio's face clotted with fury. "You facety . . . !" Antonio made to rush down the porch stairs.

"No, Daddy!" Tan-Tan put her hands out to stop him. He clouted her over her ear, the one where her implant had been. Pain exploded behind her eyes, but she managed to stay upright. She held on to her father's waist, kept him on the stairs from sheer force of desperation. "Melonhead! Go home!"

"I not leaving you!"

"She not going anywhere with you, you pissant wretch!"

"Go, Melonhead, or it just go be worse!"

"You sure?"

"Yes! I go come talk to you later."

Melonhead took an unsure step away, waiting to see what would happen. Antonio quieted, stood weaving on the stairs and mumbling incoherent curses at Melonhead.

"Tan-Tan," Melonhead called, "I go give it a hour for you and he to talk. Then I coming back with Daddy and the sheriff and we taking you from here."

Oh, please Nanny, yes. "Go, I say!"

He walked away backwards, slowly, keeping a stern eye on Antonio. Antonio found some energy and threw the bottle top at him. Melonhead ducked clear, turned and jogged down the lane.

"Come Daddy, make I clean up your feet."

Antonio grabbed her arm, so tight she felt the skin bruise same time. "Rutting whore!" He backhanded her across the face. She felt her teeth meet in her tongue.

"No, Daddy!"

"Every time I turn my back, you making time with some man! Like you turn big woman now? Eh? You smelling yourself?"

"No, Daddy! Please, Daddy! It ain't go happen again!"

But Antonio dragged her into the living room. All Tan-Tan pulled she couldn't break his grip.

"Blasted slut with a slut for a mother. You ain't too big for me to tan your behind for you!" With one hand, Antonio unbuckled his heavy leather belt and pulled it out from his pants. He doubled it up in his hand and cracked it against her shins. The pain was like a knife cut.

"Daddy!" she shrieked.

He beat her across her calves, her thighs. She could feel the welts rising. She screamed, but Melonhead was too far away to hear.

As he whipped her Antonio was dragging her by the arm through the house, into her bedroom. He threw her on the bed.

"Is man you want? Is man? I go show you what man could do for you!"

No. No. She couldn't face this again, after years free from it. He kicked her legs apart, yanked up her skirt, tore her underwear off. He pushed into her. She bawled out for the tearing pain between her legs. He grunted, "I is man too, you know! Is this you want! Is this?"

Something was scraping at her waist. Her hand found it. The scabbard. With the knife inside. A roaring started up in her ears. It couldn't have been she. It must have been the Robber Queen who pulled out the knife. Antonio raised up to shove into the person on the bed again. It must have been the Robber Queen, the outlaw woman, who quick like a snake got the knife braced at her breastbone just as Antonio slammed his heavy body right onto the blade.

"Uhh!" Antonio jerked like a fish on a hook. He collapsed onto her. His weight drove the knife handle backwards against her breastbone, gouging upwards until it was under her chin. Antonio's head fell on Tan-Tan's own. She screamed. His body convulsed, then relaxed. Thick blood gushed out of his mouth. She heard his bowels loose in death. Then she smelt it.

Her body went cold. She started to tremble uncontrollably. She lay there so under Antonio's corpse, waiting for Melonhead to come and end the nightmare.

And is there so Chichibud found her. He sniffed the air before he entered the room. "Dead," he said.

Tan-Tan felt the hysteria bubbling up. "Off me. Get. He. Off. Me."

Chichibud hopped up onto the bed and dragged Antonio's body to one side. Tan-Tan couldn't stop trembling. She couldn't even self manage to pull her skirt back down over her legs. Is Chichibud who did it for her. A low moaning was coming from her mouth. "Sh, sh, doux-doux. I could read the signs for myself. I know he attack you."

She found the words. "He did beating me." She swallowed. Her chest burned where the knife handle had gouged a track, pushed by Daddy's body. "Beating me bad, with he leather belt. Then he . . . I never mean to use the knife, Chichibud. I did only want he to stop hurting me. Oh God, Daddy dead?"

"Dead, yes. We have to leave, fast."

"No, Melonhead coming back with One-Eye."

"Then we must move now. One-Eye rules don't have no mercy. Murder will swing you from the hanging tree."

"Me?" She couldn't believe it.

"You, yes. Pack." He sent her over to her dresser drawers while he wrapped up Antonio's body in the bedclothes. She did nothing, couldn't seem to think, just watched him. He wiped her new hunting knife clean against the bedsheets and handed it back to her.

"No, no, Chichibud! Don't make me touch it! Throw it away!"

"Don't fret, Tan-Tan, don't fret." He sheathed the knife at his own waist.

He tore off a strip of the bedsheet, wiped the blood off Tan-Tan's face. He indicated the gouge in her breastbone from the knife handle. "I go bandage it later." He opened her dresser drawers himself, yanked clothes out of them at random.

She had killed Daddy.

Somehow she struggled into the clean blouse that Chichibud gave her. Her hands were shaking so badly she could only do up three of the buttons. Chichibud held out another garment. Her new skirt, the birthday skirt that Chichibud's wife had made for her. She pulled it on under the skirt she'd been wearing, tore the top skirt off her body and let it fall. Her eyes kept straying back to the bloodstained lump on the bed, wrapped in her sheet. The smell of death was thick in the air. She just kill she own daddy.

Chichibud bundled her out of the house, talking soothingly to her the whole time. "Nothing wrong, is just you and me, going for a walk like we always do. Good thing Benta come with me today. We could ride she." They went out front to the guava tree. Benta, his big, stout packbird, was crouching on the ground, large as a cow and as solid, but with green and brown feathers. She was plucking leaves off the water vine that was entwined around the wormy guava tree and sucking them down. She had a leather panier strapped to her back between her stubby wings-them and her neck, and a high leather seat buckled round her body.

When Benta spied Chichibud she got to her feet, bating her useless wings and cawing.

"Hush up, the child in trouble! Can't make everybody know we business."

"Wroow," Benta said. She butted her head gently against Tan-Tan's shoulder in her customary greeting. She nuzzled against Tan-Tan's neck and combed the girl's untidy plaits through her beak. On another day it would have made Tan-Tan smile; Benta bird was forever trying to groom her hair. Today she stood beside Benta and shook. Daddy dead. Somebody kill he. Somebody bad.

"Down, Benta girl," said Chichibud. The bird crouched low. "Tan-Tan, get in the panier."

She could do that. She could follow an order. Benta bent her neck and Tan-Tan climbed into the panier, knees pulled up in front of her nose. Her body hurt. She waited for whatever it would please Chichibud to do next. He climbed into the seat behind her. He threaded a leather strap between one handle of the panier and the other, tied it. "Hold on to this when the ride get rough," he told her. "And keep your head low."

It smelt clean inside the panier, like wood shavings. She heard Chichibud buckling his own seat straps.

"Hold on, pickney. Go, Benta. Straight to the bush." The bird stood up, shook her wings into place, and took off at a run. She pelted round the back of the house, using her wings for balance whenever she swerved. Tan-Tan closed her eyes. The bumpy, jolting ride in the confined dark...a memory nearly a decade old rose in Tan-Tan's mind, of crashing round in the trunk of the sheriffs' car while it drove her and Daddy to exile. Daddy...

Soon the sound of Benta's feet hitting the ground changed from a thud to the crackle-bounce of corn trash. Tan-Tan opened her eyes. They were in the fields around Junjuh, fleeing fast in the dusk towards the bush.

They broke into the bush proper, to the cover of the trees. When the first young branch scored the side of her face, Tan-Tan crouched down inside the panier. More withies slapped whup-whup against the panier. Tan-Tan didn't know how Chichibud was protecting himself from them. But Benta slowed only slightly, trampling what she could and avoiding what she couldn't. The roaring in Tan-Tan's head hadn't stopped since she'd impaled Antonio on her knife. Bad Tan-Tan was screaming silently: *Antonio dead, he dead. Antonio dead. You kill he.*

After some time, Chichibud called for Benta to stop. Tan-Tan heard him sniffing the air.

"Them coming for we, Tan-Tan. Bringing the dogs."

The dogs! The dogs that had made it to Toussaint had all interbred into one tough, bad-tempered mongrel strain. They would track a scent till Kingdom Come. Tan-Tan had seen animals that the Junjuh pack had torn apart. It was too much to deal with. Dumbly, she twisted back to look at Chichibud.

He said, "Benta, is up to you. The dogs must lose we scent. Tan-Tan, you strap in good? Hold on tight."

"Wroow," Benta cooed. She hopped over to the nearest big

tree and dug one set of powerful claws into its trunk. Even in
the reddish dusk Tan-Tan could see the tips of Benta's claws
sinking into the wood. The bird reached up and dug her beak
into the trunk a little higher. And to Tan-Tan's amazement,
Benta started to climb. She sidled up foot by foot, using her
beak to pull her up higher into the tree, up into the branches
where the leaves could hide them and the dogs would lose their
scent in the air.

Chichibud laughed a low *shu-shu*. "Oonuh tallpeople
don't really know what packbirds could do, oui?"

Tan-Tan held on to the sides of the panier till her fingers
cramped around it. "You should leave me, make them find
me."

"For that mad sheriff to hang? You was only trying to defend yourself."

"One-Eye would be right to hang me. I k-kill Daddy."

"Papa Bois see what really happen in that room, Tan-Tan.
He ain't judging you."

Benta had reached a thick limb high up in the tree. Before
Tan-Tan knew what was happening Benta was leaping to a next
tree, flapping her useless wings as she went. Tan-Tan gave a little scream.

"Hush. Don't make the dogs hear we."

Benta landed sure-footed in the next tree and kept climbing. And now Tan-Tan could hear the pack of dogs baying, following their scent and the clear trail Benta's tracks must have
made. The dogs were crashing through the undergrowth, with
the men shouting behind them: "Here! This way!" Lights from
hurricane lamps were dancing through the bush like duppy
lights in the dark.

Benta froze.

Tan-Tan held still like the last breath between life and
death. She didn't even dare look down. The dogs were whining
and running around, looking for the scent they'd lost. One-

Eye's voice said, "Is what the blast wrong with allyou bitch hound? Find them, I say!"

The men laid about the dogs-them with whips. The dogs yelped. But they'd lost the scent and there was no more trail.

"Let we go home," said a voice. It was Melonhead. Tan-Tan managed to stop her cry before it had left her lips. She sat in the dark with Chichibud and Benta, knuckling hot tears and grit flies from her eyes.

The lights and the sound of the hunting party were gone. Chichibud made a chittering noise with his claws. Tan-Tan knew that sound; he was worried. "I think is time," he said to himself. "We know say it would happen." Benta gave a low, grumbly series of warbles that made Tan-Tan think of nannysong. But they were only nonsense phrasings. Benta started climbing again, higher and higher up the tree till the stars were visible through the branches. She kept climbing, testing her weight on smaller and smaller branches. Tan-Tan was queasy from the swaying of the climb. Would the branch hold? She looked out over the bush. She could just make out one-one light twinkling back in Junjuh Town: the hurricane lamps people hung outside their front doors every night. The darkness was a thick blanket round her, like the blanket in the trunk of the autocar when she'd run away with . . . Chichibud's voice was barely a whisper when he said:

"Oonuh tallpeople been coming to we land from since, and we been keeping weselves separate from you. Even though we sharing the same soil, same water, same air. Tonight, that go change, Tan-Tan. I taking you far away, where Junjuh Town people can't find you. For me to do that, you go have to come and live with we douen. You go find out things about we that no other human person know, starting tonight." She twisted round to look at his silhouette, crouched on Benta's back in the clotting dark. "Understand the trust I placing in your care, doux-doux. Understand that I doing it to save your life, but you have to guard ours in return."

"I don't follow you."

"When you take one life, you must give back two. You go keep douen secrets safe? You must swear. I know you ain't feel to talk right now, but you must swear out loud."

Tan-Tan's heart was hammering hard and slow in her chest like drum. *When you take one life, you must give back two.* Tan-Tan bowed her head and accepted the obeah that Chichibud had just put on it. "I swear, Chichibud."

"Remember what you swear, child. Papa Bois listening."

What would he do now? She remembered how she used to think douen people were magic.

"In the daytime," Chichibud told her, "packbird is ground bird. But is nighttime now. No-one to see."

And he raised his voice: "Benta! Now!"

The packbird gave a squawk that sounded like joy. She puffed her chest in and out repeatedly, then started to beat her wings, hard and fast. They were shadows whipping through the dark. And they were growing. The wings that Tan-Tan had always believed were clipped were filling out, getting long and strong.

"Chichibud! What she doing?"

He had to shout to be heard above the beating wings. "The channels in she wings does fill up with air when she need to fly."

Fly? Benta leapt out of the tree and plummeted towards the ground below. Tan-Tan screamed. But one beat of the powerful wings hooked at the air and with the next beat Benta was powering them high above the bush, soaring through the air, high, higher, till Tan-Tan couldn't make out the treetops in the darkness.

Chichibud leaned forward and shouted over the rushing wind, "Since allyou tallpeople start coming to New Half-Way

Tree, packbirds only fly at night, and in places where allyou can't see. I taking you to a place no other tallpeople ever see either."

The wind sang past Tan-Tan's face. The breeze blew away her tears. The cold, crisp air cleared a little of the fog from her brain. Tan-Tan the Midnight Robber was soaring out above her kingdom, free from thought, nothing to fear. *Sweet chariot, time to ride.* She laughed out loud. But the wind blew the laugh from her mouth and carried it away. *Antonio dead,* Bad Tan-Tan hissed at her. *You kill he. When you take one, you must give back two.*

A deep swooping motion drove Tan-Tan from sleep. She grabbed at the panier's restraining strap. It was 'fore-day morning and Benta was beginning her descent. Tan-Tan looked behind her at Chichibud in his saddle. The douen was still sleeping, his long clawlike toes locked on his restraining strap where it curved around Benta's body.

Tan-Tan was cold, despite the blanket that Chichibud had tucked round her. Her knees hurt where her legs had been folded all night into the panier. Her bruises were a thought for later. She rummaged in her pocket, found a last strip of the dried tree frog meat that Chichibud had given her. She set to chewing it, working it about in her mouth to soften it.

The night had been long, oui. It had been too difficult to speak through the rushing wind of their flight, so they'd passed it in silence; Tan-Tan there in the rushing dark with the memory of the weight and smell of Antonio's corpse pinning her to she bed. She'd retreated into sleep a few times, only to be dragged out of it by her painful knees.

The day was brighter now, easier to see about her. Tan-Tan sat up tall in the panier, dashed her hand across her cheeks. Dried tears flaked off at her touch. Benta swooped down. Tan-Tan looked over the side. "Rahtid!" she cursed. They were heading straight for the forest canopy, towards a leafy circle lower than the topmost trees in the bush, but wide; big so like any village.

"Is home that," Chichibud shouted above the rushing wind.

Then they were dropping down through green, plunging past leaves and branches. Tan-Tan closed her eyes, ducked her head below the level of the panier to avoid the whipping foliage.

Benta screeched, backwinged, landed with a jolt. Somewhere in the foliage Tan-Tan heard a next packbird scream.

"Woi, Taya!" Chichibud shouted in response. "Benta sister," he told Tan-Tan. Benta bird screeched her own greeting—the nonsense nannysong again—bobbing her head and cooing back like any pigeon. She shook her wings. They shrunk down small once more. She began to preen and tuck them in.

At first Tan-Tan couldn't really take in what it was she was seeing any at all. It so big, she could only understand a piece at a time. First the half-light and the damp, heavy heat. And the sound of leaves rustling in the breeze. Shiny burgundy leaves all around them, some of them the length of her body. Then it came to her that the thing they had landed on that curved away on either side was a branch, not ground. One big mako branch, wide as a two-lane autoroute. Big branches everywhere, so big they disappeared into the shadows like trails. Smaller ones coming off them, like paths and so. This place was a massive tree, so big she couldn't see all of it.

Another screech! A multitudinous chirping, warbling, calling out of Chichibud's and Benta's names. Douens were bubbling out of the foliage, shinnying down branches, swinging in on lianas, flying in a-packbird back. Comess, Granny! Up in the air, animals like ratbats flitting from limb to limb and calling out to each other. They started to land *praps! praps! praps!* all around. Actually they were gliders, not flyers so much. They would land on a branch, push off, shoot to a next one. They chattering to each other like pickney. Mama Nanny, what a way they were ugly! Tan-Tan would have run screaming if she'd been by herself, but Chichibud was only grinning and Benta cooing a welcome.

The first of the douen men reached to them. They stared at Tan-Tan, babbled away at Chichibud. He chirped back as fast as he could. Benta screeched and flapped her wings-them, and the whole was a cacophony. How could anybody make any sense heard through that racket?

There were two kinds of ratbat things, Tan-Tan could see now. One kind had limbs like Chichibud's, with the two hind legs turn backwards. Some were covered in long hairs, some that looked older had lost the hair. Most of them had flaps of skin stretching between arms and body. Douen pickney could fly! The other kind of ratbat must have been packbird young. Their feathers were disorderly, rampfled up like slept-on hair. But is what kind of packbirds they, with beaks that were half snout and full of teeth? Some of them were walking stooped, like they'd started out being upright. They hopped like douens instead of walking or running like Benta. For the first time, Tan-Tan noticed how packbird feet and douen feet looked almost the same.

Chichibud hopped out of his saddle down to the tree branch, said to Tan-Tan, "You in a Papa Bois, the daddy tree that does feed we and give we shelter. Every douen nation have it own daddy tree. Come in peace to my home, Tan-Tan. And when you go, go in friendship."

Friendship? the bad Tan-Tan voice howled at her, louder here in douen land. *You could be friend to anybody? You was friend to we daddy?* Chichibud reached to help Tan-Tan down. She flinched her nasty self away.

"I go do it myself." She climbed off Benta's back.

Two pickney landed right by her, a douen and a packbird. Benta chirped a welcome. "Zake," said Chichibud. "Abitefa." Was the douen child his? It reminded her of Old Masque bat costumes, leathery and plain. Ugly lizard pickney. She took a step back. The pickney back-backed in the opposite direction; the packbird pickney too.

They were surrounded by the inhabitants of the tree: douen men and pickney; packbirds. Where were the mysterious douen women? The men were talking fast-fast-fast to Chichibud in their language. He screeched at them. Most of them fell silent. The pickney-them squeezed to the front and stood staring at Tan-Tan, making the nervous click with their tiny claws and pressing their little bodies against the adults as if for comfort. Chichibud called out to Zake again, and finally the pickney Zake came shuffling out of the circle, watching Tan-Tan the whole time from the corners of its eyes. Its young packbird pet followed it, walking awkwardly in its old-people gait. Benta nuzzled pickney, bird and all.

Chichibud uncinched Benta's saddle, slung it over his shoulder. One of the douen men stood in front of him, his throat frill bulging with angry air. He expelled the air with a high whistle and began the argument again, jerking his muzzle over towards Tan-Tan. Chichibud answered back softly. A few douens in the crowd said the same words, seemed to be agreeing. But the angry one looked Tan-Tan straight in her eyes, reached inside his genital flap and let go a hot, green stream of piss right there on the branch in front of her feet. Tan-Tan danced out of the way. A thin layer of the living wood curdled where the urine had hit. Chichibud hopped between her and the angry one, his throat frill blown up full. The two of them stomped from foot to foot and screeched at each other. The stranger reached for his knife belt, lunged at Tan-Tan. Next thing, something knocked Tan-Tan down. Something big and warm covered her, gently. Benta had shoved Tan-Tan down and was shielding her beneath her huge, warm body. For all her massive size, Benta's body was light. Tan-Tan could hear Benta's wings beating, the bird screaming: "Krret! Tzitzippud!"

That last sound—it had almost sounded like Chichibud's name. Tan-Tan peeked out from underneath Benta's smooth breast feathers. The douen stranger had crouched low in front of Benta. His knife was back in its sheath. His hands were empty, held out in open view, his throat frill deflated. Chichibud approached Benta slowly, murmured at her softly in the douen tongue. The packbird raised her body so that Tan-Tan could get out. But it was safe right there so in the musty dark that Benta had made. Tan-Tan didn't move.

"Come out now," Chichibud coaxed her.

"You sure? I 'fraid that man kill me dead."

"Kret? Nah, man. Benta go do for he if he try."

"Why he want to hurt me?"

"He think say me shoulda leave you in Junjuh, and leave tallpeople to deal with they own. But trust Benta to keep you safe, Tan-Tan. Woman is something else to deal with, oui?"

"Woman?"

"More douen business for you to learn. Benta is my wife."

Benta chortled. She stood right up and shoved her head under her own body to stare at Tan-Tan with one purple eye. The sounds she was making could be "welcome," if it was talk she was talking in truth. Tan-Tan scooted out from under her and glowered at Chichibud. "You making mako 'pon me?"

Benta warbled in Chichibud's direction.

"Yes, I did feel say she wouldn't believe."

The douen that had attacked Tan-Tan made a noise like a rusty hinge, stood and rejoined the crowd.

Benta sidled over, skreeked, *Tann-Tann!* She rattled her beak through Tan-Tan's wiry hair, still trying to groom it.

"No, no; wait. Back off." She was talking to a bird as though it could understand. Benta moved back. "Chichibud, I don't understand. Allyou is two different species."

The packbirds around them ruffled their feathers.

"Them find what you saying jokey," Chichibud told her. "We and them is same-same one. Only tallpeople does come in like the other beasts and them. Allyou woman does look like man, or pickney."

Tan-Tan laughed! Swallowed her laughter. Looked at Benta good. At the bird feet, so like douen feet. At how the fronds of her feathers resembled the long hair on the douen pickney-them. The bird—douen woman—regarded her calmly.

"All this time she could talk?" Tan-Tan asked Chichibud.

Talk to me! Benta warbled. This time the douen males added their *shu-shu* laughter to the packbirds' rufflings.

"I . . . I sorry, Benta."

Good.

Now that Tan-Tan knew that Benta was sentient and capable of speaking human language, she could understand the packbird a little more clearly.

Chichibud said, "Benta could always talk. All the hinte, the douen women, speak. Just not among tallpeople, is all. Them want to keep them secrets."

"What a thing," Tan-Tan murmured.

"Of course, the hinte prefer to communicate in song. Nothing sweet like when a hinte sing to you."

Benta burst into a concatenation of sound, a wordless almost-nannywarble. Chichibud went and leaned against her side.

Then Tan-Tan had to meet Chichibud and Benta's whole community. First old Res, the eldest one of them. His fangs were ground down to pegs in his mouth. His eyes were bleary. Tan-Tan wondered how long douens lived. Res sniffed her skin in greeting then climbed agilely up a vine rope to a higher branch of the daddy tree to watch. One by one she met them all. The hinte tasted her clothing and hands with narrow horny tongues. The men and the children sniffed at her. Amongst so many douens, the nutmeg-and-vinegar scent of the adults was strong. The restless, nervous pickney-them smelt something like saliva. One of the changing-into-a-packbird girls both licked Tan-Tan's blouse *and* sniffed at her skin, like a pickney and a woman. Much *shu-shu*ing and rustling all round at her adolescent confusion. The douen men sniffed Tan-Tan politely, but some of them rolled down their second eyelids the way douens did at a bad odour. Many greeted her in her language. She thought she recognised some of them. Truth to tell, sometimes the only way she could ever tell Chichibud from the other douen men who came to Junjuh was by the scar on his leg from when he'd fought the mako jumbie. Kret, he just stood to one side. When Tan-Tan met his eyes, he turned his back on her. Then all the douen men and women-them withdrew to under Res's branch. They stood talking to one another in their singy-singy language, glancing at Tan-Tan from time to time. Benta stayed with her. Tan-Tan was glad for that. She ain't think she could take much more strangeness, oui? She found herself leaning in the old familiar way against Benta's warm side. Benta leaned back and made a comforting churring sound. Tan-Tan remembered that this was a woman, not a pack animal. Her ears burning with embarrassment, she pulled away.

"Where I going to stay, Benta?"

With we. She chirruped more too besides. Tan-Tan had to apologise; it was too fast for her to catch.

Chichibud left the arguing group and came back to Tan-Tan and Benta. He tried to introduce their pickneys-them, Zake and Abitefa—for Abitefa was a douen girl, not a pet—to Tan-

Tan again, but the children wouldn't come close at all at all. Up on his branch, Res was cawing harshly at the crowd of douens. "So," Tan-Tan started, wanting desperately to make some sense of the new world in which she found herself, "douen woman does have two kind of pickney?"

Benta start to warble an answer. Tan-Tan listened hard but only caught one-one word here and there; "douen," and "pickney," and "fly."

"I don't . . ." Tan-Tan said helplessly. Chichibud took over the explanation:

"When douen pickney hatch," (*Hatch?* Tan-Tan thought) "them does all look like Zake, boy and girl both. Them have wingflaps and fur, and them could glide. As the boys mature them does lose their wingflaps and the hair. The hair on the girls does develop into feathers and them arms does crook into wings, them mouths does harden into beaks. Once them start making eggs, them could fly for real. Them get two ways of speech, one for each other, and the one that men and pickney-them use. Is the saddest thing for douen men, to remember how we used to be able to fly like them. If a douen man ever want to fly again, he have to partner with hinte."

Tan-Tan didn't want to deal with no more of this, oui? She sat down on the tree branch to try and gather her wits. Something fell through the air and landed in her lap. It was small and soft. She looked up. Old Res was directly above her. In the murky light, she couldn't tell what it was that he had thrown down for her. She picked it up, holding it to the light to try to see more clearly. It wriggled in her fingers. It was a slimy tree frog.

"Aahh!" Tan-Tan made to pitch it away but Chichibud was faster. He leapt, closed his fist around Tan-Tan's own. The tree frog squirmed in the cage of their two hands. Tan-Tan tried to pull away. She hated slimy things, they reminded of all the ways her daddy had taught her for bodies to make slime.

But Chichibud held her hands tight. "Oho!" he said out

loud, like he was proclaiming it for all to hear. "Is a gift Res give you. Raw tree frog meat is the sweetest meat it have. That mean he accept you as a guest in we daddy tree, Tan-Tan. You must thank he, and you must eat it."

Tan-Tan hissed, "You gone bassourdie, or what? Eat that nasty thing?"

"Child," the douen man answered soft-soft, "keep your voice quiet, and follow my lead if you want to sleep safe tonight. Plenty of my people already not too happy to have a tallpeople among we, especially not one who could bring trouble on we head by she kill one of she own. Them 'fraid you go bring more tallpeople here searching for you. Is a chance Res give you, and me too. So just do what I tell you, nuh?"

If you take one, you must give back two. Old Res was showing her a kindness. Chichibud too. They were trying to save her life.

"What I must do, Chichibud?"

"You go have to eat the frog."

"Raw?" Tan-Tan felt her gorge rise. The greasy frog squirmed frantically in her hand.

"Seen, but I go make it easier for you."

She set her teeth. She nodded.

"Good girl. You have courage." Chichibud called something out to Res. The old douen laughed *shu-shu*. Chichibud turned back to Tan-Tan.

"I tell he that since you ain't know we ways, I go have to show you how to eat tree frog." Before Tan-Tan could respond, Chichibud took the tree frog from her hand and bit off its head. He put the body to her lips. Tan-Tan made a choking noise. She fought not to pull herself away. "Drink some of the blood, doux-doux. Pretend you sucking it all in."

Tan-Tan took a little sip from the hot thread of blood pumping down her chin. It tasted salty, and sweet. It spread over her tongue like thick mud. Like the first time Antonio had ever ejaculated in her mouth, whispering to her the whole time. *Yes, sweetness, you want it, ain't?* Her belly rose right up into her throat, but she swallowed the frog's blood. Oh Nanny. She looked into Chichibud's eyes, praying that the torture done, but it had more for her to do.

"Take it from me, Tan-Tan. Bite off one of the limbs. If you could eat it, eat it, but if not, make like you chewing, and just keep it in your cheek."

She couldn't let herself vomit. Tears were flowing down her cheeks, but she took the tiny dead body from Chichibud. She held her breath. Closed her eyes. Bit into the tree frog. She could hear small bones snapping, feel the gristle tearing. She shut her mind against the smell, the smell of Antonio's body once she'd sliced it open. She didn't know how she managed it but she choked down little piece of the meat. She spit a small leg bone into her hand.

And is like that was the signal every man-jack was waiting for. One set of yodelling from the douen men started up in the daddy tree. The hinte bated their wings and bobbed their heads, screeching to the sky.

"What?" Tan-Tan asked Chichibud, wondering where she could run to.

"So you eat the tree frog, so you eat we secrets. We know we safe with you now."

Only Kret didn't seem too happy. He walked slowly past Tan-Tan, holding his gaze on her with cloudy eyes. He'd rolled down his second eyelids-them to stare; a big douen insult. Benta hissed. Kret gave Tan-Tan one last shrouded glare then ran for the edge of the branch they were on and leapt over the side, grabbing at a rope vine as he went.

It looked like that was that. Douens started to drift away through the daddy tree, some gliding, some hopping, some walking. Finally, only Benta and Chichibud and their two pickney remained standing there with Tan-Tan. Tan-Tan gave

Chichibud the rest of the dead frog. He popped it into his mouth and chewed it like hard candy. Tan-Tan could hear the little bones crunching. She looked away.

"It have somewhere I could lie down?" she begged. "I tired too bad."

Come, I go show you. Benta led them all to an aerial buttress vine. On a regular banyan it would have been narrow. On this mako tree it was bigger than Tan-Tan could wrap her arms round. There were handholds carved into it.

Her eyes more accustomed to the dusky light now, Tan-Tan could see how the daddy tree come in like a mangrove. It had many vast trunks to uphold its bulk. A fluorescent fungus grew everywhere, giving off guiding light. Tan-Tan gasped when Zake leapt right off the branch, opening his gliding flaps with a snap. He was heading downwards into the dark. Abitefa chirped something to her mother and started climbing down the aerial root.

"Get on Benta back," Chichibud told Tan-Tan. He grabbed a liana and swung down.

Tan-Tan looked at Benta. Benta cooed something. Tan-Tan frowned, feeling more like crying, in truth. She didn't understand. She wanted to go home. She couldn't go home. Benta sidled up to her and tried to put one shoulder under Tan-Tan's thigh, but no matter how low the douen woman crouched she was still too tall for Tan-Tan to throw her leg over the broad back. Benta warbled. Tan-Tan shook her head impatiently, running her hands over her hair. The hinte tapped Tan-Tan on the shoulder with her beak. Tan-Tan looked down where the beak was pointing. Benta had crooked one leg akimbo, making a step for Tan-Tan to climb up on.

"Climb up on your foot, Benta?"

Yes.

And is so Tan-Tan found herself straddling a hinte bareback. She had barely settled when Benta gathered herself and swooped down from the tree branch. Tan-Tan's belly did a somersault. She grabbed for Benta's snaky neck, squeezed with her thighs as hard as she could. Benta hadn't puffed up her wings!

But they glided safely, Benta landing on one branch then pushing off to fall gracefully to a next one. Tan-Tan closed her eyes against the sight of leaves rushing too fast past her face. Her ears popped, her bruised legs protested. Benta connected with a thump on a hard surface. This time she didn't immediately leap to another branch. The world was still again. Tan-Tan opened her eyes.

The structure in front of them was a cluster of room-sized spheres the colour and texture of dried leaves. Tan-Tan struggled for a childhood memory. The thing looked like a giant wasp nest. It had a halwa tree growing beside it, digging roots into the daddy tree like a parrot on a perch. Plants clustered all round the structure, feeding directly through the daddy tree's branches. Stuck into the surface on either side of the wasp nest structure were the two beak halves from the mako jumbie that Chichibud had killed many years ago. Zake was perched at the very top of one of the beak halves. Benta screeched at him and he slid down to the branch, threw himself backwards through a hole in the wasp nest structure. Chichibud came out of the same hole, Abitefa clambering clumsily after him.

Get down now, said Benta. Tan-Tan let go Benta's neck, although her arms-them felt like they wanted to lock there permanently, oui? She slid off the douen woman's body.

"So you reach!" Chichibud laughed. "I was beginning to think say Benta let you fall." Abitefa screeched and ruffled her body in douen woman mirth.

"Easy for oonuh to laugh," Tan-Tan muttered. "Oonuh make to travel this way. I ain't no ratbat, you hear?"

Come inside.

Up close, Tan-Tan could see the mudlike substance that formed the domes of the dwelling, the twigs and dead leaves mixed in for strength. A soft moss grew over it, with tiny square leaves. Probably that would make it waterproof.

The douen family had disappeared through the door hole. Tan-Tan had to crouch down to get inside. Her bruises stretched painfully.

Inside, it did spacious and airy. Glowing fungus everywhere made it bright, aided by kerosene lamps—traded from the humans—hanging from every level of the space. The domes connected on the inside in a waffle shape, rising to three-four storeys. Some of the walls had round holes knocked out of them for windows; or doors, Tan-Tan supposed, since the douens-them could fly or climb through any one they wished.

Some of the dwelling's domes had been built right around smaller branches of the daddy tree. The structure would be very stable.

Zake hopped over to an aerial root. It had the same handholds carved in it that Tan-Tan had seen before. In no time at all the boy shinnied up the branch to the next storey. He opened his arms wide and threw himself into the air, screaming with glee, to glide down to the ground level. He took off at a hopping run into another room. Tan-Tan and the others followed.

A low oval table was in the middle of the room. It had logs in a circle around it; probably they could be seat or perch, depending on who was using it. Zake dove for a pile of approximately spherical cushions against one wall, all different sizes and shapes. He gathered them round himself in a temporary nest then reached out and broke off a piece of fluorescent fungus that was growing by the wall. To Tan-Tan's surprise he popped it into his mouth and started eating it. He stared at her, saying nothing.

Tan-Tan recognised the dye-work on the fabric of the cushions; is Chichibud's wife's work . . .

"How Benta does do she weaving?"

Chichibud said, "Ask she nuh, doux-doux? I sure she go like to show you."

Tan-Tan felt her ear tips heating with embarrassment. She'd forgotten again to speak directly to Benta.

This way. The hinte led her past a room with a hole right through the floor. Tan-Tan had to pee, but she wasn't going to squat with her bottom exposed to the outside to do her business, like some kind of wild animal, a leggobeast in the bush. The room didn't even self have a door! She felt her mouth screwing up in disgust.

A next room, too dark to see good, then Benta's workspace. Weaving and dyeing were everywhere: cayenne red and ochre yellow strips were draped to dry on lines strung from wall to wall; cloth was folded into squares and stacked on one of the low tables; a sloping loom was strung with a half-finished piece. Tan-Tan could discern the dancing black figures that Benta was weaving into it. How, with no hands?

Benta waddled to the loom. In her beak she picked up a warp thread that had been dangling off to one side. The end of the thread was attached to a shuttle. Benta started shunting it through the warp, using her beak and one foot just like a parrot eating a nut. With the foot on the ground she pressed the treadle.

"But eh-eh!" Tan-Tan laughed. *Everything here so strange!*

Benta stopped the loom, chirped, ***Bath for you now.***

The bathing room was the dark one next to the piss hole room. It had one mako big flowertop growing from the daddy tree right into the space. It put Tan-Tan in mind of a pineapple top, but at least three metres across. The tips of it extended out through small holes in the side of the room. Cool, diffuse light came through the holes. A lantern hanging from one of the spiny flower petals threw a quivering mandala of light on the wall. As her eyes adjusted, Tan-Tan could see that the crown of the flower was full of water; a natural bathtub. Abitefa was strewing crushed herbs from a small bowl into the water, stirring it with her arms that were crooking into wings. The herbs smelt strengthening, like the scent of coffee brewing. Abitefa stood and from a low shelf took a little iron pot with holes cut out the sides. She waved it in the air and a sweet-smelling smoke curled from out the pot. The bathing place felt peaceful and quiet, the perfect space to cleanse your body and your mind.

Benta left the two of them alone in the room. Abitefa glanced at Tan-Tan, looked away, made to shuffle past her. "Ahm, Abitefa?" said Tan-Tan. The young hinte woman stopped and looked at her silently. Did she speak Anglopatwa? "I need to, uh, I need to piss."

Sure enough, Abitefa led her into the adjoining room that she had walked past a few minutes ago. Tan-Tan peered down into the squatting hole. There was some kind of bowl hanging below it. Her stomach roiled at the sight of the pale, fat grubs churning in the mess inside. But she was going to burst, she had to go. "You could watch the door for me?"

Abitefa warbled, then switched languages: ***Watch why.***

It was a question. "I mean, stand by the door and make sure nobody come by and look 'pon me while I peeing."

Abitefa ruffled her developing feathers in amusement, but waddled to the door and stood. She skreeked loudly, ***Nobody coming.*** There was a flurry of answering calls and cries from somewhere in the dwelling. Tan-Tan hurriedly did her business while Abitefa rustled and bustled with laughter. The acid urine stung Tan-Tan where . . . feeling Bad Tan-Tan stirring, she abandoned the thought. She quickly pulled up her clothing and said loudly to Abitefa, "I done now."

Abitefa took her back, continued preparing the bath. Not knowing what to say to her, Tan-Tan just looked round. On the floor beside the bromeliad tub it had a bowl with scrubbing husks. A handful of arm-thick stalks jutted out one side of the tub, pushed themselves out of a hole that had been cut for them trunkside of the room. Abitefa pulled one of the stalks to the inside. It was a big dark blue flower, pitcher-shaped, with a deep cup. Abitefa bent the stalk over the bath, emptied its load of water in.

"Oho," Tan-Tan said.

Bathe now, Abitefa sang. She left Tan-Tan to figure it out herself.

Tan-Tan stood closer to the bromeliad tub. She could see a trickle of condensation running from the tip that went outside down into the tub. It would refill itself constantly and the douens could top it up from the pitcher flowers if they needed to. How did they drain it?

She was alone, finally. The flicker-lace light from the lamp threw soft, gentle shadows on the leaves and branches. Tan-Tan dabbled her hand in the bath water. It was warm. The trickle sound of the water was a soothing balm. It had a scent in the room of growing things, of peace. She was tired for true, seen. She was nearly swaying on her feet with fatigue. She made to strip off her shirt—but the door, it ain't have no door!

She yelped when Abitefa shuffled back into the room unannounced. Startled, Abitefa dropped the folded unbleached cloths she'd been carrying. They stood staring at each other. Was the young hinte shy? Vexed? Indifferent? The elongated hands of Abitefa's going-to-wings arms-them retained their fingers on their ends, that's how she grasped things. Abitefa picked up one of the cloths and rubbed it against her own body.

"You mean I must dry myself with them?" asked Tan-Tan.

Yes.

She was gone again. Tan-Tan knotted two-three of the soft cloths together and tied them across the door.

Finally some quiet, oui. Tan-Tan took off her clothing and climbed into the flowertop. Her feet slid into the centre, where the wide spikes of the bromeliad overlapped to hold the water. It was warmer there. The heat seemed to be coming from the core of the flower. So strange to be inside a living bath! She lowered herself in.

As her behind hit the warm, fragrant water all her nicks and cuts from the day before awoke stinging. She sucked in air against the pain and eased in slowly. Her hands were trembling, her knees shaking. All of a sudden she felt sick. Every scratch was a memory, every gash an image. Bad Tan-Tan was screaming at her, accusing her. She could see the raised welts on her legs from Daddy's belt. Sobbing, she scooped up some water, splashed her face with it. The water made a spot on her cheek burn. She touched it gently. A bruise, from Antonio's slap. Another, a branch-whip from their flight through the bush.

The herbs in the water were soothing, eventually eased the pain of her wounds to a blessed numb tingle, but Tan-Tan was sobbing by the time she was clean. This wasn't just a day trip, an adventure. She had had home torn from her again.

Tan-Tan crouched in the tub, watching the tears dropping one by one into the water. She felt sick to her stomach. *Only good for dead,* hissed Bad Tan-Tan. Her dripping eye water made rings in the bath.

She stayed there so until the chilling of her skin from the water brought her back to herself. She was hungry, yes? She climbed down from the bath and dried her skin. She picked up her birthday skirt—today was her birthday—to put it back on. A faint smell snaked out from it, different from the cleansing scents of herbs and smoke. A smell of blood. Tan-Tan skinned up her face and dropped the skirt into the bath water. She swirled it round, wrung it, laid it over one of the flower spikes to dry. She found a dryish piece of cloth from the pile Abitefa had brought her. She tied it into a dhoti round her hips, wrapped another cloth round her chest and tied it into a halter at neck and waist. She looked down at herself with a wry smile. "But look at what I come to, ee? Living in a tree like a monkey, wearing a halter top and a diaper. Lord, if Janisette see this out-fit, she would dead with laugh."

Janisette. Tan-Tan's mind shut tight like a mouth again.

Her belly grumbled. Maybe Chichibud and them would give her something to eat? She slipped her sandals back on and left the bathroom, looking for Chichibud and his family.

The main room was empty. Benta wasn't in her weaving room. Tan-Tan couldn't find Abitefa or Zake anywhere.

"Allyou?" she called out softly. Then, a little louder: "Is where everybody gone!"

Up here, doux-doux!

Tan-Tan looked up. Three-four ropes hanging from the ceiling were threaded through a round hole. The whole family was looking down on her from a next room up there.

Chichibud called down, "I still smelling the heat from the lantern, child. Bush Poopa don't like a unwatched fire." So she had to go back and blow out the lantern. When she returned, Chichibud told her to climb one of the ropes and join them for the day meal.

The ropes had spaced knots that she could wrap her toes round, had they been long and prehensile like douen toes. But she had always liked to climb . . . She kicked off her sandals and grabbed hold of a rope. The climb seemed to take forever. By the time she stuck her head through the hole, she had added rope burns to her other abrasions. The muscles in her arms were burning like pepper. Chichibud and Benta had to pull her the rest of the way, with her grinning like a fool. She had done it. "Is a good thing I know how to tie dhoti, ain't?" she announced to the family. "Couldn't have do all of this in that little short skirt."

A piece of the daddy tree trunk formed one wall of the space in which she found herself. Two branches stuck out from the trunk along one wall surface, and then poked out to the outside. The trunk grew right up through the ceiling-self. There was a hole cut out for it. Thick, succulent daddy tree leaves grew from the trunk and branches; some hand-sized, some long as she. In amongst the branches, it had more of the flowerstalk that had been in the bathroom sticking through the windows. There was lots of water available for food preparation. Somebody had dug small pits in the meat of the branches-them, lined them with what looked like dried leaves, then planted herbs inside. Their roots probably tapped into the daddy tree's own food systems. Tan-Tan recognised peppermint and scotch bonnet pepper that the douens had probably traded with humans for, but it had a whole set of plants too besides that she didn't know.

The family was sitting or crouching on a crescent-shaped rug on the floor. It had bowls in front of them, but Tan-Tan couldn't really make out what was inside.

"Sit, Tan-Tan," Chichibud said.

He hopped over to a table that was right under the herbs. One set of wooden and iron bowls had been put on the table, and some piles of what looked like meat and plants. Chichibud picked up a cleaver, overturned one of the bowls and started chopping up the things that had tumbled out. The things tried to crawl away as he chopped. Tan-Tan's skin crawled; they were the same kind of grubs she had seen in the toilet. Maggot juice flew as Chichibud diced away with his cleaver. He caught one grub just as it wormed its way off the table. He popped it into his mouth and chewed contentedly. Tan-Tan swallowed hard to keep from spewing up her belly contents right there. Mama Nanny, is what she doing here?

"I ain't too hungry, you know," she announced.

"Well, if you ain't eat now, is hours before night meal."

Chichibud said something to Zake. The boy stood and collected two bowls and a pile of wood skewers from the chopping table. He took them over to where the family was sitting. Chichibud brought the bowl of minced grubs himself. The table was set. Tan-Tan squatted down beside Abitefa, who presented her with a gap-toothed grin; smile or grimace, who knew? The sight of Abitefa's funny half-beak-half-muzzle mouth made Tan-Tan queasy. Between these bird-lizard people and the offal they ate, is what she land-up herself in now? She leaned forward to look into the bowls-them to see is what they really expected her to put into her mouth in truth.

A tiny lizard darted from a crevice in the nest wall. It ran right over her hand, snatched a piece of salad from out one bowl, and glided back towards its hole on little wingflaps just like the ones douen pickney had. Tan-Tan yanked back her hand.

Abitefa warbled. She held out her own hand to intercept the lizard. The reptile ran right up onto Abitefa's shoulder and stood there on its hind legs, stuffing salad leaf into its mouth with tiny claws.

"Cousin," Chichibud cooed at the lizard, "good you come to visit." From one of the bowls, he picked up something that had enough still-wriggling legs for twelve centipedes, oui. He waved it in front of the lizard's face. Its eyes-them got big like cat eye when she see cockroach a-run past. It flew off Abitefa's shoulder, straight at the centipede thing. Chichibud let it go. The lizard wrestled the centipede to the ground and bit off its head one time, just like Chichibud had done with the tree frog. The lizard settled down to its afternoon meal, crunching up chitin and all.

Tan-Tan swallowed hard. "I could just have some salad? Plain salad, with nothing on it?"

Yes, said Benta. The family settled down to their food, taking from the various bowls and pushing raw meat and live insects and everything into their mouths. Every so often, one of them would dip some writhing something into a bowl of lavender paste that Abitefa had put there and pop it into their mouths, making hissing noises, like if the mess they were eating tasted good for true. A delicious smell came from the bowl of chopped-up grubs. Tan-Tan's belly grumbled at being denied. She ignored it.

"Benta," she said, "I worried about Kret. You think he go trouble me again?"

Kret jealous. Can't live good with nestmates. Ain't have no woman to take he flying. No man to share a frog with he, for he friendship always bitter. From time back, him always jealous of Chichibud, of me.

It was the longest speech of Benta's that Tan-Tan had heard. She struggled to understand the carolled words. Chichibud laughed. "Well, he been courting your sister steady, but so far, Taya ain't taking he on, oui?" He turned to Tan-Tan. "Benta done warn Kret off you. Is only a madman would face down a hinte."

Kret had looked plenty mad to Tan-Tan. She rifled through the salad bowl, pretending to look for the tenderest leaves. But really she was making sure it ain't have nothing but leaves in there. Then she chewed it all down, dry so, to appease her hunger. *You satisfy?* mocked Bad Tan-Tan. *This is your home now.*

Yes I know, doux-doux. Things changing around you too fast. But don't pay it no mind, this thing will happen without you or with you. Listen, make I sing you a next story:

In all she years of exile on New Half-Way Tree, with all the anansi stories exiles and douen people make up to tell about she life, Tan-Tan never hear back the tale about that escape she make from Junjuh Town on Benta back. It had one exile tale about a bird carrying someone away. But that tale put she more in mind of when the mako jumbie bird try to fetch away she daddy. Sometimes she wonder why the voice of Dry Bone remind she of another voice in she head:

Tan-Tan and Dry Bone

If you only see Dry Bone: one meager man, with arms and legs thin so like matches stick, and what a way the man face just a-hang down till it favour jackass when him sick!

Duppy Dead Town is where people go when life boof them, when hope left them and happiness cut she eye 'pon them and strut away. Duppy Dead people drag them foot when them walk. The food them cook taste like burial ground ashes. Duppy Dead people have one foot in the world and the next one already crossing the threshold to where the real duppy-them living. In Duppy Dead Town them will tell you how it ain't have no way to get away from Dry Bone the skin-and-bone man, for even if you lock you door on him, him body thin so like the hope of salvation, so fine him could slide through the crack and all to pass inside your house.

Dry Bone sit down there on one little wooden crate in the open market in Duppy Dead Town. Him a-think about food. Him hungry so till him belly a-burn him, till it just a-prowl round inside him rib cage like angry bush cat, till it clamp on to him backbone, and a-crouch there so and a-growl.

And all the time Dry Bone sitting down there in the market, him just a-watch the open sky above him, for Dry Bone nah like that endless blue. Him 'fraid him will just fall up into it and keep falling.

Dry Bone feel say him could eat two-three of that market woman skinny little fowl-them, feathers and all, then wash them down with a dry-up breadfruit from the farmer cart across the way, raw and hard just so, and five-six of them wrinkle-up string mango from the fruit stand over there. Dry Bone coulda never get enough food, and right now, all like how him ain't eat for days, even Duppy Dead people food looking good. But him nah have no money. The market people wouldn't even prekkay 'pon him, only a-watch him like stray dog so him wouldn't fast himself and thief away any of them goods. In

Duppy Dead Town them had a way to say if you only start to feed Dry Bone, you can't stop, and you pickney-them go starve, for him will eat up all your provisions. And then them would shrug and purse-up them mouth, for them know say hunger is only one of the crosses Duppy Dead pickney go have to bear.

Duppy Dead ain't know it waiting; waiting for the one name Tan-Tan.

So—it had Dry Bone sitting there, listening to he belly bawl. And is so Tan-Tan find he, cotch-up on the wooden crate like one big black anansi-spider.

Dry Bone watch the young woman dragging she sad self into the market like monkey riding she back. She nah have no right to look downpressed so; she body tall and straight like young cane, and she legs strong. But the look on she pretty face favour puppy what lose it mother, and she carrying she hand on she machète handle the way you does put your hand on your friend shoulder. Dry Bone sit up straight. He lick he lips. A stranger in Duppy Dead Town, one who ain't know to avoid he. One who can't see she joy for she sorrow; the favourite meat of the one name Dry Bone. He know she good. Dry Bone know all the souls that feed he. He recognise she so well, he discern she name in the curve of she spine. So Dry Bone laugh, a sound like the dust blowin' down in the dry gully. "Girl pickney Tan-Tan," he whisper, "I go make you take me on this day. And when you pick me up, you pick up trouble."

He call out to Tan-Tan, "My beautiful one; you enjoying the day?"

Tan-Tan look at the little fine-foot man, so meager you could nearly see through he. "What you want, Grandpa?" she ask.

Dry Bone smile when she say "Grandpa." True, Duppy Dead townspeople have a way to say that Dry Bone older than Death it own self. "Well doux-doux darlin', me wasn't going to say nothing; but since you ask, beg you a copper to buy something to eat, nuh? I ain't eat from mornin'."

Now, Tan-Tan heart soft. Too besides, she figure maybe if she help out this old man who look to be on he last legs, she go ease up the curse on she a little. For you must know the story 'bout she, how she kill Antonio she father, she only family on New Half-Way Tree. Guilt nearly breaking she heart in two, but to make it worse, the douen people nah put a curse on she when she do the deed? Yes, man: she couldn't rest until she save two people life to make up for the one she did kill. Everywhere she go, she could hear the douen chant following she:

> It ain't have no magic in do-feh-do,
> If you take one, you mus' give back two.

Tan-Tan reach into she pocket to fling the old man couple-three coppers. But she find it strange that he own people wasn't feeding he. So she raise she voice to everyone in the marketplace: "How oonuh could let this old man sit here hungry so? Oonuh not shame?"

"Lawd, missus," say the woman selling the fowl, "you ain't want to mix up with he. That is Dry Bone, and when you pick he up, you pick up trouble!"

"What stupidness you talking, woman? Hot sun make you bas-sourdie, or what? How much trouble so one little old man could give you?"

A man frying some hard johnnycake on a rusty piece of galvanized iron look up from he wares. "You should listen when people talk to you, girl pickney. Make I tell you: you even self touch Dry Bone, is like you touch Death. Don't say nobody ain't tell you!"

Tan-Tan look down at the little old man, just holding he belly and waiting for somebody to take pity on he. Tan-Tan kiss she teeth *steuups*. "Oonuh too craven, you hear? Come, Daddy. I go buy you a meal, and I go take you where I staying and cook it up nice for you. All right?"

Dry Bone get excited one time; he almost have she now! "Thank you, my darlin'. Granny Nanny bless you, doux-doux. I ain't go be plenty trouble. Beg you though, sweetheart: pick me up. Me old bones so weak with hunger, I ain't think I could make the walk back to your place. I is only a little man, half-way a duppy meself. You could lift me easy."

"You mean to say these people make you stay here and get hungry so till you can't walk?" Tan-Tan know say she could pick he up; after he the smallest man she ever see.

The market go quiet all of a sudden. Everybody only waiting to see what she go do. Tan-Tan bend down to take the old man in she arms. Dry Bone reach out and hold on to she. As he touch she, she feel a coldness wrap round she heart. She pick up the old man, and is like she pick up all the cares of the world. She make a joke of it, though: "Eh-eh, Pappy, you heavier than you look, you know!"

That is when she hear Dry Bone voice good, whispering inside she head, *sht-sht-sht* like dead leaf on a dead tree. And she realise that all this time she been talking to he, she never see he lips move. "I name Dry Bone," the old man say, "I old like Death, and when you pick me up, you pick up trouble. You ain't go shake me loose until I suck out all your substance. Feed me, Tan-Tan."

And Tan-Tan feel Dry Bone getting heavier and heavier, but she couldn't let he go. She feel the weight of all the burdens she carrying: alone, stranded on New Half-Way Tree with a curse on she head, a spiteful woman so ungrateful she kill she own daddy.

"Feed me, Tan-Tan, or I go choke you." He wrap he arms tight round she neck and cut off she wind. She stumble over to the closest market stall. The lady selling the fowl back away, she eyes rolling with fright. Gasping for air, Tan-Tan stretch out she hand and feel two dead fowl. She pick them up off the woman stand. Dry Bone chuckle. He loosen up he arms just enough to let she get some air. He grab one fowl and stuff it into he mouth, feathers and all. He chew, then he swallow. "More, Tan-Tan. Feed me." He choke she again.

She body crying for breath, Tan-Tan stagger from one market stall to the next. All the higglers fill up a market basket for she. Them had warn she, but she never listen. None of them would take she money. Dry Bone let she breathe again. "Now take me home, Tan-Tan."

Tan-Tan grab the little man round he waist and try to dash he off, but she hand stick to he like he was tar baby. He laugh in she mind, the way ground puppy does giggle when it see carrion. "You pick me up by your own free will. You can't put me down. Take me home, Tan-Tan."

Tan-Tan turn she feet towards she little hut in the bush, and with every step she take along the narrow gravel path into the bush, Dry Bone only getting heavier. Tan-Tan mother did never want she; Ione make Antonio kidnap she away to New Half-Way Tree. Even she daddy who did say he love she used to beat she, and worse things too besides. Tan-Tan never see the singing tree she always pass by on she way home, with the wind playing like harp in the leaves, or the bright blue furry butterflies that always used to sweet she, flitting through the bush carrying the flowers they gather in their little hands. With Dry Bone on her back and the full market basket in her arms, Tan-Tan had was to use she shoulders to shove aside the branches to make she way to she hut. Branches reach out bony fingers to pull at she dreads, but she ain't feel that pain. She only feel the pain of knowing what she is, a worthless, wicked woman that only good to feed a duppy like Dry Bone. How anybody could love she? She don't deserve no better.

"Make haste, woman," Dry Bone snarl. "And keep under the trees, you hear? I want to get out from under the open sky."

By the time them reach the thatch hut standing all by itself in the bush, Tan-Tan back did bend with the weight of all she was carrying. It feel like Dry Bone get bigger, oui? Tan-Tan stand up outside she home, panting under the weight of she burdens.

"Take me inside, Tan-Tan. I prefer to be out of the air."

"Yes, Dry Bone." Wheezing, she climb up the verandah steps and carry he inside the dark, mean one-room hut, exactly the kind of place where a worthless woman should live. One break-seat chair for sit in; a old ticking mattress for when sleep catch she; two rusty hurricane lamp with rancid oil inside them, one for light the inside of the hut, and one for light outside when night come, to keep away the ground puppy and mako jumbie-them; a dirty coal-pot, and a bucket full of stale water with dead spider and thing floating on top. Just good for she. With all the nice things she steal from people, she ain't keep none for sheself, but only giving them away all the time.

Dry Bone voice fill up the inside of she head again: "Put me on the mattress. It look softer than the chair. Is there I go stay from now on."

"Yes, Dry Bone." She find she could put he down, but the weight ain't lift from off she. Is like she still carrying he, a heaviness next to she heart, and getting heavier.

"I hungry, Tan-Tan. Cook up that food for me. All of it, you hear?"

"Yes, Dry Bone." And Tan-Tan pluck the fowl, and chop off the head, and gut out the insides. She make a fire outside the hut. She roast the fowl and she boil water for topi-tambo root, and she bake a breadfruit.

"I want johnnycake too."

So Tan-Tan find she one bowl and she fry pan, and she little store of flour and oil, and she carry water and make dumpling and put it to fry on the fire. And all she working, she could hear Dry Bone whispering in she head like knowledge: "Me know say what you is, Tan-Tan. Me know how you worthless and your heart hard. Me know you could kill just for so, and you don't look out for nobody but yourself. You make a mistake when you pick me up. You pick up trouble."

When she done cook the meal, she ain't self have enough plate to serve it all one time. She had was to bring a plate of food in to Dry Bone, make he eat it, and take it outside and fill it up again. Dry Bone swallow every last johnnycake whole. He chew up the topi-tambo, skin and all, and nyam it down. He ain't even wait for she to peel the roast breadfruit, he pop it into he maw just so. He tear the meat from the chicken bone, then he crunch up the bone-them and all. And all he eat, he belly getting round and hard, but he arms and legs only getting thinner and thinner. Still, Tan-Tan could feel the weight of he resting on she chest till she could scarcely breathe.

"That not enough," Dry Bone say. "Is where the fowl guts-them there?"

"I wrap them up in leaf and bury them in the back," Tan-Tan mumble.

"Dig them up and bring them for me."

"You want me to cook them in the fire?"

"No, stupid one, hard-ears one," Dry Bone say in he sandpaper voice. "I ain't tell you to cook them. I go eat them raw just so."

She own-way, yes, and stupid too. Is must be so. Tan-Tan hang she head. She dig up the fowl entrails and bring them back. Dry Bone suck down the rank meat, toothless gums smacking in the dark hut. He pop the bitter gall bladder in he mouth like a sea grape and swallow that too. "Well," he say, "that go do me for now, but a next hour or two, and you going to feed me again. It ain't look like you have plenty here to eat, eh, Tan-Tan? You best go and find more before evening come."

That is all she good for. Tan-Tan know she must be grateful Dry Bone even let she live. She turn she weary feet back on the path to Duppy Dead Town. She feel the weight on she dragging she down to the ground. Branch scratch up she face, and mosquito bite she, and when she reach where she always did used to find Duppy Dead Town, it ain't have nothing there. The people pick up lock, stock and barrel and left she in she shame with Dry Bone. Tears start to track down Tan-Tan face. She weary, she weary can't done, but she had was to feed the little duppy man. *Lazy,* the voice in she head say. *What a way this woman could run from a little hard work!* Tan-Tan drag down some net vine from out a tree and weave sheself a basket. She search the bush. She find two-three mushroom under some rockstone, and a halwa tree with a half-ripe fruit on it. She throw she knife and stick a fat guinea lizard. Dry Bone go eat the bones and all. Maybe that would full he belly.

And is so the days go for she. So Dry Bone eat, so he hungry again one time. Tan-Tan had was to catch and kill and gut and cook, and she only get time to sneak a little bite for sheself was when Dry Bone sleeping, but it seem like he barely sleep at all. He stretch out the whole day and night on Tan-Tan one bed, giving orders. Tan-Tan had to try and doze the long nights through in the break-seat chair or on the cold floor, and come 'fore-day morning, she had was to find sheself awake one time, to stoke up the fire and start cooking all over again. And what a way Dry Bone belly get big! Big like a watermelon. But the rest of he like he wasting away, just a skin-and-bone man. Sometimes, Tan-Tan couldn't even self see he in the dark hut; only a belly sticking up on the bed.

One time, after he did guzzle down three lizard, two breadfruit, a gully hen and four gully hen eggs, Dry Bone sigh and settle back down on the bed. He close he eyes.

Tan-Tan walk over to the bed. Dry Bone ain't move. She wave she hand in front of he face. He ain't open he eyes. Maybe he did fall to sleep? Maybe she could run away now? Tan-Tan turn to creep out the door, and four bony fingers grab she round she arm and start to squeeze. "You can't run away, Tan-Tan. I go follow you. You have to deal with me."

Is must be true. Dry Bone was she sins come to haunt she, to ride she into she grave. Tan-Tan ain't try to get away no more, but late at night, she weep bitter, bitter tears.

One day, she had was to go down to the river to dip some fresh water to make soup for Dry Bone. As she lean out over the river with she dipping bowl, she see a reflection in the water: Master Johncrow the corbeau-bird, the turkey buzzard, perch on a tree branch, looking for carrion for he supper. He bald head gleaming in the sun like a hard-boil egg. He must be feeling hot in he black frock coat, for he eyes look sad, and he beak drooping like candle wax. Tan-Tan remember she manners. "Good day to you, Sir Buzzard," she say. "How do?"

"Not so good, eh?" Master Johncrow reply. "I think I going hungry today. All I look, I can't spy nothing dead or even ready to dead. You feeling all right, Tan-Tan?" he ask hopefully.

"Yes, Master Buzzard, thanks Nanny."

"But you don't look too good, you know. Your eyes sink back in your head, and your skin all grey, and you walking with a stoop. I could smell death round here yes, and it making me hungry."

"Is only tired I tired, sir. Dry Bone latch on to me, and I can't get any rest, only feeding he day and night."

"Dry Bone?" The turkey buzzard sit up straight on he perch. Tan-Tan could see a black tongue snaking in and out of he mouth with excitement.

"Seen, Master Buzzard. I is a evil woman, and I must pay for my corruption by looking after Dry Bone. It go drive me to me grave, I know, then you go have your meal."

"I ain't know about you and any corruption, doux-doux." John-crow leap off the tree branch and flap down to the ground beside Tan-Tan. "You smell fresh like the living to me." Him nearly big as she, he frock-coat feathers rank and raggedy, and she could smell the carrion on he. Tan-Tan step back a little.

"You don't know the wicked things I do," she say.

"If a man attack you, child, don't you must defend yourself? I know this, though: I ain't smell no rottenness on you, and that is my favourite smell. If you dead soon, I go thank you for your thoughtfulness with each taste of your entrails, but I go thank you even more if you stay alive long enough to deliver Dry Bone to me."

"How you mean, Master Crow?"

"Dry Bone did dead and rotten long before Nanny was a girl, but him living still. Him is the sweetest meat for a man like me. I could feed off Dry Bone for the rest of my natural days, and him still wouldn't done. Is years now I trying to catch he for me larder. Why you think he so 'fraid the open sky? Open sky is home to *me*. Do me this one favour, nuh?"

Tan-Tan feel hope start to bud in she heart.

"What you want me to do, Master Crow?"

"Just get he to come outside in your yard, and I go do the rest."

So the two of them make a plan. And before he fly off Master Johncrow say to she, "Like Dry Bone not the only monkey that a-ride your back, child. You carrying round a bigger burden than he. And me nah want that one there. It ain't smell dead, but like it did never live. Best you go find Papa Bois."

"And who is Papa Bois, sir?"

"The old man of the bush, the one who does look after all the beast-them. He could look into your eyes, and see your soul, and tell you how to cleanse it."

Tan-Tan ain't like the sound of someone examining she soul, so she only say politely, "Thank you, Master Johncrow. Maybe I go do that."

"All right then, child. Till later." And Master Buzzard fly off to wait until he part of the plan commence.

Tan-Tan scoop up the water for the soup to carry back to she hut, feeling almost happy for the first time in weeks. On the way home, she fill up she carry sack with a big, nice halwa fruit, three handful of mushroom, some coco yam that she dig up, big so like she head, and all the ripe hog plum she could find on the ground. She go make Dry Bone eat till he foolish, oui?

When she reach back at the hut, she set about she cooking with a will. She boil up the soup thick and nice with mushroom and coco yam and cornmeal dumpling. She roast the halwa fruit in the coal pot, and she sprinkle nutmeg and brown sugar on top of it too besides, till the whole hut smell sweet with it scent. She wash the hog plum clean and put them in she best bowl. And all the time she work, she humming to sheself:

Corbeau say so, it must be so,
Corbeau say so, it must be so.

Dry Bone sprawl off on she bed and just a-watch she with him tiny jumbie-bead eye, red with a black centre. "How you happy so?"

Tan-Tan catch sheself. She mustn't make Dry Bone hear Master Johncrow name. She make she mouth droop and she eyes sad, and she say, "Me not really happy, Dry Bone. Me only find when me sing, the work go a little faster."

Dry Bone still suspicious, though. "Then is what that you singing? Sing it louder so I could hear."

"Is a song about making soup." Tan-Tan sing for he:

Coco boil so, is so it go,
Coco boil so, is so it go.

"Cho! Stupid woman. Just cook the food fast, you hear?"

"Yes, Dry Bone." She leave off singing. Fear form a lump of ice in she chest. Suppose Dry Bone find she out?

Tan-Tan finish preparing the meal as fast as she could. She take it to Dry Bone right there on the bed.

By now, Dry Bone skin did draw thin like paper on he face. He eyes did disappear so far back into he head that Tan-Tan could scarce see them. She ain't know what holding he arms and legs-them together, for it look as though all the flesh on them waste away. Only he belly still bulging big with all the food she been cooking for he. If Tan-Tan had buck up a thing like Dry Bone in the bush, she would have take it for a corpse, dead and rotting in the sun. Dry Bone, the skin-and-bone man. To pick he up was to pick up trouble, for true.

Dry Bone bare he teeth at Tan-Tan in a skull grin. "Like you cook plenty this time, almost enough for a snack. Give me the soup first." He take the whole pot in he two hand, put it to he head, and drink it down hot-hot just so. He never even self stop to chew the coco yam and dumpling; he just swallow. When he put down the pot and belch, Tan-Tan see steam coming out of he mouth, the soup did so hot. He scoop out all the insides of the halwa fruit with he bare hand, and he chew up the hard seed-them like them was fig. Then he eat the thick rind. And so he belly getting bigger. He suck down the hog plum one by one, then he just let go Tan-Tan best bowl. She had was to catch it before it hit the ground and shatter.

Dry Bone lie back and sigh. "That was good. It cut me hunger little bit. In two-three hour, I go want more again."

Time was, them words would have hit Tan-Tan like blow, but this time, she know what she have to do. "Dry Bone," she say in a sweet voice, "you ain't want to go out onto the verandah for a little sun while I cook your next meal?"

Dry Bone open he eyes up big-big. Tan-Tan could see she death in them cold eyes. "Woman, you crazy? Go outside? Like you want breeze blow me away, or what? I comfortable right here." He close he eyes and settle back down in the bed.

She try a next thing. "I want to clean the house, Master. I need to make up the bed, put on clean sheets for you. Make me just cotch you on the verandah for two little minutes while I do that, nuh?"

"Don't get me vex." Tan-Tan feel he choking weight on she spirit squeeze harder. Only two-three sips of air making it past she throat.

The plan ain't go work. Tan-Tan start to despair. Then she remember how she used to love to play masque Robber Queen when she was a girl-pickney, how she could roll pretty words around in she mouth like marble, and make up any kind of story. She had a talent for the Robber Queen patter. Nursie used to say she could make yellow think it was red. "But Dry Bone," she wheeze, "look at how nice and strong I build my verandah, fit to sit a king. Look at how it shade off from the sun." She gasp for a breath, just a little breath of air. "No glare to beware, no open sky to trouble you, only sweet breeze to dance over your face, to soothe you as you lie and daydream. Ain't you would like me to carry you out there to lounge off in the wicker chair, and warm your bones little bit, just sit and contemplate your estate? It nice and warm outside today. You could hear the gully hens-them singing *co-corico,* and the guinea lizards-them just a-relax in the sun hot and drowse. It nice out there for true, like a day in heaven. Nothing to cause you danger. Nothing to cause you harm. I could carry you out there in my own two arm, and put you nice and comfortable in the wicker chair, with two pillow at your back for you to rest back on, a king on he own throne. Ain't you would like that?"

Dry Bone smile. The tightness in she chest ease up little bit. "All right, Tan-Tan. You getting to know how to treat me good. Take me outside. But you have to watch out after me. No make no open sky catch me. Remember, when you pick me up, you pick up trouble! If you ain't protect me, you go be sorry."

"Yes, Dry Bone." She pick he up. He heavy like a heart attack from all the food he done eat already. She carry he out onto the verandah and put he in the wicker chair with two pillow at he back.

Dry Bone lean he dead-looking self back in the chair with a peaceful smile on he face. "Yes, I like this. Maybe I go get you to bring me my food out here from now on."

Tan-Tan give he some cool sorrel drink in a cup to tide he over till she finish cook, then she go back inside the hut to make the next meal. And as she cooking, she singing soft-soft,

> Corbeau say so, it must be so,
> Corbeau say so, it must be so.

And she only watching at the sky through the one little window in the hut. Suppose Master Johncrow ain't come?

"Woman, the food ready yet?" Dry Bone call out.

"Nearly ready, Dry Bone." Is a black shadow that she see in the sky? It moving? It flying their way? No. Just a leaf blowing in the wind. "The chicken done stew!" she called out to the verandah. "I making the dumpling now!" And she hum she tune, willing Master Johncrow to hear.

A-what that? Him come? No, only one baby raincloud scudding by. "Dumpling done! I frying the banana!"

"What a way you taking long today," grumbled Dry Bone.

Yes! Coasting in quiet-quiet on wings the span of a big man, Master Johncrow the corbeau-bird float through the sky. From her window Tan-Tan see him land on the banister rail right beside Dry Bone, so soft that the duppy man ain't even self hear he. She heart start dancing in she chest, light and airy like a masque band flag. Tan-Tan tiptoe out to the front door to watch the drama.

Dry Bone still have he eyes closed. Master Johncrow stretch he long, picky-picky wattle neck and look right into Dry Bone face, tender as a lover. He black tongue snake out to lick one side of he pointy beak, to clean out the corner of one eye. "Ah, Dry Bone," he say, and he voice was the wind in dry season, "so long I been waiting for this day."

Dry Bone open up he eye. Him two eyes make four with Master Johncrow own. He scream and try to scramble out the chair, but he belly get too heavy for he skin-and-bone limbs. "Don't touch me!" he shout. "When you pick me up, you pick up trouble! Tan-Tan, come and chase this buzzard away!" But Tan-Tan ain't move.

Striking like a serpent, Master Johncrow trap one of Dry Bone arm in he beak. Tan-Tan hear the arm snap like twig, and Dry Bone scream again. "You can't pick me up! You picking up trouble!" But Master Johncrow haul Dry Bone out into the yard by he break arm, then he fasten onto the nape of Dry Bone neck with he claws. He leap into the air, dragging Dry Bone up with him. The skin-and-bone man fall into the sky in truth.

As Master Johncrow flap away over the trees with he prize, Tan-Tan hear he chuckle. "Ah, Dry Bone, you dead thing, you! Trouble sweet to me like the yolk that did sustain me. Is trouble you swallow to make that belly so fat? Ripe like a watermelon. I want you to try to give me plenty, plenty trouble. I want you to make it last a long time."

Tan-Tan sit down in the wicker chair on the verandah and watch them flying away till she couldn't hear Dry Bone screaming no more and Master Johncrow was only a black speck in the sky. She whisper to sheself:

Corbeau say so, it must be so,
Please, Johncrow, take Dry Bone and go,
Tan-Tan say so,
Tan-Tan beg so.

Tan-Tan went inside and look at she little home. It wouldn't be plenty trouble to make another window to let in more light. Nothing would be trouble after living with the trouble of Dry Bone. She go make the window tomorrow, and the day after that, she go re-cane the break-seat chair.

Tan-Tan pick up she kerosene lamp and went outside to look in the bush for some scraper grass to polish the rust off it. That would give she something to do while she think about what Master John-crow had tell she. Maybe she would even go find this Papa Bois, oui?

Wire bend,
Story end.

Tan-Tan's first day in the daddy tree, her birthday, her first day as an adult, the douen family realised that something in her urine was poison to the food grubs. After she'd pissed in the pot all the grubs-them had floated up to the top of the effluvia and died, bloated and discoloured. Like them hadn't been nasty-looking enough already. Benta contemplated the mess. Tan-Tan felt to die from shame.

From now on, Benta said, ***I go take you down to the ground to do your business.***

"Nanny bless, Benta; ain't that is plenty trouble?"

Trouble yes; me and Chichibud know is trouble we would get for picking you up. Don't pay it no mind.

That night, Benta gave her a pallet stuffed with dead leaves to sleep on. It was comfortable, but sometime in the night Tan-Tan felt something in her hair. Half asleep, she put her hand up to brush it away. She woke up one time when she felt a tiny body wriggling out from between her fingers. Her screams brought the whole nest to see is what do her.

"Is only a house cousin, child," Chichibud told her. "Them like to sleep warm against we bodies."

House cousin. Flying lizard. Vermin. Tan-Tan asked Benta for a piece of cloth. She wrapped up her hair tight-tight, and that is the only way she got any more sleep that night. But the dreams, the dreams. Antonio beating her, flailing at her legs with the buckle end of the belt. She grabbing the belt to hit him back, only the belt had become a cutlass as she swung down with it. She slashed off his pissle with one stroke. He hadn't been naked before. The bloody tube of meat dropped to the ground and turned into one of the maggots from the douen pisshole; a big one. "Eat it," Antonio ordered her in a voice like the dead. "It good for you, you just like your mother." She felt his hand on the back of her neck, pressing her head closer and closer to the writhing pissle on the ground.

She woke up sweating, to the sound of tree frogs singing out sunrise. She felt unreal. Is which world she living in; this daddy tree, or the nightmare daddy world?

Benta flew her down the forest floor. Tan-Tan's belly still didn't like the feeling of dropping down through the daddy tree branches. It was a relief when they slid smoothly into a corridor made by two of the giant buttress roots of the daddy tree, at the foot of one of its massive trunks. The root corridor was almost a storey high. Tan-Tan held up her lantern against the darkness, wishing for a flashlight from back home, Toussaint home. She slid off Benta's back. Her alpagat sandals-them sunk ankle deep in leaf mould and dry twigs. The buttress roots took a long, low slope to the ground, gradual enough to run up them if she had felt to.

Mind where you step.

It was humid here on the ground, not like the leaf-rustling breeziness of up in the daddy tree. The heat weighed on Tan-Tan. It was dark. And damp. It was like breathing in warm water. Sweat was already running down between her breasts. Her thick hair was holding in the heat, twisting into locks in the dampness. Shy of Benta's eyes, she took the long walk round to the other side of one of the buttress roots to do her business. No such thing as paper. And when her period came? Blood cloths from Benta, she supposed. She wiped herself with some dead leaves, wincing as they scraped her. Benta took her back up in the daddy tree.

That morning, Benta and Chichibud's family foraged for their breakfast. Abitefa climbed onto Benta's back and the two of them went winging off through the daddy tree to get grubs from a neighbour to replace the ones that Tan-Tan had poisoned. Chichibud gave Tan-Tan a carry pouch woven out of vine. He and Zake took her out into the daddy tree and showed her where to find tree frog nests to raid. Zake shyly tried out his Anglopatwa on her, pointing out edible shoots and the best hand and foot holds for climbing. When they found tree frog eggs, Chichibud and Zake just sucked out the raw contents from the shells right there, embryos and all. Tan-Tan felt queasy watching them.

"Oonuh have any way to cook in your home?" she asked. "I could take some of these eggs back and make a omelette."

"We have a coal pot in the kitchen, doux-doux, but we don't use it plenty. We can't make flames catch the daddy tree. You could use it today, but you go have to learn to eat your food raw. It better for you so; you could taste the life in it."

She preferred her food good and dead. Trying to keep her find of eggs safe in their pouch, she climbed clumsily down towards the level where Chichibud and Benta had their nest. Two-three douen pickney saw her struggling. They consulted with each other then leapt into the air to swoop past her on their wing flaps, laughing *shu-shu* and tapping her on the head as they rushed by. She yelled at them to stop. They didn't listen. Twice she nearly lost her balance. When she finally reached to the nest level most of the eggs were broken. Their slime dripped through the carry sack down her leg. She was trembling with anger and effort. She went inside to climb the rope to the eating room. Three eggs survived that jaunt. She had to pick out yolky, budding masses from inside them before she could finally make herself something to eat. Tree frogs were small animals. The omelette she got from the three eggs would have just filled a tablespoon. There was no salt.

She chewed down the omelette determinedly—she'd burnt it, and Chichibud had made her put out the fire. She wasn't going to go hungry all the time, oui? She couldn't bring herself to eat living beasts or compost grubs that grew in douen people's mess, but there must be a way to cook for herself. She spat out a sharp piece of tree frog shell.

The forest floor; she could go down there and forage and cook what she found, the way Chichibud had shown her and Antonio their first day on New Half-Way Tree. She was going to be going down into the bush regular anyway. Best make some use of the trip while she'd be down there.

Could she make the climb down by herself? She got her knife and carry pouch, found a lantern and a stoppered container into which she poured the lantern's oil. There were matches—that new creation from the settlement of Bounding Makak—beside the lantern. Oil, matches and lantern went into the carry pouch, which she slung across her body.

Outside, she contemplated the daddy tree trunk nearest Chichibud and they's nest. She'd climbed it today, a little bit. It had been hard work, but she would get used to it. She set her hands and feet in the first set of holds and started down. Douen people were only stopping what they were doing to stare at her. No-one greeted her, no-one spoke. She clambered down past a douen man climbing up the other way. They did an awkward dance of exchanging hand and foot holds. "Tallpeople," he muttered as he edged round her. "Chichibud and Benta bring misfortune 'pon we heads when they bring you here." He was far above her before she even thought to reply.

He right, said the Bad Tan-Tan voice. *You is a trial, you is a wicked crosses for people to bear.*

Why that hinte over there watching at her? Scrutinizing her business. Tan-Tan waved mock-cheerily at the douen woman and skinned her teeth in a pretend grin. The hinte flew away. Tan-Tan kept climbing. More douen people came out of their nests to ogle. Anger heat rose in Tan-Tan, took over her voice and tongue. She stopped where she was and shouted out to them:

"Morning, sir, morning, ma'am, howdy lizard pickney. Oonuh keeping well this fine hot day? The maggots growing good in the shit? Eh? It have plenty lizards climbing in your food? Good. I glad." She waited. Some of them went back into their homes, others found other reasons to be busy. They dispersed. The rhetorical words had stirred the Robber Queen deep in Tan-Tan, quelled the Bad Tan-Tan voice a little. Nobody else stared at her for the rest of the climb down, except one or two irrepressible pickney. She didn't know how the douens got word to one another to leave her alone and she didn't care. The Robber Queen had triumphed.

The climb down was a good half an hour of skinned-up knees and blistered hands before she reached the forest floor again. Legs and arms trembling with the effort she'd made, she fumbled in the dark for her lantern. She spilled much of the oil, but finally managed to get it lit. She stepped out from between the buttress roots into the womb-close dark.

It had a jumbie bush right in front of her. She edged round the sharp poison thorns. The thorns caught light her lantern threw on the bush, created a warning glow of fuzz on the underside of each leaf. And there, not far off, was jumbie dumb cane. The forest was thick all round her; between foliage and the dark she could scarcely see more than a few metres in any direction. The sombre bush swallowed her lantern's weak light. She just hoped it was enough light to keep away mako jumbies, yes.

A straggly passion fruit vine hugged on tight-tight to a dead tree, using it as a ladder up to the sun. So much Earth-type flora the exiles had invaded this world with already.

She could see a path leading off into the distance, but that would be douen-made. She didn't want to see any of them right now. She went in the opposite direction. She heard a crackling noise like feet scuffling the dead leaves on the forest floor. She froze, peering round her into the darkness. Is two trees that, growing close together? Or is the legs of a mako jumbie? No, must be trees, she could see the leaves on them. And is what the hell just moved at the corner of her eyesight? Oh. A manicou rat humping along a low branch. Tan-Tan relaxed a little at the sight of the small, familiar animal. It looked plump and nice. She wished she knew how to trap. Roast manicou was some of the sweetest meat in the world.

It happened too fast for her to calculate. A step forward, onto one end of a long piece of dead wood hidden under leaf mould. The other end levered up from the forest floor. Yapping, a ground puppy leapt out from under it: two handfuls of dirty yellow bristle hair; teeth imbedded in it. Red maw, ring of fangs all round it. Tan-Tan screamed, flailed away. The ground puppy bounced off her knee, slashing briefly at her thigh as it went. It ran off into the darkness on all twelve legs.

"Shit. Is what the rass ever make my people name that thing a 'puppy,' eh? Blasted thing look like a hair ball with teeth." Jittery with fright, Tan-Tan knelt to inspect the bite it had given her. A circle of tooth marks in her knee was bleeding slightly. Ground puppy bites could fester. She would ask Chichibud for something to put on it.

This close to the ground, she could see other things scuttling out from where she'd disturbed the piece of dead wood. A handful of red crablike insects. Something else that favoured a bright green leaf with a million tiny legs running, running, running under it. The way its body undulated made Tan-Tan's stomach writhe in sympathetic motion. It ran up a tall, thin tree, turned sideways, and slid its body under an edge of bark.

She just wanted to be somewhere safe, somewhere familiar, where people looked and spoke like her and she could stand to eat the food. She crouched on the ground like that for a while, breathing, remembering when she was a girl-pickney and she'd had a home.

Her belly growled. Memories weren't going to fill it. She stood. Balancing on one foot at a time, she took off her alpagat slippers and shook them out: she didn't feel to have no red-crab thing or million-leg leaf-thing clambering about in her footwear, oui? What had made her think she could come down here wearing only canvas rope slippers? *Stupid bitch,* said her internal voice. Maybe Chichibud and Benta could bring her back some hiking boots next time they went into a prison colony to trade.

She found a long stick to probe the forest floor with as she walked. She'd learned her lesson, she took her time, only putting her feet down once she was sure there was nothing dangerous where she wanted to step. She found some nice big mushrooms and put them in her carry pouch. Little farther on she spied a weedy halwa tree, small and struggling in the shade of the daddy tree. Her mouth sprung water at the thought of the sweet gizada-smelling fruit. In two-twos she was up in the tree. Nanny was finally smiling on her; there were two small but ripe fruit. On the ground again she cleared a space in the leaf mould. It went down calf-deep and she didn't want to think about the disgusting things she flushed from it. One of them had looked like a dried sack of bones, oui. She used fallen twigs to build a fire and roasted the halwa fruit. She ate until her belly swelled, baked the mushrooms over the remaining coals. She would have them and the remaining halwa fruit for dinner.

Time to climb back up the daddy tree.

She couldn't find it. In the engulfing darkness she couldn't make out any of its trunks. Is which way she had come from? She couldn't remember. Maybe from over there so? She took a few steps that way, dead leaves crackling underfoot. She tripped over a log. It hadn't been there before, she was certain.

Is not this way she had come from. She turned a next way, peering into the dark in front of her. She walked one hundred paces, two hundred. Still no daddy tree trunk.

"Chichibud," she whispered. That twist-up vine looping from one jumbie bush to the next; had she passed that before? She couldn't remember. That hollowed-out trunk? That waist-high fan of glowing purple fungus? Her head was completely turned round. She didn't know is which way she'd come from or which way to go. She couldn't stop the whimpering sound coming from her throat. She stumbled off to the left, poking the stick into the ground in front of her as she went. Still nothing didn't look right. She ducked at a rustling sound in the leaves above her head. She looked up. A dead leaf was falling, falling slowly to the ground to add itself to the mulch on the forest floor. A big leaf. A red leaf. A juicy leaf. The whimper almost managed to turn itself into a little laugh.

"Cho. I too fool-fool. Ain't is daddy tree branches right there above me so?" The daddy tree was wide as a village and she'd been under it all the time.

She held the lantern high, studied the pattern of the daddy tree branches above her head, the way they rayed inwards. Where the branches met, she'd find one of the daddy tree trunks. It was so simple. She headed in the direction that the branches pointed. When she saw the buttress roots of the main trunk looming out of the darkness she nearly laughed out loud with relief.

Chichibud was there! Lying along one of the buttress roots, hind claws digging into the daddy tree wood, waiting for her. Tan-Tan called out joyfully to her friend.

"I name Kret," he said. "Tallpeople could never tell we apart."

Kret. The one who disapproved of her being there. So he could speak creole. Tan-Tan stayed where she was. Kret's muzzle hung open, sharp douen fangs gleaming in the half-light. He jumped down and came towards her. Tan-Tan grasped her stick firmly in her hand, ready to defend herself.

"Girl, you making enough noise to give the dirt and all headache," he said. "Is what you doing down here?"

Tan-Tan held out her carry pouch for him to see.

"Is what you have in there?" he asked.

She wasn't mookoomslav enough to get close to show him. "Mushrooms."

He tasted the air. "And roast halwa. Like you too good for the blessings of the daddy tree. You coulda find those things growing up there."

She could have. It wouldn't have suited, she'd wanted to be by herself. And right now her business was how to get past Kret.

"Benta bring me down here," she lied. She pointed off somewhere into the blackness. "She over there. She tell me to come here and wait for she."

Kret looked where she was pointing. He twitched his snout up in a strange way, like a dog would if it were barking. But he was making no noise.

"Liard pickney," he said. How did he know?

He jumped back onto the buttress root. "Cho. Me ain't business with disrespectful tallpeople. Play down here if you want, me wouldn't bawl if mako jumbie take you." Smoothly as a snake he headed back up to the light.

When she couldn't see him any longer, she began the climb up herself.

Poison, Benta declared when she'd seen what Tan-Tan proposed to eat for dinner. With her beak she flipped the mushrooms out of one of the window holes. Poison.

"Shit." Tan-Tan blew cool air on her hands where the climb had rubbed the skin off. She could still feel the trembling in her thighs from the ascent back up to the nest. "I can't eat the way allyou does eat, I can't move about the daddy tree the way allyou does do it, I can't even take a piss without it causing somebody some botheration!"

Chichibud said, "We don't mind. You is guest. You need to give your body and your mind time to heal after what Antonio do to you."

No, not that. Talk about something else. "But none of the other douen want me here."

"Old Res say you could stay, so none of them go do nothing, no matter how much them chat. Don't worry your head about that. The pickney-them just mischievous. Them will tease you, but don't pay them no mind."

"And what I go do for food? I sorry too bad, Chichibud, but I can't eat all the raw egg and live centipede allyou does eat."

Of all the things to do, Chichibud laughed. "I know. Tallpeople does remove all the life from all their food before they eat it, but them still ain't satisfy with that. Them have to burn it too, and make it deader than dead. None of we douen understand how allyou could taste anything what you eat after allyou done burning everything to coal. I sorry, darling, but we have to be careful about fire in the daddy tree. We don't cook plenty up here."

Benta warbled, *You could go down with Abitefa.*

"How you mean?" Tan-Tan strained to understand the warbling patwa.

*Is Abitefa alone time, last season and this next two. She leave she friends and she testing sheself every day in the bush. Go with she. The climbing go be good practice for you, and spending time with tallpeople is good practice for she for when she become a packbird. The two of allyou find and cook food while you down there. Abitefa go take care of you. So you go be spending time

away from the douen-them who ain't easy with having you here. Understand?

It could work, maybe. "Yes, Benta; I understand. That sound good."

But when Abitefa came for supper and Benta repeated the plan, the young hinte made a growling sound. Benta hissed something back; Abitefa spat out her reply in whistles sharp like glass. Benta screeched, stamping one foot on the ground. Her wings filled out one time. She beat them through the air, knocking one of Tan-Tan's halwa fruit off the table. It broke open on the floor, spraying Tan-Tan's ankles-them with the brown jelly inside.

"Chichibud, what them saying?" Tan-Tan asked.

"Not to worry. Abitefa go do what we tell she."

Chichibud spoke to Benta and Abitefa slowly, calmly. Abitefa continued to protest. Chichibud and Benta cut her off. Benta cawed out once more. It sounded like a command.

"That settle that," Chichibud said. "Abitefa go take you down in the bush whenever she go."

Abitefa was making quiet skirling noises. It was clear she wasn't looking forward to playing babysitter.

That night Tan-Tan filled up her belly on salad and leftover roast halwa fruit. Come time to sleep, she banded up her head again with the cloth Benta had give her. She curled up on the pallet and stared into the dark, praying for a peaceful sleep.

Prayers didn't do no good, oui. Antonio chased her all night.

Abitefa jumped from the lowest branch of the daddy tree, about six metres up. She fell like a bullet, dipping her backwards-knees to land silently on the forest floor. She hadn't even self jiggled the two kerosene lamps she was carrying. Tan-Tan clambered down to a buttress root, tried to balance along its top, lost her balance and slid the rest of the way. She landed *braps* on the ground, leaves tangling up in her hair. Abitefa barely even threw a glance her way. The hinte lit the two lamps-them, pushed one at Tan-Tan, then just turned her back and strode off into the bush. Her step was quiet like breeze passing. Tan-Tan struggled to her feet and rushed to follow Abitefa, crunching loud-loud through dead leaves with each step.

"Cho!" she muttered to herself. "You would think say me is the one with the foot big like shovel." Somehow she managed to get her lamp lit as she scurried. She caught up with Abitefa standing by the passion fruit vine Tan-Tan had noticed the day before. The vine was heavy with ripe fruit, filling the air with their sweet, tart smell. Yesterday it hadn't even had blossoms.

"What a way things does grow fast here," she remarked to Abitefa. The hinte didn't reply. Tan-Tan put down her lantern to free her hands. She picked all the ripe passion fruit she could reach. With her teeth she broke the smooth yellow rind of the last one. She sucked out the fragrant, tangy juice and swallowed the tiny black seeds. She thought of Toussaint.

She opened her eyes. Abitefa was gone. She couldn't see her in the swallowing gloom, couldn't hear her. She called her name. No answer.

She wandered round in the dark, peering through the circle of light from the lantern, calling for Abitefa, trying to bite back the panic that was fighting in her throat, threatening to spill out her mouth in a scream.

Calm down, Tan-Tan, she said to herself.

Stupid, said Bad Tan-Tan. *You go dead from stupid one day.*

Cool down, girl. Remember what Chichibud tell you, your first day on New Half-Way Tree. How you does survive in the bush?

She stopped and stood still, calling back to mind Chichibud's lessons. *You have to learn to use all your senses; is that what he say.*

Tan-Tan looked all round her, turning in a complete circle. No Abitefa. All she could hear was the rustling of the beasts and insects in the bush, going their own quiet ways. Nothing to taste that might help her, nothing to touch. Feeling like an idiot, she put her nose in the air and sniffed. *And is what that you doing now?* jeered Bad Tan-Tan. *A chop-head chicken would have more sense.* Nothing to smell but clean air. And the passion fruit juice on her hands. Huh. Maybe smell could work after all. Tan-Tan closed her eyes and drew in another long, deep breath. She smelled the salve that Benta had put on her bites and bruises this morning—like pine and mint. A heavy-sweet smell wafted through the air from over to her right, where the halwa tree was dropping its overripe fruit. Yesterday they were just ripening. The slight breeze was bringing her stories. She let out the breath, sucked in another. So, so faint, the odour of decay. She looked to where it was coming from. A thick clump of browny-pink fungus was growing, perhaps feeding on the body of a small dead beast.

And then she caught a thin thread of scent that didn't quite belong in the bush. Is what that? She could almost recognise it . . .

Tan-Tan walked towards where the scent was coming from. It got a little stronger. What, what? Some kinda chemical. Ah. She smiled. She blew out her lantern, tiptoed as quietly as she could towards the smell. Just a few more metres, and round that big rockstone with the blue moss shining on it . . .

Abitefa was sitting on the ground, back against the big rockstone, using her teeth and wingfingertips to weave something out of vine. She barely glanced up when Tan-Tan stepped round the boulderstone. She'd probably heard Tan-Tan coming through the bush. Tan-Tan played it cool. She sat down beside Abitefa and pulled off one shoe. She shook a million-leg leaf-thing out of it and said, "Your lantern go out just now, ain't? I smell the matches when you strike them."

Abitefa's shoulders shook with laughter. *What the rass . . . ? Oh, so is game she think it is?* Tan-Tan coulda get eat by mako jumbie out there by herself in the dark, and this ugly ratbat think say is funny! Furious, Tan-Tan shoved Abitefa's shoulder: "Bitch! You think is joke! Eh?"

One time, Abitefa rolled to her feet and crouched to face Tan-Tan, stretching out her nearly-wingflaps in a fighting stance, flexing her sharp claw tips-them. Abitefa made a threatening noise in her throat. But Bad, heedless Tan-Tan had come to the fore. She leapt at Abitefa, dragging her to the ground. The two of them crashed round in the leaf mould, each one trying to land a good blow. Tan-Tan boxed Abitefa in her ugly mouth; Abitefa bit Tan-Tan's hand. Tan-Tan felt the skin tear, but rage flared higher than caution. She trapped one of Abitefa's wingflap arms under one knee and slapped her face again. Abitefa screeched and drew back one of her big bird foot-them. She kicked Tan-Tan solid in her chest, sending her flying to land up against the big rockstone.

The blow made Tan-Tan dizzy. She tried to get up to go after Abitefa again, but her legs were wobbly beneath her. She felt her body inclining down, down to the ground. Is like it took forever till she was stretched out on the forest floor. Her head touched the leaf mould bed, soft like dreams.

Water trickled into Tan-Tan's mouth, slightly acidic; daddy tree leaf juice. Before she came good into her senses a pungent smell jumped into her nose. She coughed and tried to sit up. Too-long fingers were touching her face. She grabbed at Abitefa's arm and pushed it away. "Rahtid, woman; is what that you put under my nose?"

Dangling from Abitefa's claw tip it had a crushed millionleg leaf-thing.

"Cho," Tan-Tan said. "I never like them things from first I see one. What a stench! Is a smelling-salts bottle on legs, oui?"

Abitefa warbled something at her and moved back in close. Tan-Tan looked at her warily in the juddering lamplight. Slowly Abitefa reached towards her, put gentle hands on the back of her head. She was checking Tan-Tan's head where she'd bucked up on the rockstone.

"I all right," Tan-Tan told her, pushing the hands away. Abitefa settled back on her shovel feet, making worried cooing noises. Tan-Tan frowned, sat for a while with her thoughts. Then she had to smile.

"I guess I kinda ask for this, eh? Who tell me to pick a fight with a four-foot ratbat?" She laughed. "Daddy always tell me I was too much of a tomboy." Antonio. Suddenly she felt serious again. "Anyhow, Abitefa, I sorry, eh? You understand?"

Yes.

She rarely said anything to Tan-Tan. It came out more like a trill than words, but Tan-Tan understood. Abitefa rose to her feet. She sang something at Tan-Tan; could have been an apology or a curse, Tan-Tan didn't know, but it was softly spoken, and with no threatening movements.

"No problem." Hinte speech sounded so much like nanny-song. On an impulse, Tan-Tan sang at Abitefa the Anansi Web's phrase for "sunny and fine," the way Nanny responded most often when asked about the weather. Cockpit County people would sometimes hum the song snatch to mean, "everything all right between me and you." But Abitefa didn't respond, just stared at her. Tan-Tan shrugged. Her carry pouch was lying beneath her, the passion fruits broken. She offered a crushed one to Abitefa. The hinte ripped it apart, shook out the seeds and the pulp and chewed up and swallowed the tough yellow rind. Tan-Tan giggled. Abitefa picked up the thing she'd been weaving when Tan-Tan had located her; a next carry pouch, plenty bigger than the one Tan-Tan had, with a sling to put it over one shoulder. Abitefa gave it to her with a warble.

"For me?"

Yes.

"Nanny bless. Let we go hunting then, nuh?"

Abitefa led her through the bush. She showed Tan-Tan a thing like a badjack ant but big as a berry, and the nest it made in a type of small, weedy tree that dripped sticky sap. Dozens of the grey ant-things were running round in the sticky cluster of bubbles that was their nest. Abitefa rolled a daddy tree leaf into a cone and stuck the open end right into the sap nest. One time, one set of the ants ran right up into the leaf cone to investigate. Abitefa tore off the closed tip of the leaf and emptied the ants straight into her mouth, chasing runaways with her tongue. She handed Tan-Tan a leaf to try it with.

"No thanks."

They walked on. Suddenly Abitefa put a hand over Tan-Tan's mouth, stopping her and muffling her voice same time.

"Wha—" But Abitefa just clamped down harder. Tan-Tan looked where Abitefa was pointing.

The beast was entering a clearing where tinselled sunlight made it visible. It looked like an armoured tank. High to Tan-Tan's shoulder, wide so like a truck, covered in overlapping scales each the size of a dinner plate. A snout with six tusks poked forward. It moved slowly through the bush, tramping right over anything in its way. Behind it, it dragged a massive tail, as big around as Tan-Tan's two thighs put together. The tail had a morningstar of spikes at its tip. Tan-Tan was never coming down here alone again. The monster disturbed some of the undergrowth with its passing, and a ground puppy leapt out yapping and landed on its tail. It must have found some-where sensitive to bite, for a shudder went through the tank beast's tail then its whole body before the monster slammed its tail to one side, smashing it into a tree. The spikes left finger-deep gouges in the tree trunk. The beast bent its head to root through the underbrush. Abitefa pulled Tan-Tan in another direction, motioning to her to walk quietly.

When she judged that they were out of earshot Tan-Tan whispered to Abitefa, "I never see something terrible so in all my born days! Is what that was?" Abitefa's response sounded like a hacking cough. Yes, that was a good name for the monster.

Abitefa took them out of the overhang of the daddy tree, into the bush proper. There was a definite path; a lot of douens went this way. Maybe they were going to a human settlement? Tan-Tan got excited at the thought of seeing people again, until she remembered why she'd left Junjuh Town.

She heard the noise before they reached a next clearing; a banging and a clanging and a pounding, like somebody hitting metal against metal. A blast of heat washed over them. "Mama Nanny wash me down! You mean it could get hotter?" The sound was familiar. Yes, they came into sunlight to see a makeshift foundry inside the wide clearing in the middle of the bush, a grey cement dome of a building with big round window-holes all round it. Tan-Tan frowned. Those were douens she could see through the man-height windows; she thought they didn't know anything about building with cement or forging metal. But is metalworking they were doing for true. Tan-Tan watched at all those douens and them working obeah magic with hammer and fire, turning lumps of rockstone into shining metal. Perched on a log outside the foundry, a douen woman was lashing a sheet of weaving into an iron frame. With beak and claws she tightened the lashing, stretching the piece of cloth into the frame. The mud-coloured wad of cloth pulled taut to reveal a story in pictures: a figure walking all bent over like the weight of the world was weighing the person down. Some kind of small beast clung to its back. Flying above the two was a big bird or bat circling, circling in the air. The hinte gave one last pull of the lashing and the frame gave way, weak joints warping it into a diamond shape. The hinte let it fall with a clang. Two douens came hopping out to see what had happened. Chichibud and Benta. Tan-Tan ran towards them, Abitefa hopping beside her.

"Chichibud! Benta! You wouldn't believe what we just see in the bush!"

The other hinte shrieked and hurried into the foundry. Chichibud barked angrily at Abitefa, who sat back on her heels and ducked her snout into her breast. Benta stomped. Tan-Tan didn't pay them no mind. Excitedly she described the mako tank-like beast. Benta warbled a question at Abitefa. The young hinte responded with the cough-hack word. Benta cocked an eye at Tan-Tan and said, **"'Rolling calf.' That is what tallpeople does call it.***

Rolling calf! Another anansi story folk tale come to life. That last Jonkanoo Season on Toussaint, when Tan-Tan had gone for parang with the Cockpit County Jubilante Mummers. Mummers go on foot, is the tradition. And as they walk the distance between house and house in the dark, is the tradition to pass the time by telling scary stories. The rolling calf was a giant duppy bull with eyes of red flame. Its body was wrapped round in chains. It snorted fire and pawed the ground. The rolling calf left behind smoking tracks of burnt earth. If one only caught you outside late at night where you had no business to be, it would turn into a big ball of flame and chase you, chase you, chase you till you dropped dead of fright and exhaustion. Walking in the dark with the Mummers, the little Tan-Tan had hoped say the rolling calf understood that them had business out there, that them wasn't up to no good. She had grabbed hold of Ione's hand tight-tight.

Chichibud said, "Rolling calf bad-minded for so. Them does attack just out of spite. Only a master hunter could kill them."

"How, with all that armour?"

"Them have a soft spot under them jaw. You have to jook a machète up under the jaw into the brain. If you miss you likely won't live to try again. You see why we ain't want you coming into the bush alone? You keeping your lantern light to keep away the mako jumbie-them?"

With her beak Benta rummaged in the hard-pack earth. She picked up a splinter of kindling and handed it to Tan-Tan. Without a word, Tan-Tan used the splinter to relight her lantern from Abitefa's own.

"And now our own-way pickney show you a next douen secret," said Chichibud.

"This foundry," Tan-Tan replied.

Yes. We trying to teach weselves, for tallpeople refuse to teach we.

"Why you want to learn it, when you could trade for it with we?"

Chichibud stared at her for a long time. Tan-Tan fidgeted, unused to her friend scrutinizing her like a stranger. Finally he said, "What you could make with fire and metal?"

"How you mean? Plenty things. Hooks and so for hanging things up. Baby buggies. Frames like that hinte was trying to string . . ."

"Guns. Bombs. Cars. Aeroplanes. Them is all words I learn from tallpeople."

"I don't understand."

"Is part of the reason why Abitefa come down here with you. She was supposed to keep you from learning this thing, not to lead you right to it. Stupid, defiant pickney. Tan-Tan, if douens don't learn tallpeople tricks, oonuh will use them 'pon we."

"Don't talk stupidness!"

He moved closer. Little though he was, she sensed the easy strength of him. He wasn't someone to defy. "Girl child, believe what you want to believe. We see how allyou does act, even to-wards your own, and we preparing weself."

Tan-Tan thought of the dogs that One-Eye had set on her, how he and her friend Melonhead had hunted her in the bush. *We see how allyou does act, even towards your own.*

We going away for two-three days, Benta chirruped. ***Abitefa go look after you.*** Abitefa remained with her snout burrowed sullenly against her breast.

"Away? Where? Why?" Tan-Tan felt a little panicky at the thought of them not being around.

Trade, Benta replied. ***Over there.*** She swung her head to indicate where she meant.

"With who?"

"Tallpeople village, not far from here," Chichibud an-swered. "We have goods to deliver in return for lamp oil and some seeds them have that we never see before. When oonuh climb the half-way tree, oonuh does bring some wonders with you for true."

But Tan-Tan wasn't paying no mind to all that. "A village? A human village? I coming with you." Her heart started to beat fast at the thought of seeing people, of hearing speech she wouldn't have to strain to understand.

No, doux-doux, Benta murmured soft-soft. ***Too much danger.***

Resentment spewed out of Tan-Tan like bile. "How you mean, dangerous? You just think I going to be too much trou-ble, ain't? I bet you would take Abitefa."

A douen passing by them with a length of raw iron stopped at that. "Tallpeople pickney, wings ain't even start for sprout, what you know about wisdom? Look at Abitefa. What you think allyou people would do if them see something that look to them like half douen, half packbird, that can't talk to them in them own language, that big enough to defend itself if them attack? Eh? If Abitefa only set foot in tallpeople lands, she dead. Is so allyou does do anything that frighten you."

She didn't care. "But why I can't go? I is human, just like them."

Chichibud replied, "The danger is you, not them. We can't take the risk that you tell them about we."

Tan-Tan felt cold. They would never let her go.

Through the days of foraging in the bush, a friendship sprang up between Tan-Tan and Abitefa. Abitefa taught her how to trap small beasts; gave her lessons in yelling and stick-throwing to startle prey or frighten off the bigger beasts-them; how to smoke meat. Tan-Tan tried to learn to speak as the hinte did, but the sounds were too liquid and complex for her mouth to form. Abitefa would only jiggle with laughter when Tan-Tan tried. When she was in the flowertop bath up in the nest, Tan-Tan would watch at the reflection of her face in the water, pursing up her lips-them and skinning up her teeth-them, trying to trill like a hinte. She rolled her tongue into a tube, she chirped, she whistled; all she do, her words came out dead and flat. Tan-Tan singing hinte favoured a lonely tree frog croaking in the darkness. She got so frustrated trying make the sounds come out right! She started to wish she had a beak like Benta's, even a snout-turning-to-beak like Abitefa's. When she listened to mother and daughter warbling and cooing at each other she felt invisible, like she didn't have a mouth to speak for people to hear her.

Abitefa and tallpeople speech was a next story, though. In no time Abitefa was fluent. She and Tan-Tan got along well. And Chichibud and Benta had an easier time of it with the rest of the daddy tree people when Tan-Tan was out of sight. Abitefa and Tan-Tan spent most of their days together down in the bush.

• • •

Tan-Tan elbowed Abitefa aside on the daddy tree trunk. No time to explain. She slid down a buttress root fast-fast, jumped to the ground, holding her hand to her mouth. She sank to her knees just in time to spit up the halwa fruit and cold roast frog she had eaten for breakfast up in the nest. The sour taste burned the back of her throat. She made some more saliva to spit the taste out of her mouth with. Then she cotched up against the buttress root and just stared off into the distance.

Abitefa dropped down beside her, second eyelids still flickering in surprise. She handed Tan-Tan a lantern. Tan-Tan glanced up, took it, glanced away.

"Hot down here," she said, as if that explained what had just happened. She took a breath, let it out slowly. "And every day I come down, I does feel it more. Like my body making more heat."

You sick? Abitefa asked.

Tan-Tan dashed her eyes clear with the back of one hand. "Not sick; pregnant. I ain't see my courses for a month now. Oh, God; I making baby for my own father." *Again.* She leaned back against the daddy tree root. "What I go do? Tell me what?" A bitter laugh broke from her throat: "And what I go call it, eh? Son or brother?" She looked at her friend. "I can't give birth to this thing, Abitefa. Is a monster. I rip one of the brutes out of me once, I could do it twice."

Abitefa's arms were more like wingflaps now, feathered and longer. The feathers puffed out in shock. *Why? You make egg, you must lay it; is a gift from the daddy tree.*

Gift. That squeezed another bitter laugh from Tan-Tan's lips. "We don't lay," she corrected Abitefa. "We does push out we babies live and screaming. And this ain't no gift, is a curse."

No egg? Oho, Abitefa said, peering at Tan-Tan's stomach. *So is that why I can't see no egg . . . skin round the baby.*

Tan-Tan goggled at her. "See it? See it how? What you talking about?"

In the whiney voice that meant she was puzzled Abitefa replied, *Same way I see when a halwa fruit good to eat.*

"I don't understand."

I call out to it. Little bit like the cry when I want to catch small meat. I just call, so . . . She raised her snout in the air and opened and closed her mouth like she was screeching, but Tan-Tan didn't hear no sound. A tree frog dropped out from the canopy above them and lay stunned for a split second before it hopped on its wobbly way.

"Abitefa," Tan-Tan whispered, "is you do that?" Abitefa would do the same silent motion when she was showing Tan-Tan how to startle beasts. She'd always followed it up with a throwing stick. Tan-Tan had thought it was just alien body language. Was Abitefa actually making a supersonic sound?

Yes, the hinte replied. *You don't hear it? If I call high-high the sound does confuse small meat; tree frog and thing. If I do it soft, I does see things inside things. I see the baby in you.*

"To rass! Allyou got sonar!"

Sonar?

"Yes, man. Sonar and echolocation too, I bet you. Abitefa, you could see in the dark down here?"

Not good, no. Not with my eyes. So I call. I does hear if something in my way. When my wings grow in, is so I go fly at night.

"See what I mean?" Tan-Tan laughed, happy to latch on to this new thing instead of her troubles. "Girl, you is a ratbat for true!" An idea hit her. She'd always wondered . . . "Tell me this. How allyou does always know where the next group of exiles show up?"

It does make a big, high noise, Abitefa chirped. *It does hurt we ears. You never hear it?* The hinte's second eyelids flickered in surprise.

"No. I never hear a shift pod materialise. No human could hear it."

Oh, Abitefa replied matter-of-factly. Plenty of things tallpeople couldn't do, after all. She held up her lantern, looked round. **You feel better now? Ready to go?***

"Yes, the nausea does go away once I vomit. Plenty women not so lucky." Lucky. Tan-Tan scowled. She rubbed her hand over her belly, imagining she could just dig her fingers inside and pull out the thing growing in her. "Sonar not going to help me, Tefa. What I need is to lost this baby. I need to kill it before it grow any more."

No, Abitefa insisted.

"Oh, God, Abitefa, what I going to do?" Tan-Tan leaned against Abitefa's warm body, comforting as Benta's. Tefa's feathers were coming in. Tan-Tan wished she had wings too, and a sharp beak like Abitefa was getting. For all her bones were probably hollow to aid flight, Abitefa would come in bigger and stronger than any man of her people. She could defend herself.

"Abitefa," Tan-Tan said one evening while they were climbing back up to the daddy tree, "if you only know how sick I getting of roast manicou and halwa fruit, eh?" With her feet Tan-Tan curled a length of the vine rope she was climbing into a knot round her instep and stopped for a rest. She was already experiencing the shortness of breath of pregnancy. Abitefa leapt to a nearby branch to wait until Tan-Tan was ready to go again.

I go give you some of my tree frog tonight,* the hinte suggested.

"Nah, man. After it go be raw?"

Is good that way, not burnt like you does do it. Daddy must be mad, eating tallpeople burn-up food.* Abitefa had once tasted some of Tan-Tan's cooking. She had spit it out one time.

"Taste nasty, you mean. Uncooked. Me can't get used to

the kaka oonuh does eat, you hear?" Tan-Tan untangled her feet again and continued climbing. Abitefa followed her in silence. Tan-Tan stopped.

"I sorry, girl. I ain't mean to insult you. All I could think about is this baby eating out my insides." She sighed. "Tefa, you want to go with me tomorrow to the village?"

We already living in the village.

"No, the tallpeople place, not this douen place; the village nearby where Chichibud and Benta did going that time. You want to come with me?"

Is too dangerous for me.

"Yes, you right," Tan-Tan replied gloomily. "Them will take you for some leggobeast out of the bush and throw two cutlass chop in your head one time." They climbed a bit more. "But you don't have to come all the way with me, Tefa. Just show me how to get there nuh, and wait in the bush for me? I ain't go stay long. I only have to find them doctor and make she give me something to abort this baby."

Do what for the baby?

All she tried, Tan-Tan hadn't really been able to make Abitefa understand. Easy for her. When Tefa came of eggbearing age, if she couldn't or wouldn't look after one of her own pickney, her chosen nestmates would, or another nest. "Take it away from me. You go help me?"

I can't go. You shouldn't go neither. You hear what Daddy say.

Tan-Tan hauled herself up onto a younger, narrower daddy tree branch and lay there puffing. The monster child was taking away her wind and all.

"Abitefa, I tell you true, if I don't lost this baby, I go kill myself." Abitefa looked at her, feathers puffed out in alarm. "So," Tan-Tan asked her again, "you go help me, or what?"

When Abitefa said her reluctant ***yes,*** is like a weight lifted off Tan-Tan's chest. She laughed out loud, ignoring the douen pickneys wheeling through the branches around them. "Oh, Tefa, you is a real friend, you hear?"

They didn't waste any time, oui. Next morning self, barely dayclean, the two of them were down in the bush. *Sorry I can't fly yet,* Abitefa said. *Else I coulda carry you.*

They took the regular path. Abitefa led the way and Tan-Tan clambered after her, prodding the ground ahead of her with a stick as she went. Like everything in douen territory, the path grew over quickly. Ground puppies sprang out and snapped at Tan-Tan; dead branches reached up and jooked her calves; grit flies pestered her; a manicou shat on her head from a tree above. But Abitefa? Grace covered her like a blanket. Nothing could touch her. She saw branches before they snagged her skin, dodged the ground puppies-them before they could land. The trip was pure cool breeze to Abitefa. Two-three times Tan-Tan nearly said, "Let we turn back," but the nausea was burning in her belly like acid this morning, driving her to her purpose. They pressed on. Every few minutes, Tan-Tan felt for the gold ring she had knotted into a corner of the dhoti she was wearing. Antonio's wedding band. The one he had give her for her ninth birthday. All those years of wearing it, and every time her hand had brushed it, it had propelled her back to that birthday night, to Antonio touching her, hurting her, to the smell of liquor on his breath. She had taken it on its leather thong off her neck the second day in the daddy tree. She could use it to buy herself freedom from the monster child. Bad Tan-Tan within accused her of being ungrateful. She kept hiking doggedly along the overgrown path.

The pink sun rose, shooting the occasional beam of light through the sombre bush. With it came the heat. At least that sent the grit flies away. They walked another hour or two, stopping twice for Tan-Tan to lose her breakfast. They stopped beside a tree, a weed compared to the daddy tree.

Walk through there so, Abitefa hissed, pointing. *You reach.*

Tan-Tan couldn't see anything but more bush.

Little more and you go be there. I go wait in this tree. Abitefa nicked the bark with her claws in a particular pattern to help Tan-Tan find her again. She climbed up into the tree. *Be careful,* she trilled.

"Yes, man." Tan-Tan took a minute to untie her dhoti and wrap it into a sarong round her hips. She patted at the knot that concealed the ring. Then she set off the rest of the way. So long now she hadn't seen people! Once she traded the ring, maybe she would have enough money left over after seeing the doctor to get some real food. Her mouth sprang water at the thought of stewed gully hen with yam and dumplings and sweet, red sorrel drink to wash it down. Her belly rebelled, though. She had to stop once more to spew.

A few minutes later the trees started to thin out. Then it had low bush, then some picky-picky brown grass trying to grow in the hard earth under the hot sun. Beyond that it had a cornfield. The feathery spikes were brown for lack of water. It look like nothing grew easy in this place. Nobody was working the corn for it was day hot. So she got through without anybody seeing her.

Her heart started to pound when she got out of the cornfield. To see people again! A dirt track led off to her right. She followed it to where it stopped a little farther on, making a T junction with a cobble street that ran off perpendicular to it. On the street to her right were two-three broken-down farmhouses in a row. To her left the cobble street meandered into the distance, probably leading into the town. Tan-Tan checked out the farmhouses again. The two goats tied up in the yard of the closest one scarcely raised their heads to look at her.

A woman came out from round the side of the house. Tan-

Tan started, looked round for somewhere to hide; then checked herself. This is what she'd come for.

The woman swayed with the weight of a bucket balanced on her head. She spied Tan-Tan, stopped and watched at her. It was too far to discern her expression, but for a little bit Tan-Tan just stood and stared at the strangeness of her; her round face with neither beak nor snout, her two legs-them that bent to the front not the back. She would use them to walk, not hop. It came in strange to Tan-Tan. She felt her own body beginning to remember that it was human not douen, that her feet-them were made to walk on ground, not climb through trees. She smiled at the woman. "Morning, Compère," she called out.

The woman just turned away and headed off for the compost heap with her slop bucket. What for do, eh? Some people just ain't have manners. Tan-Tan shrugged and headed down the cobble street, looking for the town proper.

The street was lined with run-down wattle-and-daub houses, stink from the reek of the goat dung that formed their plaster. The front stairs to one bungalow had rotted away completely. Somebody had put a piece of warped board over the crumbling wood to make a ramp. A little farther on it had one mako midden heap, everything in it from a mashed-up baby cradle to rotting entrails, rank in the sun. Tan-Tan could hear the flies buzzing round it. A goat was standing on top of it, ripping and eating the leaves out of an antique paper book. The sight was shocking. Who had thrown away knowledge like that?

Eyes malice-bright, the goat watched her go by, twitching its ears to keep off the flies. It wrinkled up its nose like if is she who smelt bad.

In the front yard of the house after the midden heap it had a scruffy man digging in a half-dead kitchen garden. Tan-Tan patted the knot that hid her ring. She went to greet him. Like all the rest, his house was small and lopsided. Something had been split or maybe spewed against one of the mud-coloured walls; the dried residue was orange-yellow and looked gritty. Bits of it were flaking off into the pack earth. Half the steps up to the house had fallen away. It had a mangy, meager dog tied up in front with a piece of knotty rope. The dog start to bark when it saw her; a wheezy, resentful yipping.

"Morning!" Tan-Tan called out in a cheerful voice.

The man straightened up, stretched out his back, and looked at her. His eyes got wide. He cracked a big grin. Three of his front teeth were missing. His mouth looked just like his own front steps. His hair was snarled and matty-matty.

The dog was still barking. He went over to it and gave the rope round its neck a vicious yank. "Shut up!" The dog yelped and crouched down low on the ground. It stopped its noise.

The man flashed Tan-Tan a next gap-tooth grin and pulled up his pants that had been riding so low on his hips she'd seen the beginning of pubic hair peeking out above the waistband. "Ah," he sighed. "What a way morning time bring me a piece of sweetness to grace my yard today."

He was ugly like jackass behind, but she had to ask someone where to find the doctor. Tan-Tan remembered tallpeople ways. Bad Tan-Tan put on her coyest smile. "Morning, mister," she cooed. "I lost, you know? Ain't this is the way to the doctor?"

The man scratched his head, popped something between his fingers. "Like you new to Chigger Bite, doux-doux?"

Naturally the place would name after a parasite, Tan-Tan thought sarcastically. But she just giggled and played with her hair. "Yes, mister. I just visiting from over the way," she said, pointing vaguely out beyond the opposite side of the village.

"Oh. From Wait-A-Bit?"

Wait-A-Bit. Must be the name of the next settlement. "Ee-hee," she agreed. "And what you name, mister?"

The man stood to attention. He pulled down the shirt hem that had crept up over his paunch to expose a belly soft like a mound of mud; a bloated paunch on a meager man. He accidentally released the hoe handle; grabbed for it; it flew back and rapped him on the ear. Tan-Tan had to bite her lips to keep from laughing.

"Me?" the man said, rubbing the banged ear ruefully. "I name Alyosius. Alyosius Pereira. Al for short. And you, my girl, you must be name Beauty to match your nature, for I can't tell when last I see anything so pretty as you."

To Tan-Tan's surprise, the look in Al's eyes was warm and genuine. But what a way the man fool-fool! Her smile faded. She asked again:

"Is which part the doctor stay?"

"Make I take you, sweetness. I go give you the tour of Chigger Bite." He leaned his hoe up against the side of the house, beckoned her to follow. Up close, he smelt of days-old sweat and rotten teeth. Tan-Tan fell in beside him, taking shallow breaths. They started off down the cobble road again.

"Chigger Bite Village," Al said in a sunny voice, "is the nastiest, meanest of all the exile settlements on New Half-Way Tree, oui? In Chigger Bite, is every man and woman for themself."

They passed a next flyblown midden heap. Al smelt sweet in comparison. He nodded in its direction: "Say you have a goat; a smelly, mangy goat, thin so till you swear you could see the sun shining through it flanks, but still, it does give milk when it have a mind to, when you could catch it before it bite you. Now, say a next feller put him eye 'pon your goat for some nice goat curry for him dinner; well then you best watch your back, oui? You could be walking your goat down the dirt trail to river bank good-good to get her some water, minding your own business, when next thing you know, one machète stroke chop the rope you leading your meager goat by, and if you make fast and try and stop the feller from running off with your property, well. Half hour later, them could find your carcass facedown in the river, fouling the water with the blood running from the slash in your throat."

Tan-Tan stared at him. Al just pointed to a house they were passing, even dirtier than his own. A woman was hanging up raggedy laundry to dry on a line strung from the house to a dried-up lime tree nearby. Two snotty-nose pickney no older than two years were hanging on to her dress hem. One of them picked up a twig and threw it in the direction of Al and Tan-Tan, but the little arm didn't have plenty power. The twig dropped to the ground right in front of the pickney's foot. Without even self looking, the mother slapped it across its head. The pickney didn't seem to notice.

Al continued with his story. "And it ain't have nobody who would feel sorry for you, oui? Once you dead, your woman go praise God that it have one day in this land she ain't have to slave for no man. Only one day, for you know that tomorrow some next man who couldn't find a woman before this go be sniffing round she skirts. Your pickney-them go run wild, for now it ain't have nobody to lash them and stripe their legs with no greenstick switch. And friend? Nobody in Chigger Bite have any friends. It only have two kind of people: them who would like to kill you on sight, and them who can't be bothered with you."

Tan-Tan decided she'd better get to her business and get the rass out of this place. "Al? Is which part the doctor living?"

He stopped and looked her up and down, drinking her in like a thirsty man guzzling water. "Oh, sweetheart, you look too strong and healthy to need medicine. If I was a different man, maybe you and me could be medicine for each other, oui." He brushed her shoulder with his hand.

Tan-Tan yanked away. She pulled in a breath, hard, then a next one. *Antonio tear off she underclothes with one hand. He shove into she with a grunt.* She made a noise like the chick seeing the mongoose.

Alyosius looked confused. "Is what do you, doux-doux?"

Tan-Tan snapped back into the world. "Nothing . . . nothing, Al. I just need to find a—"

"Alyosius? Alyosius Pereira! All this time I calling you, you lazy so-and-so, and you ain't answer me, ain't even prekkay 'pon me. Is what possess you to leave the gardening and gone traipsing down the road, eh? I give you permission to go chasing skirt? Eh? Ain't I tell you to tie up all the bodie beanthem?"

The old woman waddling down the path after them could have doubled as a mountain in her spare time. Her dirty calico dress didn't quite manage to contain the masses of her breasts. They pushed out of her bodice like dough rising. Her belly rolls swayed from side to side as she hustled towards them. Her jowls wobbled. Someone was keeping this woman well fed, oui. Under a raggedy piece of head wrap, sweat was beading down her forehead, bathing her face in salt. She was waving a switch at Al.

"Mamee!" Alyosius said. He shrank closer to Tan-Tan. All of a sudden, he seemed to her like a small boy. "I wasn't going far, Mamee, just showing the young lady to she destination."

Al's mother glared at Tan-Tan. Her face went dark with anger. "You business with any woman? Eh? Any woman go want you? Sweat-stink, big belly, no-tooth excuse for a man? Who go want you, eh? Just a tramp like this!" The woman slapped her switch down on the ground right by Tan-Tan's foot. Tan-Tan jumped. The woman cut the switch against Al's calf. He howled, danced out of range. She followed, slicing at his legs, hissing, "Is woman you want, eh? Tramp? Leggobeast? Bitch in heat? Eh? I go show you heat. I go heat up your behind for you with this switch!"

A crowd of grimy, run-down Chigger Bite people had gathered round to watch the show. Somebody shouted out, "But eh-eh, Alyosius; how you could dance so?"

Antonio unbuckled his heavy leather belt and pulled it out from his pants. He doubled it up in his hand and cracked it against Tan-Tan's shins. The pain nearly made her faint.

Something in Tan-Tan broke loose, howling. Her skin felt hot. She pushed Alyosius to one side, grabbed the switch from his surprised mother and fetched her one slice *swips* on her leg.

"You like how that feel? (*Swips*) Eh? You think he like it any better? (*Swips*) Eh?"

The woman was only twitching heavily away from the blows, crying, "Have mercy, lady, what you doing! Allyou stop she nuh!" Somebody in the crowd sniggered. Tan-Tan didn't let it distract her. Is like a spirit take her. A vengeance had come upon her, it was shining out from her eyes strong as justice. Not one of them would dare try and prevent her. She whipped the woman's legs, she whipped them. She made the bitch prance. She knew how it felt to dance like that. She knew how it felt to cry out so, to beg mercy and get none. So the woman wailed, so Tan-Tan licked her. So she begged, so Tan-Tan cut her. Alyosius was hovering about them, asking her to stop, to have mercy. Nobody had had mercy on her. She yanked the switch out of his reach when he grabbed for it.

The woman bawled out, "Lord Mistress, don't do me so! Please, don't hit me no more!"

Please Daddy, don't hit me no more.

Just so, the anger left Tan-Tan. She lowered the switch and stood there, breathing hard. Alyosius snatched it out of her grasp and threw it out of her reach. He ran to his mother, wrapped his two arms round her. "Is all right, Mamee, is all right. I sorry, Mamee. Come, I go take you home. I go put healing oil on it for you, eh? And it go stop hurting. Don't cry, Mamee. Come." The woman leaned on him, whining about the welts that were rising on her legs.

Al cut his eyes at Tan-Tan. "Best find your meddling behind somewhere else, oui? Before my blood rise."

He left with his mother, cooing soothing noises at her.

How could he stand to touch that woman? How could he love her when she hurt him like that?

"How you could . . ." She was, *somebody* was speaking out loud. Words welled up in the somebody's mouth like water. Somebody spoke her words the way the Carnival Robber Kings wove their tales, talking as much nonsense as sense, fancy words spinning out from their mouths like thread from a spider's behind: silken shit as strong as story. Somebody's words uttered forth from Tan-Tan's tongue:

"Stop and stand forth, O Jack Sprat and his fat, fat, fat mother," said the Robber Queen.

Alyosius and his mother stopped, turned to hear the Carnival Monarch. People in the crowd started to grin again.

"Woman, what a way your son lean; lean 'pon you, lean because of you, inclined to be a mama-man for love, for loviedove. What a way your son love you, like two cooing doves in a cote. I go coat my throat with words of wisdom; come, and pay me heed."

"But she mad!" Al's mother whispered loudly. She took Al's hand and started to pull him away. The Robber Queen leapt in front of them, held up an imperious hand:

"Nay, stay, knaves and pay me mind. I shamed to be of your kind, oui? You treat he worse than dog, yet he love you like hog love mud. My father was a king, and my mother was he queen. Them carry me in chariots that float on air to take me anywhere, from my silken boudoir to my jasmine-circled pagoda. Them give me invisible servants to do my every bidding, and even with all that, I never feel a love like this man just show for this woman he mother. Compère, don't wear it out."

A wondering smile was wavering on Al's face.

"Yes, Compère," the woman said, backing away like you

does do from mad dog. "Sometimes my temper does run away with me, you know? That is all."

The woman-of-words, the Robber Queen, stared at the woman long. "Me tell you, don't hurt your son no more. Me will know. Me, Tan-Tan, the Robber Queen."

Mother and son made haste down the road.

She was back in her body. The somebody had gone. Tan-Tan felt weary. In a small voice she said to the crowd, "Please, it have a doctor in this place?"

They backed away. "No," somebody muttered.

"Mad like France," said another.

"No? So is where Al was taking me?"

"For a ride, oui? Me nah know. It ain't have no doctor. If we sicken, we does dead, that is all."

No doctor. No-one to take the parasite out of her. Tan-Tan spat on the ground. She turned on her heel and strode away. She could feel their eyes on her.

As she passed the hut of Alyosius and his mother she saw the movement of someone inside drawing back the faded curtains a little to peek at her.

Hiking back through the corn to meet Abitefa, Tan-Tan began to feel proud of herself, so full up of pride she could have burst from it. She remembered the voice that had come from her, it must have been her. She, all by herself; she'd taught that woman a lesson, and she'd spoken her mind with confidence, and she (yes, this is how she would tell it to Abitefa), she had ruled a mob of people who could easy have pelted her with rockstones if they had had a mind to. She didn't even self feel like the same Tan-Tan.

And for once, Bad Tan-Tan was quiet.

When she reached the tree with the gouge in it she called out, "Abitefa-oi! You still there?"

The hinte poke her head out of the branches and looked round. She did her silent call and seemed satisfied. She climbed down, gave Tan-Tan a hat she'd woved from flexible twigs while she was waiting. *The baby gone now?*

Tan-Tan frowned. "No, man. That is one backward place, you hear? Them ain't have what I want." She brightened up again. "But Abitefa, make I tell you what happen to me in Chigger Bite Village. Girl, it sweet can't done; Tan-Tan the Robber Queen just done make masque 'pon Chigger Bite!"

That night she lay on her pallet in the dark, staring at the lantern flame. She was jittery for some reason, she couldn't get restful. What was eating at her so, what? She tried to lull herself to sleep with the pictures leaping in the flickering light: *She and Melon-head up in a wet sugar tree, arguing happily about whether it was humane for the Nation Worlds' to exile their undesirables to a low-tech world where they were stripped of the sixth sense that was Granny Nanny. She and Quamina years younger, un-dressing their dollies and making them play doctor. The look of amusement on Aislin's face when she found them. Chichibud on that first day on New Half-Way Tree, showing her how to roast meat on a spit and never saying that he hated it cooked. Her mother, Ione, letting her play with her colourdots, trying on lip colour after lip colour with her and laughing at the effect. The house eshu from Toussaint, singing her lullabies when she'd woken in terror from nightmares.*

She missed the eshu. She hadn't thought of the a.i. in years. She wondered what had happened once people had realised she and Antonio were gone off Toussaint, gone from out of that di-mension for good.

She had acid stomach. The parasite baby again. She wrig-gled on the pallet irritably, trying to get comfortable. Her mind was only running backwards, backwards in time. The lantern flame guttered, flared with another image. *Antonio, screening a*

*picture book for her and rocking her to sleep as her eyes closed
on the bright images.*

The tears were sudden, the flood of them hot down her
cheeks. Benta must have heard. She *wheek*ed a question from
her part of the nest. "I all right!" Tan-Tan called back. She quieted down, fixed her eyes on the flame, on the heavy-lidded little girl dozing securely in her father's arms.

Daddy dead. You kill him.

She dropped her head to the bed, put her neckroll over her
ears. But she could still hear the evil voice in her ears.

She longed to have the good daddy back. Her mind skittered over his attack the day before her birthday. Could she
have prevented it? Stopped him? If she had come back early
from running errands and kept him from the liquor-soaked
fruit? If she hadn't lingered with Melonhead out on the verandah? Her daddy was gone. She wept and rocked, despising herself. Bitter silent Tan-Tan howled accusations at her, and they
were true, every one. Her doing, all hers.

Not a bit of sleep that night.

The sun was beginning to lay dapples of pink wash on the
daddy tree leaves when she realised what she had to do to quiet
the inner voice that never ceased. Bad Tan-Tan had given her
peace for a while when she'd been saving Al. Chichibud had
said, "When you take one, you must give back two." She had
to make up doublefold for what she'd done to Antonio. Helping Al had been the first small step. She had to go back to Chigger Bite.

Tan-Tan wrinkled up her nose, trying to make it smaller so she
might inhale less. The evening air was a little chilly. She pulled
the shawl that Benta had given her closer round her shoulders.

The alley behind Chigger Bite's rum shop ran rank with
slops. The door that led into the alleyway opened. Tan-Tan

moved farther back in the shadows, trying to ignore the squelching feeling underfoot. Her alpagats would soak through soon.

A young woman with a hard, scarred face was standing in the doorway. She pulled aside her clothing, put a hand inside. A stream of urine jetted outward in a precise curve, guided by the two fingers she would have inserted between her labia. Arcing liquid caught the dying sunlight to glow a soft and glittering tangerine. The woman pulled her hand free and shook it. She put the fingers into her mouth, sucked meditatively. She wiped the hand dry against her overalls and rearranged her clothing. "Cookie!" she yelled into the rum shop, turning from the darkening evening to go back inside. "You motherass so-and-so, bring me a jerk pork and some stew peas there!" She slammed the door behind her, cancelling out the rhomboid of light that had been thrown through the open doorway onto the ground.

Full dark soon. Benta and Chichibud no longer worried when Tan-Tan was out this late, though. She climbed down the daddy tree at all hours now to relieve herself, stayed down on the ground in the bush quiet as long as it suited her. They'd given her a machète as tool and weapon, for she wouldn't touch the knife that had been Janisette's birthday present to her. Too besides, she knew how to wield a machète from years of farming corn.

She pulled her feet free of the putrid suction of mud, crept closer to the finely meshed wet sugar tree bark that made the rum shop's back windowpane. She peered in. The shop owner was cutting slices off a cured haunch of meat, tossing them into a sizzling frying pan. Flames jumped in the brick oven. The man swiped his brow with one hand, took a swig from a mug beside the cutting board.

"Cookie!" a deep voice called from the rum shop's front room. "Two pimiento liqueur!"

He put down his mug, wiped his mouth with his hand back. "Strong or weak?" he shouted.

"Your behind, I ever take weak yet? Strong!"

"Soon come, Japheth." Cookie scooped the fried meat onto a plate, spooned a ladleful of stewed peas from a big pot onto the plate. Tan-Tan's belly rumbled. From an earthenware urn the owner ladled garnet red pimiento liqueur into two mugs. He took the lid off his water bucket and topped up the pimiento liqueur with water. He took the plate and the two mugs into the front room.

Giving them weak but charging for strong. Oho; Tan-Tan had felt she would find something to entertain herself with this night. She go do for he. She tied her shawl around her body like an apron—easy thing to hide her machète in its folds. She tied a knot in a corner of the apron; let the owner think she was carrying money, he would be less suspicious.

The ground was dry where she was standing. She bent, paddled three fingers in the grime of the alleyway and rubbed it into her face. Chigger Bite people never seemed quite clean, oui. She wouldn't want to stand out.

Her heart was starting to throb with the excitement of what she was about to do. She breathed in deeply for calm, pulled her scarf down low on her forehead to hide her features a little. She hunched her shoulders and cast her eyes meekly down, then put on the exhausted shuffle of someone who did manual labour from dayclean to daylean. She went round the front and limped into the rum shop. A few people glanced up but went right back to their drinking.

Tan-Tan stood for a second, blinking in the flickering lamplight. The woman who'd taken a piss out back was laughing and talking at a table with three other women. One of them had the Toussaint-style clothes and the lost, frightened look of the newly headblind; a recent exile. Singletons or with their compères, people were taking their rough ease from the day's labour. Wisdom weed smoke choked the air.

The owner was at the bar now, wiping out some ashtrays. Tan-Tan shuffled over. The owner frowned at the dirty, down-pressed woman in front of him. "Compère," Tan-Tan asked in a trembly voice, "beg you little liqueur, nuh?"

"You mad or what?" the man growled. "It ain't have nothing for free in here."

"No, no, Compère, I could pay," she said, fumbling with the knot in her apron. "I have gold."

"Real, or gold wash? Make I see," he ordered, bending over the bar to see better in the gloom.

Yes, just so. Lean just a little closer. She fumbled with the knot a little more, chatting the whole time like she was trying to cover up nervousness. "I ain't too like coming out in the dark, oui, but my woman tell me say I must bring she pimiento liqueur tonight, only she forget to give me any money, you know, so is a good thing I have this gold ring my mother give me . . ."

She untied the knot and started to open the folds of cloth. The shop owner stretched his neck quite over the edge of the bar trying to see what she had in there. *I have you now, you son of a bitch.* Tan-Tan grabbed his collar, jammed his head against the bar. Her machète was out and against his neck before he knew what had happened to him. A man cried out and made a move towards her.

"No! Anybody even self blink, I cut he."

Two people were sneaking up on her. She could hear them. They would never survive in the bush. Tan-Tan said, "This man been cheating oonuh, you know." The footsteps behind her stopped.

"Cheating? How you mean?"

She chanced a quick look at them. "Is oonuh just order the pimiento liqueur?"

"Seen."

"Him a-use water to weak it, and a-tell you is the strong he giving you."

The people in the rum shop started one set of *ssu-ssu,* whispering to each other. "Cookie," someone called out, "is true what she say?"

The shop owner started to curse. He surged up towards her and got a shallow slice on his neck back for his trouble. "Ow! Fucking leggobeast!"

Tan-Tan grinned to see the thin line of blood. This was what she needed, this desperate, sharp joy. She had the crowd's attention now. She sang out to them, "Oonuh want to see if is true what I telling you, or is lie?"

"Yes, lady," they responded gleefully. The two men behind her came up and held Cookie's arms.

"Elroy!" he blustered. "Christopher! Is what the rass wrong with allyou? Let me go; hold she instead!"

"Never you mind that," one of them replied. "Two years I been coming in here. If I find out you been cheating me from since . . ."

Tan-Tan warbled out, "Oonuh want to know the truth?"

"Yes, lady," the crowd chanted.

"Oonuh want to be sure you getting the right goods for your rupees?"

"Yes, lady."

"All right. Well, watch me then, nuh?"

At machète point, Tan-Tan walked the shop owner back into his own kitchen. His customers followed, squeezed tight-tight into the kitchen to see sport. Tan-Tan pointed with her chin: "Koo the strong liqueur there." She turned to the two men who were holding Cookie. "Where the one he give all-you?"

"I go get it!" someone said. The mugs were brought into the kitchen. There were still some dregs in them.

"All right. One of you two; ladle out a taste from the barrel."

"No!" said Cookie. "If too many mouths touch it, it going sour!"

"Don't fret," she said. "More time, it won't have none left to sour."

One of the men ladled himself a good taste from the barrel, then took a swig from the mug Cookie had brought him. "Pah!" He spat it right into Cookie's face. "Piss water." Unable to use his arms, Cookie blinked and blinked to get the burning alcohol out of his eyes.

"So you really been cheating we, Joseph," said an old woman. "When I think how I does work hard all day," she addressed the crowd, "and I come in here nearly every evening and give Joseph my money to ease some of my sorrows, and this is how he do me. Joseph, man, you make my heart hurt too bad."

The shop owner didn't reply.

"Too right," a next somebody say. "What a way the man is a swindler, ee? What you going to do, lady?"

"This." At machète point, Tan-Tan made shop owner Joseph drink from the bucket of water.

"Drink, you cheating swine, drink it all down. Drink down your swindlement, drink down your defraudation. Swallow, now! And again!" All the customers cheered as they watched him struggling to gulp until he'd drunk all the water. But Tan-Tan ain't done yet. "Nah, man, like you slowing down. I know you have enough water in this kitchen to last you a full day. Yes, here so." The barrel stood as high as her hip. "Fill your bucket. Now drink again. Drink, I say." Looking slightly green, Joseph put the bucket to his head. "Drink a swallow for every one of these populace you defraud. Swallow, don't spill none! Drink three times more for every member of this fine population who had was to choke down your thin, watery concoction and trade you them hard-earned goods for the favour."

The barkeep started to cough back up the water, out of his nose and all, but Tan-Tan made him choke down another bucketful, and another. He fell to his knees, vomited copiously onto the floor, gouts of slimy liquid with the thready remnants of his supper floating in it. Few spared the time to laugh at him. They were too busy helping themselves to the pure, sweet stash of pimiento liqueur.

Cookie groaned, glared daggers at Tan-Tan from reddened eyes. She smiled sweetly back. "When them ask you is who bring about your ruination this day, tell them Tan-Tan the Robber Queen, the terror of the bad-minded. I come into this life further away from here than your imagination could stretch. I born behind God back, under a next sun. My mother was the queen of queens, and my father was she consort, and he bring me to this place in a mighty engine. The birds of the air raise me. The lizards in the trees feed me. Them teach me how to be invisible, man, so if you start watering your drinks again, you won't see me, but I go know. Is Tan-Tan telling you."

She ladled out a half gallon jug of the strong for herself. The rum shop patrons cheered. She turned to breeze out the shop. Al and his mother were standing together in a corner, watching her. Tan-Tan's heart leapt like firecrackers, but they made no move to stop her. The hatred in Al's mother's face could have burned flesh off bone. Tan-Tan didn't care, she just laughed. She blew Al, clumsy, coward, stink, sweet Al, a kiss. He looked down, but it didn't hide the bow of the smile forming on his face. Spirit singing, Tan-Tan strode out into the dark. Behind her she could hear the people fêting on Cookie's good liquor, laughing and singing and making old-talk.

Abitefa was mad to know the story when Tan-Tan reached back to the bush. The two of them sat on the ground and Tan-Tan related the tale by the light of two kerosene lamps. "If you only see the shop owner, Abitefa! I sure he never going to feel thirsty in he life again, oui."

With a flourish Tan-Tan unscrewed the cap from the liqueur. She put it to her mouth and spat it out again immediately. "Bloodcloth!" The smell, the taste was making her belly roil.

What? asked Abitefa.

"It spoil! How it could spoil between there and here?"

Smell fine to me, Abitefa said.

"You mad? You try it then."

They poured the water out of Abitefa's drinking calabash, replaced it with pimiento liqueur. Abitefa dipped her beak in it, tossed back her head to let the liquid roll down her throat. *Good. Like fruits, but better.*

To rass, what was she talking about? Tan-Tan sniffed the alcohol again, took a small taste of it. Still nasty. But the people in Chigger Bite had been drinking it fine-fine. They didn't know strong from weak, but for sure they would have known spoiled from fresh, ain't?

Is the baby, the monster baby that was round and hard now like a potato in her belly. Her two months' pregnancy had changed her body chemistry so till alcohol tasted and smelled bad. Resentfully Tan-Tan dug her fingers into her stomach. The defiant thing inhabiting her didn't yield. Her head pounded with anger. She could only drink what it let her, eat what it permitted. And strong? She was making the climb from the daddy tree in two-twos nowadays. Poopa, this thing inside her was keeping her strong and healthy like horse, a good horse to carry it.

Abitefa had never tasted pimiento liqueur before, just the salty, fermented grogs that douens made. She got herself good and drunk. She ended up running round in the bush, holding up her kerosene lamp and flapping her free arm, trying to fly. Tan-Tan nearly perish with laugh at the sight. Giggling, she led

Abitefa deeper into the bush so the Chigger Bite people wouldn't hear her. Nanny witness, that night was joke for true! Tan-Tan laughing as she guided Abitefa into the bush, one hand on the hinte's neck, the next hand holding her kerosene lamp up high to keep away the mako jumbies. Abitefa only whistling and warbling the whole time in douen talk mixed up with creole. Then every so often Abitefa would stop and say, *Story, Tan-Tan! Tell me again how you frighten them in Chigger Bite.*

And Tan-Tan would tell it all over again. The hectoring inner voice didn't plague her once. That there night was sweet, seen.

She got too confident. She had started sneaking into Chigger Bite all hours of the day and night, doing a deed here, a deed there. By now people were recognising her, but so long as they weren't the butt of her crusadering, her appearance was cause for a fête and a merriment. She was beginning to hear whispers: how she was a duppy, the avenging spirit of a woman who'd been beaten and left in the bush for dead; how she was a hero like Nanny and Anacaona of old, come to succour the massive-them, the masses that the Nation Worlds had dumped out here behind God's back; how she was a witch who sucked the blood of sleeping pickneys. She could scarce recognise herself in the stories. She wasn't paying none of it no mind. She was working off her curse, keeping her nightmares at bay.

But she took on too much that night, three men who had chivvied an old man into an alleyway to rob him. Addled with fear, the old man had forgotten his earbug was dead to Nanny, and was yelling for his eshu to help him. He must have been a newcomer. Tan-Tan surprised the three nasties good, got them backed into the dead end and was holding them at bay with her machète. Their victim recovered his wits, snuck away as soon as his road was clear. Good. But when Tan-Tan launched into her Robber Queen speech, waving the machète round, she got mesmerised by her own elocution. She never even self saw the fourth man who had been their lookout until he dropped down on her from a rooftop. She let go her weapon. All four of them were on her one time. Somebody boxed her in her head so hard she felt consciousness fading. They were holding her down, they were hitting her, hitting her. It come in like her sixteenth birthday again, like she was back under Antonio's body, fighting for her life.

Then it stopped. One of them shouted, "Rasscloth! A-what that? Run, allyou, run!"

Tan-Tan was still too bassourdie to make out is what going on. One mako claw closed round her upper arm. She tore weakly at it. Another supported her head. Abitefa!

Stand up, Tan-Tan! the hinte screeched. *Arms round my neck!* Somehow they managed, Tan-Tan muttering punch-drunkenly all the while into Abitefa's ear, "My gros bonange, sweet guardian angel." They made their exit fast from Chigger Bite, Tan-Tan hanging on to Abitefa's neck and the hinte running hopping dropping, for her body hadn't changed enough yet to allow her to fly off proper with Tan-Tan. Abitefa 'buse she off good for that little escapade, oui?

Lying in the cornfield outside Chigger Bite, Tan-Tan was barely listening to Abitefa's rant. Her head was still spinning from how the man had lashed her. She half-heard Tefa, noticed how the young woman's words getting to sound more like when Benta spoke. Abitefa nearly turn woman already, oui?

Tan-Tan poked at her calabash belly with the demon inside. Three months. Maybe the fight had knocked it loose? She lay back again, listening to Abitefa carry on. She prayed for the cramps to start that would miscarry the demon. But nothing. When she woke up next morning, Antonio's child was still with her.

She'd lost her machète over that one. She crept back into

Chigger Bite next night to thief another one, even though Abitefa was frantic over her going.

Daylean was when she went, the prettiest time of day on New Half-Way Tree. The dying sun had turned all the light lavender. The evening air felt cool on her skin as she emerged from the bush into the field of high corn. The waving leaves drew against her face as she went by; the same way so Antonio would pass his dry, papery fingers across her cheeks, like he was trying to remember when his flesh felt young like that. Tan-Tan shuddered and put a hand out in front of her to ward off the corn leaves. The corn swayed and rustled in the breeze. Sneaking through it in the puss boots Chichibud had brought her, Tan-Tan heard her feet landing quiet-quiet like lovers whispering secrets to one another. With her big shawl and her boots on, she felt like Tan-Tan the Robber Queen for true.

She lifted a machète easily from the barn. She could have gone back then, but from where she was she could see the flickering oil lamps in Chigger Bite. Her heart started to pump faster. She went creeping round the village, just to see what was doing. Seemed she couldn't fill up her eyes enough with the sight of tallpeople going about their business. The stories she heard people whispering about her round the kerosene lamps in the rum shop nearly made her dead with laugh. She hurried back and told Abitefa about it round the fire they had built:

"If you could only imagine: them say how Tan-Tan the Robber Queen have eyes like fire, how she ain't even human! I supposed to have ratbat wings like Shaitan out of Hell heself, and two heads, one in front and one in back. Somebody have it to say how they see me spit green poison and fly off into the night! God girl, that too sweet."

She grinned at Abitefa. She took a bite of the manicou haunch that she'd roasted on the fire. The hot fat oozed into her mouth and ran down her chin. She tried to imagine what tallpeople saw when they looked at her, that they would describe her as duppy and ratbat and ravener. Was she? Mad? A scary thing from a anansi story? Or just herself? She ain't know. For now, food hot in she belly and friend strong by she side. For a little while at least, life was good.

Tan-Tan knew she had to wait couple-three weeks before making a next excursion to Chigger Bite. Give the village people time to relax and stop looking out for her. But the waiting got her to feeling so restless she couldn't stand it. Benta tried to show her how to weave, but she was only snarling up the loom. What weaving had to do with her any at all? Chichibud took her from level to level in the daddy tree to introduce her to their neighbours, but she didn't pay plenty mind to who was who. She was barely polite. Douen people didn't want her among them anyway. Days in the daddy tree didn't suit her, and she was frightened of the nights too bad. She would lie in the darkness with her head wrapped up from the house cousins, holding her eyes open wide-wide against sleep, trying to stay awake until dayclean. But all she do, her eyelids-them would lock eventually, and then, Antonio would be there waiting for her.

"*Soon, doux-doux,*" he would whisper, running his hands over her body. She couldn't squirm out of his grasp, he was too strong. "*I go be with you again soon. Four months gone. Just a few more. Soon, Ione.*"

Every morning Tan-Tan would wake up in a cold sweat, her belly churning. She was going to go mad in this place. She passed the time by weaving herself a hut down on the bush floor from pliant green withies she cut from the trees. She really didn't know much about it, but she was learning as she went, occupying her mind and body. The hard work soothed her spirit. One day she swung at a young sapling with her machète, and something moved inside her belly. She dropped the machète and put her palms to her stomach. She felt the baby roll under her hands, once.

Anger filled up her mind, buzzing in her head like bees. She picked up the machète again and started to chop, chop, chop like if she could chop down every tree on this motherass planet. Abitefa found her a little later, blowing hard, her sweat-soaked clothes sticking to her like sensé fowl feathers when it rain, but still chopping strong. And cursing! If curse word was machète, Tan-Tan would have chopped down that whole bush by herself with her mouth alone. She glared down Abitefa, but what tallpeople body talk mean to a douen? Damn mangy not-yet-hinte didn't see the warning in her look. With one claw foot Abitefa calmly took the machète from Tan-Tan's hand. ***You tired. Rest.***

Tan-Tan felt her mouth start to tremble. She sucked in breath after breath, trying to catch more air. The breaths turned to sobs.

"He rape me, Abitefa. He put this baby in me, like the one before. He was forever trying to *plant* me, like I was his soil to harvest."

Abitefa scratched her two feet-them a little on the ground. ***Why?***

"How the rass I am to know? Eh? Tell me how! I only wish I could have stop he—kick he with my claw foot-them, jook out he eye-them with my pointy beak!"

You not a hinte, Abitefa pointed out.

The sobs erupted, harsh as coughs. "Not a hinte, not nothing with value. Better I did dead, oui."

Abitefa folded up her backwards knees to plump herself down on the ground beside Tan-Tan. She rocked from side to side, making a humming sound in the back of her throat. Thinking.

The baby was jooking into Tan-Tan's side. She put a hand

to the place. The baby moved away from it. It really had a living being inside her for true.

Abitefa cocked her head to look at Tan-Tan. *No need to wish for dead, it will happen soon enough. It does come to all of we.*

Tefa just couldn't understand, oui. "Is all right, Abitefa."

That had been a good lime, a nice piece of entertainment. That poor, tired woman sleeping like the dead in her break-down little hut was going to be so surprised to wake up and find a big pot of curry goat on her kitchen table. Tan-Tan wondered if the people at the cookstand had missed it yet.

It was early evening. Lights were being lit all over Chigger Bite. Maybe she would go back early up the daddy tree tonight.

She was nearly to the outskirts of the town when she heard a noise from a side street: *Putt-putt-putt.* It sounded familiar, and it was coming closer. Frowning, Tan-Tan waited to see what it was.

Ahead of her, a car turned from the side street onto the one she was standing on. A *car!* Big and loud and smelly; body made of rusting sheets of iron held together with rivets; and large, lumpy wheels made from tree sap or something. The car's exhaust pipe was pumping out one set of black smoke, clouds of it rolling up into the clean air. The exhaust is where the explosions were coming from. And look, is bad-minded Gladys she behind the wheel, oui.

At first Tan-Tan didn't even self have the presence of mind to be frightened. *So is that Gladys and Michael was making in them iron shop.* Michael was beside Gladys, fanning away smoke from her face with a palm leaf fan.

And in the back of the car, sitting high on the caboose? Tan-Tan's stepmother, Janisette.

"Look she there!" Janisette shouted. Gladys turned the car

towards Tan-Tan. Janisette aimed a rifle at her stepdaughter. Tan-Tan jumped behind the corner of a house. *Pow!* A spray of plaster flew into Tan-Tan's eyes from the bullet that hit the wall right beside her head.

Phut-phut-phut. Tan-Tan ran, dipping through people's kitchen gardens, ducking behind chicken coops and thing. The baby bounced like a watermelon in her belly, slowing her down, like it wanted her to get caught. Antonio's duppy self, haunting and hunting her from within. Tan-Tan put two fists to her belly bottom to hold it still. She ran, she ran, she ran. "Nanny, Granny Nanny, help me now . . ." She was only sucking in air, but she couldn't get enough. The autocarriage stalked her, *phut-phut-phut.* She crashed through somebody's bambam pumpkin patch. Her foot smashed *clomp!* right through a ripe pumpkin. She had to stop and shake it off. Through frightened tears she saw a face in the kitchen window, smiling a vampirish soucouyant smile in the guttering candlelight: Al's mother. She nodded a greeting in the direction of the autocar.

Phut-phut-phut.

Tan-Tan ran.

The car was getting tangled in the ropy pumpkin vines, it didn't have enough power to tear free. Janisette pulled off another shot, missed. Fire burning in her throat, Tan-Tan headed for the cornfields. She could hear the whine of the carriage straining against the bonds that held it, the coughing of the engine as the wheels spun pumpkin trash up into it. She lost them in the tall corn, escaped into the bush and ran, ran, ran till every breath was like sucking in ground glass and her limbs were whip-striped from branches she had fled past. She collapsed to the ground, chest heaving for air. How, how? Too frightened for words, she couldn't complete the thought. Were they still following? She tried to still her breath, listened hard. No car sound. On foot, maybe? Sneaking up on her right this minute? Tan-Tan peered back the way she thought she'd come.

Outside the bush the sky would be still deepening to oxblood dark, but here in the bush night had already come, solid as a lump of coal. She couldn't see a rass. Cooling sweat made her shiver. A grit fly nibbled painfully at her eye corner, but she didn't dare slap it away. Was that a light? The sound of a footstep? No. She waited minutes more. No, they weren't coming after her.

Where was she? She hadn't entered the bush at her usual spot, hadn't had been able to spare a moment to even think about her lantern, much less collect it from where she'd hidden it.

The grit flies were gathering, drawn by her heat. She could hear their whining. She was bitten, then again. Dashing furious fingers at her eyes, she fumbled with her other hand in her carry pouch, found the precious matches. It felt like a stinging age of stumbling round in the dark before she put hands on a likely brand of wood. When she moved it she disturbed a ground puppy, which took a good bite out of her arm before it bounced off into the night. Damned things glowed purple in the dark.

By now the grit flies were worrying so badly at her eyes that she could barely stand to take her hands away to light the brand. It took a long time to catch, nine or ten tries with the matches. By the time it was burning well, her eyes were swollen nearly shut.

The brand flared, driving away the grit flies. Blessèd, blessèd relief. She heard a sound moving *away* from her, away from the light; a massive crushing of the undergrowth. Then another. Mako jumbie? Rolling calf? She began to tremble.

It was hours before she came upon the douen path. She could have wept with relief, but she didn't dare; she was hardly seeing out of her tortured eyes any more. She careened along the path. When her shins finally crashed into a buttress root of the daddy tree, she thought it was the sweetest pain she'd ever felt. She extinguished the burning branch by stabbing it into the damp loam and, eyes shut, scrambled exhaustedly up until the first douen lights flickered against her eyelashes. She was home. She climbed to Chichibud and Benta's nest. Chichibud was up, waiting for her. "I thought is you that I could hear crashing through the leaves," he said. "Why you let grit fly do you so? What happen to your lantern?"

"I lost it. I put it down somewhere and didn't mark good where."

"I go get you some balm. Go on to bed."

The soothing balm worked, as so much douen medicine did. The itching and burning faded quickly and the swelling subsided. Tan-Tan fell into an exhausted sleep. She ran in her dreams all night, chased by a thing she couldn't see. When she clambered out from sleep, she realised: Janisette and them hadn't seemed surprised to see her there in Chigger Bite. They must have been asking the settlements round Junjuh for news of her. Had Al's mother betrayed her?

Next morning she was helping Benta fold some newly woven cloths. **You could have come to grief last night,** Benta clucked.

Grief come to me long time. "But nothing happen, I was all right."

No, you prove you is still a bush baby. You my charge and Chichibud's, we can't put you in danger. From now on, you must only go down a-bush during the day.

And all Tan-Tan protested, she had to obey. The rest of the douens told on her if she tried to escape, and somebody from the nest would come and get her. For a week her curfew made her shamed and furious. She big woman, making baby, and two ratbats telling her what to do!

She couldn't stand it. One morning she decided to talk to them about it. They were in the kitchen, Chichibud gouging holes in the daddy tree to transplant new herbs into, and Benta trimming back new daddy tree growth with her sharp beak. Tan-Tan opened up her mouth to talk to them.

BANG-bang-bang! rang out through the daddy tree. Tan-Tan threw herself prone to the floor. Benta was by her side in two-twos, sweeping Tan-Tan to safety beneath her body. She screeched for Zake and Abitefa, who scrambled up into the kitchen to hide under her too. *BANG-bang-bang!* It was coming from groundwards. Chichibud yelled that he would see what the racket was. He leapt for the hole in the floor, grabbing at the rope as he did. There came the slap of his feet hitting the floor downstairs, then running outside.

Zake was only wailing, "Uhu! Uhu!" Benta whistled softly to him. The daddy tree branches were thrumming with the impact of douens running, hurrying down to the bush floor to see is what really going on. Tan-Tan, Zake and Abitefa squatted under Benta's breast like baby birds in a nest. What strangeness was happening this time? Tan-Tan's mind skittered in fright.

The bowl of centipede things had spilled. The nasty yellow-green insects that had been released were scuttling hell-for-leather to freedom. And all the while, all you could hear was: *BANG-bang-bang! Splutter-splutter-phut-phut.*

Then the patter of feet running back inside the nest. *Chichibud?* Benta sang out. Chichibud warbled back. His head appeared in the hole in the floor. "Allyou make haste come and see. Down on the forest floor. You too, Tan-Tan; this have to be tallpeople business."

No time for the harness once they reached outside the nest. Chichibud climbed up on Benta's back, grasped her feathered sides with his feet claws. Tan-Tan clambered up behind him and wrapped her arms round his waist. The banging noise was driving out all logic. Chichibud's nutmeg-and-vinegar smell was strong; he was agitated. Abitefa threw herself down a daddy tree trunk, heading fast for ground level. Benta pumped up her wings and flung herself off the branch. Tan-Tan fought down nausea as the plummet seemed to turn her belly right away round in her body.

All round them douen people were heading down, quiet like duppy spirits as they reached the lower levels. Benta landed on the lowest branch. It was wide like an avenue. Its edge was crowded with douens four deep, but Benta pushed to the front. Tan-Tan and Chichibud slid off her. A few douens climbed up frantically from ground level to join them; the ones who'd been at the foundry. What were they running from?

The sound of explosions was coming from off in the bush, from the direction of Chigger Bite. It was getting closer. Could never happen, say it couldn't be. Tan-Tan bent and whispered into Chichibud's ear: "What we looking for?"

"Wait. It coming into sight now. Keep still."

Is like he give the order to everybody. Every man-jack of the douen people became still and invisible. They slid into shadows or put themselves behind big daddy tree leaves. Is as if nobody was there.

Tan-Tan sank into a crouch and watched at the place where the noise was coming from. Closer. Louder. It broke from the bush into the space beneath the daddy tree. *Splutter-splutter-phut-phut-phut*. It was the car, limned by the lanterns its occupants were carrying. Tan-Tan squeaked, clapped a hand to her mouth. They had tracked her from Chigger Bite!

The car rolled to a stop. They had wrapped chains round its wheels. The chains had bitten into the loam and tossed up deep chunks of it, leaving a plowed trail all the way from the daddy tree back to Chigger Bite.

"What a way the something ugly!" Chichibud whispered.

Sitting up on the caboose, Janisette was wearing a low-cut black peasant blouse today and tight black dungarees, with a big black straw hat and veil protecting her face and bosom. She favoured La Diablesse, the devil woman. She put her lantern down beside her and rolled the veil up over the hat to look round. For all her widow's weeds she didn't look like nobody in mourning, oui? More like a woman on a rampage. Is so thunder cloud does look before the hurricane, so rolling calf does gather heself into a big black ball before he strike. She looked up, up at the height and breadth of the daddy tree.

"What a ugly, obzocky-looking thing! It come in more like a mountain than a tree. Michael, you sure is here the bitch went to?"

"Is here the trail dead out," Michael responded. "Best we check it out. Rahtid! You ever see a tree big so?"

"What you think Tan-Tan would be doing *here?*" Janisette looked round, her mouth pursed up in disdain. She cupped her hand to her mouth and sang sweetly out over the bush, "Tan-Tan! You out here? You all right? Come, doux-doux; everything forgive. Mamee looking for you!"

Gladys said, "You know, you is a two-faced woman. Trying to mamaguy the pickney with sweet words."

"Is no pickney that, is the bitch that killed my husband."

"Nobody know that for sure."

Janisette spat over the side of the car. "So is who do it, then?"

"Maybe Antonio get into a fight with one of Tan-Tan man, oui? He had a unhealthy way to be jealous of he own pickney."

"Hush your mouth!"

"No, Compère. Making this car for you was a good challenge, we learn plenty, but me fatigued with this nonsense now. Me and Michael want to go home."

Michael smiled at Gladys, shrugged apologetically in Janisette's direction.

Scowling, Janisette pointed back the way they'd come. "You want to leave, get out and go then, nuh?"

"Like you forget who construct this vehicle? We ain't see no payment yet."

Janisette kissed her teeth, looked away.

But Gladys wasn't done. "Maybe you bring we on this chase for nothing. That woman-pickney pants too hot for she own damn good, but I tell you, coulda be anybody do for

Antonio. Anybody he cheat or insult. Cuffee, for instance.
Chichibud. The rest of allyou does trust douen people too
easy."

"And you does run off your blasted mouth too easy. Shit
flowing out of it like out of duck behind."

"Oonuh don't fight, nuh?" Michael pleaded with them. "It
ain't go help nothing."

Tan-Tan knew what she had to do. This was about her, she
couldn't make the douens get mixed up in it. She made to start
down the nearest trunk, but Chichibud held her back.

Michael got out of the car. He had to vault over the side;
look like they hadn't had time to make doors. He walked over
to a trunk of the daddy tree. Is like tout monde in the daddy
tree turned to stone. You couldn't even self hear breath whisper
from anybody's lungs. Michael squinted up through darkness,
cocking his head to one side. He laid a hand on the buttress
root, made an enquiring noise. "Gladys, bring a lantern for me
there."

By lantern light, the scuff marks on the buttress root were
clear. "You see? Like if somebody went up there so." He shone
the lantern as high as he could, but it didn't reach them that
were hiding.

He gave Gladys the lantern and jumped up onto the root.
"Careful, dumpling," she said.

"Nah, is no problem; like walking up a ramp." He reached
the trunk, touched it. "Koo ya! It have handholds here so."

Quiet-quiet, the douen women started guiding pickneys
and half-formed adolescents up onto their backs. Some of the
little ones piped up to know what was going on.

"You hear that?" Janisette asked.

"Yes," Michael replied. "Like birds chirping." He was
climbing the tree now. Those women with pickneys started flitting away under cover of the shade. The rest stayed with the
men.

Michael was well on his way to the first branch. Too close for anybody else to get away. Tan-Tan crouched on the branch next to Chichibud, praying to any god she could think of that Michael wouldn't come no closer. She heard a soft *swips* from beside her. Chichibud had pulled his knife out of his belt. The other men did the same. The hinte-them had their beaks and claws to jab and tear. *Oh, Nanny; like more blood going to get shed for me.*

Michael squinted up into the darkness of the daddy tree leaves. Janisette called out:

"You see anything?"

"Not too good," he shouted back, frowning. Then his face went clear with astonishment. "But eh-eh! If you only see the size of the wasp nests it have up here, Gladys! Whatever live in there have to be almost as big as me!"

"Nanny save we!" Gladys exclaimed. "You must careful, you hear, doux-doux? I don't think you should go up any further. Suppose one of them sting you?"

"Only a little more, sweetness. I go mind myself."

He took two more steps up.

With a screech, a hinte launched herself right at his chest. Gladys screamed. Michael and the hinte plummeted to the ground, the hinte flapping her shrunken wings furiously. Michael landed with a thump. The hinte covering him was Taya, Benta's sister. "Taya!" shouted Kret. Taya held Michael down with one clawed foot, pecked viciously at his eyes. Michael was only screaming, holding up his arms-them to protect his face. Blood streamed down his forearms.

Fast as flight, Tan-Tan flung herself down the daddy tree trunk. "Taya! Stop it! Stop!"

As her foot touched the ground the air round her exploded, a concussion so strong is like somebody had clapped two hands against her ears. She turned towards the noise. Scraps of blood, bone and beak were fluttering in the bush round the daddy tree.

Gladys was standing up in the car, still looking through the sights of the rifle she had used to blow Taya to bits.

"Taya!" Kret hurled himself from the daddy tree to the ground to where Taya's severed head was lying, the beak still opening and shutting; reflex action as her brain died. Michael was curled up in terror on the ground like an unborn baby. Startled by all the movement, Gladys aimed the rifle first at Kret, then at Tan-Tan. Janisette pulled it out of her hands. "Don't shoot she. She coming back to Junjuh with we. I want to hear she voice bawling out of the tin box, getting weaker and weaker for days." Janisette brought her gaze like knives to bear on her stepdaughter Tan-Tan; cutting eyes on Tan-Tan's person, like if she moved too sudden they would slice her.

Squatting on his haunches, Kret picked up Taya's bloody head and mashed it to his chest, cawing Taya's name the whole time. The severed head's second eyelids rolled over its eyes. The beak stopped moving. Kret put the head down, gentle, gentle, like putting a baby in her bassinette for the night. In terrible swift silence he rushed across the clearing at Gladys; a deadly shadow brandishing a knife. Calm like slow water, Janisette sighted down the rifle and shot him. The gunclap thundered. More blood. More scraps of bone and tissue flying through the air.

"No, no, no! No more!" Tan-Tan shouted. Deafened by the sound of the rifle, she couldn't hear her own words. The acrid smell of gunpowder got up in her nose with the sweety-salt smell of douen blood. A rage came on her, a fire in she belly. She forgot fear, forgot reason. In two-three strides she was on Janisette. She snatched the rifle away and trained it on Janisette. Janisette's fearsome gaze never wavered. Uncertain, Tan-Tan dipped the nose of the rifle to the ground.

Her hearing was coming back. Behind her, Chichibud was saying, "You just hold still now, Mister Michael. It have more douen here than you want to tackle with." Tan-Tan glanced behind her. Michael cowered on the ground, surrounded by the sharp knives and beaks of douens.

Janisette said to Tan-Tan, "So is here you is. Playing in the trees with the monkeys. Murderess."

Sorrow ground down Tan-Tan's voice like river water does grind rockstone. "You know what he do to me? You know what my father been doing to me for the past seven years? I couldn't take it no more, Janisette!"

Janisette clenched her fists and leaned into Tan-Tan's face: "You think I ain't know? Slut! You woulda screw anything in sight, including your own father!"

Shock filled Tan-Tan's mouth up with bile. She started to shake. Janisette continued, "Is you drive he to it! You know what I had was to live with, knowing my own husband prefer he force-ripe, picky-head daughter to me? Eh?"

To Tan-Tan, is like she could feel Antonio's hands on her again, Antonio's mouth, Antonio inside her, tearing her up. She had to spit sour slime from her mouth before she could choke out, "Is not so it go, Janisette! Is not my fault! Daddy *hurt* me!" All she could think was to erase Janisette's words, to make sure she couldn't say them any more. She raised the rifle and aimed point blank at Janisette. The blank look of fright that came over Janisette's face was pure pleasure to Tan-Tan. With a surge of joy she pulled the trigger, *blam!* just as Chichibud's clawed hand forced the rifle down towards the ground. A spray of dirt and leaves blinded Tan-Tan. She went cold with horror at what she'd just done. She let go the rifle into Chichibud's hands. When her eyes cleared again Janisette was leaning against the side of the car, face grey with shock.

I just try to kill my stepmother. Is what kind of monster I is any at all?

"What a stupid-looking thing, only a tube with a handle," Chichibud said. There was a slight trill to his voice. He wasn't as calm as he sounded. "Who woulda think it could cause so much pain? What you call this, Tan-Tan?"

"Is a gun," she told him absent-mindedly. Suppose Chichibud hadn't pulled her hand away in time? "Mind you don't pull the trigger; you could shoot off your own foot." Gladys was returning to consciousness, struggling to her feet inside the car.

"And you point it and shoot it . . . so?" Chichibud aimed the gun at Michael where he was sitting.

Gladys shouted, "Don't shoot! Please, Mister Douen— don't shoot my husband!"

She didn't recognise Chichibud. She saw him almost every month when he brought goods to trade, and she still couldn't tell him different from any douen man. *But me any different?* Tan-Tan's mind fastened on the thought, rather than dealing on what was in front of her. *Sometimes me hard put too to tell he from the rest.*

"I can't shoot at he? Not even for practice?" Though without human intonation, Chichibud made shift to sound regretful, ironic. "You don't think when I bring this . . . gun to we ironsmith, I should be able to tell him how it work?"

"I beg you, mister, I go do anything, only don't kill he."

"And if I had beg allyou same way not to kill my people, what you woulda say?"

He sighted down the barrel of the gun. Michael looked Chichibud straight in the eye, put his chin in the air, and just waited. Nothing else for him to do, Tan-Tan realised. The douens were in charge of the situation now—Chichibud and she and the rest of them.

"Chichibud, let them get in the car," she said. She heard a sharp breath in from Gladys:

"Rahtid! Is Chichibud that?"

Tan-Tan watched Michael climb in. Janisette seemed to have recovered from the shock. She stood glaring at Tan-Tan until the other two pulled her into the autocar. Tan-Tan told the hunting party: "Leave these people in peace and go your ways. You don't have no quarrel with them. As for me, I tell you; I do what I do in self defense." *Liard! You kill he in cold blood!* She shook her head a little to dispel the voice. "Leave me in peace, I going to a settlement where Junjuh laws can't entrap me."

Chichibud still had the gun trained on Michael. Michael started up the car. It failed twice, started the third time with noxious poops of black air. With much yanking at the steering wheel he turned it round. Janisette pointed a threatening finger at Tan-Tan. "One day I go find you lying slutting self when it won't have no leggobushbeasts to protect you," she promised. "Then I bringing you back to Junjuh to roast like chicken in the box." They left, the car farting every few metres of the way.

The douens watched until they were good and gone. Oddly, Tan-Tan wished she could have asked after Melonhead.

The hinte and some of the adolescents that had fled were starting to return, having left the children safely in the high branches of the daddy tree. Benta's grief at her sister's death filled the skies. It tore at Tan-Tan's heart.

"I have to leave oonuh and go," Tan-Tan said to Chichibud.

"How them know to find you here?" he asked.

Don't make no difference, now them know is where we is, warbled a douen woman. ***Best allyou men had listened to we and never fast up yourself in tallpeople business.***

Chichibud lowered the gun. He dropped his arms to his sides and said nothing. ***Because you help that girl child,*** the woman continued, ***them will bring more tallpeople back here to hunt we down. Them will fight we with more of them gun and thing. We ain't go have no peace from tallpeople again!***

Chichibud said sadly, "How them know, Tan-Tan?" She couldn't meet his gaze. "Oh, girl child," he continued, "the time had to come when tallpeople come into the bush to look for we, but I ain't know was going to be my actions that bring it."

"But you could fight!" Tan-Tan told him.

The hinte replied, *We could fight, yes, but allyou tallpeople mad like hell. I think plenty of we would dead in that fight, and allyou would win.*

She couldn't stand it, she couldn't take it. Everywhere she went she brought trouble, carrying it like a burden on her back.

From behind Chichibud, the old douen Res growled out something in their language. Chichibud whipped round and chirped out a response. From his movements Tan-Tan recognised that he was amazed at what he'd heard, and he wasn't the only one. Man and woman, the other douens gathered round Res, screeching and chirruping at him. Res tried to answer back. He couldn't make himself heard. The douens were cawing and crowing at their elder. The women beat their wings in distress. A couple of the adolescents started to cry, that *uhu-uhu* sound that Tan-Tan had heard Zake make earlier. Even Abitefa was in the middle of the discussion, clicking her claws together in alarm. Res just held his ground, responded calm-calm.

Tan-Tan touched Chichibud's shoulder. "What he saying?"

"He say we don't have to make no more tallpeople find we."

Hope was like a bird in Tan-Tan's throat. "How?"

"We have to destroy we home and move away."

"What, your houses?"

Chichibud didn't answer, just went and huddled with his family. The argument with Res continued, but in the end they all agreed with him: they would cut down the daddy tree.

All the rest of that day, everybody stripped their houses and made small packs of the things they would need most, only what they could carry on their backs. Benta's eyes on Tan-Tan were cold like duppy heart and sad, so sad. Finally, everyone's goods were packed up inside the foundry for them to pick up once the tree had been chopped down.

Benta waddled over to Tan-Tan. Tan-Tan looked at her warily, sorrowfully. *Taya gone. We hatch from one shell, and she gone.*

"Benta, I sorry too bad!"

Is not you make the gun, is not you fire the gun. But is your actions bring she to this path, so is good you sorry. She squatted back on her heels, looked up at the daddy tree. *This work going to take we all night,* she said. *You stay here in the foundry, out from under the shadow of the daddy tree.*

"What I could do?"

Help mind the babies.

Which she would have done, if they had let her. The douens had set up the foundry as a nursery for all the pickney-them, with the adolescents and the old people to look after them. But every time Tan-Tan moved towards a child, someone would sweep it out of her reach. Finally a douen man being harried by four pickneys of varying size thrust the youngest one into a startled Tan-Tan's hands. The baby instinctively wrapped his toes round one of her arms and tangled his fingers in her hair. "I feed he already, he should sleep now. I have to go and help them chop. Somebody else will look after these three. Mind he good."

She would mind he like her life itself, she was so grateful to be trusted. She sat down on an anvil to rock the baby. He curled up his free hand into a fist on his chest and started to drop off to sleep one time. He didn't look as ugly to her as when she had first set eyes on douen pickneys.

A chopping sound was coming from up high in the daddy tree. Still rocking the baby, she went and stood in the door of the forge. In the dusk, she couldn't see through the branches of the daddy tree, but she could hear. Up at the top of the tree, the douens were hacking away at its trunks. It was a shocking sound. With loud cracking noises, the tops of the tree broke off in rapid succession, letting in the dying light. All the douen women were in the air, circling, circling. Quick-quick, teams of them grabbed branches in their talons, tugged at them until they came away from the tree. The hinte flew away beyond her sight.

The noise had startled the baby awake. He whined, "Uhu, uhu," little ratbat face wrinkled up in distress.

"Shh," Tan-Tan whispered, rocking him. She sang, "Captain, Captain, put me ashore / I don't want to go any more." Then she clamped her mouth shut. Not that song. She stroked the baby's forehead with a fingertip instead, like she'd seen the douens doing. He calmed down little bit. Tan-Tan stared out at the let-in sky. Benta had told her that the hinte would take the tree piece by piece to the sea and drop it in. She had never seen the sea on New Half-Way Tree, never thought to wonder what its oceans were like. Keeping body and soul together kept tallpeople too busy to think of exploring.

Another level of daddy tree was taken away. Thick brown sap was welling up out of the chopped-off trunks. It dropped in gouts to the forest floor. The rest of the hinte kept circling, circling.

The team of douen men with axes climbed down a next level and started chopping again. This level had some douen houses in it; the men just left them there so. Their owners had already abandoned them. Wasp nest houses. Tan-Tan had scorned them when she'd first seen them. Now, she would give anything to be safe back in Benta and Chichibud's house; anything for the douens not to have to do this thing.

The men chopped and chopped till they cracked off a next section of the daddy tree. Another team of douen women made off with it, heading seawards. And is so it went, level after level, until all that was left was the big stumps and buttress roots of the daddy tree. It had sticky sap all over the forest floor, and shards of douen houses.

It had a mako big hole in the bush canopy in the place where the daddy tree crowns used to be. Tan-Tan looked up at the cerulean blue of the evening sky. *Is you do this, you worthless one; is you let the sky into the bush like this.*

All through the new-made clearing the douen people gathered in circles round the weeping stumps of what used to be their daddy tree—waiting, waiting. Some of them had lit their lanterns already. Lantern light, sky light; when last had this part of the bush been so illuminated?

Finally the last team of douen women had flown back from the sea. They fluttered down to join the rest of the village in the circles. Benta started to rock from foot to foot. Everybody followed suit. Res began a chant deep in his throat, a wail that resembled a douen baby crying. Tan-Tan caught the words for "home" and "food" and "thank you." The wail got louder. So a child would lament a dead parent. Other douens joined in, some chanting low and passionately like Res, some screaming, ululating, crying. They keened their loss to the sky. Each one was thanking the daddy tree for sheltering them, mourning its loss. The sound filled up the air, pierced into Tan-Tan's ears like knives, beat against her body like fists and slaps. The baby she was holding woke up crying again. She let him go on this time. Now is the time for him to bawl. Tan-Tan felt say she didn't have any right to be part of their mourning, but the tree had held her in its arms too. Quietly she whispered, "Thanks. I so, so sorry. Thanks."

Slowly the douen wail died down, leaving only the children still sobbing. Next thing Tan-Tan knew, Res pulled out his pissle from his genital flap and peed on the stump in front of him—a green, thick piss that curdled the raw wood wherever it landed. The rest of the douen men did the same, wherever they were standing. The daddy tree stumps were dissolving!

"Papa God!" Tan-Tan exclaimed. "Is what them doing?"

Burying the daddy tree, Abitefa explained. Her words-them were mushy, for her teeth were falling out as her mouth grew into a beak. Tan-Tan had to strain to understand her.

I never see this before, I only hear about it, Abitefa continued. *Them making the burning water. It go hide the old tree and help the new tree grow in faster.*

"So then how them does piss without melting down the whole place all the time?" she asked. Kret could have burned off her leg that day!

Them body water don't always burn, only when them wish it to. What Kret do you, he wasn't supposed to do.

"And how it is that no boys ain't there helping them?"

Too young. Boys can't make the burning water yet, them have to turn man first.

Tan-Tan clicked her tongue in wonder. "And we does say a man not a man until he old enough for he pee to make froth."

The light of day was almost gone. The men finished their job. All that was left of the daddy tree was a green soup, smelling like ammonia and blood. It made a rank mud on the forest floor. Picking his way carefully round the redolent pools, Chichibud hopped over to his family. Tan-Tan had known him from she was a small pickney. She knew how to read his emotions in his body language. She'd never seen him sadder than this night. But all he said when he reached to them was, "All-you have any of the tree sap on you? On your foot bottom, anywhere? Wipe it off careful with dead leaf. Don't touch it! Throw the leaf-them down here so then let we get out of the way. The little teeth coming any minute now; the smell of the sap does call them."

Little teeth? Tan-Tan gave the baby back to its father. She made haste and obeyed Chichibud. All round her douen people were wiping any trace of sap off themselves and moving briskly out of the clearing into the tree cover. They clustered together.

Nine-ten of the douens dipped some long sticks in the sap and piss soup and made a trail out of the clearing, away from where the rest of the village was standing. Tan-Tan went to stand with Chichibud and them.

We safe upwind. We could watch from here, Benta said. With her beak she gently pulled Abitefa to her, tucked the young douen woman beneath her breast. Abitefa hunkered down into a ball, warm against the deep keel of her mother's body.

One-one, more light from lanterns sprang up in the darkness; bouncing, disembodied glows. Tan-Tan remembered the douen myth from back home, about how people could be drawn into the bush by douen lights and the sound of their voices, going deeper and deeper until they were lost for good. And Tan-Tan knew she was lost for true, so far away from herself that she couldn't know how to come back.

Nobody spoke. What was going to happen? Tan-Tan asked Chichibud what they were waiting for, but a voice from out of the darkness said in a deliberate, contemptuous Anglopatwa, "Chichibud, hush that tallpeople up, you hear? None of we want to hear she voice tonight." Pressed down with shame, Tan-Tan clamped her lips together.

A hissing sound was coming from the darkness beyond them; a hissing that turned into a rustling that became a chittering then a crunching. A bright red wave poured into the cleared space where the daddy tree had been. From the lantern light Tan-Tan could see a gleam here and there of a thousand thousand shiny carapaces: the little teeth. The wave moved closer. Tan-Tan strained to see. They looked like lobsters, an army of scavengers each the size of her hand, climbing over one another in their eagerness to get to the mixture of daddy tree sap and piss. The noise was their feet running, climbing over anything in their way, even their compères. The noise was their mandibles; cutting and biting, tearing up anything that had sap on it and bearing it away: pieces of wattle and daub; daddy tree leaves and branches that had been left behind; a scrap of some hinte weaving; a leg ripped off one of their own; anything, anything. And so them tear it up, is so them eat it.

Tan-Tan felt a whimper in her throat but she couldn't hear herself over the noise of the little teeth feeding. She shrank away from the sight in the clearing and leaned up against Benta's side. She heard an animal scream; the little teeth were taking down a mammal that had been foraging in the clearing and had probably gotten some sap on its feet. The beast was the size of a small dog, but the little teeth bore it down to the ground with the sheer weight of their piled bodies. Tan-Tan couldn't take her eyes off the roiling mass that hid the beast. It stopped screaming. Seconds later the little teeth that had attacked it were moving on again. Only gnawed bones were left.

And quick as it start, it finish. The little teeth gobbled up everything in their way, followed the trails of sap out of the clearing, and disappeared into the night bush. The ground in the clearing was bare, but for the bones of creatures that had been caught in their path.

"The little teeth does leave nothing behind but them guano," Chichibud said. Is true; in the lamplight Tan-Tan could see the droppings everywhere, little pellets littering the clearing. And then the most astonishing thing of the whole night; as Tan-Tan watched, shoots started to push up through the ground, growing right before her eyes!

"Koo ya!" she gasped: *Look at that!*

Chichibud told her, "Is the little teeth guano doing it. When them eat the sap mixed with we burning water, them guano does cause things to grow fast-fast-fast for a few hours. By tomorrow morning, it ain't go have no clearing here, just a young new daddy tree. Anybody come looking for we might find we foundry in the middle of all this bush, but it go be just a empty, break-down building. No daddy tree. No douens to hunt. We gone."

Chichibud turned to Abitefa and Tan-Tan. "And you two can't come with we." The words beat at Tan-Tan's ears like Carnival bottle-and-spoon.

"What? Is what you a-say?"

Abitefa cried out. Trembling, she tried to bury herself deeper under her mother's body. Chichibud warbled at her, took a step towards her, but Res barked out something and Chichibud drew back. Benta nuzzled her, then stepped away. The ring of douen lights moved away from where Tan-Tan and Abitefa were, pulled closer together farther back in the bush.

They couldn't mean it! "Chichibud," Tan-Tan asked again, "what you telling we?"

"My job to tell you, for is me bring this misfortune. Is so we does do things, Tan-Tan. You cause harm to the whole community, cause the daddy tree to dead. Abitefa aid you by helping you find Chigger Bite. She shoulda been keeping we secrets, not you own. The two of you too dangerous to carry with we. You going to have to make your own way somehow."

In frenzied silence Abitefa was plucking out her new feathers, one by one.

The new daddy tree was man-height now, its treetop beginning to knit together. Its growth had slowed, was no longer perceptible to the eye.

All round Tan-Tan and Abitefa, douens were sniffing one another's skin in the way they did for hello and goodbye. They were splitting up into groups, going separate ways. Other daddy trees would take them in. They all knew how to live off the bush; no need to carry much in the way of provisions. Instead everyone was packing what they treasured most: a douen man was squatting on the ground, repacking a wood box full

of ironworking tools; a hinte went by with what looked like
two tallpeople books in her beak—she must have learned written patwa. Tan-Tan wondered what she made of the alien
worlds described in the pages. "Abitefa," she asked timidly,
"what you taking with you?"

The young woman seemed to have recovered a little from
her shock. She opened a pouch round her neck and showed
Tan-Tan some pieces of what looked like wrinkled hide, thick
as orange rind.

***The shell I hatch from. When I mate, my partner go carry
piece in he genital pouch. My first chick go have a anklet from the
rest.***

Tan-Tan's belly felt like it was full up of ice. How was Tefa
going to find a mate if she was exiled from her people? *Is you
do this, mash up another life.*

Chichibud came over to them. He extended something to
Tan-Tan: her sixteenth birthday present from Janisette.

"Me nah want it!" The leather scabbard was well-oiled.
Chichibud slid the knife partially out so that she could see how
he'd kept its edge clean.

"Is a gift, you must think before you throw those away," he
told her. "You go need it now, the one machète not enough. It
could lose, or break. This knife get you out of danger once,
remember?"

"It kill Daddy!" *Is you kill Daddy.*

"Yes, it had a cost. Present that could cut will cut. And
sometimes the tree need to prune, oui? Take it."

She reached out and touched it, shut her eyes against the
memories that came with it. That only made them clearer. She
opened her eyes again, took the knife from Chichibud, fastened
it in its scabbard round her waist, beside her machète. She had
to sling it low round the tummy pot she'd developed. The flesh
touched by the scabbard crawled.

"Doux-doux, I sorry too bad it come to this. Maybe your people and mine not meant to walk together, oui."

But still is your ratbat pickney you leave me with. "Is all right, Chichibud. I going find a settlement I could stand to live in. Them can't all be rough like Junjuh, right?"

"A next daddy tree will take Abitefa in. We will find she again. But I tell she not to leave you until you settled." He hadn't answered her question.

He turned to walk away. They were really leaving her and Tefa here in the bush! Tan-Tan ran to Chichibud and Benta. Tefa beat her to it at a hop, nibbled at Zake's neck and huddled with her family. Benta cocked an eye at Tan-Tan, lifted one wing. *Come.* And for the final time, Tan-Tan leaned against Benta's warm side, submitted to Benta grooming her jungly dreadlocks. Then Res snapped out an order and she and Tefa had to separate from the rest again.

Clusters of douens were abandoning the place: by air; on foot. Tan-Tan and Abitefa crouched together on a boulderstone and watched them leave, group by group. They were all gone by the time the sun had risen. The new daddy tree was some two metres tall. Tefa stood, stretched her arm/wings. *Time to leave here before those tallpeople come back with their killing things.*

You must understand, my darling: Abitefa and Tan-Tan was practically children they own self. They know plenty about how to survive in the bush alone, but not everything. Before too long, the two of them did living in misery: not enough to eat, the rain and dew keep coming in on them through the grass thatch Abitefa weave, and the fire only going out all the time. Them have chigger worms digging into them foot. Abitefa had a sore on she toe that wouldn't heal, from where a ground puppy had bite she one night when she wasn't careful where she step. Abitefa was doing all right for food, but Tan-Tan was only eating raw mushroom and whatever fruits she could find, for that she didn't have to bother to make a fire for. She start to weaken on the poor diet. She belly was running all the time.

"We can't go on like this," she tell Abitefa. "Every time the fire go out, I frighten mako jumbie go come and hold we. We need some lamps and some kerosene. We need grain alcohol to put on your foot, and a shovel to dig a good fire pit, and a axe to cut wood. Too besides, I could kill for some roast gully hen, oui!"

Tan-Tan convince Tefa to come with she closer to where tall-people living. "Just for a little while. Just until we scavenge what we need." That is how them find themselves in the bush outside the settlement named Begorrat.

Tan-Tan didn't recognise the food crop growing in the fields that circled Begorrat. It was tall with long, scratchy leaves like corn, but the segmented stems were thick as her wrist, bowed with their own weight. She elbowed through it, trying to keep the leaves from touching any exposed skin. She stepped out from between the planted rows right into the path of a young woman about her own age. Her heart fired like a cap gun. "Pardon, Compère."

The young woman smiled a tired, friendly smile and stayed where she was, centred and calm. Her brown eyes twinkled, matching the red highlights in the drizzled, unruly hair. Two of her front teeth were cracked. "You have to be careful, eh? Don't make Boss catch you pissing in the cane."

Boss? That was a word for machine servants to use, not people. "How you mean?"

"You miss lunch. You want some of mine?" She held out a burnt bammy with a bite out of it. "I does take longer to eat, because of the teeth, you know."

Tan-Tan tore off a bite of the sticky cake of grated cassava. Somebody had soaked it in gravy to soften it before cooking it on the tawa griddle. The outside was overcooked and the inside was hard, but after weeks of cold food with grit in it, the still-warm bammy was glorious. "Thank you."

"Piss does burn the cane roots," the woman said. Tearing awkwardly with one side of her mouth, she took a bite of her lunch, chewed it cautiously. She made a small noise of pain, stopped chewing. "Can't eat too good now since Boss lick me in my mouth that time." She resumed eating. "Me know one-one dead cane not plenty, but me does do it too. Me figure every one me kill is one less me have to cut, seen?" Her conspiratorial grin was warming, her face beautiful, even deformed round the lump of bammy she was trying to consume. Her look appraised, approved what it saw. Tan-Tan grinned back, dashing away a fleeting image of bandy legs in khaki shorts, a head too big for the strong, wiry body it topped.

"Cane, you call this? Why oonuh want it to dead?"

A triple whistle blast echoed out over the cane field. The woman turned to look over her shoulder, never moving from the spot where she'd chosen to stand. "Time to get back to work. Me will have to finish eat this as me chop." She stuffed the bammy into a pouch at her waist. "From I get send to this New Half-Way Tree, me never could learn all you have to do to survive without Nanny, oui? This way, me chop little piece of cane, and mind what Boss say, and me get shelter for me head and food for me body. Some of we saving up we earnings until we could do better, but me ain't able fight up myself more than so. Where you from, that you don't know what it is to be indentured?"

Indentured. A word from her history lessons. "Is what; somebody making allyou work like this?"

A deep, rumbling woman's voice was ordering people back to work, calling them lazy, willful. The young woman took Tan-Tan's two hands urgently, held them hard. The warm touch was startling. Tan-Tan gripped the human hands that held hers. The woman looked earnestly into Tan-Tan's face. "Prettiness, me nah know where you come from, but if you have it better there, best you get your fine behind out of this Begorrat Town. For me, this place is my best chance for a stable life."

Tan-Tan was only half-listening. The woman's mouth was plump, shiny with bammy grease.

Over her shoulder the woman yelled, "Coming, Boss, I coming!" She turned and shambled away. She was dragging one leg; it was hampered by a ball and chain. It had been hidden in the short grass. Gooseflesh rose on the back of Tan-Tan's neck. She pelted back through the long cane, oblivious of it nicking her skin, to the freedom of the bush.

All night as she shivered in the chill and dark next to Abitefa her inner voice berated her. What kind of Robber Queen was she, that she just turned tail and ran from real evil?

In Corbeau she traded her mother's ring for three lanterns, oil, matches, grain alcohol, an axe, five kilos of flour and two chickens. She watched the last evidence of Ione's existence disappear into the shopkeeper's apron. She gave half the flour and one of the chickens to a wizened family living in a shanty beside the trash heap; it was too much to carry, anyway. "Make soup and dumplings," she told them. "It will stretch for all six of all-you." The father asked her her name. "Robber Queen," she told him, before heading back into the bush. Tefa hissed at the way the alcohol burned her toe, but her sore dried up overnight.

In Babylon A-Fall Tan-Tan stayed a week, having two specially thick blankets woven in return for some manicou she trapped, killed and smoked. She cursed herself for having given away Ione's ring when she could have used her survival skills to produce goods like smoked manicou to trade.

She liked Babylon A-Fall. They had no tin box torture. She would go back and tell Abitefa she would stay here. On the day her blankets were ready, she collected them and was going to speak with a woman who had a room she would let. She saw a new headblind exile about to step into the town well. She shoved him out of danger, and got an earful of obscenity for her trouble. And one of her blankets fell into the water. As she was dragging it out of the well, she heard a familiar *phut-phut-phut*. Open road, nowhere else to hide. She jumped into the well, hung on by her fingers to its edge. Her blanket landed soundlessly again in the water below.

The sound came closer, moved past her. Tan-Tan poked her head out of the well. Janisette had found her. Her stepmother was alone. She was driving a jeep this time, obviously made of parts that Gladys and Michael had stripped from the autocar. The jeep was heavier, rode smoother. There was no bleating from its engine.

There came a screech of brakes, the sound of Janisette cursing. Then to Tan-Tan's dismay, she heard the jeep returning. Biceps burning, she lowered herself into the well to the extent of her arms. The weight of the baby pulled at her, made the tendons in her groin cramp. Her feet paddled in the ice-cold water. The jeep stopped. Tan-Tan could feel the rough brick of the well's edge scraping the pads of her fingers. Her boots were filling with frigid water, making her shiver. How deep was the well? Her arms screamed for her to let go, just let go. She could swim, ain't? She would be all right? But she held on. She could see the muscles of her arms twitching involuntarily. Her feet were blessedly numb now, but the weight of the water in her boots was an extra drag. Her fingers were beginning to slip. The babyweight was dragging her down. Soon only her fingertips held her.

Janisette made an impatient noise. "Cho. After is here them tell me I could find she." The jeep started up again, *phut-phut-phut*ted its way away.

Gasping with the pain in her abused arms, Tan-Tan scrabbled with her feet against the sides of the well until she found purchase on its uneven bricks. She worked her thighs apart to make room for her bellybulge, braced her feet and her back against the sides of the well. Slowly, by pushing with her thighs and arching her back, she levered herself up. Eventually she was able to roll out onto the ground, much to the shock of two little girls who had come with their bucket for water. They stood wide-eyed and watched her. "Careful there," she told them. "Mind you fall in."

Her arms wouldn't work to push her upright. They trembled and ached. Tan-Tan rocked to her knees, then her feet, wept with the effort of tossing the remaining blanket over her shoulders. She smiled her brightest smile at the little girls. They stared solemnly. She hiked back to Abitefa and the safety of the bush. She couldn't make a home in tallpeople lands. Janisette would follow the trail that gossip about her laid, hunt her out wherever she was. She should stay away from settlements altogether, but sometimes she just longed for tallpeople faces.

In Poor Man Pork she had the remaining blanket made into a cape to hide her seven-month belly. Hard living in the bush had made her so lean, the bulge didn't show if she wore bulky clothes. But it was getting bigger.

The seamstress tried to substitute a cheaper fabric for the one Tan-Tan had given her. So Tan-Tan stood over her while she sewed. She pilfered every single candle the woman had in the place, tucked them into her carry pouch. When her cape was done she paid for it and took it away. She had supper in a rum shop, etched "Tan-Tan the Robber Queen" with her knife point into the longest candle. She made sure to leave just as the sun was beginning to think about going down. She meandered through town until she found a house that was in darkness. She put the candles down on the front step, rapped smartly on the door, and ran away, cape flaring behind her.

She began to notice little girls playing at Robber Queen in the settlements.

•   •   •

You feeling pressure, eh doux-doux? Don't worry, that normal. Not too much longer, promise you. Then a whole new life going to start for you.

No, don't fight it so, relax. Or it does hurt more. Yes, relax. And make I continue, the story will take your mind off it.

So. Little time after she start up she escapades regular in the New Half-Way Tree settlements, Tan-Tan start to hear back the first anansi stories 'bout sheself. I think you going to like this one, sweetness. Is the only one Tan-Tan would sometimes repeat sheself:

Tan-Tan and the Rolling Calf

One time, Tan-Tan was on the run again, oui, barely ahead of the bounty hunters. She did just done kill a man; a pimp who used to specialize in young young girls, and a pusher too besides. Truth to tell, nobody on New Half-Way Tree was sorry he dead, but murder was murder, and Tan-Tan had to pay. So she run. She bind up she locks so nobody could recognise she, and she head for the bush, like always when she in trouble. She hike for hours, until she was far, far from home, and tired. Night was coming on, but Resurrection Town was just over the next mountain. It had a woman there named Pearl who would feed she and hide she for the night. So Tan-Tan head up the mountain path, dragging she feet with tiredness, but keeping she eyes open for trouble.

It had a nice evening breeze blowing soft through the trees beside the path. Is the same song the breeze used to sing in the trees on Toussaint planet, when Tan-Tan was a little gal pickney. Walking along, she almost forget she was a exile on New Half-Way Tree with a curse on she head from the douens-them: every time she take from somebody, she had was to give back twice as much to a next somebody. But she couldn't really forget the curse, nuh? All like how she just take a life, she was going to have to save two more, just to even up. Tan-Tan could hear the whispering of the douens starting up in she head again:

> *It ain't have no magic in do-for-do,*
> *If you take one, you must give back two.*

Tan-Tan sigh and keep walking. Up ahead, she spy a form in the dark, someone hurrying to get home; a woman in long skirts. The woman was walking fast-fast, she shoulders all scrunch up together. She looking from side to side into the bush every minute, as though she could see trouble before it reach, oui? A tree frog shout "Breck-eck!" into the night, and the woman jump like jumbie on she tail, and start to make haste even faster. Tan-Tan see a chance to do somebody good, and quiet down some of the whispering in she head. She shout:

"Evening, sister: is home you going?" The woman cry out, "Lawd ha' mercy!" and whip round to see who coming up behind she.

Tan-Tan say, "Don't frighten, lady, don't frighten. I just going over the mountain, past Resurrection Town to Juncanoo. I going to spend some time with my old grannie; she ain't too strong any more, oui."

As Tan-Tan get closer, she could see the woman shoulders relax, but she voice still tremble when she reply, "Thanks God, you is a honest woman. Bounty hunters tell we Tan-Tan round the place, and I frighten to walk this lonely road by myself so late at night. I stay too late in the market. I 'fraid Tan-Tan hold me and cut me throat like hog!"

Tan-Tan smile to hear somebody call she a honest woman. "Is alright, lady, I could walk a little way with you to keep you company. Is where you going?"

Sadie was going to Basse-Terre, a village beside Resurrection Town. Tan-Tan agree to walk with she until the path fork at the bottom of the hill. As they walk, they talk about things: how ackee dear in the market now with the drought; and what a sad thing it was for a woman to turn outlaw and have she heart so hard like the Robber Queen Tan-Tan; and what a way pickney-child wouldn't mind their elders nowadays. Little-little, Sadie start to laugh and joke with she like them was old friend. It was hard work for Tan-Tan; long time since she just make old-talk. Sadie almost catch she out when she ask, "And what about you, my dear? You think your nen-nen going to get well again?"

Which nen-nen? Tan-Tan almost answer, but she remember she story in time: "I ain't know. She old now, you see. Every time she get sick like this, she never come back as strong as before." Tan-Tan bow she head to shake it in pretend sadness over she pretend nen-nen.

That is when she see a shadow shifting right where Sadie was about to step. Tan-Tan yell out, "Mind you foot!" but too late: Sadie step down hard; the shadow yelp; Sadie scream "Oh God oh God!" and jump back behind Tan-Tan. Tan-Tan make haste and pull out she machète, but when she look good at the shadow, she only start one set of laughing. It ain't nothing but a small beast, cringing on the ground in front of the two women, growling a baby growl and waving a tiny tail back and forth in the dust on the path. Tan-Tan re-sheathe she machète and bend down to pick up the beast. She show it to Sadie:

"Don't 'fraid, Sadie; is just a rolling calf baby. See, the tail spikes too small to have any poison yet. It can't hurt you."

"Jeezam," Sadie say, coming closer to get a better look, "you ain't frighten it bite you?"

"Nah, man. Is only the big ones you have to watch out for. Them miserable, will mash you just for so. This one going to be big like a bull calf for true, and the four legs going to have some wicked claws. And you see these tiny scales all over the body? They going to get thick and hard, like leather armour. Let we leave it right here. It will find itself back home when it ready." She put the baby back down on the path, and the two women start to walk again.

Well, doux-doux, Sadie couldn't get over what just happen; she start to chat like she mouth is a pot with no kibber. "Lord, anybody see my crosses? I just walking down the road, minding my own business, when one wild beast nuh try to bite off my foot? I tell you, missis, I don't know what I woulda do if you wasn't here to help me! Jeezam!" Tan-Tan try to tell she rolling calf does only eat bush, but Sadie carry on so till Tan-Tan couldn't take the noise no more. She start to walk a little ahead, trying to leave some of the jibber-jabber. And Sadie scream again. Tan-Tan turn round, just in time to see one big mako something rush at Sadie and slam she to the ground. Rolling calf! Big one this time! *The mother come to protect she baby,* Tan-Tan think as she fetch out she machète again and run to help Sadie. The rattle of the rolling calf tail remind she that she shouldn't get too close; the spikes in the tail could kill she easy. Tan-Tan jump back; the massive tail just miss she. In the dark, she could barely make out Sadie, twisting round under the beast, trying to get away from the snapping jaws.

"Sadie! I coming, gal!" Tan-Tan fetch one blow to the rolling calf tail with she machète. The spikes went flying off. The beast scream and left Sadie to come after Tan-Tan. She couldn't see it good in the night, but she could smell it. Yeasty breath, like bread dough a-spoil. Rolling calf-them does have they snout full of grinding plates, and sharp eyes, for the half-way tree jungle dark like the Blackheart man soul. Them have hard scales all over the body. When them move fast, the scales and the tail spikes does rattle. That is why the first colonists did name the animal "rolling calf"; the rattling noise remind them of the scary anansi stories they grannies tell about the Rolling Calf, a jumbie bull calf all wrap up in chains, with eyes of fire, that does chase people travelling alone at night.

The rolling calf lunge and snap at Tan-Tan. It catch she by she sleeve, and she had was to tear it free. "Ai!" She leave some of the flesh of she arm in the rolling calf jaws. Tan-Tan could hear Sadie sobbing on the ground, and praying steady steady, but she couldn't mind that; the beast swipe she with it injured tail and send she slamming down. The fall knock out all she wind. She try to roll away, but the rolling calf grab she foot. She feel the bite of it grinding plates scraping down she leg nearly to the bone. She scream and she jerk the foot away, but she shoe leave behind in the rolling calf mouth. *Don't tell me I go dead right here tonight,* Tan-Tan think. She had was to move fast; the way to kill a rolling calf was to stab up through the brain, but she only had one chance. If she miss and it trample she, she would dead anyway. The rolling calf haul back to lunge again; Tan-Tan roll to she knees under the snapping jaws. With two hands, she drive the machète upwards, praying she hit brain. She feel the machète shudder. Rolling calf blood start to spray from the wound, all over she hands, and the beast crash down right on top of she. The blow almost knock she senseless. She couldn't move. She hear Sadie cry out, "Lady, you alright? Oh God, lady, don't dead!"

"I ain't dead, Sadie. Help me, nuh?"

Sadie limp over and drag Tan-Tan out, crying the whole time, and calling on God to save they life. Tan-Tan didn't mind. She let Sadie rip up she kerchief to wipe off the rolling calf blood and bind up she foot. It feel nice to have somebody fretting over she. Sadie had was to help Tan-Tan stand up, for she still bassourdie from the blows she catch, but they couldn't stay there. Tan-Tan drag she machète out of the carcass, and use it to pry out she shoe from the jaws. The shoe was slimy when she put it back on. Tan-Tan give Sadie a shaky smile:

"But look at the two of we, eh? My foot chew up, your bodice rip, both of we cover in bruises, and is where the hell your market basket gone to?" They find where the basket did drop when the rolling calf attack. Most of the goods was still inside, though all but three of the eggs break. They start walking again, with Tan-Tan leaning on Sadie shoulder to ease the pain in she foot (when was the last time she trust anybody so?) Sadie only carrying on about how they almost dead, but Tan-Tan let she talk; it was the voice of a friend.

By now, they was heading downhill, and them reach a fork in the path. On the right hand was the lights of Resurrection Town. On the left hand, Tan-Tan could see Basse-Terre. Tan-Tan stop and stand up by sheself, but Sadie didn't want she to go.

"Lady," she say, "words alone can't thank you; you save my life this night! My home not far; you want to come? You could spend tonight with we."

Tan-Tan was dog-tired. She couldn't make Sadie know who she was. All she want was to be in Resurrection Town, where she could speak she name and be welcome, and rest she head for one night. "No, thank you, darling. My grannie waiting in Juncanoo, and I don't want to leave she alone tonight."

"Alright, I understand, but I will come and visit you while you there. Lemme give you a little something to go with, nuh? I still have some nice naseberry from the market." Sadie reach into she basket to give Tan-Tan the fruit, but Tan-Tan decide to end the masquerade right there. She couldn't make Sadie come looking for she. She reach up and dash she scarf from she head, and the dreadlocks tumble down she shoulders, black like eels in river water. Sadie gasp and drop the two naseberry-them. Them split open on the path. The black seeds remind Tan-Tan of the eyes of the douens; all dark with no centre. She say to Sadie:

"You could stop calling me 'lady': I name Tan-Tan! Go your ways in peace, darling, and let me go mine. Tell the people in Basse-Terre that is Tan-Tan save your life this night."

"Oh, God, oh God: I going! Don't hurt me, nice lady, Devil Lady, do . . ." Sadie turn and run off down the hill, looking back every minute to make sure Tan-Tan wasn't following. Tan-Tan watch she run. She feel a sadness weighing she down; she alone in the night again. She turn down the fork towards Resurrection Town, but before she get far, the whispering start in she head again:

No obeah there in do-for-do,
If you take one, you must give back two.

"Oh, God, oonuh leave me alone, nuh? I already save one life tonight, and I tired! Let me rest a little? Please?" But the voices in she head only saying, *not one, but two* . . . Tan-Tan drop to she knees on the path, sobbing with fatigue. *Two . . . two . . . two . . .* Finally, she get up again, and limp back along the path. As she reach the carcass of the dead rolling calf, she hear something whimpering in the dark. The rolling calf baby was huddling against the mother dead body, crying for she. When it see Tan-Tan, it start to hiss and snarl.

"Oho," Tan-Tan say to the baby, "if I leave you here, mongoose bound to eat you before morning come." She pick up the baby. It try to snap at she, and the tail swipe she in she face.

"You little bit, but you tallawah," Tan-Tan say with a smile. She tuck the baby under she arm, where the tail couldn't do no harm, and start off again, humming a tune to calm the rolling calf baby. It kick and fight and scratch up Tan-Tan two arms-them, but it was company. Finally, it get tired and fall asleep, just as they reach Resurrection

Town. It was almost 'fore-day morning. Tan-Tan was the only one out on the streets. She make she way towards Pearl house, with the rolling calf baby getting heavy in she tired arms. The douen voices in she head was quiet for now, but how the ass to convince Pearl to let she keep a wild animal in she clean house for the night?

A rumbling noise woke Tan-Tan. Exhausted, she peeked out from sleep, blew one of Tefa's breast feathers out of her face. The piteous rumbling came again. Tan-Tan struggled to her knees, leaned over the side of the nest. Yes, the rolling calf pup had overnight eaten every leaf in a six-metre circle round where her leash was tethered, and was demanding breakfast. In the weeks since Tan-Tan and Tefa had been looking after the pup, she had grown quickly, now stood nearly as high as Tan-Tan's hip. The chain that held her was stretched taut. She was leaning towards a patch of shoots that was just out of reach, mouthing her flexible beak at it and crying for help.

Time to let she go soon.

"You think so?"

She nearly big enough to fend for sheself now.

Tefa distrusted the rolling calf pup, had tried to convince Tan-Tan to release her into the bush as soon as her teeth plates had come in. But she cost them nothing to keep, beyond the initial cost of her chain. Is only leaves she wanted. They had plenty of those, oui. Hard to believe that something that looked so able to hunt and kill for its supper was a folivore, harmful only if you frightened it or threatened it. Or got in its unmindful way. Tan-Tan's foot was still sore from where the beast had stepped on it yesterday.

The pup grumbled again.

"Yes, I coming just now, hold your horses, nuh?" She clambered awkwardly out of the nest, sat straddling the branch while she got her breath. Her centre of gravity shifted almost daily as her belly grew. She'd lost track, was it seven months?

Seven and a half? More, maybe? Her back hurt all the time, she couldn't get a restful sleep. Damned baby. And like it had heard her, it kicked. Ai. Vicious brute's legs were getting stronger. She swung heavily out of the tree, wincing as the impact of landing made her belly pull at her crotch tendons. The rolling calf pup hurried over to her, making a noise like three grown men with bellyaches. It tried to lean against her leg; she stepped away. "No, you too big, you have to stop that now!" Its armour-plate skin had hardened as it had grown. It could scrape her skin raw. It swiped its spiked tail back and forth, making a thumb-deep groove in the dirt. She slid the choke chain loose from its neck. It shook its blocky tricorned head and lumbered off in search of greenery. One day she knew it wouldn't come back. Tefa was right, it was old enough. She no longer needed to keep it near so she could watch over it at night. But she didn't want to set it free. It was the first thing whose life she'd really managed to save so far, the first step in lifting the douen curse from her head. If she let it go and it died, would she have to start all over again?

Tefa had fluttered down from the nest, was giving herself a dust bath to stifle mites. She was kicking up an opaque cloud. Tan-Tan coughed and stepped back, fanning dust away from her face.

Tefa was another one who didn't have to be leashed to her any longer. There were other daddy tree communities about. Abitefa had made a point of searching them out and warning them not to lay down obvious trails to tallpeople settlements. Humans were curious animals and now that they had really begun to wonder about how douens lived, some brave ones were venturing farther and farther into the bush. Janisette's posse had made it the farthest so far, but they had become a laughing stock. Almost no-one believed their tale about a tree as big as a mountain that had shrunk to a sapling overnight. Tefa had refused to stay with any of the other douen communities because Tan-Tan refused to join her, or to try and live with tallpeople. Was only a matter of time before Janisette caught up with her. She didn't want to bring her fate on anyone else. Abitefa should leave her too, in this shadow place between two peoples. And then where would Tan-Tan be? And what about when the devil baby got born?

Circles, her mind was forever going in circles lately and always came back to this. "Tefa," she shouted, "I going into the settlement it have over there so."

The dustcloud stopped its dance. Abitefa peeked out. ***Why?***

"I need new blouses—the belly poking out again." Which was only partly true. The last set of clothing she'd got would fit until she delivered. She was just restless, wanted to see people going about their lives round her. She hadn't checked out this particular settlement yet. She puffed her way back up into the tree—soon she'd have to nest on the ground, and what would she do then? Later, think about it later. From higher up she marked the path of the sun, then jumped back down to the ground. "I go come back by nightfall, all right?"

Seen. Walk good.

Tan-Tan marked her way as she went; notching a tree here, building a small pyramid of boulderstones there. Aside from the discomfort of her baby belly, it felt good to exercise her body. Adult exiles to New Half-Way Tree often never came into the full satisfaction of feeling their muscles work to move the world around them.

It took her about two hours to start to see the middle bush that signalled a settlement. She hid her lantern in a shrub at the border of the bush. She thrust her face out of the bush. About a metre sunward was a wisdom weed field. It would hide her entrance and exit from the settlement. Staying in the bush, she worked her way round to it.

There were people who had been working the field this morning. She could see them in a hut nearby, taking shade from the noonday heat and eating their lunch. One of them was holding court with a Tan-Tan story, the one about Kabo Tano and the evergiving tree. Tan-Tan smiled wryly to herself. It was a simple thing to sneak past them through an uncut section of the field.

What a thing those Tan-Tan stories had become, oui! Canto and cariso, crick-crack Anansi back; they had grown out of her and had become more than her. Seemed like every time she heard the stories they had become more elaborate. Anansi the Trickster himself couldn't have woven webs of lies so fine. She kept trying to discern truths about herself in the Tan-Tan tales, she couldn't help it. People loved them so, there must be something to them, ain't? Something hard, solid thing other people could see in her; something she could hear and know about herself and hold in her heart. *Know you is a no-good waste of space.*

She found the road and asked a passer-by if there was a tailor. There was. She followed the man's directions through the streets. One or two people looked at her curiously. Some nodded a greeting. She had almost forgotten what the gesture meant. She'd been walking a few minutes when she realised what was odd about this settlement—it was clean. No smell of sewage in the streets. No open middens. Pickney-them only as frowsty as diligent parents would allow.

And this must be the tailor shop here, right where the man had said it would be. The door of the small hut was open. She walked inside. The tailor looked up from his ancient treadle sewing machine. "Good afternoon, Compère. How I could help you today?"

Tan-Tan goggled at him, tipped her sombrero down so its shadow hid her face. "Is okay," she said in a voice she made deep, and rushed out of the shop.

"What . . . ?"

She didn't answer, kept moving. What settlement was this?

She must have asked it out loud. A young boy replied, "Sweet Pone, Compère." She hurried by him without thanking him. Her heart was triphammering, the weight in her belly dragging her down. Hurry!

She turned down a side street, found herself in a market. Hurry! Her cape dragged a gutted foot snake down off someone's counter. She heard its liver wetness smack against the ground. The vendor shouted.

"Pardon, beg pardon," Tan-Tan apologised. "No time."

She was half running now, as much as the monster baby would let her. She got her legs tangled in a goat's leash, overturned a heaped pyramid of halwa fruit. The vendors were shouting at her to take care, the noise was calling attention to her. She ran smack into a little girl child, knocked her bawling onto her behind. "Lady, what the rass wrong with you?" the little girl's mother demanded to know. She bent to her child.

The girl's lip was cut, Tan-Tan could see the blood. She stopped. "Oh. I didn't mean to hurt she . . ."

"Why you can't watch where you going?" said the woman. And to the child, "Don't mind, doux-doux. Is just a stupid lady."

She was hunting for something to wipe the girl's mouth with. Tan-Tan bent, used a corner of her cape. "Sorry, sorry."

Running footsteps. A shadow fell over her. "Compère?"

No running from it any longer. Tan-Tan looked up into Melonhead's face.

"Take off that cape and hat, nuh? I could see you sweating under there."

"No thanks, me all right."

Melonhead shrugged doubtfully. Tan-Tan remembered that expression, the one he got when he didn't believe her but wasn't going to push the point. To be looking at his face, so dear to her! She kept imagining brushing it with her fingers. She reached for her glass of wet sugar tree water instead, concentrated on drinking one swallow at a time. She felt nervous, sitting still in a rum shop like this. Keeping on the move was survival. But her camouflage drab worked. People were ignoring her.

"I thought you did dead in the bush," Melonhead said softly.

"No." He had been with One-Eye and the dogs that were hunting her down. What was he up to?

Even softer he said, "I thought if maybe you didn't dead, you would try and meet me up here in Sweet Pone, like you did promise."

"No." Covertly she scanned the place, plotting her escape route. The exit on her left led to the main street, busy enough to disappear in, if no-one was really looking for her. She shouldn't have come here in broad daylight. *Stupid girl. You go dead of stupid.*

"Why you won't talk to me, Tan-Tan?"

What he really think this is any at all? What he trying to trap her into? "Nothing to say. You not going back to work?"

"You have a next partner?" he asked.

Enough. "Is what it have with you, eh? All you could think about is partner this and partner that? You and me story never start, now it finish. It finish when you come with dogs to hunt me."

The hurt and shock on his face wrenched at her. "Me? Hunt you? Tan-Tan, I follow One-Eye to try and make sure he ain't do away with you right there!"

Horse dead and cow fat. She wasn't going to believe no anansi story.

Melonhead must have seen the doubt on her face. "Is true! Me and Daddy come back later that night to try and find you. I come back next morning, and the morning after that. For a week I went back to that same place, hoping to find you. Then I think say you dead."

An old grief saddened his face. No, not so old; it had only been seven months, eight? since she'd seen him last. To her it felt like years.

"You don't believe?"

She sighed. She had no business with regret. "Seen, I believe you."

"So what make you ain't come to find me?"

"Janisette hunting me down."

"What?"

"I can't rest any one place, seem like she have people in every settlement who she pay to look out for me. She think I kill Daddy in cold blood."

"Rahtid. Nobody in Junjuh think that. Everybody know say him been beating you like dog from since."

They all had known? "Worse than that."

"Worse how?"

Shit. That had slipped out. "Never mind. You not going back to work?"

But he wouldn't leave her, wouldn't be distracted. He pressed her for details of what had happened that night, how she'd survived in the bush this long. She wove half-truths, trying frantically to keep her own story straight. She'd thought Antonio was going to kill her with blows, had lashed out blindly with her new knife. She'd run away into the bush, had climbed a tree to throw the dogs off the scent. She'd made her way to other settlements somehow, had begged and borrowed and stolen and had been settling down when Janisette had found her.

Nothing about the rape. Certainly nothing about Chichi-bud and Benta, or about the daddy tree. She had drunk tree frog blood; drunk douen people's secrets with it. She owed them her silence.

Melonhead bought her lunch. They laughed and talked over a meal like they hadn't done in so long. Quamina had been well when Melonhead left Junjuh, though she would still cry with missing Tan-Tan. Aislin too. Glorianna had given birth to twin girls, fathered by Rick. "Two pickney pretty for so, you see? I help Daddy sew the nine night-gowns for them, from lace Quamina make."

Shooting the breeze with Melonhead was sweet. Tan-Tan realised that she didn't want to leave his company, didn't want to go back to her cold nest in the bush with no humans for company. Guilt flared at that thought. Abitefa was her friend.

"Oh! Let me tell you this one, Tan-Tan! You go like it, for it have your name in it. Long time, Tan-Tan the Robber Queen used to live on the moon . . ."

The thing in Tan-Tan's belly kicked and rolled like Jour Ouvert morning. "Nah man, pretend story that. Tell me, tell me . . . how people here does cook foot snake meat. After it so rank." He obliged. She breathed again.

The shopkeeper brought them mug after mug of sugar tree water, bowls of salted dry-fried channa peas. Other patrons of the rum shop smiled indulgently at them as they sat with their heads together. She and Melonhead talked and talked, her spinning lies, him caught in their web.

The sun was beginning its descent down the bowl of the sky. If she wasn't back at the nest by daylean, Abitefa would be frantic. So would the rolling calf pup. "Come Melonhead, make I walk you back to the shop. Must be time for you to lock up and go home."

"Is right there so I live."

But the shop she'd seen was one room with a narrow pallet bed rolled up in the corner. "What, you not keeping house with nobody?"

His face crumpled. "Tan-Tan, like you don't understand. I been grieving."

So had she, for so many things. "Come, I walk you back." He looked at her, sighed, shook his head, lips pressed hard together as though he were keeping words in. He got to his feet.

She stood. Felt like the blasted duppy pickney had grown in the few hours she'd been sitting there. She stretched out her legs, did her best to affect the walk of someone who wasn't pregnant. She would be an easy target if people thought her ability to move was hampered. They walked along the main street. She saw new deportees, identifiable by the softness of people unaccustomed to physical work and by the distant, frantic look of the newly headblind. But for the most part people looked content; thin and wiry from manual labour, but healthy. The basics were there: running water nearby, a market, and the tradespeople—healer, carpenter, blacksmith, Melonhead the tailor. Runner people skills flourished in Sweet Pone. People greeted Melonhead happily, called him Compère Charlie. So is that was his name. He kept stopping to introduce her to people, till she had to take him aside and explain how she couldn't afford to have people start to recognise her. His face fell, but he said nothing. They kept walking. "You like living here?" Tan-Tan asked him.

"Yes, man. These people working hard to build a new life, you know? We nearly finish putting up a Palaver House where we Mocambo could meet people and talk. We even have a little library! Nearly a hundred books! Them solar-powered texts could run forever if we care them right."

Books, manuals. So many they had! No wonder people could develop skills here, they had books to teach them. Tan-Tan noted how Melonhead said "we."

They were at his home. A neat pile of folded clothing lay on his pallet. He shook the pieces open. They were tiny, a child's clothing made from unbleached fabric. "Rehan must be bring these while I wasn't here. Is his little boy pants these, I recognise the tear I mend from when he fall down and bust he little knee open on a rockstone. Look, the bloodstain never come out. Is my stitches these."

Proudly, he showed her the small pair of pants, the neat, well-made stitches that darned the torn edges of fabric back together. "Nothing ain't wrong with them, so the pickney must be just outgrow them again. I have to let out the hems for he." Tan-Tan had a brief flash of a girl with her face, dancing and laughing in the sunlight. She used to be a pickney too, who would tear out the knees of her pants while playing. She shut the vision out, moved to look round the rest of the hut. There was nothing much to see beyond Melonhead's orderly tools: needles, awls, thimbles, scissors, a small spinning wheel.

Melonhead inspected the rest of the clothing, noting a rip here, a missing button there. He folded the clothing, unfolded it again, draped it over a chair. He looked uncomfortable. "Um, you want to stay little bit?"

"No thanks, I have to go." Did he look relieved?

"Where you staying?"

She sighed. "Don't ask me, Melonhead, I done tell you I have to live in secret, I don't settle anywhere for long. I will come and visit you again, seen?" She turned to leave.

"I could come with you?" he asked quietly. At her look he blustered, "Not to stay or nothing, not to give you grief, just to walk you back to your home, talk to you little more. Then I leave you alone, promise. So long I ain't see you, girl."

Home. He thought she had a home. This was breaking her heart, this longing. "You could hike in the bush?" she said, before she could have time to think about what she was offering.

"Nanny save we, is bush you living?"

She couldn't stand the pity on his face. "Bush today yes, a different place next week, maybe bush again the week after that. Is so I does live, take it or leave it."

"Nah, I ain't mean nothing by it." He was searching through his room. "Let me just find my good boots."

"We taking the side routes, so you know. Can't make any-body see where I go."

He straightened up from tying his laces. She'd forgotten his short, sweet, bandy legs. "All this secrecy really necessary, girl?"

Panic fluttered in her throat. "Yes! And if you can't honour that, tell me now and let me go my ways."

"I never break word with you yet, Tan-Tan."

But she'd broken hers to him. "Make we go." She tipped her sombrero low on her head.

He followed her uncomplainingly, dipping into side streets, taking the least observed routes. He followed her through the cover of the eveningtime cornfields, through the middle bush to where she'd stashed her lantern. He just raised an eyebrow at how quickly she found it. It would be dark before she got back, Abitefa would be worried. She shouldn't have stayed this long. How would she let Tefa know she was bringing company? How would Melonhead react to the hinte? To the rolling calf pup? She didn't know what she was doing, or why. "We have to go quick."

"Seen."

He hiked along quietly with her for almost an hour, a soothing presence by her side. He held the lantern for her while she lit it, handed it back to her, said, "You making baby, ain't it?"

"You could tell!" she stuttered, too shocked to dissemble.

"Not at first, no. That cape does hide plenty. But it start to show in your walk once you get out of Sweet Pone."

"Huh." She strode off, leaving him to keep up.

Another half hour of silence, not calming this time. Tan-Tan's brain was seething over, too fast for sense. She was aware of every step Melonhead took, every inclination of his head. She nearly jumped out of her skin when he took a preparatory breath in. He was going to speak. He said, "Tan-Tan, don't vex at the question: is Antonio baby?"

"Why you would ask me something like that!" She stomped on ahead of him, horrified herself with the fleeting thought that she could abandon him here in bush, like in the douen stories. She had let him get too close.

He caught up to her, gazed at her, waiting. Fucking man, always waiting, waiting for her to say what was on her mind. She said, "I can't talk about it, don't ask me."

He nodded. "Seen." They kept walking. In a few more minutes, he reached slowly for her hand. She took it and held on, tight-tight like creeper vine.

"Is really your home your taking me to, Tan-Tan?"

"My camp, yes."

"It dark out here like backra soul, oui. You not frighten in this bush come nightfall?"

She felt pleased with herself. "Not any more."

In another hour they were approaching the place where she and Tefa had made camp. Tefa had left pork-knacker signs, bush prospector signs, to tell her that she'd made that night's nest in another nearby tree. They did that every night; it gave the rolling calf pup somewhere new to graze. Tefa was probably already hearing two sets of feet tramping through the bush, was wondering is what a-go on. "Tefa!" she skreeked. Her hinte talk was getting better. "A tallpeople with me! No danger!" Tefa carolled back that she was prepared.

Melonhead had jumped when she began calling. He halted dead where he stood. "What you make that noise for?" he asked.

"I have a packbird with me," she said. The story she and Tefa had prepared if they were to need it. She hoped they could pull it off. "Just letting she . . . it know I coming." Now she could see through the trees the flicker of the campfire. "Melonhead I have, ah, a pet."

"You mean the bird?"

It took her a second to understand that he was calling Abitefa a pet. "No, a next beast. Don't 'fraid when you see she."

By the lamplight she could see him smiling. "You got what, a hunting dog or something?"

"No, more like a ankylosaur."

"How you mean?"

"She getting big, all right? And she scary looking, but she won't mean you no harm. Just don't get where she could step on your foot."

They stepped into the campsite. Snuffling with joy, the rolling calf pup rushed Tan-Tan, narrowly missing her with one of its horns. Melonhead shouted and froze. "What the blood-cloth . . . !" Inquisitive, the pup went to sniff at him. Melonhead put out warding hands, his face grey with alarm. The pup sampled a bit of his sleeve.

"Stop that!" Tan-Tan scolded her, pulling on her horns. "Sorry Melonhead, she growing; she is nothing but appetite."

"She going to get *bigger?*" The pup chewed meditatively, spat out a button.

"Little bit, yes. Watch out for she tail there. She mother reached to my shoulder. I killed she, the mother I mean, but is my fault. I frighten she and she attack. I couldn't abandon the pup after that."

Some of the fear had gone from Melonhead's face. Carefully he reached out a hand and stroked one of the pup's horns. "In all my born days, I never."

Abitefa fluttered down from the nest. Melonhead straightened, smiled. "Now, here something I more familiar with. Coo-coo, bird-oi." He made dove noises at Abitefa, holding out his hand. She looked to Tan-Tan for guidance.

"Ahm, she not used to strangers. She won't come to you."

He dropped the hand, pulled it out of reach of the pup's

nibbling mouth. In her beak Abitefa picked up a log of the wood she had gathered to stoke the fire. She must have thought better of it, for she dropped it again and stood looking at Melonhead. She didn't get to see plenty tallpeople.

Melonhead glanced round the campsite. "Nanny bless, Tan-Tan; is here you staying? And all because of Janisette?"

"I like it here," she lied. "You hungry?"

That was a long night; long in good and bad ways. There was the moment when Tan-Tan realised she couldn't really expect Melonhead to make his way back home through the bush in the dark. He was going to have to stay there with them. How come she hadn't thought of that before? It pleased her and frightened her to have him stay. She showed him how to climb up into the nest and he praised her ingenuity at training her bird to build it for her. Abitefa's neck feathers had bristled. Tan-Tan had told him how she slept snuggled next to Abitefa for warmth and he'd said sweetly, "You don't have to do that tonight, sweetheart. I here." Tan-Tan had gaped at him, looked helplessly at Tefa, who just gazed back, puzzled. Finally Tan-Tan had had to ask her in awkward hinte to please sleep somewhere else for the night. Abitefa had made a peculiar noise and climbed up higher in the tree. Leaves and twigs had rained down on she and Melonhead for a while as Tefa had woven herself a new nest.

Yes, a long, long night alone in a confined space with Melonhead, which she had managed by pretending to fall asleep almost instantly. Melonhead had called her name softly a few times, then sighed and curled himself round her. She'd lain like that for hours, feeling the slow beat of his heart against her spine, his arm curled round her belly.

Come morning time Abitefa didn't show up. Trying not to worry, Tan-Tan had shared with Melonhead her breakfast of smoked tree frog and dried halwa fruit. Things were awkward between them, shaped by the silences she insisted on. He said he had to get back to his shop. She walked him to the edge of the bush, made clumsy small talk the whole way. Before stepping back out into Sweet Pone he took her hand and said, "You going to be moving on soon?"

"Yes. Nuh must?"

"I not convinced, but if is so you want it. Come and see me before you go?"

"I promise."

"Don't promise, just do it."

True, her promises were no good. Sadly she watched him thread his way through the corn. She had disappointed him again.

When she got back to the camp, Abitefa was waiting. ***You partnering with that tallpeople now?***

No, she wasn't. But she found herself back in Sweet Pone two days later, looking for excuses to keep passing and repassing the front of Melonhead's shop, too jittery to just walk in. She stared wistfully at the people who did: the old man in the anachronistic suit; the bongo toughy little girl who was clutching a rubber ball in one hand and holding the torn seat of her dungarees closed with the other; the preoccupied-looking young woman who had a bag full of either cloth or mending. She was pretty, that one—fat and firm with a high, round behind. She stayed in Melonhead's shop too long for Tan-Tan's taste, left with too big a smile on her face.

And who was she Tan-Tan to care? Standing there in patched-up, leaf-stained clothes; no pot to piss in, no roof over her head. Who was she to be scrutinizing who Melonhead was entertaining?

She was preoccupied, that's why he caught her. Another day and she would have zwipsed into the shadows as soon as he set foot out of his shop. Damned baby was slowing her down, yes.

"Tan-Tan!" he called, waving. She gasped. He was coming over, face alight with joy. "You come to see me!"

"Ahm, yes, I suppose so." She couldn't meet his eyes for long. She felt dirty, plain.

He looked glum. "Is 'cause you moving on?"

"Soon, yes. Not right now. I come, I come . . . because I want you make me some clothes," she continued, happy to have thought of something that would make her feel less homely. "I need a new outfit that would hide this belly."

This time his smile had some mischief in it. She knew that smile well. That smile had got her behind warmed for her one time when she had gone along with his suggestion that they knot all Compère Ramdass's yellowed singlets together as they flapped on the clothes line behind his cottage. "If I going to sew for you, I have to measure you," Melonhead said.

Her ears were burning. She just nodded. "Let we start then, nuh?"

She followed him into the shop. Pity that having clothes made would slow her down, waiting for him to finish them. She'd have to delay moving camp.

Melonhead closed the door. "You could take off the cape, people know not to come in while I measuring."

Thankfully she shucked the heavy unbleached fabric she wore all the time now if she was among tallpeople. She should wash it soon; it was smeared with leaf and road stains. She rolled her shoulders luxuriously, stretched her neck.

Melonhead sat at his workspace and started pulling things out of a press beside his sewing machine: a tape measure, a pencil, some scraps of paper. "Why you want to hide that you making baby, Tan-Tan? Begging your pardon, but who go care?"

"I can't make nobody . . ." she started, then stopped. No words to speak about Tan-Tan the Robber Queen. That was another self, another dimension. "I alone on the road. If people know say I pregnant them might try to take advantage."

He looked disturbed at that. "True thing. Maybe you could stop here little bit till the baby born. I don't think Janisette will find you. Come, stand over here." He draped the tape measure over his neck and stood to face her. His hair smelt of sweet oil. Cheeks flaming, she let him take her measurements and write them down. She looked round the room to distract herself.

To stop in one place. Sweet Pone was nice. With a start of surprise, Tan-Tan realised that she hadn't played Robber Queen on the Sweet Pone people yet.

There was more fabric in Melonhead's shop than there had been the last time. Plenty more, and bright bright colours too besides. Her sister Quamina would have loved it in here, all the shiny needles and gorgeous cloths. "Like somebody give you a big job, eh?"

He laughed. "Sweetness, you been in the bush so long you ain't even know what time of year this is?"

She did. Time for the mako jumbies to migrate to the poles. Time for the foot snakes to moult. She was trying to work out a way to tan the shed hides they left behind. Maybe she could make wallets with them to sell. She frowned. What did tallpeople do this time of year?

He took her by the shoulders, turned her to face him. "Tan-Tan, Carnival is three weeks from now. What you going to wear?"

Tan-Tan stopped for a minute behind the new Sweet Pone Palaver House before turning the corner into the town square. The Robber Queen cape felt good on her shoulders, a comforting weight. Melonhead was a genius, oui? He'd pieced together precious ends of black velvet, made style by outlining the joins with iridescent shell buttons. The cape was edged with brightly coloured ribbons, ends left long and fluttering. It fastened in front with ornate brass frog closures, had two long slits through which she could thrust her arms. The round jutting collar had a support under it that also served to hold the cape away from her belly. Her soon-to-be baby was well-hidden.

And there was more. Melonhead had made her a fine Robber hat from goat wool felt that he'd dyed black and blocked into shape. There was a belt, extra-large to extend round her belly, with two holsters and sheathes for her knife and machète. He'd even found cap guns and caps! She did an experimental turn. The cape flared out satisfyingly. She wished Melonhead were there to see, but he'd stayed at his shop to make some last-minute adjustments to costumes. He'd said: "I catch up with you later, doux-doux. In the square, all right? Girl, you looking fine too bad!"

She'd leaned over her baby belly and kissed his mouth, gratified at the pleased look of surprise on his face before their lips touched. "Later, yes." She'd waved happily and left, her body tingling from the contact of his skin. She stopped, stood knowledge-struck in the street. Touching Melonhead made her feel good, an unalloyed pleasure untainted by fear or anger. So different than she'd ever felt before.

But the feeling of well-being deserted her quickly. She didn't belong here, amongst people like this. As she approached the square she could hear the music. A steel pan band was playing what should have been a sweet, sweet road march. The bass pans-them were beating out their deep, low notes like heartbeats: *Boom, boom-boom-boom-boom.* How come it sounded to her like "doom"? Over the beats, the tenor pans were working the melody hard: pure, tinny notes dancing up into the sky—a tune to make you want to wind your behind, shuffle in time, and take a swig out of the flask of red rum in your back pocket—*Ting ting, ting te-ting ting ting.* And all Tan-Tan could hear in the music was *"Tan-Tan; doom, doom-doom-doom-doom."*

The square was full up with people. Even with the music she could hear the shuffling feet, the laughter, and every now and again, a joyous voice shouting out, "Koo fête, Papa! Wind your waist!" Melonhead had been busy these past few weeks, making costumes for those who couldn't make their own. She saw Jab-Jab devils cracking whips, sporting horns on their heads; the Fancy Indians jumping up in their soft moccasins, hanging on to their feather headdresses so they wouldn't fly off; the bats, silent and scary in skin-tight brown and black, waving their huge ratbat wings to and fro through the crowd; even the occasional Midnight Robber wearing a velvet sombrero, brim a metre wide, trimmed with pom-poms and papier-mâché skulls all round; leather chaps with plenty fringe; a noisemaker and fake guns. The Robbers carried sacks to hold the Carnival pounds and pennies people would throw them if they speechified well. Some of them were even pretending to be Tan-Tan, New Half-Way Tree's Robber Queen. She was hiding in the best possible way, masquerading as herself! The smile that cracked onto her face was nearly a foreign thing, a half-forgotten thing. *Just join the fête, stupid gal. When last you have a good time?*

Still, something was holding her back. Months of living in the bush with Abitefa had made her sensitive to the slightest sounds. Too much noise in a town. Underneath all the shouting and the pan playing there was a sursurus: maybe a tiny cross-breeze, a little warmer than the rest of the air, skittering past her shins; there was a low thrumming that didn't seem to be coming from the steel band. There was a barely audible staccato tattoo that wasn't noisemakers. What was wrong?

Truth to tell though, nothing could be completely right about Carnival in this shadow land of New Half-Way Tree. Everyone here was an exile; this could only be a phantom of the celebration they would have had on Toussaint.

Cho! She couldn't hang back like this all day. Time for fête, yes!

Tan-Tan took a deep breath and stepped round the corner of the new Palaver House, into Carnival in Sweet Pone.

Mama, if you see Masque!

The steel pan band was on a stage in the middle of the square, a whole side of about thirty pan men and women, beating the tune out of the steel drums with sticks wrapped in rubber. And dancing! The pan people-self couldn't help stamping their feet to the music they were making. The whole stage was only jerking up and down to the beat.

Tout monde in Sweet Pone and the surrounding settlements must have been in the town square jumping-up to the music. Carnival was bringing people together on New Half-Way Tree. Tan-Tan revelled in the finery of the Bats and Jab-Jabs and Fancy Indians. It even had a few small bands, oui? A Pissenlit band inna Old Masque stylee: one set of hard-back men dressed off in women's white petticoats, twisting and jutting their hips to show off the red stains painted on their panties; a Sailor band, every man and woman wearing navy and white naval uniforms with bell-bottom pants, and swaying from side to side like drunken sailors; a tiny Burroquite band, just two people—the King in satin and rhinestones, wearing a papier-mâché horse round his waist to look like he was riding it. Beside him came the Queen in her sari, passing round the brass plate to collect money. To the tune of the steel band the two of them were chanting:

> *Raja, Raja Hindako*
> *Dhal bhat, dhal bhat Hindako*
> *Soo, Mary, Soo Danka.*

Midnight Robbers were holding up people to make their speeches. People were laughing at the verbal garbiage and handing over booty: calabashes of liquor; silver jewelry; taking off their good leather shoes even and giving them to the robbers.

The people who didn't have on costumes had dressed for show anyway: their tightest bodices, their brightest bandanas. And plenty of people were beating bottle and spoon in time to the music.

"Oi-yo-yoi! Oi-yo-yoi!" chorussed two men in front of Tan-Tan, winding down each other, belly to behind. The man in front had on the tiniest pair of shorts Tan-Tan had ever seen. His brown skin was glistening from sweat and the gold glitter he had dusted all over his body. The cords in his thighs were like steel cable winching him low. He gyrated his hips against his dance partner's crotch. The man in back was wearing a loincloth and nothing else but a pair of alpagat slippers. His hair was chopped off at the sides. He waved round a wooden tomahawk as he danced. His round belly rolled and jumped in time. Tan-Tan smiled to see the two of them.

"Lower! Match me, come on!" Clustered in a circle, four people were having a contest to see who could wind down nearest to the ground without falling over. They spread their knees wide apart, worked their twisting hips lower. Squealing and giggling, three of them toppled into the dust. The one left on her feet was a woman wearing a halter top with an eye painted on over each bubby. She stood from her crouch, did a little victory dance, hands sketching curlicues in the air. The three rivals laughed, got up, brushed themselves off. One of them squirted a drink into the winner's mouth from a leather bottle. Arm in arm, the four of them danced off to the middle of the square. Mama, this is Masque! Today, tout monde forget all their troubles. Music too sweet, oui!

Tan-Tan cocked her hips to one side, then the other. They felt rusty. How could she have forgotten how to *dance?*

The rhythm soon caught her up in it, though. Swaying to

the music, she worked her way past the two men, right into the comess of Carnival. She swung her sack over her shoulder and just lost herself in the music for a while. Was that Melonhead over there? No. She'd probably buck him up soon.

Time to try to earn her coppers this Carnival day. She moved to the outskirts of the square, chipped along until she spied a likely target for her first speech; an old man dancing at the edge of the crowd. She unholstered her cap gun, presented herself in front of him, and shot off *plai! plai!* into the air.

"Papa-oi! Stand and hear my tribulation."

The old man grinned and folded his arms, waiting to judge if her speech would be good enough for him to drop some coppers into her sack.

"Stand and deliver up your tears and your pounds," said the Robber Queen, "else your tears and your life for my grievous and sad accounting!"

Her voice swelled with power as the Robber Queen persona came upon her. She spun him the tale, about being born a princess among men. "My father, Lord Raja, was the King of Kings, nemesis of the mighty. He command the engines of the earth, and they obey him. My mother, Queen Niobe, cause the stars to fall out the sky at her beauty and the wind to sigh at she nimble body as she dance. How I could not be joyful? How I could not be blissful?" She wove her deft weave about being kidnapped and stolen away. About fleeing her captors, stealing to survive, helping those worse off than herself. "A mere snap of my fingers jook terror into the hearts of the dastardly!"

A small crowd of people had gathered to hear the speech. A few of them flipped coins of copper and brass into her sack. Finally the old man tossed her two coppers too. A good first take. They honoured her as they should. The Midnight Robber bowed graciously, accepting their beneficence. Her small audience clapped, dispersed. Tan-Tan blinked to find herself just a woman in a costume once more.

She went on a little farther, performed her piece a few more times, gathered more coin and gifts. Was going to be hard taking all this back to Abitefa, and her back was hurting her today. Maybe Melonhead would help. She danced some more, but the underlying hum it seemed only she could hear was throwing her off. She wasn't going to let it get in the way of her first fête in years. She worked her way to the front, right up close to where the band was playing. Music so loud it danced in her blood like her very own heartbeat. Yes, like so. She put her hands on the stage, her behind in the air, and gyrated to the rhythm. "Put your hand in the air!" she shouted with the chorus. Yes, allyou; watch the Robber Queen dance.

A loud tone blatted out over the square. The tenor pans stopped first. People in the crowd started to complain. Then the bass pans fell quiet. The trumpet cut out with a rude noise. What wrong with them? Tan-Tan looked up at the stage. All the musicians were staring open-mouthed behind her. The crowd was silent. There was a controlled purring noise coming from behind her back, a slight hiss. Tan-Tan turned round.

The bullet-shaped tank was sleek as a cat. Its metal body had been buffed to a reflective shine. Rivets made a stylish punctuation along its sides. Nothing on all of New Half-Way Tree looked like it. It advanced slowly on her, thrumming low in its belly, oiled treads whispering over the dust of the town square. Sunlight bounced needles of light off its mirrored hide. Its headlights tracked back and forth as they searched, searched for her. Its horn brayed again. Her fate had found her. Petrified, Tan-Tan could only watch it come.

The crowd backed away. Tan-Tan could hear the band members abandoning the stage. She dropped her sack. The tank stopped inches away from her in a menacing crouch. Its top opened.

Janisette jumped out, sleek in a tight red one-piece with black boots, her hair slicked back from her forehead and confined in a black bandana. "Oho! Koo the two-faced devil there, the woman that kill my husband."

"It was self-defense . . ." Tan-Tan whispered. Her voice had no strength. Her belly was dragging her to the ground.

Janisette stalked over to her. "You come from Junjuh, is Junjuh justice you must face. You coming back with me." She reached for Tan-Tan's wrist, snapped one half of a pair of handcuffs shut over it. The ring of metal had the strength of Antonio's fingers. *Yes, is this you good for. You must get punished.*

Numbly, she reached out her other wrist for the cuffs. "Yes," cooed Janisette, fingers stretching for her. "Is the right thing to do. Tin box for you."

A movement caught Tan-Tan's eye. She looked up to see her reflection in the tank's grinning face. A bedraggled woman in a jokey, wilting hat and a silly cape of motley. The image made her short and made her middle bulge. Tan-Tan remembered the baby-to-be hidden under her cape. *Not just one life, but two.*

She jerked her chained wrist out of Janisette's hand, flicked the handcuffs. Janisette had to duck. "Fucking bitch!" she spat at Tan-Tan.

"Mind your mouth!" Tan-Tan hollered. She twisted free of Janisette's grasp, kept dancing backwards away from her clutching hands. She opened her mouth again, and Bad Tan-Tan let the harangue tumble from them: "You not shame, you reddened trollop, to stanch this fête and jubilation with your scurrilous calumniation?"

"When I catch you, you leggobeast!"

Power coursed through Tan-Tan, the Robber Queen's power—the power of words: "I you will never catch, for I is more than a match; I will duck your base canards; I will flee and fly to flee again." Nanny, sweet Nanny, yes. Tan-Tan bad inna Robber Queen stylee.

"You going to come with me, woman!" Janisette lunged

for her, caught the brim of her hat. Tan-Tan zigzagged out of reach.

"Not wo-man; I name Tan-Tan, a 'T' and a 'AN'; I is the AN-acaona, Taino redeemer; the AN-nie Christmas, keel boat steamer; the Yaa As-AN-tewa; Ashanti warrior queen; the N-AN-ny, Maroon Granny; meaning Nana, mother, care-taker to a nation. You won't confound these people with your massive fib-ulation!" And Tan-Tan the Midnight Robber stood tall, guns crossed at her chest. Let her opponent match that.

Someone in the crowd blew a whistle in approval. "Kaiso! Tell it make we hear, Tan-Tan!"

Tell it? The Robber Queen opened her mouth to gift the populace with more word science. A man's voice shouted, "Is pappyshow! Tan-Tan is old-time story, not real!"

No, not real. He right. Just a pregnant bitch in a costume. The glamour faded like a dream. She was only Tan-Tan. "I real as you," she croaked. Her voice shredded in the air. She was trying, trying to tell the real story, but she was tiring, Janisette was only steps away. Too much baby, too much guilt weighing her down. Janisette leapt. Missed. Tan-Tan flipped away, dropped the guns, launched into a heavy jog round the square that felt as though it would tear her groin tendons loose. The handcuffs clanked at her wrist. No way to get through the press of people. Where would she run to, anyway?

Janisette kissed her teeth, ran and clambered up into the tank. It roared to life, headed straight for Tan-Tan. *She going to run me down!* Tan-Tan took two desperate steps, stumbled to her knees. Death rushed to crush her.

The tank was upon her. She rolled in the dirt, feeling her weapons in their scabbards scrape against her flesh. Her cape snagged under the tank's treads. It dragged her for a few ago-nizing metres before the button at her neck gave way, leaving her gasping, her side scraped raw. Janisette was turning for an-other pass. The baby in Tan-Tan pounded to get out. *When you take one, you must give back two.* She had two lives to save; hers and the pickney's. She struggled to her feet, belly pushing out big for all to see. Someone screamed, "Nanny save us, she making baby!" The tank was bearing down on her again, its headlights full on her. Nothing to do. She stroked her belly, waited. The headlights blinded her.

The tank's brakes screeched. Janisette stopped centimetres from Tan-Tan's navel. Tan-Tan concentrated on sucking in air sweet as life could sometimes be. Her side burned. Her lower back pulsed with pain. She waited, calm as a queen.

Janisette opened the hatch to the tank, stuck her upper body outside. "Is who pickney that filling up your belly, murderess?"

Whose? She'd carried the monster all this way. The damned pickney was hers. Tan-Tan took another breath, rubbed her belly again. "Is love that get the Robber Queen born," someone said softly out of her mouth, "love so sweet it hot." Janisette frowned. The crowd pulled in closer to hear. Someone in Tan-Tan's body took a breath, filled Tan-Tan's lungs with singing air, spoke in her voice:

> *Her beauteous mother,*
> *Was another,*
> *Not this Janisette with she fury-wet lips and she*
>   *vengeance.*
> *Tan-Tan Mamee Ione, the lovely; Tan-Tan woulda do*
>   *anything to please she,*
> *But she wasn't easy.*
> *Her pappy,*
> *Was never happy with all he had, oui?*
> *He kill a man on Toussaint, leave he family to wail,*
> *Then he grab his little girl and flee through plenty*
>   *dimension veil*
> *And bring her here, to this bitter backawall nowhere.*

People, she was seven.
Them say the Robber Queen climb the everliving tree.
I tell you, that little girl was me.

"What the rass?" cried someone in the crowd. "Is what kind of paipsey robber talk this is any at all? Look, best make we get on with we jump-up, oui?"

Cho, the populace and them trying to get rowdy. How dare the bold-face man not believe her story? Regally she pulled her machète, brandished it at the heckler. She was the Brigand à Miduit; they were *going* to hear her! She roared:

Is me, I tell you! Tan-Tan the Robber Queen! The one and
  the same,
She warm the poor with candle flame
And spirit the lame from harm.

"Oho!" the heckler said. "I know you now. You is Charlie crazy girlfriend. Doux-doux darling, you might be name Tan-Tan, but that don't make you a legend."

To rass it didn't.

You nah believe is majesty you talking to?
Me won't blame that on you;
From your face it plain you
Ignorant. What for do?

Somebody sniggered. "A-true, Dambudzo, you know sun don't always shine as bright for you as for the rest of we." People laughed. "Lewwe hear she story little bit." Dambudzo frowned. Janisette revved the engine of the death car. Her Majesty the Midnight Thief stepped prudently back a step or two.

Wait! Me ain't done relate
to you the full monstrosity of this man, Tan-Tan pappy.
She ain't come here by choice,
He never give she any voice
in she fate.
He use he wiles to trick she, a seven-year-old pickney,
Into exile, oui?

Now even her supporter had lost interest. "Cho man, we ain't business! Everybody life hard here. You coulda come up with a nicer speech than that, girl. Come Selector: start up the music again."

"No, answer me, bitch," yelled Janisette, climbing out onto the running board of the vehicle. She leaned and spat the words into the face of this body the Queen was wearing: "A who-for pickney that a big-up your belly?"

Oh, and fury made the Brigand Queen flare:

Like you ain't know, steplady?
Is she father who fuck she.

The restless crowd went still. Even from where she was, the Queen could see shock at her crudeness on some of the revellers' faces. This was too nasty to be a Carnival mako. She didn't care.

Yes, he inject Tan-Tan with he child,
She sister or brother.
And you one
Come to accuse she? Of what then, nuh?

Tears started from Janisette's eyes. "I accuse you of loose-ness," she said. "Of sluttery. Is you tempt Antonio with your leggobeast ways."

Oh, Mama Nanny, the woman was lies incarnate, and right in the face of royalty!

Is that you believe, Antonio wife?
Is she tempt he?
Then why for her birthday you give her one knife?

The Midnight Robber pulled Tan-Tan's blade from its sheath, turned it so that it winked in the light. She held knife and cutlass at the ready, daring Janisette to rush her.

Someone moved forward from out of the crowd. Short legs, knobby knees, a head too big for its body. "You recognise that, Janisette? Why you give your stepdaughter a blade, if not to protect sheself from she own daddy?"

The Robber Queen's heart danced in her breast to hear Tan-Tan's friend speak up for her. But this story had to sing as her own soul, oui? Knife still in hand, she held up her arm to shush Melonhead.

People, oonuh must understand. The Robber Queen father
    was a slick, sick man.
The first time she did making baby for he, she was fourteen.
He uses to beat she too, and
this Janisette, who he woo at first with sweet words,
Then give she the back of he hand.

Janisette put a trembling hand to her face, where Aislin's stitches traced a scar from cheekbone to chin.

Tan-Tan couldn't take it. When she turn sixteen, she and
    allyou tailor make a plan
To leave and come to Sweet Pone,
To love each other on their own,
Away from Antonio.

Janisette pushed out her bottom lip. The look she flashed Melonhead was pained, unreadable.

Could the Robber tell the rest? Rough with emotion, her cracked voice came out in two registers simultaneously. Tan-Tan the Robber Queen, the good and the bad, regarded Janisette with a regal gaze and spoke:

> That plan for love never come to transaction.
> When Antonio find out, he rape she, beat she, nearly kill
>   she.
> Lying under he pounding body she see the knife.
> And for she life she grab it and perform an execution.
> She kill she daddy dead. The guilt come down 'pon she
>   head,
> The Robber Queen get born that day, out of excruciation.

Hanging on her every word the crowd was frozen, most in attitudes of horror, but a few just looked wary, their faces clearly saying *what if them catch me?* She couldn't cipher that there one, though. Brer Mongoose does look watchful, seen, but Brer Fowl does do so too.

Janisette was shaking with tears, with fury. She made to climb back into the cab of the tank.

"I defend myself," said the Robber Queen, dropping out of the free rhyme and back into herself. "For the first time, I defend myself, Janisette."

Her stepmother turned at the sound of her name, one foot suspended in the air.

Tan-Tan said, "Is you give me the knife to do it with. Don't tell me you never used to hear what Antonio was doing to me. Is you see my trial and never have courage to speak up. So why you hunting me now, woman, when I only do what you give me tools to do?"

Then Tan-Tan knew her body to be hers again, felt her own

mouth stretching, stretching open in amazement at the words that had come out of it. Is she, speaking truth; is truth! *"Sans humanité!"* she spat at Janisette—"no mercy!"—the traditional final phrase of the calypsonian who'd won the battle of wits and words. Tan-Tan gasped, put a hand up to her magical mouth.

Her song had echoed out over the square. All were there to hear her sing the story true. She'd said them, spoke the words. Admitted to the murder. Let the people-them witness. She dropped her eyes to the ground, waited for the sound of Janisette's machine springing. *Nanny, strike me dead now.*

But nothing happened.

She looked up.

The sorrow and love on Melonhead's face was like healing balm. He nodded at her, a grim smile on his face. Janisette was standing on the running board, arms limp at her sides, a woman listening to her own condemnation. Her face had crumpled like a passion fruit that get suck dry.

The crowd erupted in cheers. Carnival pounds and pennies rained on Tan-Tan's head. She re-sheathed her blades. Stood in the rain of money, just being Tan-Tan, sometimes good, sometimes bad, mostly just getting by like everybody else. She felt the Robber Queen relaxing into a grateful slumber. Daddy was dead, her baby was alive. Now was time to put away guilt.

Melonhead came and held on to her, his eyes glistening. He was holding the guns she'd dropped. "You all right?"

"Yes," she said, meaning it.

Janisette clambered down from the tank, heavily and awkwardly. Her face was a mask of grief. She approached Tan-Tan, threw the handcuff key at her, spat on the ground at her feet. "You give me bitter gall to eat," she said. "I hope sorrow consume you like it consuming me."

"Sorrow was my father, my mother. I know sorrow good."

The band was back on the stage again, taking up their instruments. The crowd flowed back into the square. People looked at Tan-Tan uncertainly. Some smiled. Many scowled. Somebody asked a friend, "So is Masque that was, or real?"

Melonhead picked up the key, used it to free Tan-Tan's wrist.

A man approached Tan-Tan with her sack. "Lady, good kaiso that. I done pick up all your change I could find and put in it."

Melonhead took it and thanked him. "Come home with me, Tan-Tan." The music started again. As they left the square, Tan-Tan heard the thrum of the tank starting up, turned to see it moving despondently through the crowd, going away.

They were almost at Melonhead's door when a sudden pain wrung out her insides. She gasped, took a deep breath. "Melonhead, I have to go home."

"What home? Where?"

"I have to go back in the bush to Abitefa."

"You mad or what? You turn bassourdie? You need to lie down and rest."

"I will lie down when I reach back in the bush. I have to go right now." Holding her belly protectively, she turned on her heel and started walking, with or without him. "Soon," she whispered to her tummy. "I take one life, and I just save two."

Oh, sweetness; this is the hardest part, the last part of labour. I right here with you, don't fret. I know it feel like your mamee trying to crush you dead, but is only she body pushing you out into the world. No, she can't hear you yet, only I could hear you. Yes, that was a big one. Rest little bit; another one coming.

Is really your mamee we should be talking to, me and the Grande 'Nansi Web. When Granny Nanny realise how Antonio kidnap Tan-Tan, she hunt he through the dimension veils, with me riding she back like Dry Bone. Only a quantum computer coulda trace she through infinite dimensions like that, only Granny Nanny and me, a house eshu. And only because Tan-Tan's earbug never dead yet. A fearsome journey, little one; nearly as fearsome as the one you on now. Ai, ai; this push strong! I know, doux-doux. Try not to frighten. See? It stop now. Only a few more.

We try to contact your mamee when we find she nine years ago, but the nanomites growing she earbug did calibrate wrong for Nanny to talk to them across dimensions. Eight years it take Granny Nanny to figure it out, and then was too late. Tan-Tan reach maturity, the earbug harden, and Nanny couldn't talk to she again. Another contraction sweetheart, hold on.

Antonio was a sick, needy man, but in he own way, is he provide the method for we to contact Tan-Tan. By the time she get pregnant with you, Nanny had figure out the calibration. She instruct the nanomites in your mamee blood to migrate into your growing tissue, to alter you as you grow so all of you could *feel* nannysong at this calibration. You could hear me because your whole body is one living connection with the Grande Anansi Nanotech Interface. Your little bodystring will sing to Nanny tune, doux-doux. You will be a weave in she web. Flesh people talk say how earbugs give them a sixth sense, but really is only a crutch, oui? Not a fully functional perception. You now; you really have that extra limb.

Whoops! It coming, it coming! That feeling is your head crowning, sweetheart—that is air on your skin of your scalp. Welcome into one of the worlds, pickney!

Tan-Tan lay back, bassourdie with fatigue, and looked at the little bit of person in her arms. His eyes wavered over her body, fought for focus when they came to her face. For a second he stared right at her. He had Antonio's face, but they were her features too, *hers*. Her son was not a monster. He yawned crookedly and worked his mouth. Squeaky sounds came out.

"He singing," laughed Melonhead. He touched the baby's cheek.

"No," Tan-Tan replied. "I think is only gas."

Abitefa thrust her beak into the nest of blankets that Melonhead had brought, sniffed the baby's skin in greeting.

"What you going to name he?" Melonhead asked. He stroked some of the tiny curls of the baby's hair.

"Tubman." Tan-Tan surprised herself, coming out with it so quickly. She hadn't been thinking of what to call him. She smiled up at Melonhead.

Tubman: the human bridge from slavery to freedom. She give you a good name, doux-doux. A seer woman might have name you that. Sleep, Tubman.

Call that George, the story done.
Jack Mandora, me nah choose none!

Acknowledgments

Thanks are due to the Ontario Arts Council, the Canada Council and the Multiculturalism Programmes of the Department of Canadian Heritage, for financial assistance while I completed this project.

For patient, insightful critique, encouragement, invention and general correction of my wacky concepts of science and social systems, thank you to Bob Boyczuk, Laurie Channer, Debbie Donofrio, Candas Jane Dorsey, David Findlay, Peter Halasz, Brent Hayward, Dora Knez, Kelly Link, Pamela Mordecai, Peter Watts, and my agent Don Maass and editor Betsy Mitchell.

Appreciation to David Findlay for permission to quote "Stolen." Thank you, doux-doux.

Love, respect, blessings to my mother, Freda, and brother Keïta for their boundless support and enthusiasm.